More . . .

THE TWO CHINATOWNS

"*The Two Chinatowns* has clearly been written by an author with real procedural experience . . . The main virtue of Mr. Mahoney's fine detective story is the strength of the illusion it sustains that things could have happened almost the way they happen in this book."

—Richard Bernstein, *The New York Times Book Daily*

"Mahoney . . . knows the nuts and bolts of a sweeping multi-jurisdictional police operation. He is also able to portray complex, believable characters struggling mightily with their own muddled lives. Fans of William Caunitz, Robert Daley, and Ed McBain will savor this top-drawer procedural."

—Wes Lukowsky, *Booklist*

"A complex plot is no deterrent to enjoyment of Mahoney's ambitious thriller . . . Mahoney's characters are always solid, and this tale is almost a primer on Chinese community dynamics. He pulls no punches and speeds to a perfect ending."

—*Publishers Weekly*

BLACK AND WHITE

"Mahoney gives compulsive procedural buffs exactly what they crave."

—*The New York Times Book Review*

"*Black and White* is as gripping a novel about a police investigation as you can get . . . a top-notch thriller."

—*Chicago Tribune*

"Few authors map the political minefields faced by cops on a high-profile case with more realism than Mahoney . . . a brilliantly twisted plot."

—*Publishers Weekly*

"Exact and fascinating."

—*Kirkus Reviews*

"Compelling, graphic."

—*Booklist*

"Mahoney does a great job of showing us an insider's view of a cop's world."

—*Rocky Mountain News*

"Mahoney . . . draws on his twenty-five years as a cop to provide blow-by-blow description of how homicide detectives do their job."

—*The Free Lance–Star*

"Suspenseful . . . graphic details . . . the finale is a shocker."

—*The Sunday Oklahoman*

ONCE IN, NEVER OUT

"Mahoney doesn't sell his readers short. He keeps the action moving."

—*Chicago Tribune*

"Mahoney . . . knows the drill on conducting a manhunt . . . and he takes us through the crime-scene photos, the morgue visits, the criminal profiling, the computer searches, and all the rest of it with scientific precision and absolute authenticity."

—Marilyn Stasio, *The New York Times Book Review*

"Gripping . . . With absorbing exotic background and richly developed characters, Mahoney . . . delivers an unusual procedural that rises far above the genre norm."

—*Publishers Weekly*

"Succeeds wonderfully . . . A superb effort from an emerging master of the genre."

—*Kirkus Reviews*

"A nonstop roller-coaster ride of a thriller . . . Fast-paced and lean."

—*The Irish Echo*

**St. Martin's Paperbacks Titles
by Dan Mahoney**

THE PROTECTORS

THE TWO CHINATOWNS

BLACK AND WHITE

ONCE IN, NEVER OUT

HYDE

EDGE OF THE CITY

DETECTIVE FIRST GRADE

JUSTICE

DAN MAHONEY

St. Martin's Paperbacks

JUSTICE

Copyright © 2003 by Dan Mahoney.

Cover photo montage by Herman Estevez.

Library of Congress Catalog Card Number: 2003041399

ISBN: 0-312-98736-6
EAN: 80312-98736-7

Printed in the United States of America

St. Martin's Press hardcover edition / August 2003
St. Martin's Paperbacks edition / October 2004

St. Martin's Paperbacks are published by St. Martin's Press, 175 Fifth Avenue, New York, NY 10010.

10 9 8 7 6 5 4 3 2 1

For my Peggy Taggart

JUSTICE

JUSTICE

ONE

Gaston awoke suddenly, feeling nervous, and he automatically reached for the pistol under his pillow. Without knowing how he knew, he still knew: There was someone in the house, someone who didn't belong there. He checked the clock on the nightstand at the side of the bed: 3:06 A.M., an hour when criminals were up and about. He listened intently, trying to detect any sound. Then he heard it, a faint tapping downstairs that lasted only seconds.

Gaston placed his hand gently on his wife's back. Lela was sleeping soundly in her usual position, rolled up into a ball with her back to him and her hands clasped between her knees, breathing rhythmically. She purred at his touch, and he felt the muscles in her strong back tighten beneath the silk nightgown, then relax again.

Gaston considered waking her but decided against it. It was man's work that had to be done. Someone foolish was trying to prey on a predator, and that wasn't allowed. He sat up, swung his feet off the edge of the bed, and stood up in one fluid motion with his pistol extended in front of him, and aimed at the bedroom door. He was wearing cotton pajamas that didn't hide his physical attributes; he was a compact, muscular man who moved slowly and gracefully. The house was dark, but he could see well enough as he silently headed for the door in his bare feet. He had grown up in the jungles of Colombia, and was used to hunting at night.

Gaston's first thought was his children, so he checked their bedrooms first. His six-year-old son, Gaston Junior, was asleep in his bed with his covers thrown off. The central air-conditioning was turned on high, and Gaston thought the room too chilly. He covered his son, then checked his daughter's bedroom.

Three-year-old Alicia was also sleeping, sucking her thumb as usual. Her young nanny, Linda, was asleep in her bed across the room from Alicia's, and Gaston took a moment to admire her form under her sheet. *Linda* meant "pretty" in Spanish, and she was just that: seventeen, pretty, and always smiling, especially when he was around. A distraction, Gaston thought, especially since Lela had noticed and commented on it. Just once, but that was enough. Gaston was a man of few virtues, but marital fidelity was one of them. He considered Linda a test of that virtue, a test he wasn't sure he would always pass if she remained, so he decided just then that he would pay her a year's wages and send her back to Colombia.

Gaston returned his attention to Alicia and eased her thumb from her mouth. She stirred but didn't wake up, and he smiled when she put her thumb back in. He left the bedroom, intending to take the back stairway, but something on the landing five steps down stopped him. His German shepherd, Peligra, was lying there, apparently asleep. He whistled soft and low, just once, but the dog didn't stir.

Drugged or dead, Gaston thought, and he cautiously descended to the landing. The dog didn't move as he stood over her, but her eyes were open and she was panting. He moved her head with his foot, and found what he expected. The dog had vomited, he felt the slime on his bare feet. Peligra wasn't let out at night, so her presence there told Gaston that he was right: There was an intruder.

Gaston considered going back upstairs and calling the police but quickly rejected that idea. He didn't want inquisitive cops running around his house again, and he preferred to deal with the intruder in his own way. Once he did, the cops would have a puzzle to worry them, a tortured body found far from his house with sensitive parts missing.

There was a window at the landing, and Gaston opened it

without making a sound. He felt the warm, moist night air rush in, then stuck his head out the window and looked around. The house was set on half an acre in the fashionable Malba neighborhood and it was completely surrounded by a brick wall. The property was tastefully illuminated by dim lights designed to show off the house and the grounds, but security had been foremost on Gaston's mind when he had them installed. He could see both the four-foot wall in front of the house and the eight-foot wall in the rear. The electric driveway gate was closed, and nothing he could see appeared suspicious. Both the front and rear yards were crisscrossed by hidden infrared motion detectors that should have alerted his bodyguard Carlos to the presence of any intruder. He saw no sign of Carlos outside, so he focused on the garage. It was twenty feet from his window, and the side door was slightly ajar. He couldn't be sure, but Gaston thought he saw a dim source of illumination coming from inside the garage.

Gaston opened the landing window wider and slid out feet first. It was a fifteen-foot drop, and the ground stung his feet when he landed, but he ignored the pain as he rolled once, then sprang to his feet in a crouch with his pistol aimed at the garage door as he advanced toward it. He pressed himself flat against the garage wall and took a quick look to his left and right. He had a better view of the front and rear yards from his new position but still saw no sign of the intruder. Then he detected a faint odor, and knew at once what it was. Burning flesh, inside the garage. He lowered himself flat on the ground and peered around the doorjamb.

Carlos was the source of the odor. He was lying on his back on the hood of Gaston's BMW, and his shirt was the fuel for a smoldering fire that went out as Gaston watched. He strained his eyes as he searched the dark recesses of the garage. He saw only Carlos, but thought someone else inside might be lying in wait behind either the BMW or the Mercedes.

Gaston would have preferred a more cautious approach, but he didn't have the time. He stood up and entered, hugging the wall with his pistol held ready. It took him another minute to determine there was no longer a threat, and then he examined Carlos's body with anger welling up inside him. People would pay dearly for this, he promised himself.

Carlos had been more than just a trusted, faithful bodyguard; he was the closest thing to a friend Gaston had ever had. They were from the same village and had come to the United States together to pursue Gaston's business interests.

Carlos had been killed by a single shot to his right eye, but death had not caught him by surprise. Gaston figured Carlos had begged for the bullet to end his suffering. He had also been shot in both kneecaps, his hands were handcuffed behind him, his mouth was stuffed with a roll of gauze, and he had been tortured with a blowtorch.

It was an interrogation technique Gaston knew well, because he had seen Carlos himself perform it. His face was burned, and there was nothing left of his eyebrows and mustache. That was where the flame had been applied first, Gaston figured, because that was the way Carlos used to do it. First the face, to get the victim's total attention and show him that the interrogation was to be a serious affair, and next the armpits. Carlos's shirt was burned away at both armpits, and that was probably when he had been offered a chance to talk. Carlos hadn't, and the procedure had continued, starting at his navel and working down to his groin. His shirt and pants were burned away in a straight line from his fourth button to the bottom of his fly, his flesh was charred black, and all his pubic hair had been burned away. That was when Carlos had talked, Gaston knew, because the next step in the procedure hadn't been applied to him. Carlos's shoes hadn't been burned.

Carlos was a big man, strong and tough, so even though he had been shot in both kneecaps, Gaston figured it still took two men to hold him down during that painful session. That meant two or more opponents, with at least one of them in the house. Tough odds, Gaston realized, but he would have the element of surprise on his side.

Or would he? In a near panic, Gaston rolled Carlos's

body off the car, and saw at once that the situation was even worse. Carlos always wore an electronic wristband while guarding the house, and the device was keyed to the motion detectors. An LED display told him when a beam had been crossed and which beam had picked up the motion. The wristband was gone, and Gaston realized that he had crossed a beam when he went from the house to the garage. If his opponents knew how the device operated, then they knew they had trouble brewing near or in the garage.

Carlos had told them everything they wanted to know, Gaston decided, so they knew he was there. Worse, Carlos's pistol and cell phone were also missing. The hunter had become the hunted, and he needed a little time to think in a more secure place. His opponents would know every move he made, so the alarm system meant to protect him had to be disabled before he could go back on the offensive—and he had a way to do that. A remote-control device in each car activated or deactivated the alarm system, and Gaston used the one in the glove compartment of the BMW to shut the system down. He then put the remote control in the pocket of his pajamas.

Leaving the garage in a running crouch, Gaston zigzagged across his rear yard to the safety offered by a stand of pine trees planted along his west wall. He surveyed his house from the rear and saw nothing out of place. There wasn't a light on in the house, the back door seemed to be intact, and every window he could see was closed. Then Gaston realized there would be no need to break a door or window to get in. The house locks were accessed by means of a code, and Carlos had surely given them the correct numbers to punch in.

But for what other reason did they torture Carlos? What information did Carlos have that they so desperately wanted to know? Carlos ordinarily wasn't included in the planning stages of any of Gaston's deals. Of course, Carlos had possessed enough incriminating information to send Gaston to prison for life, but Gaston was sure that whoever had tortured Carlos had nothing to do with the law. Even in Colombia the cops would never use such advanced and painful interrogation techniques.

Then who was he up against? He hadn't heard the shots that had wounded and killed Carlos, and he was sure that the sound of a shot would have awakened him instantly. They're using silenced pistols, Gaston reasoned, but how had they gotten the jump on Carlos? Carlos was like a watchdog, suspicious of everything, and alert to every sound and movement.

Then Gaston saw a flashlight shine for an instant in his dining room, and he knew what Carlos had told them. The safe was in the dining room, so carefully hidden beneath the floorboards that the police had failed to find it when they had executed the search warrant on Gaston's house—but Carlos had known where it was. The safe didn't contain much at the time, maybe four or five hundred thousand, but Gaston was sure that was what his opponents were after—and knowing their target placed them square in the bull's-eye of *his* target.

Gaston crawled along the wall until he reached a point near the corner of the house. He was just about to dash for the house when he saw it, a pinprick of red light on the hand that held his pistol. He knew what it meant, and dropped to the ground—but not fast enough. He heard the dining room window break, and felt the sting in his hand at the same time. It took him a second to realize that he had been shot and that he no longer held his gun. He searched the lawn in front of him, looking for it, but he couldn't see it.

His opponents showed him where it was with another pinprick of red light focused on the butt of his pistol, ten feet to Gaston's left in the pachysandras bordering the lawn. Gaston crawled for the pistol, and was just about to grab it by the barrel when another pinprick of red light focused on the offending hand. Gaston froze, staring in fascination at the two pinpricks of red light, inches apart. Then he looked up at the window, but in the darkened dining room he couldn't see anyone inside. Two of them, at least, he realized. Two men in my dining room at the window, and they're armed with laser-sighted, silenced pistols. Options?

Surrender was the only one that came to mind, and he slowly withdrew his hand. The red dot stayed on it, and Gaston was surprised to see himself get shot again. The bullet passed through his hand and buried itself in the ground underneath. Although he was aware of the pain in both his hands, Gaston was still able to think clearly. "Don't shoot me again," he said. "I give up, and I'll give you anything you want."

There was no reply, so Gaston decided that if he was going to die, it wouldn't be while he was on his hands and knees. A painful effort pushed him up onto his elbows, then he stood and waited.

Gaston finally got his reply, but it wasn't what he expected. One red dot remained on the butt of the pistol, but the other moved up Gaston's left arm until he could no longer see it—but he knew where it was because he could finally see the source of the laser beam. One of his opponents had sighted on the point directly between Gaston's eyes, and Gaston could see the laser sight mounted on top of the pistol. He raised his hands, and felt the blood running down his wrists. "Don't shoot, and I'll give you the combination for the safe," Gaston tried.

"Quiet, you idiot! If you wake up your wife and kids, I'll have to kill them, too," was the low reply from inside.

That simple statement gave Gaston a few pieces of information. One was that the man inside intended to kill him, no matter what. And, since he said *I'll* have to kill them, not *we'll* have to kill them, he was probably acting alone. But what makes me an idiot? The answer hit him at once: After I turned the alarm system off, Gaston realized, he turned it back on with the wrist control. He always knew where I was.

The news was all bad, but Gaston still felt a sense of relief. He would die, but his wife and kids would live. That relief ended a second later when Gaston was able to see the second laser sight on the pistol his opponent held in his other hand. Both pistols were sighted on the bridge of his nose.

Gaston involuntarily closed his eyes and waited for death to claim him. When that didn't happen, he opened his eyes

again and found he could no longer see the source of the
laser beam. Then he looked down: There was a red dot on
each of his knees, and then his kneecaps exploded. Gaston's
legs buckled, and he hit the ground hard. The pain was intense, but he didn't move, and he didn't scream. He wasn't
thinking clearly, but he was still trying to assess his situation
when he lost consciousness.

When Gaston came to, he kept his eyes closed. He knew
he was lying on his back, he knew he was handcuffed from
the rear with his hands under him, and he felt the air-
conditioning, so he knew he was in the house. He suddenly
became aware of the pain in his hands and knees, and the
pain intensified until it became almost unbearable. Gaston
steeled his mind and bore the pain without moving. He then
opened one eye a fraction for a second, and was momentar-
ily blinded by the light. He realized that he was on his dining
room table, and the chandelier overhead was on. A big hand
slapped him across the face, hard, and he opened his eyes to
face his attacker.

It was a black man who stared back at Gaston impas-
sively. He wore rubber gloves and two shoulder holsters,
with a large laser-sighted pistol in each holster. The man had
almost no neck, just a head perched on top of broad shoulders. His face didn't show age, and although he was balding
at the sides, Gaston couldn't tell if he was forty or sixty.
There was something about the man that seemed familiar,
but Gaston couldn't remember ever meeting him. "Do I
know you?" he asked.

"If you were smart, you would. But you're not, so you
don't," the man replied, and Gaston was struck by how deep
his voice was.

"Why should I know you?" he asked.

"Because you've made yourself into my enemy, and
smart men always take the time to know their enemies."

"What have I ever done to you?"

"Figure it out."

Gaston tried, but it didn't come to him. "Can you help me
out with a name, at least?"

"Sure. You can call me Don."

"Don? Is that your real name?"

"Donald, actually, but Don will do."

The name meant nothing to Gaston, but Don didn't give him time to think about it. He grabbed the edge of the dining room table and lifted it, rolling Gaston off the table and onto the floor. Gaston landed hard, and broke his nose when his face hit the floor. He found himself lying next to the floorboards Don had removed to expose the safe. In order to remove the floorboards, the pegs holding the finished wood strips to the supporting cross beams underneath had been tapped down.

Don had gained that information from Carlos, and Gaston recognized his tools. Lying next to the opening in the floor was the rubber mallet and the dowel Gaston always used to gain access to the safe, along with a large duffel bag that appeared to be empty.

Don then used his foot to push Gaston's head to the opening, and Gaston could see some additional work he had done. Gaston's circular safe was embedded in the house's foundation, and Don had packed the space around the door with plastic explosives. A blasting cap with a radio detonator attached was imbedded in the explosives.

"Are you going to give me the combination, or am I going to have to blow it?" Don asked calmly, with no menace in his voice.

"You're going to have to blow it," Gaston replied.

"Fine, but do you know what's directly overhead?"

It took Gaston a confused moment to run the layout of the house through his mind, and then it came to him. "My daughter's bedroom."

"More precisely, your daughter's bed. What do you think is going to happen to the heavy door of that safe when I blow it off?"

"I don't know."

"I do. The way I have the charge rigged, that door will be propelled upward at an approximate speed of a thousand feet a second. It will go right through the ceiling above us, right through the floor upstairs, probably right through your daughter's mattress, and maybe right through her."

Gaston didn't know if that was true, but he wasn't going to take a chance. "Spin the dial right past zero twice and stop at nine. Then spin left to twenty, right to thirty-seven."

"Good decision." Don grabbed Gaston's legs and pulled him away from the opening with ease. Then he got down on his hands and knees, bent over the safe, worked the combination, and opened the door. He reached into the deep safe and pulled out forty-three stacks of wrapped hundred-dollar bills and three computer disks.

It seemed to Gaston that the money didn't interest Don much, but he appeared elated to find the disks under the cash in the safe. "Those disks won't help you much. Everything on them is in code," Gaston commented.

"That's all right. I have the code."

"Impossible," Gaston countered. "I devised it myself, and I'm the only one who knows it."

"Liar. Jorge Rodriguez knew it," Don replied with a smile that told Gaston that he and Carlos weren't the first victims that night. Jorge was Gaston's wholesale distribution manager, and they shared the code to keep a record of transactions that included accounts of product imported and product delivered. "What are you going to do with that information?"

"Everybody that works for you or deals your stuff is going out of business the hard way."

"You're going to turn it over to the police?"

"No, that would be the easy way. I said it would be the hard way."

"You think you can kill them all?"

"Don't know, but I'm going to find out."

"Why?"

"It hasn't come to you yet?"

"No."

"Too bad, but if you love your daughter, you have a few more minutes to figure it out."

"What do you mean by that?"

"Watch." Don removed the plastic explosive, blasting

cap, and detonator from around the edges of the safe, and placed it all inside. Then he opened the duffel bag, and Gaston saw that it hadn't been empty after all. It contained pounds and pounds of six-penny nails, and Don poured them into the safe on top of the explosives. He left the safe door open, then packed the money and the disks into the duffel bag.

Gaston got the plan at once. For some reason, Don was going to kill his daughter after all. The safe would serve as a cannon, and he was going to set off the charge and send the nails through his daughter's body upstairs.

Don pulled a roll of gauze from his pocket. He bent over, stuffed the gauze into Gaston's mouth, and stepped back to admire his handiwork. "I think you need a little more work," he announced. He took a switchblade from his pocket, opened it up with the push of a button, and he bent over Gaston again.

Gaston couldn't see what Don did to him, but he felt the cuts, four of them, two on each bicep. Finally satisfied, Don took the radio detonator from his pocket and showed it to Gaston. It was a small device that resembled an electronic garage door opener. "Once I'm away, I'm going to push this button and set off my bomb," he said. "You know what you have to do to give your daughter any chance for survival."

Don picked up the duffel bag and left. Gaston heard the front door open and close. In order for his daughter to survive when the bomb went off and blew all the nails toward the ceiling, a large part of the force of the explosion would have to be absorbed by a buffer. Gaston put it in place without a second thought. It was a short, painful crawl, but he ignored the pain as he used his shattered legs to push himself forward on the floor until his body completely covered the opening that contained the safe. Then he closed his eyes and prayed for the first time in thirty years as he waited for his loud and messy death.

Maybe it was the prayer, or maybe it was just his subconscious working overtime, but Don's face suddenly popped into Gaston's mind, and he remembered where he had seen it before. On a TV news show, he was sure, but he couldn't remember if Don was a reporter or part of a story.

It didn't make much difference to Gaston, but Don's face was the last conscious image on his mind.

TWO

It was to have been a three-week family vacation away from New York City and the NYPD, and it should have been a wonderful one. Detective First Grade Brian McKenna had rented a Fort Myers Beach condo at a great off-season rate from Mike McCormick, a retired cop who had started a real estate business there. McKenna and Angelita had lived briefly in the same Fort Myers Beach condo complex, and they knew and liked many of their neighbors, most of whom were retired cops from one Midwest city or other. McKenna also appreciated many of the restaurants in town, so Angelita would get a break in the cooking and cleaning department.

To make everyone even happier, included in the rental package were three jet skis and a twenty-seven-foot motor-boat docked right outside the condo on a canal that accessed the Gulf of Mexico. The kids especially enjoyed outings on those toys, and there was an easy eighteen-hole golf course across the road to keep McKenna entertained during the early mornings.

The first week had been great. McKenna used the condo's pool to teach his four-year-old twins how to swim, and they had learned well enough to impress him. The condo had the Disney channel and the cartoon channel to amuse the twins when McKenna and Angelita needed some quiet time, and seven-year-old Janine was no problem at all. Two of the neighbors had grandchildren visiting, so Janine had formed a friendship with one of them, another seven-year-old girl.

Perfect vacation, and then Cisco had arrived with his girl-

friend, Agnes. As partners in the NYPD's Major Case
Squad, McKenna and Cisco frequently took their vacations
at the same time. However, since McKenna thought of it
more as a vacation from Cisco than a vacation from the
NYPD, he had never considered asking Cisco to join him in
his travels. He and Cisco were great friends at work, but they
had entirely different interests and lifestyles, so they rarely
socialized together.

McKenna was considered the NYPD's most famous detective, and that annoyed Cisco no end. Cisco considered
McKenna to be an exceptionally lucky detective—lucky to
have him for a partner and lucky to have the police commissioner, Ray Brunette, as his longtime best friend. Because of
that friendship, as Cisco was never reluctant to point out,
McKenna was frequently assigned the big cases that received the press attention that had made him so famous, and
McKenna conceded whenever asked that Cisco was right.

McKenna also conceded that having Cisco for a partner
helped him solve those big cases. Cisco was the greatest natural athlete McKenna knew; he was hardworking, dedicated,
glib, and sometimes practiced his detective craft so well that
even the chiefs who loathed him admitted that he just might
be as good as he thought he was.

Cisco had known where McKenna was going on vacation, which was unfortunate since Cisco also knew Mike
McCormick. Agnes had given Cisco the idea of joining
the McKennas. Agnes loved Cisco and desperately wanted
to marry him, and Cisco loved her in his own way, but
McKenna considered him a confirmed bachelor with an eye
for and a way with the ladies. Agnes had thought it would be
nice to show Cisco the way happily married people lived,
and she had pestered him for days to take her to Fort Myers
Beach. She and Angelita got along well, and the McKenna
kids thought Cisco was the greatest thing ever. Since Cisco
could easily adopt the attitudes and actions of a spoiled ado-
lescent, he understood kids and loved entertaining them—as
long as they were other people's kids. So Agnes had prevailed, and on the seventh night of their vacation McKenna

and Angelita had discovered that Cisco and Agnes were their new next-door neighbors.

The misery began the next morning when Cisco joined McKenna for his morning round of golf, breaking up McKenna's usual foursome. McKenna considered himself a fair golfer and played about twenty times a year. Cisco, on the other hand, played once every couple of years, so McKenna had been happy to pair off with Cisco to teach his younger partner a thing or two about how the game was played.

McKenna shot his best round of the year, but Cisco beat him by eight strokes, and he had been ungracious enough to give McKenna a few pointers and lessons along the way. After golf, Cisco had devoted himself to a few hours of amusing the kids at poolside with his juggling routines, his magic tricks, and his handstands and back flips. The kids loved it, of course, and their joy increased when Cisco prevailed upon their father to come out and join in the fun.

Cisco had shown the kids the secrets behind his magic tricks and then used McKenna as his assistant. Cisco pulled quarters from McKenna's nose and eggs from his ears. The eggs broke in McKenna's hands when he handled them, and Cisco topped even that routine when he pulled a lady's bra and panties from McKenna's pockets. In Cisco's shell game, McKenna could never find the pea, and he never did figure out how Cisco performed his card tricks. The end result was that the kids were convinced Cisco was a genius but feared their father might be a boob.

But McKenna was still game, and he enrolled with his kids in a juggling lesson. Janine picked it up quickly and was soon juggling two items without a problem. McKenna was able to do that as well, and then the lesson advanced to three items. In McKenna's case, it was his keys, a tennis ball, and his wallet, and McKenna thought he had it down pat until he juggled his wallet into the pool. He immediately jumped after it, fully dressed, with an excellent dive intended to recover some prestige with his kids. He grabbed the wallet, but hit his head on the bottom of the pool and put a bloody knot on his forehead that gave him an instant headache. Cisco insisted on driving him to the hospital to have his head checked, and McKenna reluctantly agreed. "You shouldn't be playing so hard at your age" was the unsolicited opinion of the young intern who processed McKenna through the emergency room and discharged him with a bandage on his forehead that the McKenna kids dubbed his "Juggling Contest Last-Place Patch."

For dinner that night, Cisco had insisted on cooking for everybody. He was proud of his culinary talents and prepared his new recipe for a spicy Indian dish, chicken vindaloo. It turned out that Cisco's dish was delicious—maybe a trifle more spicy than they preferred but still good enough so that both McKenna and Angelita had allowed themselves a second helping. The kids had loved it, too, and ate their fill.

Right after coffee, McKenna had been the first one to feel an uncomfortable growling low in his stomach, and he excused himself to head for the bathroom. Ten minutes later he still hadn't returned, and then Angelita excused herself to visit the other bathroom. For that night and the next day, McKenna and Angelita suffered through the worst cases of diarrhea they had ever experienced. Cisco, Agnes, and the kids were all fine, and Cisco explained to the kids that their parents just hadn't been blessed with strong constitutions.

The next morning Cisco had filled in for McKenna, playing golf with McKenna's usual foursome, and he beat them all out of their bridge and pinochle money. That night Cisco had further exasperated McKenna's neighbors when he enrolled himself in the condo complex's shuffleboard tournament. He won it to the applause of Agnes and McKenna's kids, but they were the only ones clapping when Cisco was presented with his trophy.

McKenna had never considered his neighbors to be great sports, and that night he received calls from two of them. After very little in the way of chitchat, both had presented McKenna with the same pointed question: When is that pain-in-the-ass pal of yours going home?

• • •

It wasn't Cisco's fault, McKenna knew. Cisco had done
nothing wrong—he was just being Cisco—but McKenna
didn't know if he could take another day of being shown up
in front of his wife and kids. Since Cisco's arrival,
McKenna's head hurt, his kids thought he was an uncoordi-
nated dullard, his neighbors avoided him, and Angelita was
barely speaking to him. McKenna was absolutely certain
that he would lose in a physical confrontation with Cisco,
but he was almost ready to smack his partner anyway.
Ridiculous idea, he knew, but at fifty-one years old he was
prepared to take a beating in front of his wife and kids just to
experience the satisfaction of getting in that one good shot.

THREE

McKenna had canceled the morning golf game with Cisco, and he had no idea what Cisco was doing at the moment. Angelita and the kids were down at the pool. McKenna figured he'd make himself some breakfast, do a brisk five-mile run, then take a jet-ski ride by himself. There was a knock at the door, and McKenna opened it. It was Cisco, carrying two New York newspapers, the *Times* and the *Post*. "Got some interesting things happening back in town," he announced as he brushed past McKenna. "Four murders in two days, all good ones."

"What makes a murder a good one?" McKenna asked.

"Victim and manner of execution. There's a new killer in town, a guy with a sense of style."

Cisco took a seat at the kitchen table, and spread the newspapers on it. The *Post*'s headline was MURDER IN MALBA, and the first three columns of the *Times*'s front page titled the story DOUBLE TORTURE-MURDER IN QUEENS.

"I thought you said there were four murders," McKenna said.

"There are, but the second two aren't headlines. Brooklyn murders, probably drug-related. Page B-three in the *Times*, page thirty-six in the *Post*."

"And you think they're related to the Malba murders?"

"Maybe," Cisco said. "I'd be interested to hear what you think."

So it's to be a challenge, McKenna thought. Good. It's about time I beat this guy in something. He read the *Times* story first while Cisco reread the *Post* account.

The *Times*, as usual, was straightforward and contained no speculation. There was an aerial photo of the scene of the crime, the million-dollar home of Gaston Cruz in the very-fashionable Malba neighborhood on Queens's north shore. Dead were Gaston Cruz, age 39, and Carlos Montoya, age 41. Cruz and Montoya were both Colombian nationals, and according to Mrs. Lela Cruz, her husband was the founder and president of the American branch of Exito Seguros, Ltd., a Colombian insurance and investment company with offices in Manhattan, Miami, Bogotá, and Panama City. The last time she had seen her husband alive was when they had gone to bed together that evening. Montoya was her husband's longtime driver, and he lived in his own small apartment on the third floor of the house.

Mrs. Cruz had been awakened at 6:00 A.M. by the sound of the family dog whining downstairs. She went down and found her husband's body in the dining room. He was gagged with a roll of gauze rag in his mouth, handcuffed, and lying on top of an open safe hidden under the dining room floor. Montoya's body was discovered in the garage five minutes later by Mrs. Cruz, and she then called the police. When the first units arrived, they discovered that the safe under Cruz's body contained what appeared to be an antipersonnel bomb. The Bomb Squad was called, and all the houses on the block were evacuated. Members of the Bomb Squad, however, determined that although the device in the safe appeared to be a bomb with a plastic explosives charge, it was not. In the opinion of Detective Dennis Hunt of the Bomb Squad, the "plastic explosive" was Play-Doh, and later testing at the police lab proved him right.

According to Detective George MacFarlane of the Queens Homicide Squad, Cruz had been shot four times outside the house, once in each hand and once in each knee, and then had been carried into the dining room. None of the gunshot wounds by themselves would have been fatal, but Cruz had also been cut through the arteries of each arm, and he had bled to death. An S&W .44-magnum pistol had been found in the rear yard, near the spot where Cruz had been shot by a person standing inside the house at the dining room window. The dining room window had been broken by the shots, but that was not how the killers had gotten into the house; there was a rosebush under the window surrounded by mulch, and there were no footprints in the soft mulch.

Montoya had also been shot in the kneecaps, then tortured with a blowtorch, and finally killed with a shot to the head.

How the killer or killers had gained entry to the house was still under investigation by the Queens Homicide Squad. The house and grounds were protected by an alarm system, which had been on when Mrs. Cruz awoke. She told police that her husband had no enemies she knew of and that she didn't even know of the existence of the safe in the dining room. She, her two children, and a nanny had slept through the murders of her husband and his driver. She also stated that her husband did not own a gun.

McKenna decided to learn everything he could about the Queens murders before reading about the ones in Brooklyn, so he waited while Cisco continued reading the *Post*. Cisco was absentmindedly fiddling with his detective-shield ring as he went through the articles, and McKenna knew he only did that when he was deep in concentration. Cisco wasn't just reading, he was studying.

So we're in a real contest here, McKenna thought, but what's the point? We're both in Florida on vacation for another week, and homicides aren't ordinarily handled by the Major Case Squad.

Cisco then noticed McKenna watching him, so he quickly closed the *Post*. "Don't tell me you read about all those murders already," he said.

"No, just the Malba murders," McKenna replied. "First Malba, then Brooklyn."

"Sensible," Cisco said as he passed the *Post* to McKenna. Then he took up the *Times* and began reading it again.

On the front page of the *Post* was a photo of Cruz's covered body being removed from the house on a gurney by two morgue attendants. Mrs. Cruz was standing in the front yard, watching, with a large German shepherd sitting next to her. She was dressed in dark slacks, a light-colored blouse, and heels, and she casually held the dog by the collar. To McKenna, she appeared to be a very attractive woman, tall and in shape, and he also noticed the key pad at the side of the front door.

The story filled all of pages three and four, and was continued on page twenty-six. The byline was Phil Messing, and the front pages had another photo of Lela Cruz, along with file photos of Dennis Hunt and George MacFarlane. There was also a file photo of Detective Joe Walsh of the Crime Scene Unit, which didn't surprise McKenna. Walsh hadn't even been mentioned in the *Times* article, but the *Post* typically covered sensational crime stories in more depth than the *Times* did. Since Walsh was the best crime-scene detective in the business, and a real glory hound besides, McKenna found it quite natural that he would involve himself in a case as big as this one was shaping up to be.

McKenna found it interesting that he and Cisco knew everyone involved in the case, and he thought that might explain Cisco's interest in it. Phil Messing was an old-time *Post* crime reporter and a good friend to them both; Dennis Hunt had been involved in a past case of theirs in which bombs had figured prominently; and George MacFarlane had worked in the Major Case Squad for years before accepting an assignment to the Queens Homicide Squad. McKenna noticed that the big case was already loaded with first-grade detectives—Hunt, MacFarlane, and Walsh—and he knew that Cisco detested two of the main players.

Cisco detesting Joe Walsh was easy for McKenna to understand, because almost everyone did. The role of the crime-scene detective was to assist the lead detective assigned the case, which Walsh did very well. But Walsh was a blowhard who had many reporters in his pocket. After a case was over, people reading about it in the papers could easily assume that Walsh was the real star of the case. The story would insinuate that Walsh had brilliantly gathered, correctly interpreted, and scientifically analyzed so much evidence at the crime scene that his lackey—technically, the lead detective—had nothing more to do than throw the cuffs on the villain and bring him to Central Booking.

George MacFarlane was another story altogether. MacFarlane was competent, hardworking, and he possessed a trait rarely found in a first-grader—modesty. Five years before, Cisco and MacFarlane had been working a kidnapping case together in the Major Case Squad. MacFarlane had been a second-grader at the time, and Cisco a first-grader. Cisco had been the assigned detective in the case, and after it was solved, he didn't mind if MacFarlane got the ink since the case was big enough to give him a shot at first grade. So Cisco had arranged for Phil Messing to interview MacFarlane. However, when Cisco read the *Post* in the office the next day, he was quick to notice that his name hadn't been mentioned even once in the article. Everything was MacFarlane, with pictures.

Not everybody knew that Cisco was offended, but McKenna did—and soon so did MacFarlane. He got his promotion to detective first grade, but wondered if it was worth it. Cisco went out of his way to torment MacFarlane in ways only Cisco could. He went to work early to go over the files on MacFarlane's active cases, and left little notes attached with small criticisms or suggestions. MacFarlane had been proud of the fact that he had been voted the most valuable player in his softball league, so Cisco joined another team in the league and took MacFarlane's most-valuable-player honor three years in a row. MacFarlane was also the goalie on a hockey team in an amateur league, so Cisco joined another team in the league just for the chance to send a high-speed puck MacFarlane's way.

Since MacFarlane was too proud to explain or apologize to Cisco for what had happened during that interview, he had been left with no choice but to leave the Major Case Squad in order to preserve his sanity. That he had done two years ago, and he hadn't been seen much in the newspapers since.

Phil Messing's *Post* story contained all the information the *Times* piece did and much more, which meant to

McKenna that MacFarlane had quite naturally spoon-fed
Messing in payment for the article that had gotten him promoted. Walsh, another frequent source of Messing's, was
also quoted in the article.

Messing first dealt with the times of death of the two victims. An assistant medical examiner had responded to the
scene. He estimated that Montoya had died around 3:00
A.M., and Cruz an hour and a half later, at 4:30 A.M.

Six of the spent bullets in the shootings had been recovered, along with seven ejected cartridge cases. Two pistols
of the same make, model, and caliber had been used, Beretta
Model 92F 9-millimeter automatics. All three slugs recovered from Montoya's body were from the same gun, but the
slugs recovered from Cruz's knees were from two different guns, and that led MacFarlane to assume there were at
least two killers involved. Strands of fine steel mesh and
burnt cotton fibers found by Walsh embedded in the spent
slugs suggested to him that the killers had used silencers on
their pistols. In the pocket of Cruz's pajamas was an electronic device, which Mrs. Cruz identified as a remote control
used to activate and deactivate the alarm system. MacFarlane ascertained that the device had been taken by Cruz
from the glove compartment of a car parked in the garage,
Mrs. Cruz's BMW.

Two pools of Montoya's blood had been found on the
path leading from the side door of the house to the garage.
One ejected 9-millimeter shell casing turned up on the path
near the garage, and another was found by Detective Walsh
in the garage gutter. According to Walsh, that meant at least
one of the killers had shot Montoya in both kneecaps from
the garage roof.

There was a blood trail on the path that began at the place
where Montoya had first been shot, and it led to the side
door of the garage and then into the garage. Bloodstains indicated that Montoya had been tortured, then killed, as he
lay on the hood of Cruz's BMW. Since Montoya weighed
220 pounds and his wounds would have prevented him from
walking, MacFarlane concluded that it would have taken

two men to drag him into the garage, place him on the hood of the car, and hold him down while he was being tortured.

Cuts on Montoya's wrists and scratches on the hood of the BMW suggested that he had been handcuffed with his arms behind his back during the torture process. Montoya's blood was found on the handcuffs on Cruz's body, so the killers had used only one set.

Also found on the landing of the back staircase was a pool of vomit containing small pieces of raw hamburger. According to Mrs. Cruz, their dog was never fed raw hamburger, so Detective Walsh concluded the dog had been drugged by the killers to keep it quiet and out of their way while they went about their murderous business. A vomit sample had been sent to the police lab, but chemical analysis to determine whether or not the dog had ingested a short-term stupor-producing drug was not yet complete.

The house was protected by an elaborate security system, with a total of nine infrared motion detectors hidden on the grounds around the house. Mrs. Cruz stated that the system was operable and still activated after she had discovered her husband's body. An alarm sounds in the house when three sensors pick up motion outside, and according to Mrs. Cruz, the alarm hadn't gone off the night before. She stated she had no idea how the killers got into the house and left with the system still activated, and MacFarlane didn't comment on that. No fingerprints of any persons not living in the house had been found.

On page twenty-six the *Post* provided sketches of the crime scenes, with layouts of the property, the garage, and all three floors of the Cruz home. McKenna noticed the sketches were labeled in Walsh's small, distinctive scrawl, and he knew that favor to Messing was another reason why Walsh had been mentioned so prominently in the article. As with all Walsh crime-scene sketches, these contained every detail a prosecutor, a chief, or another investigator would ever need to know: The locations of the bodies, the blood trails, the recovered cartridge cases, the hidden alarm sensors, and anything else Walsh had considered pertinent were there, along with precise measurements on the distance from one object to another.

As McKenna studied them, a number of questions arose. Then he noticed Cisco intently staring at him and smirking. He ignored Cisco and kept his mind focused on Walsh's sketches. Nothing else grabbed his attention, so he closed the paper. He was ready to play.

"So what doesn't make sense?" Cisco asked.

"The wife, for one," McKenna replied. "She's married to a Colombian living in a house wired to the hilt, with another Colombian bruiser living upstairs who's supposed to be a driver, and she says her husband has no enemies she knows of? And then she's saying she knew nothing about her husband's gun and the safe in the dining room?"

"The forty-four magnum found outside was the husband's?"

"Of course."

"So we'll agree it's drugs?"

"Someone has to take a close look at that Exito Seguros company," McKenna said, "but I'm ready to go with drugs— and I'm sure his wife knows that's her husband's business. They have two kids together, so they've known each other a while, and I'd bet she doesn't have too many misconceptions on how they all wound up living in that fancy house."

"And the company's a front?"

"An assumption, but I'd be surprised if it wasn't. I'd also be surprised if we don't have Gaston on file somewhere. If so, he came up the hard way, and he considered himself a tough guy."

"Not tough enough, apparently," Cisco observed.

"No, and I'm sure that surprised him, but let's consider his conduct anyway. Something wakes him up in the middle of the night, something suspicious enough to make him grab his gun and go investigate. Would your normal, run-of-the-mill Malba millionaire ever do that?"

"No, they'd call the cops."

"Especially after he found his dog drugged, he would. But not Gaston. He still figured he'd take care of business himself."

"How do you know he found the dog?" Cisco asked. "Maybe he took the front staircase down."

Point one for me, McKenna thought, and he tried to hide his smile. "You better take another look at Walsh's sketches," he said, pushing the *Post* toward Cisco.

Cisco ignored it. "No need, Cisco has already sufficiently studied the sketches," he said. "Footprint in the vomit pool, and I'll bet the M.E. will come up with traces of dog vomit on Gaston's foot."

Damn! Scratch the point, and now I have him up on his high horse, McKenna thought. Time to go on the offensive. "Another reason Gaston didn't call the police?" he asked.

"Aside from the fact he thought he could handle whatever himself? Simple. With his history, he doesn't like cops, and he doesn't want them in his house, poking around and asking questions. Maybe he had some second thoughts when he found Montoya, but by then he was already committed."

"How do you know he found Montoya?" McKenna asked.

"Easy one. His wife's remote was found in his pocket, and she kept it in the glove box of her BMW."

"And that's the easy answer."

"So it is. You want the extra-points answer?"

"Please."

"All right," Cisco replied. "The window on the landing is open, but the air-conditioning in the house was going full blast. Gaston went out that window, and I'll bet he left his fingerprints on it. Besides, a couple of drops of Montoya's blood trail between the window and the garage are smeared. Montoya was a burned mess, and that must have smelled. So Gaston went in to take a look. It's not in the sketches, but I'm betting he picked up a bit of Montoya's blood on his feet when he did."

"The autopsy will tell whether he did or not, but I'd say you're probably right."

"Wouldn't you say that *we're* probably right?" Cisco asked.

"Okay, *we're* probably right. Agree on everything so far, but here's the big question," McKenna said. "How did at least one of the killers get to the garage roof without tripping the alarms outside?"

"Do you know?"

"I think so."

"And so do I."

Since Cisco was an avid sky diver, McKenna was sure he did know, but the idea still sounded incredible to him. "That killer skydived onto that roof," McKenna said.

"Very good, Brian," Cisco said, and he graced McKenna with an approving nod. "Didn't expect you to get that one, but it's the only way he could've gotten there without tripping a couple of beams and waking up Mrs. Cruz."

"Could you do that?"

"With no wind and a wide two-car garage without much slope on the roof? Sure, nine times out of ten. The house is lighted up nice, makes for a landing zone that's easy to find," Cisco said confidently, and McKenna believed him. "What's he do next?" Cisco asked.

"Montoya's fully dressed, so let's assume he's on guard duty. One killer gets him out of the house and shoots out his kneecaps from the garage roof."

"How does he get him out of the house without waking up everybody else?"

"We need to make some assumptions about that alarm system, but let's say he has some device that somehow notifies him when one beam is tripped. This device also lets him shut the alarm off and on so he can investigate. The shooter throws a rope—maybe even his parachute—across one beam, reels it back in, then waits for Montoya to come out."

"Montoya's armed?" Cisco asked.

"Gun not recovered, but presumably. Does him no good when he's kneecapped as soon as he comes out. The alarm's off, so the other guy on the hit team . . ."

"If there is another guy," Cisco said.

"You don't think there is?"

"No."

"Why not?"

"The Brooklyn murders. After you read about them, you'll agree. Same guy, acting alone, did them all."

"Okay, if you say so. Now we have this one very strong shooter who jumps off the garage roof after he kneecaps Montoya. Then he drags him into the garage, hoists him onto the hood of the car, and goes to work on him with the blowtorch. By the time he's done, he knows all about the alarm system, he knows how to use whatever device Montoya has for turning the alarm off and on, he knows the lock code for the house, and he knows where the safe is."

"Do you think Montoya told him the combination?"

"He would've if he knew it, but I don't think he did," McKenna said, and Cisco gave him another approving nod. "Then he kills Montoya and goes into the house to deal with the dog."

"By drugging her, after he tortures and kills Montoya? A little strange, wouldn't you say?" Cisco asked.

"Yeah, I'll give you that *is* strange. He knows about the dog, but he doesn't shoot it. Instead, he comes prepared, and feeds it that hamburger laced with knockout juice."

"So what we have is a cold-blooded killer who can burn a guy's face and dick off, but he won't kill a dog? Matter of fact, goes out of his way not to kill the dog."

"That's what it looks like," McKenna agreed.

"You ever hear of a cold-blooded killer like that?"

"No. You?"

"Nope. Never came across a killer that nice."

McKenna knew Cisco was an animal lover, but Cisco's description of the killer was too much for him. "Nice? Nice, after what he did to Montoya?"

"Maybe Montoya got what he deserved," Cisco said. "I bet when his history is known, we'll find out he was a real murderous lowlife."

"Nobody deserves to die like he did."

"We'll see," Cisco said, unimpressed. "Let's get on to how he killed Gaston."

"Knew he was coming and ambushed him," McKenna said.

"How did he know Cruz was coming?"

"Because he planned it that way, and he needed Cruz for the combination. He probably made some little noise in the house, just enough to wake Cruz up, and he knew Cruz well enough to know how he'd react. Cruz was sharp, realized that the alarm was on and that the killer had taken Montoya's device. Cruz wanted to sneak up on him, so he turned the alarm off."

"Didn't help him much, did it?" Cisco asked.

"No, because when the killer saw the alarm go off, he just turned it back on. Knew where Cruz was the whole time and ambushed him."

"With two pistols?"

"A little strange, but if there's just one killer, he probably did that to confuse the police into thinking there's at least two on the hit team."

"That would make him pretty smart, wouldn't it?" Cisco asked, smiling.

"We already know he's smart. This whole operation reeks of brains. It's more than a bloody burglary; it's a revenge killing."

"So the killer knew Cruz?" Cisco asked.

"Sure he did. The killer wanted whatever Cruz had in the safe, but this was a revenge hit done with a perverse sense of humor."

"The Play-Doh?"

"Yeah. You know what's directly over the dining room?"

"Cruz's daughter's bedroom," Cisco replied.

"And that's the key. Once the killer had Cruz wounded and in pain, he needed the combination from him. Maybe he told him he'd shoot through the ceiling to kill his daughter if he didn't get it, but this guy's a joker. I think he wrapped the Play-Doh around the safe, and told him he was going to blow the safe into Cruz's daughter's bedroom."

"I agree. Cruz gives him the combination, he takes whatever's in the safe, and then he does what he really came to do. He kills Cruz, but that's not enough for him. He kills him with a twist, which is . . . ?" Cisco asked.

"He gives Cruz a choice on who lives and who dies," McKenna replied, responding to the challenge. "His daughter or him. He loads the safe with what Cruz thinks is an antipersonnel bomb, and tells Cruz it's going to go off soon. Then he leaves, chuckling to himself. There's a phone twenty-one feet from where Cruz is lying in a blood pool, so he can still crawl to it and maybe save himself."

"He's handcuffed and gagged," Cisco said.

"Makes no difference, he can still moan. Crawl over, press nine-one-one with his nose, moan into the phone, and the cops might get there in time to save him. But he does the noble thing instead. Crawls to the safe and covers it with his body so that maybe his daughter will live when the bomb goes off."

"And that's the joke. The killer tricked him into dying for nothing," Cisco said with a broad smile on his face.

"You think that's funny?"

"Call me a bad guy, but yeah, I think it's funny. Maybe when we get Cruz's history, you'll think so, too."

"Why would we get Cruz's history?" McKenna asked. "This is a Queens Homicide case, nothing to do with us."

"It's big now, and it's gonna get bigger," Cisco countered. "This guy's smart—too smart for MacFarlane—and he's far from done."

"So what do you wanna do? Get involved so you can throw some more darts at MacFarlane?"

"No, I like MacFarlane," Cisco said.

"You do?"

"Sure I do. Basically a good guy, he just needed a few lessons in propriety. He got them, and it's over."

"So why do you wanna get involved?"

"For the glory," Cisco admitted. "I predict there will be many more dead drug dealers, and the Major Case Squad's gonna be called in to assist. We're gonna wind up with it."

"Maybe the squad, but not us. We're on vacation for another ten days, and we're prepaid in these condos."

"Vacation's gonna be cut short. You can leave Angelita

and the kids here, and I'll leave Agnes," Cisco replied. "Read the Brooklyn case."

McKenna did, first the *Times* account and then the *Post* version. There was no byline for the *Times* story, and the one in the *Post* was written by John Schneider, a young reporter McKenna knew only by sight. Although it was also a double homicide, it didn't get anywhere near the coverage the Malba murders had. That didn't surprise McKenna; murders of rich people in mansions always garner greater public attention than the almost-routine Brooklyn killings involving drug dealers eliminating their competition. In truth, McKenna also recognized that those types of "drugs involved" murders didn't get much more than cursory, by-the-book treatment from the police, with many detectives categorizing them as "misdemeanor murders" or "public service homicides." Unless there were innocent victims caught in the carnage, drug-related murders were rarely front page or high priority.

The double murders in Brooklyn seemed to fit into that mold, but there were still a few things about them that attracted McKenna's interest. They had occurred in the Classon Hotel between one and two o'clock that morning, and, since Cisco thought the same man had committed both the Malba murders and the Brooklyn murders, McKenna first put the time sequence in order. The Malba murders had been committed the day before but had been discovered too late to make the morning edition of the newspapers. It was a good story, so the papers had still treated those murders as breaking news, even though McKenna was sure TV journalists in New York had covered them in some depth yesterday. On the other hand, the Brooklyn murders *were* breaking news, an early morning story that put the papers on a par with the local TV news stations. If both sets of murders had been committed by the same man, he had given himself almost a full day to rest up between them.

McKenna also knew the Classon Hotel but acknowledged that he hadn't so much as passed by the place in years. It was located in Bedford-Stuyvesant, a neighborhood where the white people were some of the cops. McKenna remembered it as a short-stay hotel, where rooms were rented for four hours in a nice setting for those with romance on their minds. The small hotel had been renovated ten years before. It boasted an intimate bar, and the building was located on a tree-lined plot that provided parking in the rear. The hotel also employed a small security force of large men, and McKenna had never heard of any serious police problems occurring there.

Dead were Ruben De Sales, age 41, and Raymond Ramsey, age 39, and the case was assigned to Detective Steve Chmil of the Brooklyn North Homicide Squad. De Sales's and Ramsey's bodies had been discovered by one of the hotel's security guards, Clarence DuBois, after the front desk received numerous calls from guests on the third and fourth floors that there were screams coming from one of the rooms on the fourth floor, possibly room 409. When DuBois knocked on the door of room 409, it was quiet inside. A big, well-built black man wearing a ski mask opened the door, placed a large automatic pistol to DuBois's nose, and invited him into the darkened room.

Under the circumstances, DuBois had immediately accepted the invitation, but the room was too dark for him to see the source of the screams. The host placed a handkerchief to DuBois's nose, instructed him to breathe deeply, and that was all DuBois remembered until he woke up in the large, heart-shaped bed in room 409. On either side of him in the bed were De Sales and Ramsey, both dead and very bloody, and each was holding a blow-up plastic mannequin. Cause of death for each was a single shot to the head, but both had been beaten before they died. There was blood everywhere in the room and signs of a violent struggle.

On the bureau opposite the bed were eighteen one-kilo wrapped packages of cocaine and two one-kilo packages of heroin. On top of the bags were a loaded MAC-10 machine pistol and two envelopes. One of the envelopes was addressed to the police, the other to the hotel management. Detective Chmil declined to reveal the contents of the envelopes, ar DuBois refused to be interviewed for the newspapers.

Without cooperation from Chmil and DuBois, the papers
had nothing else to report except to list De Sales's and Ramsey's criminal histories. At 41 years of age, De Sales had
managed to spend more than a third of his life in prison. He
had been arrested seven times and convicted four. Except for
a robbery committed when he was seventeen years old, all of
his arrests had been for sale of drugs. He had been released
from prison in 1999 after doing a six-year stretch.

Ramsey had also been arrested seven times, and his criminal history contained more violent crimes than De Sales's.
He had spent sixteen of his thirty-nine years in jail and had
been convicted for an assault, a robbery, and an attempted
murder with a firearm. The attempted-murder conviction
had gained him eight years in prison, and he had been released in 2001. He was scheduled to have remained on parole until 2005 before the killer had lightened his parole
officer's caseload by one.

The case had McKenna's interest, and there was much
more he wanted to know about it. He could find out everything about it with a call to either Brunette or Chmil, two old
friends. But which one? Chmil, he decided, because a call to
Brunette might indicate that he and Cisco wanted to work
the case, and McKenna didn't want to give Cisco that satisfaction just yet. He had known Chmil for many years, since
the time they had worked together as partners in the Street
Crime Unit.

Cisco also knew Chmil and had worked with him on a
case when both had been assigned to the Joint Organized
Crime Task Force. Cisco always talked well about Chmil but
considered him to be an unusual detective; Chmil was a first-
grader who had worked in a few other prestigious units, but
his heart was in the place he had made his bones, the Brooklyn North Homicide Squad, and he always returned there.
Since Chmil had condemned himself to solving murders that
    't generate much press interest, Cisco thought Chmil
        insane.

        McKenna and Cisco knew Chmil as a likable, easy-
         who got along well with the press, so the fact that

he wasn't talking about these murders told McKenna that the official lid was on. For some reason, Chmil had been strongly instructed not to talk, which was unusual in Brooklyn drug-related murder cases.

So there's something big brewing here, McKenna thought, but is Cisco right? Is it the same killer in both cases? Strong possibility, he concluded, if both sets of murders are drug related. In both cases the killer had inside information that had enabled him to pull off the murders. In the Malba murders he knew about the alarm system and the bodyguard, and in the Brooklyn murders he knew about a meeting that apparently involved a wholesale drug deal. In Queens he had executed Montoya with a single shot to the head, and in Brooklyn he had executed Ramsey and De Sales in the same manner. In both sets of murders, a prankster left clues that must have given both MacFarlane and Chmil a giggle: In Queens it had been the Play-Doh bomb, and in Brooklyn it had been the blow-up sex toys.

"Same guy?" Cisco asked, breaking McKenna's train of thought.

. McKenna ignored him because there were still two glaring issues to be thought through. He stared at the *Post* article, but he wasn't reading; he was thinking as Cisco watched him with that know-it-all smile that McKenna had found particularly annoying during the past week.

In the Brooklyn murders the killer had left drugs on the scene. McKenna didn't know the wholesale value of the drugs, but he knew it would be a big number. Very unusual conduct in any drug-related murder case, McKenna thought. Why had he done that? Either we're witnessing the beginnings of a big-time drug war, or the killer is some kind of vigilante.

But which is it? Enforcer or vigilante? McKenna wondered. Vigilante, he decided, and that was why the lid was on. The notes had told Chmil that there was more activity planned, and nothing shakes up a police department as much as a righteous, capable, active vigilante causing well-publicized mayhem. Cisco was right. The Major Case Squad was going to be assigned to assist the homicide squads, and if the vigilante wasn't caught in the next ten days, he and Cisco were definitely going to be involved.

McKenna closed both newspapers and folded his hands in front of him.

"Took you long enough," Cisco said. "Are you ready to put your infallible glamour-boy reputation on the line and risk an answer?"

"Same killer, and you're right about everything," McKenna replied.

"That doesn't make me right about everything," Cisco countered. "I said that it's going to be *our* case."

"Then you're wrong about that. We're on vacation for another ten days, and there are already good people assigned. The Job is going to give MacFarlane and Chmil everything they need to catch this guy, and they will—and it's not going to take them ten days to do it."

"Then you're wrong," Cisco said. "Chmil can't sit on those notes forever. The next time this guy hits—and he will hit again—those notes are going to have to be made public. Before that happens, your phone is gonna ring."

"Ray?"

"His back will be to the wall, and he's gonna call to ask his old pal how he's enjoying his vacation. Since I'll still be here with you, you'll say, 'Funny you should ask. I'm not really having much fun. Cisco wants to work this case, and he's driving me out of my mind.'"

"Cisco, are you planning to make me even more miserable than you already have?"

"That is Cisco's intention, and he will succeed. He plans to seek a new crown to add to his many others. Cisco will want to be known as The Most Annoying Prick God Ever Created."

"You already have that crown."

"I do?" Cisco asked, and he seemed to be surprised.

"Except for the kids, ask anybody here. We're ready to crown you in any kind of royal ceremony you desire, as long as you promise to go away after we do."

"Cisco will not go away, and now you have hurt his feelings."

To McKenna, it didn't appear that Cisco's feelings were hurt at all. He looked content and confident, like a man who knew he would win. But win what? To give up his vacation, it has to be more than just getting his picture in the papers a few more times. "Mind telling me why you want this case so much?"

"Because I want to meet this killer. Interesting person, class guy, but he has made a mistake, which he has to pay for. He has shown contempt for us and issued a challenge, which we will answer."

"What challenge?" McKenna asked. "The notes?"

"Yes, the notes."

All right. The notes contain something that has Cisco going, but how would he know what they say? McKenna wondered. Then the answer came to him. "I guess you called Chmil."

"You guessed right."

"What do the notes say?"

"The one to the police says, 'Stay tuned and stay sharp, because there's more fun in store. I intend to make the world a better place, and I know how to do it. Catch me if you can.' Used a laser printer to write it, untraceable, no prints."

Now that is a challenge, McKenna thought, one that has to be answered with the best the NYPD has—and Cisco naturally thinks that means him. He will be truly unbearable until we're assigned. "Were there any good prints recovered at the scene?"

"What do you think?"

"No."

"Then you're right again. This guy is much too sharp for any careless slipups."

"What did the note to the management say?"

"Another example that this is a classy opponent worthy enough to be engaged and bested by us. It said, 'Sorry for the mess, but it was unavoidable. This should cover the damages.' That note was wrapped around five thousand dollars in cash, and there's yet another classy note that wasn't reported in the papers. DuBois didn't know it until Chmil noticed a bulge in his shirt pocket, but he also got paid for his trouble—and his embarrassment."

"Embarrassment?"

"When he woke up in the middle of the dead clowns and the blow-up toys, he was holding a teddy bear clutched to his chest."

"How much, and what did the note say?"

"Three thousand dollars in hundreds, with the note wrapped around it. Said, 'Sorry to leave you like this, but I'm one of those guys who will do anything for a laugh. I hope there's no hard feelings.' Same deal: laser printer, no prints."

"So he printed the notes before he set out for the evening," McKenna observed.

"Apparently."

"So this guy knew exactly what he was gonna do and had the job planned down to the smallest detail. Knew he was going to make a mess killing Ramsey and De Sales, and he figured there would be some attempt at intervention from the hotel's security people."

"He knew more than that. Knew his targets well enough to know that De Sales was gay."

What does that have to do with anything? McKenna wondered, and then he knew. "De Sales was holding a male blow-up doll?"

"That he was, and if you think dirty and let your imagination run wild, you'll know just how he was holding it," Cisco said, and the thought obviously amused him.

McKenna did think filthy, but he didn't want to give Cisco the satisfaction of saying it out loud. "How about Ramsey? What kind of position was he in with his doll?"

"More conventional, female doll, but still amusing. He was on top of his and had his tongue in that little round mouth."

"Both victims naked?"

"No, just had their pants pulled down. Incidentally, Ramsey had a holster on his belt for a large pistol."

"So it was Ramsey's MAC-10 the killer left," McKenna said. "He left the gun just to show how bad a guy Ramsey really was."

"Good assumption."

"And since nobody at the hotel reported hearing shots, we can also assume he's using a silencer."

"Another good assumption," Cisco said.

"Were De Sales and Ramsey tortured?"

"Bruised and battered, but Chmil doesn't think so. He thinks they just got an old-fashioned beating by someone with rage to spare."

"Restraints?"

"Both of them had cuff marks on their wrists, and they struggled against the steel while they were getting their beatings."

"And they weren't gagged?"

"Mouths taped. There's glue residue on both their faces. Our killer didn't leave their mouths taped after he killed them because he had use for their tongues when he set up the bodies."

"Then where did the screams come from?" McKenna asked. "With a guy this careful, it doesn't make sense that he'd let them get a bunch of screams out before he taped their mouths shut."

"Chmil doesn't think he did. He thinks it was our killer screaming as he enjoyed himself beating De Sales and Ramsey to a pulp."

"So he wanted the security guard to show up?"

"Yeah, and he was ready for him. Gave him another opportunity to demonstrate his generosity for the press."

And he'll sure succeed at that, McKenna thought. These obscure Brooklyn murders are going to be front page when the contents of those notes come out. Big problem brewing here for the Job, especially if this guy hits again before he's caught. The public loves this vigilante stuff. "Anybody see this guy enter or leave the hotel?" he asked.

"Chmil is sure people did, but the desk clerk screwed him. Probably many of the guests are married, but they're not there with the people they're married to. The desk clerk knocked on all the doors before he called the police, and by the time the first units arrived, they thought the place must be on fire. Everybody's running out, and nobody's going in."

"How about the guest register?" McKenna asked, but the look Cisco gave him made him instantly regret the question. "Forget I asked," he tried, but it was too late.

"No, let's pursue that for a moment. While I'm busy thinking of ways to catch this guy, you can help me out by running down George and Martha Washington, Romeo and Juliet Jones, Adam and Eve Smith, Donald and Daisy Duck, and all the other names I'm sure are signed into the guest register. That would sure be a big help to me, and I'd love to hear what those folks have to say about our killer."

Stupid question, McKenna conceded to himself, but when this case gets big enough, we *will* be hearing from those people. They've already bragged to some friends that they were there and told them what they saw, and it's just a matter of time before some of those boasts are brought to our attention. "How about the desk clerk? Was he able to provide anything helpful?"

"Nothing. Sixty-four units, people in and out every four hours, and almost everybody's black."

We would still have plenty go on, McKenna thought, and he began thinking about how the vigilante would know so much about the victims. Then the phone rang, and cut short his thought process. "Hey, Buddy. How are you enjoying your vacation?" Brunette asked.

"Funny you should ask," McKenna replied. "I'm not really having much fun."

FOUR

The bump on McKenna's head had subsided to the point where he felt it was hardly noticeable, and it had been a nice flight, so he and Cisco were feeling good and eager to get to work. Inspector Dennis Sheeran, the CO of the Major Case Squad, ignored the small bandage on McKenna's head when he gave him the expected message as soon as they arrived at the office: The police commissioner wanted to see him.

"He doesn't want to see me?" Cisco asked.

"Definitely not, and I'd say it's a good thing for you," Sheeran replied. "He's not in a great mood, and I don't think you and your antics would go over too well right now."

Cisco appeared to be surprised at Sheeran's assessment, which surprised McKenna. Doesn't this guy realize how annoying he can be? McKenna wondered as he went upstairs to Brunette's office on the fourteenth floor of One Police Plaza.

Brunette's secretary, Camilla Wright, told McKenna that the PC was waiting for him, and he went right in. Brunette was seated behind Teddy Roosevelt's big desk, taking notes while he talked on the phone. He smiled at McKenna and indicated with a wave of his hand that he should sit in the chair facing his desk. McKenna did, and while waiting for Brunette to finish his conversation, he noticed that his friend was finally beginning to show his years.

Brunette was a tall, handsome man in good shape, and although he was ten years older than McKenna, his jet-black hair, his straight posture, his ready smile, and his energetic manner had always made them appear to be about the same age. However, now there were new lines at the corners of Brunette's eyes, his sideburns had a gray in them McKenna hadn't noticed before, and his shoulders were drooping. To McKenna, he appeared to be tired and worried.

Judging from the files he had faxed them on Cruz, De Sales, and Ramsey, McKenna and Cisco figured that Brunette had a lot to worry him. De Sales and Ramsey had been bad enough characters—De Sales was the top drug dealer in Brooklyn, and Ramsey was the sharpshooter suspected in the sniper-murders of three of De Sales's rival dealers—but it was the newcomer on the scene, Gaston Cruz, who presented the biggest problem for Brunette.

Cruz had been born rich, the son of a Colombian aristocrat whose family had owned vast farms since the time of the conquistadors. After his father died, Cruz apparently decided that farming and the traditional lifestyle wasn't for him. He sold his ancestral lands and bought an air transport service in Panama. He spent ten years there, attracting some official notice as he built an elaborate drug transportation network, and then moved to New York to expand his operation into the distribution end of the drug trade. After two years spent supplying a superior product to major drug dealers, and eliminating most of his competition by one means or another, it was suspected that Cruz had made himself the top heroin and cocaine distributor on the East Coast. The NYPD, the DEA, and the FBI had all investigated him, at one point executing search warrants for his Malba mansion and his Exito Seguros company office that turned up nothing. On the surface, at least, Cruz was clean, a man without a criminal record.

But Brunette's biggest problem was internal. A DEA informant had reported that Cruz had a mole in one of the agencies who kept him informed and one step ahead of their ongoing investigations into his operations. The speculation was that besides using information gathered by all the agencies to keep himself safe, Cruz also used it to identify and target his business rivals.

Despite intensive internal investigations by the FBI's Office of Professional Responsibility and the NYPD's Internal Affairs Bureau, the source of the leaks hadn't been uncovered and, while the agencies targeting him were running in circles, it was suspected that Cruz had further solidified his position. Two NYPD informants had disappeared, and a third, the DEA informant, had turned up dead in Sheepshead Bay, burned in a line from his chest to his crotch.

"Okay, Phil. Thanks for the heads-up. Brian just came in, so he'll be over to get it and fill you in," Brunette said and then hung up. He took a minute to read his notes over before turning his attention to McKenna. "Good to see you, Buddy, and thanks for coming back. We have a real problem shaping up here," he said. "This guy's killing people and acting like he's on our side. And now we're not gonna be able to keep a lid on this."

"He's been busy again?" McKenna asked.

"Sent a letter to the *Post*, addressed to Phil Messing. Gave him a description and the location of a house just outside of Kingston, says that's where De Sales processed his cocaine into crack. Also gave him a list of the dates, amounts, and prices of De Sales's wholesale drug buys from Cruz, and the name and address of Ramsey's girlfriend. Says she's holding the rifle Ramsey used to shoot De Sales's competition."

"Were any rounds recovered when Ramsey shot those folks?"

"Two, including the round that went through the drug dealer's head."

"So our killer's helping out the Brooklyn North Homicide Squad. Match the rifle to the spent slugs, and they've cleared a homicide and two other shootings."

"Yeah. He's a real nice guy."

"Who you gonna send for the rifle?"

"One guy I'm sure who'll get it. Steve Chmil. Don't know yet if that Ramsey shooting was one of his cases, but it is now."

Good choice and a wise decision, McKenna thought.

"But here's the worst part," Brunette continued with a grimace. "Justice."

"Justice?"

"That's the name he's given himself. Signed it at the bottom of the note he sent Messing. The press is really gonna run with that."

Justice? They sure will, and Ray is in a bind, McKenna thought. Killing drug dealers and then publicizing just how bad his prey was by giving Messing a story he couldn't—and certainly wouldn't—sit on. For some reason, the killer had made Messing his minister of information, and that'll be a big boost for Messing's career. "Where's Messing now?" McKenna asked. "His office?"

"Yeah, but he doesn't want to meet you there. He's got a big scoop he's not ready to share yet with his editor and nosy pals. He'll be at The Wicked Wolf in an hour," Brunette said, and then he took an envelope from the top drawer of his desk and passed it to McKenna.

"The hotel notes?" McKenna asked.

"Copies. Since the killer made Messing his spokesman, we have no choice but to keep him well informed."

"How much should I tell him?"

"As much as you think you have to."

"What's my role going to be in this case?"

"For now, case coordinator, the guy helping out Chmil and MacFarlane with your thoughts."

"And if it gets worse?"

"Just worse? Then it's still their case. But if it gets *much* worse, I'll assign the whole shooting match to you."

"Chmil and MacFarlane won't like that, and I don't blame them," McKenna said. "They're both good men, and they'll look at this as a slap in the face."

"So would I, if I were in their shoes, so I'll talk to them and lay it on the line. I'm gonna be getting pressure from the press and the mayor to give it to the department's glamour boy, the one with the proven track record on big cases—and that's you," Brunette said. "The longer this goes on, the more pressure I'll get, so I'm gonna save myself some trouble and cave in before it comes to a boil."

"Is Cisco in this with me?"

"You want him?"

"He's been driving me crazy with this case, but yes, I want him," McKenna said. "Matter of fact, I'll go one better. I'll say I need him."

"Then you have him."

"You have any idea on what Justice is up to?" McKenna asked, then noticed that Brunette grimaced again at the mention of the name. He decided it would be better to call him *the killer*, not *Justice*, whenever Brunette was around.

"Got a few ideas, but I'd like to hear your opinion first," Brunette said.

"I don't have a theory I can go with yet," McKenna admitted. "All we know is that this guy had so much information on Cruz, Montoya, De Sales, and Ramsey that he has to be an insider in the drug trade."

"You think he knew them personally?"

"What else is there to think? Let's look at the Cruz case first. Knew about the alarm system, the dog, the safe, the layout of the house, and enough about Montoya to torture him the same way Montoya tortured others for information. That's pretty detailed knowledge, so I'd say he's known Cruz for years and must've visited him at home."

"That's what MacFarlane thinks, too," Brunette said. "Thinks the key to this is delving deep into Cruz's life, but we have a problem."

"We don't know much about his life?"

"Or his organization. Don't know who his friends are, so finding out who his enemies are will be even harder."

"Then there's a lot of legwork to be done."

"Starting where?" Brunette asked.

"Lela Cruz. She's a victim, but she can't be permitted to lie to us through her tears anymore."

"How are you going to handle her?"

"Don't know yet, but we have some homework to do before we confront her. Has any work been done on Exito Seguros yet?"

"Big job, but we have copies of the company books from the case the Narcotics Division was working. MacFarlane has Gary Bessmer going over them now."

The perfect choice, McKenna thought. Bessmer was an FBI agent assigned to the Joint Organized Crime Task Force. He was their top forensic accountant, and the legend was that he could tell if a set of books was cooked just by touching them. "Is he making any progress?"

"He says that, so far, the books look legit. The company's well funded, making a nice profit, and paying its taxes."

"So he's looking at the wrong set of books," McKenna ventured. "Exito Seguros has nothing to do with Cruz's drug business, he just set it up to make himself appear a legitimate businessman."

"That's what Bessmer says."

"And we're not gonna find the books we really need until we catch the killer."

"The safe?"

"Yeah, Cruz's safe," McKenna said. "The killer has the real set of books. That's how he knew all about Cruz's drug sales to De Sales, dates, amounts, and prices."

"And then he beat the rest of the information from De Sales and Ramsey?"

"Yeah, a bonus for us," McKenna said. "He sure gave them a tough time—and a surprise. They apparently thought they were going to a meeting to do another wholesale drug buy," Brunette offered.

"I'd say."

"How did he arrange that?"

"Can't say for sure. Either he has somebody on the inside in Cruz's operation, or he was the inside man himself."

"Motive?"

"You're not going with the vigilante theory?" McKenna asked.

"Not unless I'm left no choice, only because it's the worst

possible scenario for me. I'd much rather have a running drug war than a vigilante running loose."

So he's hoping the notes are just a cover for a very competent man inside Cruz's operation who's turned himself into a hired assassin, McKenna thought. Don't think so, but Ray's the boss—and his wishes have to be addressed. "If this is a drug war we're seeing, then who's this killer working for?" he asked. "Cruz's competition?"

"Presumably. Maybe somebody still operating in town, or maybe somebody who isn't happy in retirement."

"Then why the helpful information to Messing—which is really meant for us—on Ramsey's gun and De Sales's crack factory? Why leave money for the Classon Hotel management to pay for damages? Why leave money to the hotel guard to pay for his embarrassment? Why let Cruz's dog live? Why all the bizarre pranks? Seems to me this guy's looking for good publicity as he proceeds in his mission, whatever it is. You ever see a drug war before where the assassins want their work played out on the front pages?"

It seemed to McKenna that his rapid-fire questions had the effect intended. Brunette didn't answer right away, but McKenna hadn't expected him to. Before his eyes, Brunette snapped out of his malaise as he pondered each of the questions in turn. Then he smiled. "No more wishful thinking?"

"Can't afford any, because this is only going to get worse."

"Okay. We have a vigilante."

"Doing what?"

"Killing drug dealers."

"How?"

"Pain and torture, with a few chuckles thrown in."

"That's true, but that's not what I mean. How is he able to do it?"

"Inside information."

"And why's he doing it?"

Brunette pondered that question for only a moment before bouncing it back. "I don't know, so why don't you tell me."

know, either," McKenna admitted. "But that's
the three keys to catching him."

"And the other two?"

"How is he getting his inside information? Tough question to answer, so I'd start working hard on the third key first. Who's the pilot who dropped him over Malba?"

"The pilot? He skydived onto the Cruz place?" Brunette asked.

"That's what we figure. Beat the alarm system by skydiving onto the garage roof."

Brunette accepted the theory at face value. "Then the pilot's a good place to start," he said, "because this guy has to know the killer."

"Of course he does, and you can list him as an accomplice. Nobody would drop a sky diver over a Queens neighborhood in the middle of the night without a good reason."

"And his reason is that he knows exactly what's going on?"

"Good assumption."

"Then I'll get MacFarlane working on that angle right away—if he isn't working on it already."

"MacFarlane's sharp enough, but I don't know if he figured out the sky-diver angle. He'd need some experience in that sport to know whether or not it's possible to land on a garage roof in the middle of the night, and I've got Cisco to tell me it is possible."

"Could Cisco do it?"

"I'm sure he can, given the same conditions: no wind and a lighted house," McKenna said. "I've watched him jump three or four times, and he always lands right next to me."

Brunette looked at his hands as he thought that over for a moment, and then he looked at McKenna with a smile. "You feeling confident?"

"We answer those three questions, and the rest is just routine police work before we throw the irons on him and get him out of your hair."

It appeared that Brunette liked McKenna's scenario, and then the smile left his face. "And you'll answer all those questions of yours?"

"Eventually."

"Before he kills again?"

What do I say to that? McKenna wondered, but only for a moment. He knew his friend was in for some tough times, so he should be ready to face it with the correct scorecard. To do that, he needed the plain truth. "Probably not. He has a carefully planned agenda, and he's working fast. The press is gonna have your feet to the fire, and they're gonna be bright red before this is over."

"But not charred?" Brunette asked, and the smile returned.

"Maybe charred, even, but we'll have the last laugh. He's got a head start, but we'll get him. Now, for the record, say it again."

"For the record?"

"Our killer has put Messing in the loop, so there will be no lying to him. Might as well get used to it; your feet start steaming with the morning edition. So say it to me, for the record, and I'll repeat it to Messing for you." McKenna took out his notepad and pen, ready to write.

"Okay. For the record, and official," Brunette said, and then he stood up to make his speech. "For reasons we don't yet understand, over the past couple of days a very competent killer has been targeting drug dealers in our city. While those lowlifes won't be missed much, murder is murder, and it's not allowed while I'm the police commissioner. He'll probably kill again before we get him, but we *will* get him."

Brunette sat back down, placed his hands in front of him, and waited for McKenna to finish writing. "How's that for a statement?"

"Concise, but *lowlifes*? How about I say *victims* instead?" McKenna asked.

"Only if you can say *poor, misguided* victims."

"I can't."

"Then lowlifes it is. Give my best to Phil."

FIVE

When McKenna returned to the office, he had expected that Cisco would still be miffed and cantankerous, but Cisco was all smiles. "Do we have it?" he asked.

"We're working it, but we don't have it yet. For now, our job is to assist MacFarlane and Chmil."

"So when do we get it?"

"When he hits again."

"So it's ours tomorrow," Cisco said, and his smile broadened. "Fine by me. Let's get to work."

Cisco didn't make his predictions lightly, and experience had long ago taught McKenna that they shouldn't be taken lightly. "He's going to hit again tonight?"

"Or today," Cisco replied, unconcerned.

"Tougher to do what he does in the daylight."

"Tougher, but he's taken that into account. He has a plan, and he's gonna follow it. I wouldn't be surprised if this were our case before we get off today."

"Then we won't be getting off."

"Okay by me. What did Ray have to say?"

McKenna took ten minutes to fill Cisco in, and then Cisco zeroed in on the point McKenna had hoped he wouldn't. "What did Ray tell you about Cruz's informant in the narcotics operation?"

"Nothing."

"Nothing? Why not?" Cisco asked.

"Because I didn't ask him about it."

"Slipped your mind?"

"No, Cisco, it didn't slip my mind," McKenna replied impatiently. "Ray's under a lot of pressure, and he's gonna be under a lot more. We already know that investigation went nowhere, so the timing wasn't right to bring up another unpleasant subject."

"Don't you think we need to know about that nowhere investigation?"

"At this point, I'm not sure we do. Given, Cruz had either a narcotics cop or a DEA agent feeding him information on confidential informants. But Cruz is dead now, so answer me this: What good would the details on that investigation do us right now?"

"Can't answer that yet, but I still wanna know all about it."

"Then consider this," McKenna countered. "We've been instructed to come clean with Messing. I don't know if the time is right yet to give our dirty laundry a public airing if it's not absolutely necessary to catching our killer."

"So what are you saying? If you don't know the details, you won't feel obliged to tell Messing anything about it?"

"That's exactly what I'm saying. We are gonna come clean with Messing, but we're also gonna gloss over the things we don't know about."

"You realize, of course, that Messing is one very hard man to fool?" Cisco asked.

"We're not fooling him. We're just leaving out a point that would generate headlines that have nothing to do with our present mission. Let's keep it simple for the press."

Cisco appeared dubious, but McKenna thought he would let the proposal pass without further comment. Wrong. "Okay, so we're gonna bamboozle Messing," Cisco observed. "Very tough job, but we'll do it. Just tell me this. At some point are you gonna get from Ray the details of that embarrassing investigation that went nowhere?"

"Yes."

"When?"

"Right after we have some good news to give him."

• • • •

McKenna was happy with Messing's choice of a meeting place and certainly not surprised. The Wicked Wolf was Messing's primary hangout and the place where McKenna usually saw him in a social setting. It was *the* Manhattan detective hangout as well as the place where many federal agents, reporters, prosecutors, and the occasional defense attorney met to discuss in an informal setting whatever crime story was dominating the headlines. The discussions were free and unfettered because, by tradition, The Wicked Wolf was a sanctuary, one of the two places in New York where a cop could grace a reporter with a few off-the-record comments that would give that favored fellow a correct indication of how a case was going, and those comments would never be included in any story filed. It was also the place where the future of any detective in the headlines was discussed and accurately predicted, and where deals were made between detectives, agents, and prosecutors that would permit progress on their cases to proceed smoothly without the political infighting that usually existed in joint "cooperative" efforts.

Maintaining order, making the necessary introductions, and presiding over the process was Chipmunk, The Wicked Wolf's lead bartender and one of McKenna's best friends since his drinking days, twenty years before. McKenna had taken that department-mandated drastic cure, and he no longer drank, but that fact had done nothing to diminish their friendship, especially since the two men had many other friends in common. They helped each other whenever possible, and over the years they had each become famous in their chosen professions.

Chip was regularly mentioned in the newspapers' annual feature articles on Manhattan's best bartenders, but he was much more than that. In The Wicked Wolf, he was the arbitrator and final law on anything that happened there. When discussions got out of hand—a rare occurrence—Chipmunk might impose the ultimate penalty. He called it "Firing the Customer," and more than one law enforcement or legal big shot had been embarrassed by him and sent packing.

To the chagrin of most of the other steady customers, The Wicked Wolf was also one of Cisco's favorite haunts, and he frequently annoyed them with his bruising ego—but only for a little while. Then Chip would say something that had an effect that always amazed McKenna. A simple "You're out of order, Cisco" from him, and that would be it. Cisco would immediately transform himself into an agreeable person, a person McKenna hardly knew.

Messing was talking to Chipmunk at the end of the bar when McKenna and Cisco entered, and it took them a while to glad-hand their way through the line of friends and acquaintances lining the bar before they reached Messing and Chip. Messing was also beginning to show his years, McKenna noticed with some satisfaction. Messing was in his late forties, and he had black, wavy hair—actually, more hair on his head than McKenna had ever seen on any man—but he was finally beginning to go gray at the edges, and his glasses were a little thicker than they had been the last time McKenna had seen him. The effect was that Messing looked even smarter.

That could be bad, McKenna realized, since he had always thought of Messing as one of the smartest men he knew. Getting a "No comment" past Messing on any story was difficult enough, and successfully bamboozling him was almost impossible. Tough mission I've given myself, McKenna thought, and he hoped he would be happy when it was over.

Messing had a large manila envelope in front of him on the bar. He was a laid-back kind of guy, and he gave McKenna and Cisco a simple handshake by way of greeting.

Unlike Messing, Chipmunk was an effusive personality with many peculiar quirks, so McKenna expected more from him. He was ready for Chip's traditional toast to all airmen downed, soldiers killed in battle, and sailors lost at sea, but all they got from Chip was a wave, immediately followed by "You guys got a lot to talk about. Better get to it."

"You mad at us, Chip?" Cisco asked.

"Hardly ever," Chipmunk said, staring at McKenna. "It's just that I've been talking to Phil so long that I've been neglecting my other customers."

Both Messing and Cisco looked down the bar to the other customers, but McKenna remained focused on Chipmunk, so he was the only one to catch the wink and the slight nod.

Cisco and Messing returned their attention to Chipmunk. "None of them look too neglected to me," Cisco noted.

"I'll be the judge of that. They all look entirely too sober to me, and that's no way to run a business," Chipmunk said. "You get to your business, and I'll handle mine. Go eat, and we'll talk later."

An order from Chipmunk in The Wicked Wolf was tantamount to imperial decree, so Messing and Cisco did as they were told. Messing picked up his envelope, and they turned and headed for the tables. McKenna tarried a moment longer at the bar to receive the message Chipmunk wanted no one else to hear. Chipmunk grabbed McKenna's arm and leaned across the bar to whisper in his ear. "When this case is running you ragged and depression is closing in, come see me."

"And then you'll have something to tell me?" McKenna asked in a low voice.

"Yeah, if you haven't figured it out for yourself by then, I'll have something to tell you."

Many more questions formed in McKenna's mind, but the conference was over. Chipmunk released his arm and wandered down the bar without looking back.

What the hell was that all about? McKenna wondered as he caught up with Cisco and Messing at Messing's usual window table. Chip never has to wait for the morning papers to catch all the news, and he's just been talking to his old pal Phil, which means that he already knows everything Messing knows. But who else has he been talking to and what else does he know? Something big, I expect, but what?

Since Chipmunk numbered most of the city's first-graders and even more feds among his friends and confidants, McKenna accepted that Chip always knew more about any case in the news than was ever reported to the common folk. So one of his friends had told him something in confidence about this case, McKenna figured. *Something important, and Chip won't break that confidence unless absolutely necessary—even to me.*

As he sat down, McKenna put the matter out of his mind and prepared to address the next difficult issue—Messing. "You wanna order first, or talk first?" he asked.

Messing drained his martini. "Drinks first while we talk, then lunch," he said. "I'll have another martini."

Cisco signaled the waitress, and she was there in an instant. "A vodka martini and a Budweiser for the manly men, and a sarsaparilla for Brian," he told her.

McKenna had known Brenda for years, and she disregarded Cisco. "Brian?"

"Thank you. An O'Doul's, please."

Brenda left, and Messing immediately got down to business. He opened his manila envelope, extracted a smaller envelope, and passed it to McKenna. "Those are the originals. The letter and the envelope it came in, along with a fingerprint card on me," he said. "I'm the only one who touched the letter."

"How about the envelope and the folks in the mail room?" Cisco asked. "We need more than just your prints. We need prints on everyone who touched that envelope."

"And you'll get them, but I need a small favor."

"We get them tomorrow?" McKenna guessed.

"Yeah, after I file my copy. I'm keeping this story under wraps until then."

"Why? The letter's addressed to you, meaning that Justice has selected you to be his press agent," McKenna said. "You're the star, and there's no way your editor could take this story from you."

"That's not what I'm worried about, but I have some problems with this particular editor. He's one of those know-it-all whiz-kid efficiency experts Murdock brought from Australia to bring costs down."

"What costs? Yours?"

"Mine in particular. He's been breaking my balls over my expense reports. Idiot thinks I can get everything I need on any story from Public Information, like your palace guard lobolas downtown are gonna write my copy for me."

McKenna understood at once and agreed with Messing: His editor was an idiot. According to the rules, cops and detectives weren't allowed to speak to the press without permission from their commanding officers. Instead, all information on any newsworthy case was to be forwarded downtown to the Public Information Unit, and it was the mission of the functionaries working there to dispense information to the press. Good reporters recognized that the stories coming from Public Information were merely a condensed version of the real story, condensed in a fashion that would make the gullible, inexperienced reporter tend to believe that all real police work was done under the strict supervision and guidance of the one brilliant chief or another mentioned prominently in the Public Information version and that every case was proceeding smoothly and according to plan.

McKenna doubted that Messing had even once called Public Information at any time during his career, and he probably didn't even know the number. All great, old-time reporters made it their business to intimately know all the great, old-time detectives—meaning those detectives for whom the more picayune department rules didn't apply as they went about their business of solving the big cases and enhancing the department's image.

By tradition, those detectives were interviewed in restaurants over dinner and drinks, frequently in either The Wicked Wolf, Kennedy's, Elaine's, or Forlini's. They were give-and-take sessions, with the reporter getting the true and complete story. In return, the detective and his unit got the ink, with his or her CO always prominently mentioned in glowing terms. There were many times when it would impair an investigation if certain facts were publicly known, but the detective could always go off the record to give the reporter the proper picture on the case. Those off-the-record comments would never appear in print and wouldn't even be divulged to the reporter's editor.

When the restaurant bill finally arrived, the give-and-take ended. The reporter usually paid, and the bill wound up as one more item on his expense account. Messing had numbered among his dinner companions at one time or another every detective and federal agent worth knowing, and he liked to eat fine meals accompanied by many, many martinis.

McKenna knew that Messing's monthly expense account had been considered unacceptably high by a few penny-pinching editors, but Messing always brought in the story, so those editors were all history and Messing's lifestyle hadn't changed one iota.

Cisco, of course, also knew how the newspaper business worked in New York. "What happens between now and tomorrow?" he asked. "The editorial board meeting?"

"That's right. Every Wednesday afternoon," Messing answered, smiling.

"And your editor doesn't know about the letter, so he'll be complaining about expense accounts and talking bad about you to the managing editor?"

Messing took a moment to check his watch. "With any luck, my name will be dripping from the dope's lips in about two hours. He won't be looking too good after I bring in this story, along with another big expense eat-and-drink session just to piss him off."

"So we're part of your ambush? You're the king again, and your editor becomes the joker?"

"Timing's great for me, as long as you don't insist on making noise by fingerprinting people in our mail room today. If you do that, the word gets to my editor, and he won't take that wonderful opportunity to make a fool of himself at the board meeting."

"Fine, but that's a favor you owe us."

"Cisco, do I owe you more favors than you owe me?"

That stopped Cisco, and he ran the question through his mind. "I don't know," he finally admitted.

"And neither do I," Messing said. "But who's counting?"

"Phil, nobody's counting," McKenna said, seeking to get the conversation back on track. "You got copies of the letter and the envelope?"

"Sure." Messing reached into his manila envelope and gave copies of the letter and the face of the envelope to McKenna and Cisco.

At that point Brenda delivered the drinks and took their orders. It would be steaks all around, and another martini for Messing. Cisco and Messing immediately took sips from their drinks, but McKenna ignored his and opened the envelope.

The letter was what McKenna had expected, printed in black bold type with a computer printer on standard bond paper. The "Justice" signature, however, was in bright red in a neat, masculine handwriting. The location and description of the upstate house on Route 28 where De Sales had his crack factory was precisely given, as was the name, address, and the physical description of Ramsey's girlfriend, Yolanda Williams. Equally precise were the descriptions of De Sales's wholesale drug purchases from Cruz. The purchase prices were $20,000 per kilo of cocaine and $90,000 per kilo of heroin. The prices had never varied, although the amounts bought by De Sales certainly had.

De Sales's first buy from Cruz had been the previous July, three kilos of cocaine and one kilo of heroin, and that had been the smallest buy. De Sales had bought from Cruz at least once a month, and the number of kilos bought had increased with each purchase as De Sales had neutralized his competition while cornering the Bedford-Stuyvesant street-level drug market. Justice had done the math—another favor to the police—and the totals were at the bottom of each column. In thirteen separate transactions, including De Sales's last fatal purchase, he had bought from Cruz 20 kilos of heroin and 134 kilos of cocaine for a total of $4,480,800.

McKenna had never been in Narcotics, and he knew that Cisco had left Narcotics twelve years before, so he was pretty sure that neither of them had an exact idea on the wholesale prices of cocaine and heroin. However, after De Sales had cut, diluted, and processed his products for street sales, he must have had himself a narcotics operation that generated many millions in profits.

Messing's thoughts were running in the same vein. "Can you give me a fairly accurate estimate on how much De Sales was making?" he asked.

"No, but I'll find out for you," McKenna replied.

"And an estimate on how much Cruz made from his dealings with De Sales?"

"You get everything today, I promise," McKenna said. "You're gonna have yourself a blockbuster story tomorrow, and I have a feeling your pieces are gonna be a continuing series."

"Because Justice is gonna hit again?"

It was Cisco who answered. "Sure he is, and soon."

Messing was polite enough to put his hand to his mouth in an unsuccessful attempt to conceal his smile. "Yeah, I know, Phil. Great news for you but a very bad scene for us," McKenna said. "Is the *Post* gonna play the vigilante angle right away?"

"You betcha, and you just said tomorrow's one-word headline. VIGILANTE, fourteen point, probably in red."

"How you gonna treat us?"

"You mean you two, or the department?"

"The department."

"How you gonna treat me?" Messing asked.

"As long as you keep getting letters, we'll give you everything you need to keep your story running."

"Criminal histories on the victims?"

"Uh-huh."

"Ongoing progress reports on the investigation?"

"Uh-huh."

"Complete off-the-record picture on anything you don't want printed?"

"Uh-huh."

"Then, naturally, I'm gonna treat the department as good as I can. Can't speak for the op-ed people, but I'll use my influence to keep the criticism to a minimum for as long as I can."

"That's all we can ask for."

"You have any idea how long this will go on for?"

"Off the record?" McKenna asked.

"Sure."

"None whatsoever."

"Any idea on who this Justice is?"

"Still off the record. No, no concrete idea. Have a few theories, but nothing I'm ready to talk about yet."

Then McKenna took a minute to examine the photocopy of the envelope. Like the letter, the envelope had been printed in black ink with a computer printer, and, naturally, there was no return address. Then McKenna examined the postmark, Grand Central Station, but the date froze him. The letter had been postmarked July 14, after Cruz had been murdered, but before Justice had killed De Sales and Ramsey.

McKenna looked at Messing and Cisco. Cisco was sipping his drink and looking at him with a quizzical expression on his face, but Messing was staring out the window with a smile on his lips.

"Look at your copy of the envelope," McKenna told Cisco, and Cisco did. He glanced at the address, and McKenna saw him focus on the postmark for a full minute. Then Cisco looked at McKenna, and he was also smiling. "What planning and what confidence," he said admiringly. "The cagey bastard mailed Phil all the info on De Sales and Ramsey before he even got around to whacking them."

"And before what else?" McKenna asked.

McKenna was sure Cisco knew, but for some reason Cisco wasn't answering. Then McKenna looked at Messing, but Messing was still looking through the window and still smiling.

"He mailed it before what else?" McKenna repeated, sure that Messing had also already figured it out.

"Before the story on Cruz's murder went to press," Cisco said at last.

"Meaning?"

"Meaning he mailed it to Phil before he knew Phil had the byline on the Cruz murder story."

"Meaning?" McKenna asked, but then he held up his hand to indicate to Cisco that he shouldn't answer yet. McKenna then snapped his fingers in front of Messing's face to get his attention.

"I know, Brian, and don't worry about me. We're way, way off the record here," Messing said, but he continued looking out the window and smiling.

McKenna returned his attention to Cisco. "Let's hear it, smart guy. If he didn't know yet that Phil would be the one doing the story on the Cruz murder, then why, of all the reporters in the city, did he send his letter to Phil?"

"Cisco is a very smart guy indeed, so he will give you some food for thought," Cisco said. "There are a few possibilities to be considered. One: Justice might have put himself in a position near the crime scene that enabled him to see Phil there."

"Possible," McKenna conceded. "But let's keep in mind that Justice was very busy murdering De Sales and Ramsey the following night, and he needed time to reconnoiter the Classon Hotel and get some sleep in between."

"Cisco already has that in his mind," Cisco said. "Two: Justice is an avid reader of the *Post*, and he knows his reporters. He therefore anticipated that Phil would naturally be assigned to cover any murder as big as the Cruz murder turned out to be."

"If he knew Phil was working that day," McKenna said.

"An easy matter for him to ascertain. All he had to do was call the *Post*'s city desk and ask for Phil. He would have been told that Phil was in the field, and he would know just where in the field Phil was."

"Fine. We'll continue to consider that, but let's get to the third possibility. Let's assume for a moment that Justice didn't know Phil would be covering that story when he mailed him the letter that made our Philly Boy the hottest reporter in town. What might one assume from that?"

"That he likes our Philly Boy."

"That he might even be a friend of our Philly Boy?" McKenna asked.

"Might be."

"And who are Philly Boy's friends?"

"People like us."

"Thank you. Now, let's go one further. Considering how much inside information he seems to have, where would he be assigned?"

"Either Narcotics or the Joint Drug Task Force."

"Thanks again. So he would be a black man, very strong, very tough, and very smart. Someone on the inside who's very angry with drug dealers, and let's not forget to add in that he's an expert sky diver and an animal lover. Ring any bells?"

"Except for the black part and the inside part, you just described me."

"Yeah, but you have an alibi. Can you think of anyone else you know who might fit that description?"

"Not at the moment," Cisco said. "Give me a few minutes to think." If Cisco thought better while he drank, then he did a lot of hard thinking. He chugged what was left of his beer, and then looked at McKenna. His mouth wasn't smiling, but his eyes were. "Nobody specific comes to mind, but I don't know that many people in Narcotics anymore. Thankless job, no-win situation, so it never held my interest."

"How about you, Phil?" McKenna asked. "And before you answer, keep in mind that this guy might be someone you know."

McKenna was gratified that Messing finally looked at him to answer. "I've already run it through my mind. I've met thousands of cops and feds through the years, and shared dinners, drinks, and a few good times with many of them, but I don't know who this guy is. You can take that to the bank."

"I believe you, but if he's a cop or a fed, *he* knows *you*," McKenna stated.

"Maybe I've met him. If so, it slips my mind. But then again, maybe I never have. Maybe he just knows me by reputation."

"A secret admirer?"

"I must have a few," Messing said with a shrug. "Get a lot of nice mail from people who like my style."

McKenna was sure there were, but he was also sure that if Justice was a cop or a fed, he had met Messing at one time or another. Maybe at a party or in a bar late at night when Messing was a little under the weather, McKenna reasoned, but it had happened.

Then that cryptic message from Chipmunk hit McKenna. Is it possible that Chip already knows Justice is a cop or a fed? he wondered. Better yet, is it possible Chip knows him personally? After all, Messing and Chipmunk share many of the same friends, so if Justice knows Messing, there's a good chance he also knows Chip.

McKenna looked toward the bar and caught Chipmunk staring at him. Their eyes locked for a moment, then Chip smiled and nodded to McKenna before turning his attention to the customer sitting at the bar in front of him.

Yeah, Chip knows, but it does me no good. He won't tell me anything until he's good and ready, McKenna thought, and he then put that issue out of his mind for the moment. It was time to get on to the next unpleasant piece of business. From his pocket he took the notes Justice had left for the police and the hotel management, and he passed them to Messing.

Messing read the note to the police once and then read it out loud. "Stay tuned and stay sharp, because there's more fun in store. I intend to make the world a better place, and I know how to do it. Catch me if you can."

Messing folded up the note and put it in his pocket, and McKenna found the broad smile he was wearing to be particularly annoying. "Phil, this is serious business, isn't it?" he asked.

"Much more serious for you than for me, but yeah, it's serious," Messing said, still smiling broadly.

"Then could you please wipe that smile off your face before we go any further?"

"I'm trying. Believe me, I am," Messing said, still smiling. "Make you a deal. If he stops, I'll stop," he said, nodding at Cisco.

McKenna looked at Cisco, knowing what he would find. Sure enough, his partner was also smiling, but Cisco at least was making some attempt to put on a somber appearance. His face went from smile to grim to smile to grim, but then he gave up. The smile returned and remained.

"You realize, don't you, that our Job's reputation is circling the bowl and might just get flushed into the sewer over this?" McKenna asked, exasperated.

That dimmed Cisco's smile, but it didn't entirely disappear. "If he's a cop, it might dim the Job's reputation in some circles, but with the competent job he's doing, not in my circle," he stated. "He's given himself a mission: taking bloodsucking, murdering, soulless vermin off the street in a fine fashion. That's a mission we'd all like to undertake—if we were permitted to."

Cisco stopped to gauge McKenna's reaction, but all he received was a blank stare. Then he looked at Messing, but Messing had removed himself from the conversation. It appeared he was intently reading Justice's note to the hotel management and was much too busy to pay attention to whatever Cisco was saying.

Cisco returned his attention to McKenna. "All right, Boy Scout, don't say it," he said, placing his hand on McKenna's arm. "We're sworn to uphold the law, and whoever he is, he's breaking the law."

"Our most serious law," McKenna said, staring down at Cisco's hand on his arm. "He's committing murder, over and over, and he's gonna continue murdering until we get him."

"Actually, he's stepped on four smart, overstuffed cockroaches who figured nothing bad would ever happen to them, but I guess that's murder—in a technical sense."

McKenna was shocked at Cisco's statement, and he made no attempt to hide it. What am I facing here? he wondered.

Great detective, good man, but where's his head on this? "Murder *in a technical sense*? Is there such a lesser category of murder?" he asked, "Or is murder still the unlawful taking of human life, pure and simple?"

"Don't get excited, Brian. You're right," Cisco said, smiling as he patted McKenna's arm. "It's our job to get him, and we will."

"So you're really with me on this?"

Cisco appeared hurt at the question. "Of course I'm really with you. I'm your partner, and we'll get him together, doing whatever we have to."

McKenna believed, but he wanted to be sure Cisco was operating for the right reasons. "So we'll get him because he's a killer, and it's our job to catch murderers, no matter who they are and who they're killing?"

"That's one way of looking at it, and partially correct."

"Partially correct?"

"That 'Catch me if you can' business doesn't sit well with me. He issued us a challenge, so we'll answer it, and that will be his undoing."

I give up! McKenna thought. Next order of business, and he returned his attention to Messing. "You like that note?" he asked.

"Love it," Messing replied. "How much did he leave to cover the 'unavoidable' damages?"

"Five thousand dollars."

"Very nice of him."

"Do you intend to portray him in a sympathetic light?"

"If I don't do it voluntarily, my bosses will insist I do. Besides murders committed with a twist, there's a human-interest angle brewing here. Justice has given my paper an exclusive of sorts, and he's gonna double our circulation for as long as this goes on. We'll go with this story for all it's worth."

"Then while you're busy picturing him as an errant knight, you might also mention prominently that he's a robber as well as a murderer."

"The drug cash?"

"Yeah, and he stole plenty of it. By his own admission in

his letter to you, he got five hundred forty thousand from De Sales before he killed him. With that kind of cash in hand, is it a big deal if he leaves five thousand to the hotel and three thousand to the security guard if it convinces you to make him a hero in the press?"

"It's not just the cash, Brian. If you're gonna try to convince me he's just some kind of greedy, robbing bastard who spreads peanuts around to make himself look good, then first tell me why he left the drugs with the bodies?"

Not the question I wanted to hear, but this Messing is just too sharp, McKenna admitted to himself. If Justice is the greedy bastard I'd like Messing to believe he is, then what reason do I give him to explain why Justice left drugs with a wholesale value of over half a million in the hotel room when a strong guy like him could have just as easily taken both the stash and the money?

Nothing came to McKenna, and Messing was kind enough to change the subject. "What's this about three thousand to the security guard?"

"He left three thousand dollars in his pocket, along with another note." McKenna passed Messing a copy of the note Justice had left in Clarence DuBois's pocket. After Messing read it, McKenna told him about the teddy bear and next described the scene that had greeted DuBois when he had awoken in that heart-shaped bed next to De Sales, Ramsey, and the blow-up lovers Justice had left with them in unsavory positions.

"God, I wish I had a picture of that," Messing said.

"Why? You work for the *Post*, not the *Enquirer*. Your editor would never let it run."

"But it would sure look good with the other pictures in my book, the one I'll be writing when this case is over."

"Happy ending?" McKenna asked.

"Don't know how happy it'll make everybody, but you'll get this guy, sooner or later."

McKenna was able to relax for a moment when Brenda brought Messing his next martini and announced that their dinners would be out shortly.

Messing took a long sip from his drink, and then ended McKenna's recess. "I've been hearing for a while that Gaston Cruz bought a cop or an agent somewhere, in either Narcotics, the FBI, or the DEA," he said. "Is there a chance that has a bearing on this case?"

McKenna wasn't surprised that a man with Messing's connections knew about the problem, but since Brunette didn't need the pressure of appearing in the press with two black eyes instead of just one, he had been hoping that Messing didn't know the problem was connected to Gaston Cruz.

So what do I say to that? McKenna wondered, then decided that the simple truth would have to do. "I don't know whether or not Cruz's bought cop or agent has anything to do with this case," he admitted.

"Is it something you're actively looking into?"

"Not yet."

"Why not?"

It was Cisco who answered. "Let's get something straight here, Phil. Until this morning, Brian and I were on vacation in Florida. We haven't had a chance to do much of anything on this yet."

"Really? You were called back from vacation to handle this?" Messing asked.

"No, not *handle* it. We were called back to assist MacFarlane and Chmil, so they're the ones you should still be talking to, and they're the ones who should be getting the ink right now. They're good, competent people, so use what you learned from us to write nice things about them."

McKenna had never expected to hear that statement from Cisco, a man who rarely gave credit to others. Messing also paused for a moment, but then he took the statement in stride. "So how do I characterize our session here?" he asked.

"Simple. MacFarlane and Chmil were too busy working their cases this afternoon, so the police commissioner elected us to fill you in on what they've been doing. However, they won't be too busy later on, so go get some nice quotes from them."

"Will Chmil talk to me?"

"He will now," McKenna said. "Tell you everything we've told you, and maybe more."

"How about Brunette? Will he talk to me?"

"Not at the moment, but he's authorized me to give you a statement. That good enough?"

"Sure."

McKenna took out his notepad, ready to read Brunette's statement, but then he decided against it. Instead, he tore out the page and handed it to Messing.

Messing had just one question after he read the statement. "*Lowlifes?* Are you sure he wants to use that?"

"That's for the record, Phil. *Lowlifes* it is, and he sends his regards."

Brenda arrived with their orders, and conversation ceased until she left. "Just one more question from me before we dig in," Messing said. "Off the record, when will you be taking over the case?"

"You're not buying that assistants-to-MacFarlane-and-Chmil crap?" Cisco asked.

"No."

"Then, off the record, it will be Brian's case right after Justice hits again."

"Which will be when, in your opinion?"

"Like I told you, soon. Maybe very soon."

McKenna had just cut his first piece of steak when his cell phone rang. He knew what it meant when Messing's cell phone began ringing two seconds later.

So did Cisco. "Looks like you're in charge, partner."

McKenna didn't want to compete with Messing's call while they both received the same message, so he got up and walked to the back of the restaurant before he answered his phone.

"Where are you?" Sheeran asked.

"The Wicked Wolf. Where am I going?" McKenna asked.

"Close. Two-Five Precinct. Marginal Street under the FDR Drive. He did it with bombs this time."

"Bombs?"

"Two of them."

"How many dead?"

"Four."

"All players?"

"That's what it looks like, so far."

"Any witnesses?"

"One. A city sanitation worker was emptying his sweeper under the drive about a block away. He heard the explosions and saw the action that followed."

"Which was?"

"At least one, and maybe two of them were alive enough after the blasts to offer some resistance. A short gunfight ensued, but your man finished them off with one head shot apiece. He's got a laser-sighted pistol, and he knows how to use it."

"How long ago did it happen?"

"About half an hour. It took the first units there a while to sort out the mess and venture a guess about what happened. I'm still getting reports in, but I understand it's a pretty bloody scene."

"You going?" McKenna asked.

"I'll be on my way in a few minutes."

"Who else is there?"

"John Monahan."

McKenna thought that was the best news Sheeran could have given him. Monahan worked in the Manhattan North Homicide Squad, and he was widely believed to be one of the best homicide detectives in the city. McKenna knew that everything that could be done by the time he got there would be done, and it would be done correctly.

Messing was standing and in the process of paying the check by the time McKenna got back to the table, and he looked happy. Cisco, on the other hand, was still seated and eating his steak as quickly as he could, and he didn't look at all happy.

"C'mon, Cisco. We gotta go," McKenna said.

Cisco took a moment to swallow his food before answering. "I know, I know. I was looking forward to enjoying this meal, but this is all my fault."

"Your fault? How?"

"Because God loves his great detectives. What did I foolishly say when Phil asked me when he was gonna hit again?"

"Soon, and maybe very soon."

"So, so foolish. What I should've said was 'Right after lunch,' and maybe God would have arranged that for us."

Great detective, good man, but without a doubt a very strange person, McKenna thought.

SIX

Messing had his own car, so he followed Cisco and McKenna north on First Avenue. Since Marginal Street was just fifty blocks north of The Wicked Wolf, it would be a short trip, and Cisco saw no reason to hurry. He drove at the speed limit and stopped at every yellow light, which indicated to McKenna that he was thinking and wanted to have a theory in place before arriving at the crime scene.

That suited McKenna perfectly. He was ready to go with the notion that Justice was a cop or an agent, murdering, with a purpose and quite a bit of skill, mid-level and top drug dealers. McKenna figured there were many questions to be answered before they would have a chance of catching him, and he thought he was on his way to answering the first two big ones: Where was Justice getting his drugs to sell, and how was he able to arrange his sales meetings with mid-level drug dealers in order to kill them?

Justice must have somebody high in Cruz's operation under his thumb, but McKenna wanted to talk over his theory with Cisco before mentioning it to anyone else.

By the time they reached East 96th Street, Cisco had formed his own theory, and he was also ready to talk. "We're on our way to a meeting Justice arranged to peddle a whopping amount of drugs," he commented.

"Probably, and it's another meeting that went very bad for the buyers," McKenna replied.

"If he's operating to form, besides the bodies of that

greedy drug dealer and his bodyguards, what else are we gonna find?"

"All the drugs he brought to peddle to them."

"And how about the cash they brought with them?"

"Gone."

"And what did he leave?"

"A note for us."

"And?"

"A prank of some sort that will give you a giggle."

"Correct, and I'm looking forward to seeing what it is," Cisco said. "So what are the two big questions we should be asking ourselves right now?"

Good. Cisco's arrived at the same conclusion I have, McKenna thought. I'll play. "If I give you the questions, will you give me the answers?" he asked.

"Of course," Cisco said confidently, and then cast an inquiring glance in McKenna's direction. "Do you know the answers?"

"Sure I do. Easy, really, because both questions have pretty much the same answer."

"We'll see. Question Number One: Where is Justice getting the drugs?"

"From Cruz's stash," McKenna replied, and he was gratified to see a look of disappointment flash across Cisco's face. "You want the second question and answer, O Wise One, or would you prefer to keep the game going?"

"Game's over, smart guy. So we're agreed that Justice has someone high up in Cruz's operation working for him?"

"I don't know if we *are* agreed. There is somebody high up in Cruz's operation in play here, but I don't think he's working for Justice. Not willingly, anyway."

"We're agreed," Cisco said. "Justice snatched him, and he's been forcing him to do whatever he wants. I think he's another guy who's felt the blowtorch."

"We're in complete agreement. Whoever this poor slob is . . ."

"Let's get something straight right now," Cisco said impatiently. "Whoever he is, he's not a poor slob. He's the number-two man in Cruz's operation, which means he's not poor, and he's not a slob. What he has to be is a smart, devious scumbag with a history, and certainly nobody we should be feeling sorry for."

"Then here's where our agreement ends," McKenna said. "If Justice is torturing this guy with a blowtorch every day to get him to do what he wants, then I feel sorry for him—no matter who he is and no matter what he's done."

"Okay, we agree to disagree. Get on with it."

"It's this poor slob who told Justice where Cruz kept his stash, and he's the one who's been arranging the meetings with the mid-level drug dealers so Justice can whack them."

"Going further, he's also the one who's been giving Justice the history and the facts and figures on each dealer he kills," Cisco added. "I'll betcha that tomorrow Phil gets another letter giving him the drug transaction record of whoever he blew up on Marginal Street today."

"No bet."

Marginal Street is a desolate strip that runs alongside the East River in Spanish Harlem. There are no buildings on Marginal Street, and nobody lives there. For its entire three-block length, the only architectural features are the steel pillars supporting the FDR Drive, the Harlem River Drive, and the Manhattan approaches to the Triboro Bridge, all of which meet above Marginal Street and cast it in total shadow. The entire stretch is city-owned and has fallen by some unwritten rule under the purview of the Department of Sanitation. Large mounds of salt and sand are stored there for use in winter snow conditions, and the area also serves as a refuse transfer station for the Department of Sanitation's mechanical street sweepers. When a street sweeper is full, the operator heads there to disgorge its load of garbage; these piles are collected at night and loaded into dump trucks for transport to one of the city's landfills.

There were so many emergency vehicles and news vans on Marginal Street that Cisco had to park two blocks from

the crime scene, behind a long row of fire trucks, ambulances, and police vehicles of all kinds. Messing pulled in
behind them, and McKenna noted the street sweeper parked
in the lot on their right, behind a pile of refuse. The flashers
were on, but the operator was nowhere in sight. McKenna
also noted the police units represented as they walked toward the crowd. They passed a Bomb Squad truck, three
Emergency Service Unit trucks, two Crime Scene Unit vans,
and many unmarked cars, including the new and shiny black
Ford with all the antennas that indicated the presence of a
chief.

The news crews were gathered on the near side of the
crime-scene tape, chatting with a uniformed sergeant from
the 25th Precinct. McKenna knew many of the reporters,
and a few shouted questions to him, but he ignored them and
just gave a friendly wave in passing. He didn't know the sergeant, but the sergeant knew him. "Detective McKenna, the
chief wants to see you right away."

"Chief who?"

"Chief Rowe."

That was a relief to McKenna. Kenny Rowe was the chief
of Manhattan detectives, and McKenna had worked for him
fifteen years before when Rowe had commanded the Manhattan South Robbery Squad. He was likable and competent,
and unlike many chiefs, he didn't believe in interfering with
detectives as they went about their jobs.

"Talk to you later, guys," Messing said, and McKenna ad-
mired his style. Messing realized that circumstances had
placed him in a special position, but he didn't push it. Since
Messing would know in short order whatever McKenna and
Cisco learned, he was content to hang with his pals from the
press and not flaunt his new status.

McKenna and Cisco ducked under the crime-scene tape,
then stopped for a minute to take in from a distance the
scene fifty feet in front of them. There was a late-model
black BMW four-door sedan parked facing the river, and extensive blast damage was evident on the right side, centered
on the front passenger's door. There were also many small

holes in the door, and barely visible was the head of the driver hanging out his window. Even from that distance, McKenna could see he was dead, and it appeared that there were many small spikes sticking out of his head.

All the BMW's side windows had been shattered, but the windshield and the back window had remained intact. On the ground in front of the passenger's door were many long, twisted strips of sheet metal, and in front of the BMW was what appeared to be the bent trunk lid of another large, black car.

Behind the BMW, but ten feet closer to McKenna and Cisco, was a late-model two-door white Mercedes. Both the passenger and driver's doors were open, and there was a covered body on the ground behind the open passenger door. The Mercedes also showed evidence of blast damage: The front grill, the headlights, the windshield, back window, and the windows on the open doors had been blown out, and there were many tiny holes in the doors.

Among all the cops, McKenna could see Rowe standing behind the Mercedes, talking to John Monahan. He also saw Joe Walsh standing alone on the other side of the BMW, leaning against a pillar while enjoying a smoke. Walsh was a big man in his late fifties, possibly fifty pounds overweight, and he had a full head of curly white hair. Being the NYPD's best crime-scene technician meant getting dirty, so Walsh, as usual, was sloppily dressed. His sports jacket was open, his white shirt was smudged with fingerprint powder, and his tie was at half mast. McKenna would hate the look on any other detective, and especially a first-grader, but he had learned to accept it on Walsh.

On the other hand, Cisco didn't. He liked neither Walsh nor his manner of dressing, so McKenna got the comment he expected: "Would you take a look at that fat, filthy windbag? Nobody gets any work from him until somebody turns on a camera with him center frame," he observed.

Walsh saw McKenna and Cisco, and he waved at them, but he did nothing else to indicate that he served any purpose there whatsoever. The rest of his Crime Scene Unit was at work taking measurements of the scene, shooting photos, and drawing sketches.

On the other side of the lot on their left was a large crowd of local residents behind a strip of crime-scene tape that was stretched the length of four highway support pillars. Ten uniformed cops and a sergeant were lined along the tape to keep the crowd back, but the mood of the cops and the folks in the crowd appeared to be relaxed and friendly.

"What do you make of it?" McKenna asked Cisco, nodding toward the BMW and the Mercedes.

"Not much, but I can tell you that the center of the blast was somewhere on this side of the BMW and in front of the Mercedes. Doesn't make sense yet, unless those bozos drove up on a bomb Justice placed there for them."

"What do you make of the trunk and all those strips of metal?"

"Another thing that doesn't make sense yet. Maybe pieces of the car Justice was in, but where's the rest of it?"

"Don't know, but somebody does. Who's missing?"

Cisco again took in the scene before answering. "Don't see anybody from the Bomb Squad, and we know they're here somewhere. Also don't see too many Emergency Service people here, and there should be a bunch."

"Then let's go talk to the people who *do* know where they are," McKenna suggested, and they headed for Rowe and Monahan. When they got close, McKenna saw there was another covered body on the ground behind the open driver's side door of the Mercedes.

Both McKenna and Cisco believed in propriety, so they saluted Rowe, and that seemed to amuse him. He casually returned their salutes and then offered his hand to McKenna. "Good to see you, Brian. Been waiting on you before we started getting this mess straightened out and cleaned up."

Nice, but there aren't too many people around with the authority to tell Rowe what to do, McKenna thought. So why's he waiting for me? "Why the holdup, Chief?" he asked.

"Got a call from the PC. He told me I'm officially in

command here, but you're in charge. Unofficially, of course, but I'll play along with a smile." Rowe took out his wallet and gave McKenna his card. "Call me on my cell phone for anything you need, and I'll make sure you get it."

A detective in charge of a chief? Very unusual, but also nice, McKenna thought. And call him for anything I need, and I'll get it? *Very* nice.

Next Rowe shook Cisco's hand, a very unusual event when it came to Cisco and chiefs. Cisco wasn't at all popular with most of them, but Rowe was an exception. Rowe was the kind of boss who could overlook personalities and egos as long as results were forthcoming, and Cisco always produced results on any case he worked. In fact, Rowe might be the only chief on the Job who didn't look the other way when they saw Cisco coming, and the two men shared an interest in, of all things, Russian ballet.

While Rowe and Cisco were exchanging opinions and comparing reviews on the upcoming Bolshoi tour of the United States, McKenna used the time to exchange pleasantries with Monahan. The mess around them should have been Monahan's case, McKenna knew, and it bothered him that Monahan looked delighted to see him. That meant Monahan saw it as a very tough case, one that could tarnish his reputation if it hadn't been dumped on McKenna, his new best pal.

Rowe said good-bye and left to go wherever chiefs go to do whatever chiefs do, and then Cisco had the question for Monahan. "You okay with us taking over here?"

"Just fine. Since Rowe tells me that now you'll be taking over the killings in Brooklyn and Queens, you might as well take over these four as well," Monahan replied. "Makes sense. Same killer, so now you've got eight victims—and I don't envy you this case. It's a doozy."

"A doozy?" McKenna asked, not sure when he had last heard that word.

"A spectacular doozy. When you get this guy ID'd, I wouldn't want to be the first one in when you crash down his door or yank him outta his ride. He knows his cars, he knows his bombs, and he knows his guns—and he knows how to put them all together for maximum effect. It's a very dangerous man you're chasing, but he's already done me a big favor."

"He's done you a favor?" McKenna asked. "How's that?"

"Did you notice the gentleman in distress whose head is hanging out the window of the BMW?"

"Yeah, we noticed him."

"Ramon De Jesus, stone-cold killer. I have him identified as the shooter in three separate homicide cases over the past two years, but I couldn't get my hands on him. Last I heard, he was hiding out in Panama. Your killer just showed me that my info wasn't too current, but I'll still accept with a smile the three clearances he gave me today."

"Are those pieces of our guy's car scattered between the other two?" Cisco asked.

"No, that's what's left of the trunk and the left door panel of the British Ambassador to the UN's bulletproof limo, but it's the car your guy came in. Stole it last night from the ambassador's garage at his hideaway home on Long Island."

"How?"

"Forgot to mention. Your killer also knows his alarm systems and locks. Picked the lock on the garage side door, bypassed the alarm system, yanked the ignition, and drove the limo out. Replaced the diplomatic plates with a set he stole yesterday in Queens, did his lethal modifications on the car, and drove it here for his meeting with Raymond Garcia and his badass henchmen, all presently deceased."

"Where's the rest of the car?"

"He dumped it two blocks from here, Hundred Twenty-sixth Street off Second Avenue. Factory block, haven't found anybody yet who saw him dump it."

"Is that where the Bomb Squad is?"

"Yeah, and Emergency Service, too. The car's still hot, loaded with bombs your killer didn't find it necessary to use when he whacked Garcia and crew."

"Raymond Garcia is a drug dealer?" McKenna asked.

"Big time. Controls all the cocaine, crack cocaine, and heroin sales in Spanish Harlem."

"Where are you getting this from?"

"Mickey Alfonso. He stopped by to identify Garcia and the other two for me. Knew them all, even De Jesus, and all their histories. The only consolation I got outta that was that Mickey also thought De Jesus was still in Panama."

"If Mickey gives them names, then that's who they are," Cisco said, and it made McKenna smile. Alfonso was a second-grader assigned to the Intelligence Section of the Narcotics Division. He was the NYPD's recognized expert on Latin drug dealers, and, like Cisco, he was a Cuban-American. Their families were from the same town in Cuba, and the two men had been friends even before they came on the Job.

"Where is Alfonso?" McKenna asked.

Monahan smiled. "Behind you, in conference with everybody's pal and working on his next nice meal."

Both McKenna and Cisco turned around to see Messing and Alfonso. Messing had detached himself from the other reporters and was writing in his notebook as Alfonso spoke. Alfonso had a piece of paper in his hand, and McKenna knew it had to be a copy of the letter Justice had sent to Messing. As background for his story, Messing was getting from Alfonso the standard wholesale prices and the retail street values of the drugs Cruz had sold to De Sales.

So Alfonso's saving me some work, and Messing's saving me some time. I promised Phil that I'd get him those figures, McKenna thought, and then he made a mental note to talk to Alfonso soon and learn those retail drug values for his own information.

McKenna then noticed that the Crime Scene Unit technicians had finished their chores and were headed for their van, but Walsh was still leaning against the pillar next to the BMW, enjoying another smoke.

"You want me to walk you guys through it, and tell you what I think went down?" Monahan asked.

"Please," McKenna said, and then he and Cisco followed Monahan past the Mercedes to the right side of the BMW. McKenna saw that the torn metal strips on the ground near

the front door of the BMW were black sheet-metal pieces of
the ambassador's car, and he figured they were from a door
of the limo. Besides De Jesus, there was another body in the
front seat with its head lying on De Jesus's lap.

"Is that Raymond Garcia?" McKenna asked.

"That's him," Monahan replied. "He died a microsec-
ond before De Jesus, right after your guy set off the first of
his bombs. I figure De Jesus was Garcia's driver and one of
his bodyguards for the meeting, but none of them was up to
the task."

McKenna took a good look inside the car. The cause of
death for both men was immediately apparent; their bodies
had been punctured by many, many nails, and many of them
were still in place. From where he stood, McKenna counted
the heads of nine large ten-penny nails jutting from De Jesus's head, and another eight jutting from his hands and
arms.

Garcia had been closer to the source of the blast, and his
body had shielded De Jesus to a point. The right side of Garcia's shirt and the skin on his right arm and much of the right
side of his face had been blown away, and embedded in what
was left of him were too many nails for McKenna to count.
Those nails had broken the car's windows and some had
gone through the car's front door, McKenna saw, but he also
noted that a type of directional shape charge had been employed. Although the back windows were broken and there
were few holes in the back door, the bomb had been designed to destroy only the front passenger compartment of
the BMW and whoever occupied it.

Visible on the floor in the back of the car were many
wrapped one-kilo packages of drugs and something else
McKenna had expected to find. On top of the stacks of drugs
were two envelopes. "For the Police" was printed on the face
of the smaller envelope in bold black letters. The second envelope was bulky and much larger, and "For the Ambassador" was printed on the face in the same bold black letters.

McKenna suspected the message the smaller envelope
contained and was certain about what the larger envelope

contained. He moved aside to let Cisco take a look. It took Cisco only seconds to reach the same conclusions. "How very nice of him to measure up to our expectations," Cisco said. "Right after he sold them the drugs, he went about the business he really came here for. Whacked these murderous lowlifes, took his money, and left a helpful little message for us and plenty of cash for the ambassador to pay him back for his car."

"I think so, too," McKenna heard a voice say, and he looked up to see that Walsh had ended his break and was standing on the other side of the car. "Care to venture a guess on the message for you guys?"

McKenna thought he knew, but he let Cisco answer. "Easy one. 'Nailed these guys for you,' and maybe he added a helpful little hint on what he's planning next."

"You agree with me, so you're probably right," Walsh said. "Want me to dust the envelopes?"

"There'll be no prints on them, but it would be nice if you did something," Cisco replied.

It was impossible to embarrass Walsh, and he took Cisco in stride. "Then I will," he replied pleasantly. "While you gentlemen muddle around my crime scene wondering what's going on, I'll perform my expert scientific magic to clear up a few things for you." He pulled on a pair of rubber gloves, and then reached into the car and picked up the envelopes by the corners.

McKenna saw an opportunity to get even more work from Walsh. He took from his pocket the letter and envelope Justice had sent Messing, along with Messing's fingerprint card. "If you can keep a secret, I have another mission for you," he said.

"A secret from who?" Walsh asked.

"Messing's a pal of yours, isn't he?"

"He's one of my many pals in the press."

"Well, this belongs to Messing, and you can't be telling any of your other pals about it."

"Why not?"

"Because Brunette promised him an exclusive, and he

wouldn't like it if you broke his promise. Wouldn't like you much, either."

"Then Messing keeps his exclusive. I may enjoy being a pain in the ass, Brian, but I'm not stupid. What is it?"

McKenna gave Walsh the papers. Then, while Monahan listened in, he gave Walsh some background on his meeting with Messing. Walsh had no questions, but Monahan did. However, he waited until Walsh headed for his Crime Scene Unit van. "You guys have any ideas on who this Justice is?" he asked as soon as Walsh was out of earshot.

It was Cisco who answered. "Sure we do. We think he's either a cop or a DEA agent."

Monahan thought that over for a moment, then shook his head. "Glad it's not my case," he said, and looked like he meant it. "You ready to hear my thoughts on what happened here?"

"Can you start by telling us about these strips of car door on the ground?" Cisco asked. "They're obviously from Justice's limo, but I'm wondering why they don't have many nail holes in them."

"When you see the limo, you'll understand," Monahan said. "Short and sweet, it has to do with the way he wired up the trunk and every door on the car with his bombs. Sitting in that limo is like sitting in a bulletproof, blast-proof steel box, but it looks like a standard limo until you dismantle it."

"And that's what he did?"

"Professionally. Took off all the nice, shiny sheet-metal covering the doors. Underneath is the bulletproof steel, and that's where he attached his bombs. Spread his plastic explosive loaded with nails on the outside of the steel. Then he put the car back together again, and he's ready for action. The way he had it rigged, when he set off the bomb in his door the sheet-metal was the first thing to leave the car—right before the nails."

"So he wanted to get maximum damage outta his nails, I guess," Cisco said. "Very good."

Once again, McKenna found himself trying hard to ignore

Cisco and his admiration for Justice. "Are you thinking he was in the car when he blew the bombs?" he asked Monahan.

"I know he was."

"Your witness told you that?"

"Uh-huh. Joe Listorti."

"Reliable?"

"Solid. Been with sanitation for twenty-seven years. According to his foreman, he's the best worker in the district."

"That's good for us," McKenna said. "Start to finish, what did he see?"

"He first noticed the limo when he drove his sweeper to the spot where you see it now," Monahan said, nodding toward the sweeper. "The limo was the only car here then, but he didn't pay much attention to it. He goes about his business, unloading his sweeper, and I figure that was when the cash-and-drug transaction took place. Then Listorti hears the first blast, and that got his attention."

"What's the time lapse?" McKenna asked.

"From the time he arrived until the first big bang, maybe five minutes."

"Did he see these other cars arrive?" McKenna asked.

"He says he was busy, so he didn't see them get here. First time he saw them was after the first blast, and they were parked like you see them now. I figure the BMW pulled up next to the limo, and then the Mercedes pulled up behind it. I figure they thought they were boxing Justice in."

"But he was ready for them and whatever moves they tried on him. I guess Listorti saw the second blast," Cisco said, tapping the hood of the blast-damaged Mercedes.

"Sure did."

"What's the time lapse between blasts?"

"Just seconds. First, Justice pops open the limo's trunk."

"From inside the car?" McKenna asked.

"Yeah, he's inside the car. Then those two made their last big mistake," Monahan said, nodding toward the bodies next to the Mercedes.

"They didn't see the bomb Justice had rigged in the trunk

right in front of them, so they got out of the car," McKenna surmised.

"With their guns in their foolish hands," Monahan added. "That's when Justice blew his trunk bomb. Damaged them good, and blew them both off their feet."

"But the blast didn't kill them?" Cisco asked.

"I think it might've killed the driver, but that's when Justice got out of the limo. First thing he did was give the driver one round in the head just to make sure he was dead."

"So Listorti got a look at Justice?" McKenna asked.

"A look that won't help you much. He was wearing a ski mask when he got out of the limo, and a pair of white latex gloves. Listorti was almost a block away, so all he knows is that Justice is a bulky guy, but he can't even say for sure whether he's black or white."

Just great, McKenna thought. As far as we know, nobody has seen Justice's face. "I assume Justice saw Listorti?"

"Sure he did. Right after he shot the driver, he looked around. Saw Listorti, gave him a big, friendly wave, and then he got back to his business."

"What was Listorti's reaction to that?" Cisco asked.

"Hard to believe, but he said he waved back," Monahan replied.

"Justice didn't scare him?"

"He says no. Says he just got a feeling he was in no danger, like a spectator at an action movie. C'mon. I'll walk you through the shooting action, starting with the driver," Monahan said. With McKenna and Cisco following, he walked to the covered body behind the open driver's door of the Mercedes and pulled off the blanket to reveal the gory sight underneath. He was a casually dressed Hispanic, possibly thirty-five years old, lying on his right side beneath the open door with his right arm stretched out. His right hand still clutched an S&W Model 59 9-millimeter automatic, but it was obvious he had never had a chance to use it. The front of his body from his knees to his face was studded with nails and covered with small bits of broken glass from the windshield.

McKenna didn't know if the nails in his chest had proved

fatal, but he thought that the one protruding from his right
eye would certainly have rendered him unconscious, at least.
No matter; if he had still been alive when he hit the ground,
the bullet that had entered his forehead square in the middle
certainly killed him.

"Nice shooting," Cisco said, and his jovial manner continued to annoy McKenna. "Where was Justice firing from?"

"From the limo door, maybe twenty-five feet away,"
Monahan replied. "Not such a great shot, really, considering
he had a laser-sighted pistol, and this guy was lying on the
ground when he got it."

"Are you saying he's not a great shot?" Cisco asked.

"Not saying that at all. His second shot was a great piece
of shooting, laser sight or no. I think you'll like it." The detectives walked around the Mercedes to the covered body lying behind the open passenger's door. Next to the body were
three spent 12-gauge shotgun shells, and just visible on the
floor of the Mercedes was the butt of a pistol jutting from
under the passenger's side of the front seat.

Monahan bent down and yanked the blanket off the body.
It was another casually dressed Hispanic man, but this one
was maybe ten years older than his partner, and McKenna
could see the top edge of the bulletproof vest he was wearing under his shirt. He was lying on his back, and next to his
body was a Remington pump-action sawed-off shotgun. The
front of his body was covered with small bits of broken glass
and studded with nails from his knees to his waist. There
were also a few nails protruding from his arms, but the vest
had protected his torso. Although there was a nail protruding
from his neck, none of them had hit his head. What had hit
his head was Justice's second bullet, right in middle of his
forehead.

"Listorti saw all the gunplay?" McKenna asked Monahan.

"He wasn't in a position to see the other one get hit, but
he saw Justice fire the shot. He did, however, witness the de-
mise of this gent, bright and clear. Says he'll never forget it,
and he paints a pretty clear picture. Like I said, when Justice
set off his bomb, both these guys go down, but this one

doesn't stay down. While Justice is finishing off his partner, this one gets up, takes cover behind his door and gets off five rounds from his shotgun."

"Any effect?" Cisco asked.

"None whatsoever. Justice is crouched down on the other side of the limo, and this guy is firing double-oh buckshot. The pellets just bounced off the limo's bulletproof glass. Then this guy runs himself out of ammo, and when he's bending down to reload, Justice pops up. Only the top of this guy's head is visible through the shattered window of his door while he's reloading, but that was enough for Justice. According to Listorti, Justice didn't take the time to sight in. Just fired off one quick shot, and you can see where it went."

"Yeah, right in the noggin," Cisco observed admiringly. "Like I said, great shooting."

With some effort, McKenna again ignored his partner's tone of voice. "What happened next?" he asked.

"Justice takes a look around, sees that Listorti's still looking, so he gives him another friendly wave. Then he goes into the backseat of the BMW and disappears from Listorti's view for thirty seconds max. When he pops up again, he has a duffel bag. He waves to Listorti again, gets into the limo, makes a U-turn, and he drives off slow and careful. Makes a left onto Hundred Twenty-sixth Street, and that's the last Listorti sees of him."

"So after he made the cash-drug exchange with Garcia, the drugs were in Justice's duffel bag in the back of Garcia's BMW. Justice wanted that bag back," Cisco said. "He also wanted to leave his notes on top of a neat pile of drugs, so that's what he did when he went into the backseat. Dumped the drugs outta the duffel bag, stacked them nicely, and then placed his notes neatly on top."

"I think it's more than that," McKenna said. "He couldn't very well be wearing his latex gloves when he makes the exchange with Garcia, so it's possible the duffel bag has his prints on it somewhere. He takes no chances, so he takes the bag with him."

"You're probably right, partner," Cisco said. "Got to admire a man who plans ahead and thinks of everything."

"No, we don't," McKenna insisted, and then thought it was time to change the subject. "Any idea on the criminal histories of this guy and his pal?" he asked Monahan, nodding toward the body at his feet on the ground.

"Nothing I've seen for myself yet, but according to Alfonso, they've built themselves a horrible history. They've been shooting, pillaging, and plundering for most of their lives."

"What are their names?"

"This one's Jamie Velasquez, age forty-four. The one on the other side is José Vega, age thirty-six."

"You said this one got off five rounds from his shotgun. Where are the other two spent slugs? Under his body?"

"Presumably. Except for a visual search of the crime scene, I was told that nothing should be moved until you got here."

"Have the bodies been photographed?"

"Yeah. Walsh didn't do much, but his team was busy. The bodies and everything around the cars has been shot and measured."

"But not searched?"

"Nope. Not the cars, and not the bodies. Your case, remember?" Monahan said with a smile.

And McKenna knew what that smile meant. He wanted to get to 126th Street to take a look at the limo and see what the Bomb Squad was doing there, but he knew he had a big problem. He had been told he was in charge of the case, but there was a large amount of mundane detective work still to be done at the Marginal Street crime scene, followed by an enormous load of paperwork, and nobody had told him that he shouldn't be the one doing it. His case, his work.

Might as well get started, McKenna decided. He grabbed Velasquez's arm and rolled the body over onto its side. As expected, the two missing spent shotgun shells were there, and Cisco picked them up.

With Cisco taking notes, McKenna next catalogued the recovery of the five spent shotgun shells, and then they went on to the tedious task of searching the bodies and itemizing the personal possessions of the four dead men. McKenna was surveying the crime scene, trying to decide which of the many routine crime-scene tasks to do next, when he noticed Sheeran had arrived. The inspector was still on the other side of the crime-scene tape, talking to Messing and Alfonso. With Sheeran were Eddie Morgan and Bobby Garbus from the Major Case Squad. Morgan had his notepad out, and he was writing.

Then Sheeran left the group, ducked under the crime-scene tape, and walked to McKenna, Cisco, and Monahan. "What a mess this is," he said, looking around and then down at Velasquez's body.

"Yeah, a real complicated mess," McKenna said.

"But it shouldn't be your concern at the moment. What are you still doing here?" Sheeran asked.

"Where should I be? With the limo?" McKenna asked.

"Of course."

"It's my case, and there's still a lot of work to be done here," McKenna offered.

"I'm sure there is, but not by you. According to Ray, you're to do nothing but the thinking. Didn't Chief Rowe talk to you?"

"Yeah. He told me he was in command, but I was in charge. Told me he'd get me anything I need."

"Then it must have slipped his mind to tell you he'd also get you *anyone* you need to do whatever you think needs doing. You need people, you just holler, and then you tell them what you want done."

"Inspector, I'm a detective, remember? I'm not a boss, and I never wanted to be one."

"Okay, then we'll play it like this," Sheeran said evenly, but McKenna saw the disappointment in his face. "I'll do the hollering, and I'll get the people to do whatever you think needs doing. Happy?"

"That's the way I prefer we do it," McKenna said, but suddenly he wasn't so sure he was right in his attitude.

"Fine, and we'll start right now," Sheeran said, and then he turned to Monahan. "Where's the rest of your team, John?"

"One man's at the station house with the witness; Sergeant Morse and the rest are at Hundred Twenty-sixth Street," Monahan replied.

"And how about the Two-Five Squad?"

"With Sergeant Morse."

"Doing what?"

"Watching Dennis Hunt disassemble the bombs in the limo, I imagine, but I can't say for certain."

"Me neither, but that's gonna change. Go tell Morse I want him and every detective he can round up right here, and make it quick."

"Yes, sir." Monahan took off at a trot.

"You know, Inspector, you're not making Brian real popular here," Cisco said. "It's his case, and if you chew out Morse, Brian's stock is gonna plummet fast and far."

"Not important, because if we don't get a handle on this thing fast, Ray's stock is gonna plummet faster and further," Sheeran said. "This Justice character is operating quicker than us, and he just upped the ante."

Sheeran was devoted to Brunette and functioned as his strong right arm in the detective bureau, McKenna knew, but he had never seen him act quite so strongly.

So what does that tell me? McKenna wondered. Sheeran's smart, and he's worried about my best friend, so maybe it's time for me to toughen up and forget my Mr. Popularity image, especially since I think this case is turning even worse than Sheeran suspects. Time to bring him up to speed. "We think Justice is somebody in New York law enforcement, either a cop or a DEA agent," he said.

Sheeran's face went blank, and McKenna could see that the news hit him hard. "Who's *we*?" he asked.

"Cisco and I."

"And Messing," Cisco added.

"Tell me about it," Sheeran said, and McKenna did, giving him all the facts and suspicions that had led them to that conclusion.

"If you're right, and if Justice is a cop, do you know how bad it will make this department look?" Sheeran asked.

"Sure I do," McKenna replied. "If we're right, it means that he's using all the experience and training he gained with us to make a mockery of the rule of law and our justice system, the very things the NYPD is supposed to represent, support, and safeguard."

"That's right, and heads will roll. Is Messing gonna run with this?"

"Not right away, as long as we treat him right and as long as this thing doesn't drag on too long."

"Then make sure you treat him right, and make sure this doesn't drag on too long. Get to work, and make sure you're doing whatever you think is most important."

"Then I guess I won't be typing up all the paperwork on these killings," McKenna said.

"No, other people will be doing that for you. Matter of fact, you can get yourself a manicure, because you won't be breaking any fingernails typing for a while."

Police work without paperwork? Never did that before, McKenna thought, but the prospect didn't bother him in the least.

But it was bothering someone. "That's the way it should be. Inspector, should I be getting a manicure, too?" Cisco asked, smiling expectantly.

"No."

It wasn't the answer Cisco wanted to hear, and the smile left his face. All of a sudden McKenna thought it best to get off Marginal Street and away from Cisco.

SEVEN

Sheeran had taken charge of the Marginal Street crime scene, and it was a very busy place by the time McKenna left. It took him under two minutes to walk to the second crime scene on East 126th Street, a relatively quiet place in comparison. As Monahan had said, the block was in the industrial part of Spanish Harlem, and old, two-story factories lined both sides of the block. FOR SALE OR LEASE signs adorned many of the buildings, and it appeared to McKenna that many others had been abandoned.

The limo was parked at the curb in the middle of the block, and a police line had been established two hundred feet on each side of it. Uniformed cops manned the wooden barriers, and they far outnumbered the curious neighborhood spectators, but the press was there in force. Three TV news crews had their tall antennas set up on top of their vans, and they were transmitting live as a kneeling detective wearing a full-blast protection suit worked on the right rear door of the limo.

The bomb disposal truck, the Bomb Squad command van, an NYPD tow truck, many marked and unmarked police cars, a fire department pumper truck, and two ambulances blocked the street on the far side of the barrier. Uniformed cops, firemen, and ambulance attendants were lounging around in small groups at the building line, chatting and drinking coffee, and their relaxed demeanor told McKenna that the situation was just about wrapped up. Standing next to the Bomb Squad command van were Chief

Rowe and Lieutenant Finan, the CO of the Bomb Squad. Both were peering into the open side door of the Bomb Squad command van.

McKenna passed by the news crews without being noticed, and a uniformed cop moved one of the barriers to let him through. He got right next to Rowe and Finan before they noticed him, and then he saw what had been holding their interest. There was a TV monitor in the van, and McKenna surmised that the Bomb Squad detective disarming the bomb in the right rear door of the limo was wearing a helmet cam that transmitted live to the command van. Below the monitor was a VCR recording the procedure.

McKenna saluted Rowe again, but Rowe just pointed to the monitor and said, "Be with you in a moment, Brian. Looks like Hunt is about to render the last one safe."

McKenna took a closer look at the monitor and saw Dennis Hunt's hands as he removed the blasting cap from the center of the nail-studded mass of plastic explosive packed into a frying pan attached to the outside of the hardened steel plate lining the door of the limo.

"Well, that's a wrap," Finan said, and then he turned off the monitors and faced McKenna. "Good to see you, Brian," he said, offering his hand. "Dennis should be here in a minute to give you a report."

Give me a report? I guess Rowe's told the CO of the Bomb Squad that I, a detective, am in charge of his bomb investigation. "Thanks, Lou. Was it a tough one?"

"After we saw the damage on Marginal Street, we thought it would be. Three potent antipersonnel bombs, but it turned out to be a piece of cake. Never saw a case like this one before, but your bomber disarmed his own bombs when he dumped the car here. Very nice of him."

"The bombs weren't live?" McKenna asked.

"Not technically, but we had to treat them all as if they were. Never know when we're gonna run into a booby trap, but it turns out we should've believed him."

"Believed him?" McKenna asked, confused for a moment, but then he got it. "He left you a note?"

"Right on the front seat." Finan took an envelope from his pocket and handed it to McKenna. "For the Bomb Squad" was printed on the face of the envelope in the bold black letters generated by a laser printer. "You understand, of course, in emergency situations like this we don't worry about dusting for prints," Finan added.

"Of course, and not important in this case. I'm sure he left no prints. Not on the envelope, not on the note, and not anywhere in the car," McKenna said, and then he opened the envelope, took out the laser-printed note, and read:

> *Sirs:*
>   *I didn't know how many I would need, but I originally placed five bombs in this car. I placed one in the trunk, and one behind the outer panel in each door. As they are of an electronic-detonation design, I have rendered them safe by removing the firing mechanism and disconnecting the power source. As you probably will not believe me and will therefore go through the trouble of removing the door panels while wearing the appropriate uncomfortable protective gear, I am truly sorry for the inconvenience I'll be causing you.*

The note was unsigned, which McKenna found curious. Why did he sign "Justice" in his note to Messing, but not in the notes he leaves us? He came up with one possible answer that reinforced his belief Justice was a cop: Most cops would consider the name he had chosen for himself to be too melodramatic.

"Quite a literate fellow, and very considerate of him, wouldn't you say?" Rowe asked.

McKenna was sick and tired of hearing from cops just how wonderful Justice was, but it was a chief asking the question, so only one reply came to mind. "Yes, sir. He's quite literate and quite considerate. I look forward to meeting him," he said. "Have we come up with anybody who saw him drop the car here?"

"The Two-Five Squad came up with two. Two kids playing box ball against the wall near the corner," Rowe said, nodding toward Second Avenue, half a long city block away. "They noticed him drive up in the limo and pull behind an old four-door sedan, maybe dark green. He got out of the limo, got into the sedan, drove past them, and made a left onto Second Avenue."

"Was he carrying anything when he switched cars?"

"A suitcase, and they think a green cloth bag."

"Empty?"

"It looked that way."

So the money he got from Garcia is in the suitcase, and he still has his duffel bag, McKenna thought. "How many other cars were parked on the block at the time?" he asked.

"What you see now."

McKenna looked up and down the block, and saw only three cars parked inside the barriers. "Did the kids get a look at him?"

"Big and black was all they could come up with. He held his hand in front of his face when he passed them."

"Clothing?"

"Dark pants, light-colored sports jacket. Kids say he looked 'respectable.'"

"How old are these kids?"

"Eleven and twelve. They're at the station house with their parents now, in case you want to talk to them."

McKenna then noticed that Hunt was shuffling toward them in his bulky blast-protection suit with his helmet under his arm. "You've got your work cut out for you, Brian. This guy really knows his bombs and his cars," was Hunt's first comment to McKenna.

"I thought it was a piece of cake," McKenna replied.

"Disarming the bombs was nothing, once we got to them. Just a matter of removing the blasting cap. The problem was removing the door panels to get to them. He put them back on better than they do at the factory."

"Was it a shape charge?"

"Yeah, and very professionally done."

"Could you show it to me, and explain it while you're at it?"

"Sure. The C-Four's still there, so it won't be hard to explain. Just give me a minute to get out of this suit."

McKenna waited while Hunt removed the blast-protection suit with the help of Finan, and then he followed Hunt to the limo. The three remaining outside sheet-metal door panels had been removed, and the three inert bombs were clearly visible. Each consisted of a shallow frying pan Justice had welded to the outside surface of the hardened bulletproof steel, and inside the pan was a thin layer of the nail-studded C-4. The plastic explosive was held in place with strips of duct tape, and the heads of the nails were embedded in it with the pointed ends facing outward.

"Okay, how does it work?" McKenna asked.

"Pretty simple, but pretty ingenious at the same time," Hunt said, and then he reached into the car and tugged on some wires hanging under the dashboard. "He used the electronic feed from the car's radio as his power source for detonation, and his firing mechanism probably consisted of a box he made with nine FIRE buttons.

"Why nine buttons if there are only five bombs?"

"He only needed one FIRE button for the bomb in the trunk since all he had to do was pop the trunk to expose the bomb and get maximum effect, but the doors are different. He didn't want to waste his nails and explosive energy blowing off the limo's outer door panels, so he taped low-intensity blasting caps to the fittings holding them in place. First button he pushes blows those fittings, and the second one sends his nails approximately where he wants them at a thousand feet per second. The frying pan is his crude-but-effective device for shaping the direction of the force."

"Have you ever seen anything like this?"

"Seen my share of car bombs but never anything like this—and I've been in the Bomb Squad for eleven years. Never even read about anything like this."

"So he's a bomb expert?"

"I'd say. Don't forget, this guy was sitting in the car when he set off his bombs. That takes an expert with confidence and experience, or a suicidal madman suffering from an overdose of balls."

"Then listen to this description: Black, well-built, very strong, smart, educated, expert shot, knows all there is to know about bombs, and hates drug dealers. Bring anybody to mind?"

Hunt took some time to think before answering. "There's no suspected bomber loose in the country right now who comes close to fitting that description, and we get wanted circulars from all over."

"Think closer to home," McKenna said. "Maybe somebody you met or heard about."

"A cop?"

"Or a fed."

"Are you kidding?"

"Unfortunately, no. Take your time, because I need an answer I can count on."

Hunt did, and McKenna watched him closely while waiting. "Sorry, Brian. If he's a cop or a fed, I don't know him and haven't heard about him. Are you sure about this?"

"Kinda."

"Then maybe you better rethink. If this guy was ever in the Bomb Squad, he'd have been a very noticeable legend, and I'm certain we never had anybody fitting his description during my time here. We also work closely with the fed bomb guys, and I'm sure they don't have anybody like him, either. Not in New York, at least."

"Who's the senior man in the Bomb Squad?"

"Me."

"You've been in the squad longer than Finan?"

"Got the boss beat by two months. He came as a sergeant and left for a year when he made lieutenant. Took him a year to get back and take over the squad."

Is it possible I'm wrong about this, and going off half-cocked? McKenna wondered. Maybe I *should* be rethinking this cop-or-agent bit.

McKenna's cell phone rang, interrupting his ruminations.

"Just got off the phone with Sheeran," Brunette said. "How sure are you on this cop theory?"

"Not as sure as I was a few minutes ago," McKenna said, "but I still think we should keep it on the front burner."

"What's causing you this new doubt?"

"Dennis Hunt. I'm with him now, and he says the guy is a bomb expert, so I was figuring he must've gained that type of expertise in a bomb squad somewhere. Until I gave Dennis his description, I was thinking it was a local bomb squad, either ours or the feds'."

"But Dennis doesn't know him?"

"Yeah, and he's sure of that. He's been around a while, and he says that he'd know of any local cop or agent who's this good with bombs."

"Then just keep thinking, but I have another problem heading your way," Brunette said. "The press at Marginal Street are working themselves into a feeding frenzy, so Sheeran's scheduled a press conference for seven o'clock outside the Two-Five station house. His conference, but you'll be fielding the questions for him."

McKenna checked his watch. "That gives me almost three hours to prepare, but I'm sure they'll have a lot of questions we'll want to dance around."

"That's why it'll be you answering the questions. You're a pretty good dancer, you know most of the reporters in town, and they like you. With your track record, they'd be much less likely to bash you than they would Sheeran."

"I get it. Nothing about Cruz's bought cop and nothing about this Justice-is-a-cop theory."

"You're my man. When you finish up tonight, could you stop by for a chat?"

"Sure, but it'll probably be very late. You staying over?" McKenna asked.

"Until you get this guy for me, I'll be hiding out right here, getting grayer and pulling out my hair while I cry over the newspapers. See ya later."

How's that for some pressure on me? McKenna thought

after Brunette ended the call. He then returned his attention
to Hunt. "Will you be able to tell me where he got his explosives and all the blasting caps?" he asked.

"There's a code on the inside of the blasting caps, and all
C-Four has a chemical signature added in when it's manu-
factured, so yeah, I'll be able to tell you something," Hunt
said.

"Something?"

"Since it's all made in the U.S., I'll be able to give you
the dates and places of manufacture, and where the stuff was
shipped to."

"When do I get it?"

"A couple of days."

"I need it sooner."

"How much sooner?"

"Tonight," McKenna said, and then he got to see Hunt's
best greedy smile. "Entirely possible, if we had many people
working on it," Hunt said, "but first somebody would have to
authorize overtime while we worked hard at good rates ful-
filling your request."

"Chief Rowe authorizes it."

"Then give me your cell phone number, and on behalf of
myself, Lieutenant Finan, and maybe the entire Bomb
Squad, please give the chief a big, sloppy kiss for us."

At McKenna's request, Rowe arranged that the limo and the
BMW would be towed to the Motor Transport Division's
garage in Queens, where the cars would be processed for latent fingerprints. Many prints would be found, McKenna
was sure, but he was almost as sure that none of them would
be Justice's. That, however, could only be officially confirmed after quite a bit of tedious work had been done. Elimination prints would have to be taken from anyone known to
have been in the vehicles, and then compared against any latent prints recovered.

As a matter of course, the bodies of Raymond Garcia,
Ramon De Jesus, José Vega, and Jamie Velasquez would be

fingerprinted at the morgue. At McKenna's request, Rowe agreed to send detectives from the Manhattan North Homicide Squad to take elimination prints from the ambassador, his family, and his chauffeur.

McKenna was on his way back to the Marginal Street crime scene when he met Joe Walsh. "Finished dusting the envelopes and the notes, so Sheeran sent me to give you the results," Walsh said.

"Are there any results?" McKenna asked.

"Negative results. Not a single latent on either the notes or the envelopes. Plenty of prints on the cash, of course. There always are on old bills, but dusting all that money would be an enormous job that probably wouldn't yield any meaningful results."

"I agree. How much did he leave the ambassador to compensate him for the damage he did to his car?"

"Your Justice is a very generous man. Left him ten packets of wrapped hundreds, fifty thousand dollars total."

"And the note to the ambassador?"

"Short and simple, but I want to get it right. Mind if I read it to you?"

"Not at all."

Walsh took out his notebook and began flipping through the pages. "Where are the originals?" McKenna asked.

"I think Sheeran's afraid I'd be showing them to some of my reporter pals, so he made me give them to your partner."

Good thinking, Dennis. Probably kept Walsh's picture out of tomorrow's papers, McKenna thought as Walsh found his page.

"Here it is," Walsh said, and he began reading. " 'I'm sorry for the inconvenience I've caused you, and I regret damaging your fine car. My only excuse is that it was used in a good cause, and I trust the enclosed cash will be considered just compensation.' "

"Was it signed?"

"Justice."

"And what did he have to say to us?"

"Our note is even shorter, and we were right about the

message." Walsh again began to read from his notepad.
" 'Nailed these guys for you. There will be more fun to follow, but not for a few days. As you know by now, I've been
very busy, and I need some rest.' That one's not signed."

"You know how much in drugs was in the BMW?"
McKenna asked.

"Lots, all in one-kilo bags. Thirty cocaine, three heroin.
Garcia had a great business going for himself."

"Where's the stuff now?"

"At the Two-Five station house. Sheeran wants me there
to dust the bags."

"Have the cars been searched?"

"Not thoroughly. Sheeran didn't want to add any cops'
prints, or smudge any latents that might be there. Cisco just
gave them a quick look, and he found two pistols under the
front seat of the BMW. Nice guns, both nine millimeters, a
Ruger and a Sig Sauer."

"How about the bodies? They still there?"

"Bagged and gone. That crime scene is winding down."

"Reporters?"

"Except for Messing, most of them headed for the station
house after Sheeran let the photo people get close enough to
take some shots."

"What's Messing doing?"

"Waiting for you. He said if he's not there when you get
back, you can find him in Rao's," Walsh said. "What's on
your agenda after Messing?"

"Hopefully talk to MacFarlane and Chmil before the
press conference. Then, after the press has their way with
me, I'll head over to the Cruz house."

"To talk to Lela Cruz?"

"If we can. What's she like?"

"A knockout, but a basically uncooperative liar. If you put
some pressure on her, she'll seem polite enough as she lies
to your face."

"Do you know for a fact that she lied to MacFarlane?"

"Sure do, and I could put you in a position to prove it. So
now, tell me something. When you're interviewing an unco-

operative subject, doesn't it help when you catch them good in a boldfaced lie right off the bat?"

Sure does. Gives the investigator the upper hand, McKenna thought. Sometimes that shuts the subject down completely, but in most cases it's the first step for a good interrogator to get them talking. So Walsh wants to make a deal? Let's see what he's got. "Sometimes it helps," McKenna said. "Do you think she knows about her husband's business?"

"Maybe not all the details, but she knows."

"What do you want in return for this piece of information?"

"Press coverage. I want to figure prominently in this investigation, and I want everyone to know all about it when I do something good."

"Isn't your scrapbook already full?" McKenna asked.

"*Scrapbooks*, Brian, and I can always buy another one."

"Okay, Joe. You have a deal, and it's you who I want going over the limo for prints."

"Why me? Is it because I'm the best, and the limo is your best shot for getting one of Justice's prints?"

God! This man is insufferable, McKenna thought. "Yeah, Joe, it's because you're the best. What do you have for me?"

"I did a little unauthorized snooping, so this has to be just between us," Walsh insisted.

"It is."

"She lied to MacFarlane twice: Once was when she told him her husband didn't have a gun. He had one, and she knew it. The second whopper was when she told him she didn't know about the safe. She knew, and she even has the combination."

"Tell me about this unauthorized snooping."

"It was hectic in the house. Gaston is still on the floor and Montoya is still in the garage while we're waiting for the M.E. to arrive. The Bomb Squad is still there, crime-scene people everywhere taking measurements and shooting photos, and the press is already camped out near the front door. MacFarlane is in the kitchen interviewing Lela Cruz, and I hear her give him that nonsense about the gun and the safe.

Then I ask her if I can use the bathroom, and she tells me to use the one at the top of the stairs. I go up, but it's occupied, so I . . ."

"One minute. Occupied by who?" McKenna asked.

"The nanny, and I think she had the baby in there. So I use the bathroom in the master bedroom. When I'm done, I happen to notice half a box of forty-four–magnum shells."

"Where were these shells when you happened to notice them?"

"In Gaston's top dresser drawer, under his socks. So I know he had a gun, but where did he keep it? I go right to the bed, look under the pillows, and I notice oily spots on the sheet and on the underside of the pillow. It's gun oil, I figure, so I take a swatch."

"Did you have it analyzed?"

"By a pal in the lab," Walsh said. "Number-nine oil, more commonly known as gun oil."

"And the combination to the safe? Where did you happen to notice that?"

"In the most obvious spot. On a small piece of paper taped to the bottom of a tray in her jewelry box," Walsh said, and then he thumbed through the pages in his notepad for a moment until he found what he was looking for. "Nine right, twenty left, thirty-seven right."

"Are you sure it's the combination for *that* safe?"

Walsh looked hurt by the question, and then he looked at McKenna reprovingly.

"Sorry," McKenna said. "Of course you tried it before you left."

"Of course. Locked the safe, and then opened it again with those magic numbers."

"Did you give this information to MacFarlane?"

"No. No matter how big the case, he never gets enough press to suit my tastes. And besides, he's too goddamn straight. Not my kind of guy."

So I guess that makes *me* Walsh's kind of guy, McKenna thought. Can that be good?

• ▼• •

Sheeran and a few detectives were still at the Marginal Street crime scene when McKenna got back, but Messing wasn't there. Neither was Cisco and their car. Since it was Cisco who had found the pistols in the BMW, Sheeran had sent him to the station house to invoice those pistols as well as Velasquez's and Vega's weapons. On the chance the weapons had been used in other crimes, Cisco would also prepare requests for ballistic examinations, and then the pistols would be brought to the Ballistics Unit in the police lab.

Sheeran had ensured that everyone was pulling their weight, but the press conference was foremost on his mind. He was known for his attention to detail, and he wanted to be totally prepared for it. Since the Brooklyn, Queens, and Manhattan cases were all connected, Sheeran had Chmil and MacFarlane reporting to the 25th Precinct station house at six o'clock in order to brief him and McKenna on the work they had done in their cases.

McKenna was happy with that news and felt he would have enough time to prepare himself for the press conference. There were, however, a few issues to be addressed with Messing before filling in the rest of the press. Since the order of the day was to keep Messing happy, Sheeran agreed, and he dropped McKenna off at Rao's.

EIGHT

Located at East 114th Street and Pleasant Avenue in Spanish Harlem, Rao's was an anomaly: an old and fashionable upscale restaurant in a decidedly unfashionable, poor neighborhood. McKenna found Messing seated at a large corner booth with Mickey Alfonso, each enjoying a steak dinner in his own way. Messing had hardly touched his steak, but there was an empty martini glass next to his plate and a full one in his hand. Alfonso was a rotund fellow, apparently a big eater. His beer was untouched, but his steak was more than half gone.

Alfonso gave McKenna a wave and a quick hello before returning to his meal. While watching him enjoy his steak, McKenna realized that he hadn't eaten a thing all day except for a yogurt and a banana on the plane that morning, and he suddenly felt very hungry.

"Sit down, Brian," Messing said. "Since Justice forced us to miss our lunch, I took the liberty of ordering you another steak and one of those sissy beers you drink."

"I don't have a lot of time, Phil," McKenna said.

"I know, I know. You have to get ready for your press conference, but this won't take much time. You're just gonna be eating and listening while Mickey talks."

"Fine. I'll make time," McKenna said, and he sat down. Messing motioned to the waiter, and he disappeared into the kitchen. Then Messing immediately addressed the issue foremost on McKenna's mind. "You're worried that you're reneging on my *exclusive* deal with this press conference?"

"Yeah, I am. With these latest four killings and all the press attention they're generating, there's no way I can hold up my end of the bargain. Spectacular murders, public interest will be enormously high, and everybody in the press has a right to the story."

"I realize that, and I agree. Our exclusive deal is off, but I'm still not in bad shape. Once that press conference airs and you mention my letter, my editor will be sufficiently chastised. Besides, it's me who Justice is writing to, so I still have a handle on the inside story."

"As long as he keeps writing to you," McKenna added.

"Yeah, but I have a feeling he already has another letter in the mail for me."

"So do I, Phil."

"Since that would put me in a better position, would you mind if I added a little something to our deal?"

"Such as?"

"At your press conference you can say that my letter has been extremely helpful—and it wouldn't hurt if you mentioned my name many, many times—but I don't want you quoting from the letter. That letter still belongs to me, and it will be seen for the first time in my story tomorrow. It would be nice if you somehow mentioned that as well."

"I see where you're headed. Play it your way, and my press conference tonight will basically amount to free advertising for tomorrow's edition of the *Post*."

"Basically. You do it right, and our circulation on tomorrow's edition might even triple today's."

"Sounds great for you, so let's add something else to this deal," McKenna said. "While we're keeping you on the inside, there's a few things we don't want appearing in your stories yet."

"That we believe Justice just might be a cop?" Messing guessed.

"That's one. Nothing on that until we get a chance to follow up on it."

"And if it's true?"

"We take our lumps, but you'll be the one breaking the story."

"Fair enough. What else?" Messing asked.

"No speculation about Cruz's bought cop, at least until we find out for sure if there is such a person."

"Fine, but suppose this investigation of yours stretches out for a while, and Justice still isn't captured?"

"Then you can bash us in print if you feel you must, but you still don't file any story that would compromise our investigation in any way."

"I'm not going to give you editorial approval rights on my stories," Messing said.

"I'm not asking you to. All I'm asking is that you use common sense, and that you be fair with us. Not necessarily nice, but fair."

"Isn't that what I always do?"

"Yeah, that's why I don't feel uncomfortable dealing with you. Just don't change."

"I never will," Messing said, "and we have a deal."

The waiter brought McKenna's steak dinner and his O'Doul's, and he dug right in. Alfonso finished his meal by the time McKenna had barely satisfied his hunger. He took a few sips from his beer, and waited until McKenna was ready to hear what he had to say.

McKenna noticed, so he put down his fork. "Okay, Mickey, let's have it. What've you got for me?"

"Phil's gonna run with the figures involved when he files his story, and they are impressive," Alfonso said. "It's best you know about them before reading tomorrow's *Post*, so if it's all right with you, I'm gonna give you some basic arithmetic on the drug trade that'll show you just how profitable it really is."

"More than all right, Mickey, because you're doing me two favors," McKenna said. "You've already given Phil the info I promised to get for him, and now you're gonna give me the answers to some of the questions I'm sure to be getting tonight."

"Then we'll start with Cruz. He's selling cocaine at twenty grand a key and heroin at ninety grand a key—meaning that his prices are below the wholesale prices we're familiar with. Until he arrived on the scene, wholesale coke went for twenty-two a key, and heroin for a hundred grand a key."

"So he's selling it for less, but according to one of your informants, his stuff is better," McKenna said.

"Just means he's not stepping on his product like most of the other wholesalers do. What he buys is what he sells, undiluted. He's using lower price and higher quality to expand his distribution network."

"What about the people he sells to, guys like Raymond Garcia and Ruben De Sales? Don't they dilute their product before it finally hits the streets?"

"Of course they do, but they're starting with a stronger base product. End result is stronger drugs on the street, sold to freaks and crackheads who think they're happier."

"Any idea on what Cruz was paying for the drugs he wholesaled?"

"That depends on many factors, so it's hard to say for sure. For the cocaine, it would be someplace between two thousand and eight thousand a key. For the heroin, someplace between fifteen and forty grand a key."

"That's a pretty wide variance. What are the factors that would account for that?"

"First factor would be: Where is he getting it from? If he's getting it in Colombia and arranging for transport himself, then he's paying the low-end price."

"How about the heroin?" McKenna asked. "Could he be getting that from Colombia, too?"

"He could now. Colombia used to be strictly cocaine, but they've diversified. Big profits in heroin, so fifty percent of our heroin now comes from poppies grown in Colombia."

"Okay, he's Colombian and from a family that used to be involved in cocaine production, and he has experience in the transporting end of the business. For the sake of argument, let's say he was getting his stuff in Colombia and bringing it here himself. What're his costs then?"

"Going through the cost and all the trouble of setting up a transportation network? It would only make sense if he were moving a lot of product."

"Let's say he controlled distribution on the East Coast. That would be a lot of product, wouldn't it?"

"Sure would, but I don't think any one person or organization could control the entire East Coast. Too big a market, and the competition would be too intense."

"Okay, then let's say he controls half the East Coast market. That possible?"

"Maybe, and certainly profitable. It would mean he'd be bringing in at least a hundred tons of coke a year, and Lord knows how many tons of heroin."

A hundred tons of cocaine? The figure staggered McKenna. "Are you sure about that number?"

"Nobody knows for sure, but I'll go with that number. Every year we interdict about sixty tons of cocaine before it gets to this country. One reliable estimate is that we get only ten percent of the stuff coming in. That leaves five hundred forty tons, and the East Coast is the major market."

"Any idea on how much that is in kilos?"

Alfonso had a number ready. "A hundred tons comes to roughly ninety thousand keys."

"And the profit for Cruz?"

"Off the top of my head, I'd say it soon would make him richer than Bill Gates."

"Satisfy my curiosity, please," McKenna said. "Give me an estimate, if you can."

"Sure I can, but it will take me a few minutes," Alfonso said, and then he took out his notepad and pen, ready to write. "High estimate, or low?"

"Low will do."

"Okay, we'll figure he's paying four thousand a key in Colombia. If he loses ten percent in interdiction, that means he needs to buy a hundred thousand kilos to get his ninety thousand here. Hundred thousand keys costs him four hundred million. Add, say, forty percent for overhead . . ."

"Overhead?"

"Planes, boats, payoffs, and employees—the pilots, enforcers, and accountants," Alfonso said and then did the math in his notepad. "To buy his hundred thousand keys and get ninety thousand of them here, ready for sale, it costs him five hundred sixty million."

"Now for the money coming in, and I can do that in my head," McKenna said. "Ninety thousand kilos times his twenty thousand a kilo sales price makes one billion, eight hundred million."

McKenna next tried tackling the profit number in his head, but Alfonso was faster. "Total yearly profit of one billion two hundred forty million, tax free," he said.

"That doesn't make him Bill Gates," Messing said.

"We're just assuming the minimum he's making, and that's just on the cocaine end of his business," Alfonso countered. "He's making plenty of money in heroin, too."

"Enormously profitable, I'm sure, but he's selling much less heroin than cocaine. Why don't we just concede that he's making a billion and a half a year? After just one year in business, that still makes him a very rich man."

"*Made* him a rich man," McKenna said. "He's dead."

"That's right; your villain killed him," Messing said, smiling. "That very rich man is one of your victims, but I understand that the DEA and your Narcotics Division have built up quite a file on him."

"It's a file that goes nowhere, Phil, and I don't have it," McKenna said.

"But you can get it?"

"Yeah, I can get it."

"I'd sure appreciate a peek at it."

"I'll personally concede that Gaston Cruz was a real bad guy with a history, but there's nothing in his file we could've used to convict him of any crime."

"Am I gonna see it or not?"

"That depends. Are you planning to turn this Justice character into some kind of hero for taking out Cruz and the rest?"

"The rest of the lowlifes?" Messing asked, and his smile broadened.

"Answer the question, Phil. Are you going to make Justice a hero?"

"No, I'm not. All I'm going to report are the facts, and maybe a few well-founded suspicions. I'll let my readers draw their own conclusions."

"Let me think about it," McKenna said.

"What's there to think about? We have a deal, and I think that deal includes my inside look."

He's right, McKenna thought. "Okay, but I'll have to clear it with Brunette first."

"With a recommendation I get it as part of our deal?"

"Yeah."

"Then I'll get it. Next issue, and it's an unpleasant one for you gentlemen. I want you to put yourself in Cruz's very rich shoes for a minute."

"Already did this, Phil, even before I knew how much he was making," McKenna said. "You wanna know, if I were Cruz, what percentage of my income would I be willing to pay to get myself the information that would keep me safe and sound while helping me to expand my operation?"

"That's right. And remember, you're a very astute businessman who doesn't mind spending money to make money. So what percentage of your income would you be willing to pay the cop who gives you everything you need for security and success?"

"Five percent."

Messing looked to Alfonso. "That comes to seventy-five million a year," Alfonso said at once.

"Yeah, seventy-five million for payoffs, but consider this," McKenna said. "If he's managed to expand his operation to the entire East Coast, he's probably paying cops in sensitive positions in other cities."

Messing again turned to Alfonso. "Of all the drugs sold

on the East Coast, what percentage would you say are sold in New York City?"

"We're the world's biggest illicit drug market, so I'd feel safe saying fifty percent," Alfonso stated.

"I'll concede that," McKenna said.

"Then will you also concede it's possible Cruz slated fifty percent of his payoff money for that very knowledgeable cop he bought here?"

"Thirty-seven and a half million tax-free dollars a year to one cop?" Alfonso piped in. "Now that's a temptation hard for anyone to resist."

"Sure is, and I'll drink to that," Messing said. He took a long pull on his martini, and then focused on McKenna. "Conclusion?"

"Seems simple, if we're at least halfway right in our assumptions," McKenna said. "To identify our turncoat, all I have to do is find out who's secretly now the richest cop in the history of the New York City Police Department."

"Simple? So you think you'll get him?"

"I'd love to, but that's not part of my mission right now."

"Then let me phrase the question another way," Messing said. "Do you think you *could* get him, if you had to?"

"If I had help from the right people, then yeah, I think I could get him, but I'm not gonna talk any more about this."

McKenna had expected an argument from Messing, but he didn't get one. Instead, Messing just smiled, took another sip from his martini, and then focused on Alfonso. "Next issue. Please tell Brian how much Ruben De Sales made over the past year."

Alfonso was ready with the answer. "After expenses, the lowlife made a minimum of thirteen million three hundred fifty thousand, so let's just say thirteen million dollars pure profit, tax free. If Justice would have permitted De Sales to live long enough to peddle the drugs he left in the room, he would've made another two million six hundred thousand profit off that shit."

"Pretty precise figures you're quoting," McKenna observed.

"Comes from experience," Alfonso said. "Justice told us how much drugs De Sales bought from Cruz, so figuring out the profit is just simple arithmetic once you know the street values."

"For my own information, what are the street values?"

"By the time it's stepped on or processed into crack, that twenty-thousand key of cocaine has a retail street value of three hundred thousand. For each ninety-thousand-dollar key of heroin, the retail street value is eight hundred thousand."

When there's that kind of profit involved, how do we discourage people from going into the drug trade? The thought flashed through McKenna's mind, and then Messing brought up another issue. "Should be interesting with MacFarlane and Cisco working the same case, don't you think?" he asked.

"You knew about the falling out?"

"Yeah, and I had a few laughs over it. My article got MacFarlane first grade, but I hear it really wound Cisco up."

"That it did. He made MacFarlane miserable, you know. So miserable that he left the Major Case Squad, and it was all because of that article."

"No it wasn't. It was because of Cisco, MacFarlane, and their character defects," Messing countered. "Cisco asked me to write a piece that would get MacFarlane first grade, and that's just what I did."

"Without mentioning Cisco once in the piece?"

"That's because, when MacFarlane was giving me the story on the case, I got sick of hearing Cisco's name. It was 'Cisco did this' or 'Cisco did that' so many times that it got me wondering if MacFarlane contributed anything to the case. So I left Cisco completely out of the article, and I figured Cisco would make him suffer for it. Turns out I was right."

"So Cisco's character defect is his pride. What's MacFarlane's character defect?"

"Modesty."

"You don't admire modesty?" McKenna asked.

"In a professional athlete, maybe, but not in a first-grade detective."

"Why not?"

"Because it makes my job difficult. If most of you first-graders weren't dying to tell me all about your heroic exploits over those dinners and drinks my paper pays for, I'd probably have to go out and work for a living."

"And you wouldn't like that?"

Messing looked surprised at the question. "Of course not. Would you?"

"Are you telling me that I don't work for a living?"

"Brian, doing something you enjoy doing is called *fun*, not *work*. If it came down to it, I bet you'd do your job for free."

He might have something there, McKenna admitted, but only to himself.

NINE

Although it was an hour before the press conference, there were already many reporters outside the station house, and the TV news crews were setting up. Upstairs, McKenna found that every desk in the detective squad was occupied by a detective typing up one report or another that officially documented every small fact learned or every piece of potential evidence gathered at the two 25th Precinct crime scenes. Cisco occupied one of the desks, typing away on a PC keyboard at a speed that always impressed McKenna.

Although Cisco occasionally grumbled lightly over the amount of paperwork involved in any case, McKenna suspected he didn't mind it at all because it was another one of those tasks that Cisco proved over and over he could do better than almost everybody else. "Is that the end of your paperwork?" McKenna asked.

"Of course not. I finished mine half an hour ago," Cisco said. He ignored McKenna for a moment while he read the PC screen, then sat back, apparently satisfied.

"So what is it you've been typing?"

"Sheeran's script for his press conference."

"He asked you to do that?"

"Naw. I know he would've liked to, but his foolish pride prevented him. Cisco, however, is a kind soul, so this is the script he'll be using."

"Where is he?"

"In there, working hard on his own script—the one he

thinks he'll be using," Cisco said, nodding toward the squad commander's office.

McKenna wasn't surprised at Cisco's largesse, and he was sure it *would* be Cisco's script that Sheeran would be using. Cisco liked Sheeran, and as unlikely as it seemed on the surface, McKenna was sure that Sheeran liked Cisco, and depended on him. The two men didn't socialize together and treated each other professionally at work, but McKenna had noticed that whenever matters got either hot or touchy for the Major Case Squad, Sheeran wanted Cisco there with him. In return, Cisco never had a problem getting a day off, he was always assigned the newest car in the unit, he got the cases that interested him, and his antics were generally tolerated by Sheeran, sometimes with a smile he couldn't hide. "Mind if I read it?" McKenna asked.

"Not at all." Cisco printed the script, three sheets of paper, and handed them to McKenna.

As McKenna expected, Cisco's version of events was comprehensive and well-written. For the record, the public would learn there was a vigilante loose in New York who was effectively murdering suspected high- and mid-level drug dealers and their employees. This vigilante's motives were unknown, but it was noted that he had managed to gain for himself at least a million dollars in cash in the process. All the murders in Queens, Brooklyn, and Manhattan were summarized, and, without being specific, Cisco reported that the killer had left notes for the police in the Brooklyn and Manhattan murders, as well as cash to pay for damages. These notes indicated he would continue killing.

Cisco's version also reported that the killer had written a letter to Phil Messing of the *Post*, which he had signed "Justice." This letter gave information that confirmed prior police suspicion that Gaston Cruz had been a high-level drug dealer who had supplied Ruben De Sales with large amounts of cocaine and heroin for street-level sales. The letter also gave information that had led police to believe that Raymond Ramsey, working on behalf of Ruben De Sales, had been responsible for three shootings, including one homi-

cide, and it gave the location in Kingston, New York, where
De Sales had processed cocaine bought from Cruz into
crack. All information in this letter had been investigated by
the NYPD and found to be true.

At that point McKenna had a few questions for Cisco,
and he stopped reading. "Chmil got the rifle from Ramsey's
girlfriend?" he asked.

"Yeah, he got it and brought it straight to Ballistics for
test firing," Cisco replied. "Got a match on the bullets that
killed one Brooklyn drug dealer and wounded another."

"And De Sales's crack factory upstate? Have the local police verified that?"

"It took a while, but yeah, it's been verified."

"What was the holdup, getting a search warrant?"

"Yeah, their judge up there didn't think Messing's letter
constituted probable cause for a search warrant, but Chmil's
success with the rifle changed that. Made Justice into a reliable source, so they got their probable cause and their warrant. Since he was right again on the crack factory, you know
what that means to us?"

"Yeah, it means our killer has turned himself into a
proven and reliable police informant."

"Ironic, isn't it?" Cisco asked, smiling. "He's supposed
to be the bad guy, but we'll now be able to get a quick search
warrant on any information he gives us."

"Let's get this back into context, Cisco. He's not just *supposed* to be the bad guy. He's made himself into a serial
murderer, so he definitely *is* the bad guy."

"Sorry, you're right. Slipped my mind," Cisco said, but he
was still smiling. "Keep reading."

McKenna did, and found that Cisco had located a source
to state the wholesale and street-level values of the drugs
Justice had left at the scenes of his murders in Brooklyn and
Manhattan, and the numbers jibed almost exactly with Alfonso's estimates. Cisco had then summarized the extensive
criminal histories of the Brooklyn and Manhattan victims,
and he had ended his version of the script with the expected
statement: The NYPD had placed a high priority on catching

this serial killer, and all resources of the department would be utilized to do so. An arrest was not imminent, but this killer would ultimately be arrested and prosecuted for his crimes.

"What do you think?" Cisco asked.

"Very good."

"Then you're very smart. Let's go see if Sheeran is as smart as you are," Cisco said, and then he took the papers from McKenna's hands. With McKenna following, he went to the squad commander's door, knocked once, and they entered the office.

Sheeran was seated at the CO's desk, writing on a yellow legal pad. His jacket was off, his tie was loosened, and his shirtsleeves were rolled up. The page was three-quarters full, and he scratched out a sentence before looking up. McKenna saw that there were many other crossed-out lines on the page, and even more on the two completed pages spread on the desk next to the pad. In the wastebasket next to the desk were many other crumpled sheets of yellow legal paper.

"Got a present for you, Boss," Cisco said, and he offered Sheeran his version of the press conference script. Sheeran took it without a word, and he began reading. He was grinning by the time he reached page two and smiling by the time he finished. He then placed Cisco's version on the desk and gingerly smoothed it out.

"You like it?" Cisco asked.

Sheeran gathered up the three yellow pages of his own version, rolled them into a ball, and tossed it into the wastebasket. "It'll do."

McKenna and Cisco interviewed Joe Listorti, and they concurred with Monahan's assessment of him: The sanitation worker was a solid, no-nonsense guy who could be believed. They had him tell his story once again, but Listorti had nothing to add to what he had already told Monahan. He had seen the ambassador's limo parked on Marginal Street facing the East River when he had brought his street sweeper there to empty it. He hadn't noticed the arrival of the BMW and the Mercedes, and first saw them after the explosion that had killed Garcia and De Jesus. He then calmly described again the second explosion and the subsequent shootings of Vega and Velasquez.

"What were you doing while this was going on?" Cisco asked.

"Just standing there next to my sweeper, watching," Listorti replied.

"You weren't afraid?"

"Not that I recall. I guess I figured he was there to kill drug dealers, not hurt me."

"How did you know they were drug dealers?"

"I've been working in Spanish Harlem for twenty-six years, so I know what drug dealers and their tough guys look like up here. The big ones are easy to spot."

"Spanish guys driving expensive, flashy cars?" Cisco suggested.

"And carrying lots of guns they don't mind using," Listorti added. "Seen their type many times, the kind who'd kill you in a second without even thinking about it. They're dangerous vermin."

"So you thought he was doing a good thing?" Cisco asked.

"Maybe not good, but not really that bad."

Enough of this, McKenna thought as he watched Cisco smiling. "Can you help us out any more on the description?"

"Built strong, slim waist, like the good guy in a WWF bout. Kinda tall, I guess, but not a giant."

"Five foot ten?"

"Maybe."

"Six foot?"

"Maybe."

"Six foot two?"

"No, I don't think he was that tall."

"Clothing?"

"Light brown sports jacket, light-colored open-neck shirt, off-white or beige. Respectable looking."

"Pants?"

"Never saw his pants. The limo was between me and him. All I ever saw was the top of him."

"Anything else you can tell us about him?"

"Sorry, that's it. I wasn't that close to him, and with the ski mask and the gloves, I never saw his face or his hands."

"Did he do anything that indicated to you he was nervous or scared?" Cisco asked.

"Nothing at all. If anything, I'd have to say he was very confident. Except when he shot the second guy, he moved kinda slow and deliberate, like he didn't have a care in the world."

"What'd you think of that shot?"

"I wouldn't want him shooting at me."

McKenna expected to do better with the two boys who had seen Justice drop off the limo and get into the green car on East 126th Street, but before he could speak to them an obstacle had to be overcome. Rafael Gonzalez and Martin Alegro's parents had joined them at the station house, and they feared retaliation from Justice if they permitted their sons to talk further to the police.

With the aid of Listorti, it was Cisco who cleared that obstacle. Together they were able to convince the parents that although Justice was certainly dangerous, he was not the type of man who would ever consider harming two innocent boys. However, the parents still insisted that the boys be questioned together, and that they be present for the session.

Like Listorti, the boys said that Justice was tall and strong looking, and in no apparent haste, but they had a little more to say about him. Although he was still wearing the gloves when they saw him get out of the limo, Justice had removed his ski mask, and they were able to describe him as a brown-skinned black man dressed in a light brown checkered sports coat, a light-colored open-neck shirt, and dark brown pants. The large suitcase he carried from the limo to the dark green sedan was brown leather, and the empty duffel bag appeared to be a military style. By the time Justice drove slowly past them in the sedan, he had removed the gloves, but the boys couldn't get a good look at his face because he had his hand in front of it.

"So he was hiding his face from you?" McKenna asked.

"No, he went like this," Rafael said, and put his hand in front of his face and wiggled his fingers.

"He waved to you?" McKenna asked.

"It was kind of a wave."

"And what did you do then?"

Rafael and Martin looked at each other before Martin answered. "We waved back."

Cisco took a moment to grace McKenna with a smile before asking the boys the next question. "You first, Martin. Can you tell us what kind of car it was?"

"Old and dark green, kinda big, but I don't know what kind of car it was."

"Two-door or four-door?"

"Four-door. He opened the back door to put the suitcase in."

"Did you happen to see the license plate?"

"No."

"Okay, Rafael, you're next," Cisco said. "What kind of car was it?"

"A Chevy, I think, green with four doors."

"Clean or dirty?"

"Old and dirty."

"Did you notice the license plate?"

"New York plates, I think, but I didn't look at the number."

"But you looked at the license plates?"

"I wasn't really looking at it. We was just looking at the car when it left."

"Why?"

"I dunno. Maybe because not too many people we don't know wave at us."

McKenna was reading for the third time the stack of reports prepared on the Marginal Street killings when Chmil arrived in the squad office carrying a bulky case folder and Ramsey's scope-mounted rifle. He was early, but McKenna was ready for him. Rather than read his reports documenting the work he had done in the Brooklyn killings, McKenna preferred to hear Chmil himself tell about it.

Chmil was a short, balding man, but strong and built like a fire hydrant. His appearance could easily give the impression that he was plodding and deliberate, but McKenna knew from personal experience that Chmil's looks were deceptive. Chmil was a marathon runner, and they had run many marathons together. He trained hard, was a determined runner who never slackened his quick pace, and in a few marathons he had even managed to beat McKenna in the sprint at the end of their twenty-six–mile ordeal.

McKenna also knew that Chmil ran his cases the same way he ran his marathons. Once a murder was assigned to him, he worked long, hard, and smart, using all resources available to him until he had his killer identified. Then Chmil switched gears, and the bloodhound in him took over. Most of his killers he managed to arrest in short order, but those he couldn't get always knew they had a tenacious somebody dogging their trail. Chmil never slowed and never quit, and he knew every detail of those rare old cases in which his killer was still on the loose.

Chmil was ordinarily an upbeat kind of guy, but he looked elated as he greeted McKenna and Cisco. "What's the good news?" Cisco asked.

"This," Chmil said, holding up the rifle. "Ramsey was certainly a good enough shot, but he was a proud killer with a little bit of the Old West in him."

McKenna didn't get it until he noticed the line of six notches cut into the stock of the rifle. Three of the notches appeared to be fairly recent, but the weathered appearance of the other three cuts told him they had been there for years. "How long has he had that rifle?"

"As long as Yolanda knew him, and she was his main squeeze for twenty years," Chmil replied. "Has two of his kids, and she stuck by him through every jail stretch."

"Has she always held on to it for him?" Cisco asked.

"Every time he wasn't using it."

"Does she know the significance of those notches?"

"She knows. She says Ramsey never talked business with her, but she's no dope. She remembers every time he gave her the rifle back with an extra notch on it."

"Specific dates?" McKenna asked.

"No, she's not much of a record keeper. He cut the three new ones since he got out of the slammer a couple of years ago. Rifle shootings are rather rare nowadays, and I'm still checking through the unsolved cases citywide. Nothing so far, so I'm assuming for the moment that he thought a hit merited him a notch, even if his target lived through it."

"So it's likely the three new notches are the sniper shootings he did for De Sales?" Cisco said.

"That's the way it looks right now."

"And the old ones?" McKenna asked.

"Yolanda says he cut them in one by one, sometime between nineteen eighty-six and when he went in for an eight-year stretch in ninety-three. It'll take some work, but I'll run those notches down and put victims' names on them."

It would take a *lot* of work, McKenna knew. Ramsey had done those shootings in the city's bygone lawless era, that dangerous time when there were two thousand murders a year and many fewer cops to handle them. Murder was a common occurrence, and many went unsolved simply due to lack of manpower. Since then, the NYPD had increased dramatically in size, the annual number of murders had declined to six hundred, and clearance rates had soared. "Can you give me an idea on how long it'll take you to find out who else he shot with that rifle?"

"I'm off for the next two days, so say sometime next week," Chmil replied.

"Not good enough. We're gonna have the press on our asses, and I want something good to tell them every day."

"Overtime?"

"All you need."

"Then you'll have your victims' names by sometime tomorrow."

"And then some other homicide squad, probably yours, will wind up with a few more closed cases," Cisco observed.

"Did you have a hard time getting the rifle from Ramsey's girlfriend?" McKenna asked.

"Piece of cake. She tried stonewalling me at first, but she folded right after I gave her my standard accessory-to-murder pitch. After all, her man's dead, and he never had a sterling reputation, so what did she have to protect?"

"How did Ramsey treat her?"

"Pretty good, in his own way. Hasn't smacked her since they had the first kid, and he's twelve now. She has a nice house in the Midwood section, a Cadillac parked in the driveway, and no visible means of support."

"When did Ramsey get her the house?" McKenna asked.

"Last year."

"He give her any other cash?"

"She wouldn't say, but she didn't look worried."

"It's not Ramsey's cash that should concern us," Cisco said. "He was hired help, making peanuts compared to what De Sales was raking in. According to Mickey's calculations, he made millions last year, and a lot of that money has to be stashed somewhere. If Justice gives us some breathing room, it falls on us to find it."

"Suppose we do. What happens to it then?" Chmil asked.

"You were never in Narcotics?"

"No."

"Then this might interest you," Cisco said. "Illicit money recovered by us when drug rings are smashed winds up in the NYPD's general fund. From there it's dispensed as buy money in other undercover drug operations, and it's also used to buy the latest electronic surveillance gadgets and gizmos for the Narcotics Division."

"So shouldn't the Narcotics Division be charged with finding the money?" McKenna asked.

"If we weren't involved, yes. But now, no," Cisco said. "It's our job to find it."

"Why?"

"Because the current NYPD record for drug money seized in one case is three million three hundred thousand, and we're gonna beat that. We three standing next to all that cash should make a nice front-page picture."

"It sure would," Chmil said, obviously enthusiastic, and then they both looked expectantly to McKenna.

Am I getting to be as big an egomaniac as Cisco? McKenna wondered. Maybe. "I guess it would be nice. You have any ideas on where to start looking?"

"Just two," Chmil said. "De Sales has an apartment in Brooklyn we know about, but Yolanda says he bought himself a house on the water in Freeport last year."

"Has she ever been there?"

"No, but it impressed Ramsey. He told her it was a great place."

"Did De Sales live alone?"

"Yolanda said he had a boyfriend living with him at the Freeport place."

"Car?"

"Found it in the hotel's parking lot, a new BMW. Registered to De Sales, but he has a poor driving record. License currently suspended for the third time, so Ramsey did all the driving for him."

"Where's the car registered to?"

"His Brooklyn apartment."

"Let's go see the boss," McKenna said.

Sheeran also liked the idea of seizing the profits from De Sales's drug operation. Chmil was sent on his way with orders to locate De Sales's waterfront home.

When McKenna and Cisco left Sheeran's office, they found MacFarlane waiting for them outside, sitting at a desk and reading the reports in his case folder. In contrast to

Chmil, MacFarlane appeared dour and unhappy, but his mood lightened a bit when Cisco greeted him cordially. He was an athletic-looking man, meticulously dressed, with a full head of brown, wavy hair.

McKenna had a number of questions on the Queens murders, but first he wanted to find out if MacFarlane had been brought up to speed with the recent theories and developments. "Has Messing called you?" he asked.

"A couple of hours ago. Told me you gave the okay to tell him everything I've learned so far."

"And did you?"

"To tell you the truth, I've been pretty candid with Phil all along," MacFarlane admitted. "Been keeping him current on just about everything I've done."

"Just about?" McKenna asked. "What'd you leave out?"

"The plane."

"You figured out our boy's a sky diver?" Cisco asked.

"I'd like to say I did, but how he got into the house without tripping the alarms had me baffled until the PC called me this morning," MacFarlane said. "Then I got to work on the skydiving theory."

"Theory? Is that all it is? A theory?" Cisco asked, and there was a hint of annoyance in his voice. "I'd like to hear your objections to this theory."

"I don't have any, so maybe *theory* is the wrong word," MacFarlane stated, and it didn't appear that Cisco's tone bothered him. "If I call it a skydiving *angle* arrived at in a flash of brilliance, Cisco, will that make you happy?"

"Not ecstatic—but content, at least," Cisco said. "Why didn't you tell Phil about whatever work you've done on the plane?"

MacFarlane decided it should be McKenna who got the answer to that question. "Since I'm told that you're now in charge of this case, I saw no reason to tell Phil anything I haven't told you first. I'm thinking that you should be the one to decide exactly how much he knows."

"Good thinking," Cisco said.

"Thanks, George," McKenna added. "What did you find out on the plane?"

"Did some checking, but there's a lot more work to be done. An unidentified plane showed up on the La Guardia Airport radar at 2:20 A.M., flying westbound over Long Island Sound at three thousand feet. Because it was approaching a restricted area, the airspace around La Guardia, the ground controllers tried to raise the pilot by radio. No response, but since there were no flights leaving or coming into La Guardia at the time, they didn't make a big thing out of it. The plane rose to eight thousand feet along the Nassau County North Shore, circled once over Queens, and then left the way it came. Descended to under a thousand feet and disappeared from La Guardia's radar. The ground controllers filed a violation report for the FAA, and forgot about it."

"How long did they have him on radar?" Cisco asked.

"Not long. Under ten minutes."

"Could they tell anything on the size of the plane?"

"Small, probably a single engine."

"And?"

"And that's it, so far. I have inquiries in with all the airports, public and private, within two hundred miles of here. That's fifty-one airports. That means checking flight plans and interviewing pilots who took off late Sunday night or early Sunday morning, but so far I've only heard back from a dozen or so. Got nothing that fits the Malba scenario, yet. All those pilots landed at the places indicated on their flight plans in just about the time it should've taken them to get there."

"How long before you can tell me about all fifty-one airports?" McKenna asked.

"If I keep bothering them, sometime tonight."

"Then please keep bothering them. You need any help?"

"No, my lieutenant's no dope. After I got that call from Brunette he assigned my whole team to help me out. Everybody's working the phones."

"Hate to say it, but they might be working those phones for a long time if they don't come up with something tonight."

"What do you mean?"

"I mean it's also possible that our pilot took off from his own airstrip, and there would be no official record of that flight," McKenna said. "If that's what happened, I still have to know about it."

"Big job and very hard to verify if that's the case. There might be hundreds of those small airstrips within two hundred miles of here."

"But the pilot would want to stay under radar," Cisco said. "That means flying low and making noise that could be heard on the ground."

"It also means going door-to-door at houses near those private airstrips to find out if anyone heard a plane that night," MacFarlane said. "Do you know the manpower we'd need traipsing the boondocks to do that?"

"Big job, but we're the big guys," Cisco countered. "We could get local police departments to make our inquiries for us."

"I don't have the weight to get that done. Do you?"

Cisco looked at McKenna, and then so did MacFarlane. "In this case, yeah, I have the weight," McKenna said. "We'll get it done if we have to. What else you got?"

"This," MacFarlane said. He took a device that looked like a cheap, large-faced LED watch, and he gave it to McKenna. "Got that from Cruz's alarm company, and it's identical to the one they sold Cruz when they installed the system. When the alarm system is on, it vibrates and lights up when a beam is crossed. The face will show a little diagram of the house and grounds, and a flashing pointer will show which beam was crossed."

"Did you ask Lela Cruz if Montoya usually wore that wristband at night?" McKenna asked.

"Sure I did. Said she saw it on him a few times, but according to her, she didn't know what it was for. Said she saw a lot of Montoya but didn't have much interaction with him. He sometimes drove her husband during the day and pranced around the grounds at night."

"Armed or unarmed?"

"She said she didn't know."

"Did you believe her?" Cisco asked.

"I wouldn't believe anything she said if she were standing on a stack of Bibles," MacFarlane replied, shaking his head. "Good-looking woman, very polite, but evasive when it comes to answering even the most basic questions."

"And when you do get an answer, it's a lie?" McKenna asked.

"I haven't been able to pin her down on a single one yet, but I'm sure she's told me some lies with a smile."

"Do you think she knows anything about her husband's business?"

"I'm sure of it, at least sure she knew the business he was in."

"What makes you so sure?"

"Picture the scene. Her husband's dead on the dining room floor, kneecapped and sliced up. Next she finds Montoya in the garage, also kneecapped, then horribly tortured, and finally shot in the head. She was a little shaken up when I got there, but no tears and no hysterics. Once the bodies were covered up and she had a chance to throw some makeup on, she became the perfect hostess. It was like we dropped in for tea unexpected, and she served the coffee herself to everybody from the M.E. to the morgue wagon drivers."

"So what's your conclusion? That she knew about her husband's business and expected something like this would happen sooner or later?" Cisco asked.

"That's the impression I got."

"You think she loved him?"

"Hard to tell with her. Maybe she did, maybe she didn't. She made it obvious she didn't want to discuss her relationship with her husband or his business dealings, and I respected that for the moment. After all, he was lying dead on the floor in the dining room, and I figured I had time to pressure her later."

Would I have handled her the same way? McKenna asked himself. Probably. "You like her?"

"I think so. You gonna go see her?"

"Yeah, tonight sometime."

"I think you'll like her, too. A liar, but she has a kind of quiet dignity about her," MacFarlane said, and then he had another thought. "When you go to see her, keep in mind that her husband's body was just released from the morgue today. She probably spent most of the day making the funeral arrangements."

"Is he being buried here, or is she having the body shipped back to Colombia?"

"Colombia, for both the funeral and the burial."

"So we really don't have much time to pin her down," Cisco said. "She'll be leaving soon."

"But she'll be back," MacFarlane said. "She's got that big house, and her son's in school here."

"Yeah, she'll be back, as long as we don't squeeze her more than she'd like," Cisco countered. "Her husband had to have millions and millions stashed. If she knows how to get her hands on it, that house won't seem too important to her."

"That's something that's really not under our control, is it?" McKenna asked.

"We'll see."

TEN

McKenna thought the press conference had gone as well as could be expected. Sheeran had stuck to Cisco's script during his presentation, and he caused quite a stir among the reporters when he revealed that the killer had written a letter to Messing signed "Justice." They all looked around for Messing, but since he already had all the facts, he wasn't there.

McKenna fielded all the questions that came afterward, and he filled almost all the holes in Sheeran's script. He admitted it was likely that the killer would strike and kill again before he was captured, but he emphasized he would ultimately be arrested and charged with his crimes. As anticipated, he had been forced to present the killer in a good light when he divulged the contents of the notes left at the Classon Hotel and told about the payments he had left for damages to the hotel room and the ambassador's car. It didn't come up, so he made no mention of the note left for the Bomb Squad.

On the positive side, as far as McKenna was concerned, there had been many questions on the large amounts of cash the killer had taken with him from the scenes of his murders. McKenna had stressed that, whatever his motives, this killer was profiting handsomely from his crimes. The numbers spoke for themselves, and he hadn't been challenged on that point.

Of course, the term *vigilante* had come up repeatedly, and McKenna hadn't ducked it. Yes, there was a very effective vigilante operating in New York City, he admitted over and over, but he had been able to skirt for the moment exactly what made him so effective. Whenever a question had come up concerning the killer's apparent inside knowledge of the drug trade, McKenna had replied, "That matter is still under investigation," and he got away with it.

McKenna called Lela Cruz to introduce himself and tell her he would like to see her to clear up a few small matters regarding her husband's murder. He didn't expect his request would be greeted with enthusiasm, but he was wrong. "I'm totally at your disposal. If you'd like, you can come over tonight, after I put the kids to bed," Lela said pleasantly, still the gracious hostess.

That suited McKenna perfectly, and he made the appointment for 9:00 P.M. That left him and Cisco with an hour to kill, and they spent it at a desk in the 25th Precinct Detective Squad office, going over the case folders Chmil and MacFarlane had left with them.

They started with Chmil's crime scene photos, and since McKenna had promised a set to Messing, he was gratified that the folder contained two sets of the photos documenting the carnage at the Classon Hotel. There were shots showing De Sales and Ramsey's battered bodies on the heart-shaped bed in the positions in which Justice had arranged them with the blow-up dummies, and those pictures especially delighted Cisco. He thought Justice to be a very amusing character possessing an admirable degree of flair, and he managed to annoy McKenna each time he repeated his opinion as he went through the set.

McKenna tried to ignore Cisco and instead focused on his set of photos showing the evidence of the intense beatings De Sales and Ramsey had suffered before Justice dispatched each with a bullet in the right ear. Both men's eyes were swollen shut, their mouths were a bloody mess, and although both were dressed from the waist up, their chests looked caved in to McKenna, indicating to him that their ribs were broken.

Ramsey was wearing a sports coat, but it was pulled open, revealing the large, empty shoulder holster he was wearing.

The room was a mess, but McKenna didn't think the damage was extensive. Drops of blood splattered the walls, the mirror over the credenza was shattered, and the back of one of the two wooden chairs in the room was split lengthwise in two. Pools of blood were on the bedspread under the men's heads, and it had coagulated at the edges of the pools by the time the photos were taken. There were close-ups of both men's wrists that showed the cuts and bruises they had inflicted upon themselves as they struggled against the handcuffs during their beatings, and another close-up focused on the back of the broken chair to show the many scratches caused by the handcuffs.

There were also pictures of the stacked and wrapped bags of drugs on the credenza, and McKenna noted that the letters to the police and the hotel management, along with the MAC-10 machine pistol, were neatly centered on top of the stack.

Cisco was still chuckling over his set of photos when McKenna went to the autopsy reports, and he found he was right about the broken ribs. Four of Ramsey's ribs were broken on his right side, and De Sales had suffered even more damage. A total of eight of his ribs were broken, three of which had punctured his lungs. In addition, his spleen had also ruptured.

The serious damage wasn't confined solely to their torsos. Ramsey had suffered a fractured skull, and four of his broken teeth were found in his mouth. De Sales's jaw was broken, and he had also lost teeth. Three broken teeth were found in his mouth, and he had swallowed two more, which were found in his stomach. A 9-millimeter slug was recovered from the brain of each.

McKenna looked up from the autopsy report to find

Cisco smiling at him. "Broken ribs, fractured skulls, and many, many teeth knocked out?" he asked.

"Justice has a lot of rage in him, and he vented hard on those two," McKenna replied.

"Yeah, he's pissed, but I think he's pissed with a purpose. They had information he wanted, and he knew how to get it from them."

"And I'm sure he did. From Ramsey he wanted the rifle, and from De Sales he wanted the location of his crack factory, if he didn't already know it. Most important, as far as we're concerned, he wanted to know where De Sales kept his cash."

"So De Sales told him everything he wanted to know."

"What makes you think that?" McKenna asked, but all he got in reply was that Cisco know-it-all smile he was really beginning to hate. Then he noticed that Cisco had a property invoice on the desk in front of him. "Keys," McKenna ventured.

"Congratulations, partner. If De Sales kept his stash in either of his cribs, and if he told Justice as much, what would Justice have done with that tidbit?"

"He would've taken De Sales's keys."

"You can keep working with me," Cisco said graciously, and he passed McKenna the property invoice that listed everything removed from De Sales's body. Item number six was a key ring with eight keys attached, and it made McKenna smile in spite of himself. Then, for once, he decided that he would be the one to run the game. "Let's sum up what we know about him so far," he suggested.

"Aside from the fact that he's a pretty amusing guy who knows how to get good press?"

"Yeah, aside from the fact that he seems to give you a few chuckles I don't entirely understand."

"You know, Brian, it would be nice if you could reach down deep inside and find yourself a sense of humor. This guy's operating with a degree of class we don't often see."

"I don't find anything funny or classy about a guy who enjoys doing this to people, no matter who they are,"

McKenna countered, tapping the crime-scene photos. "What do we know about him?"

"Okay, we'll play it your way. All business," Cisco said, and he allowed the smile to slip from his face. "He's smart, black, and bad; probably well-educated, and he's good with guns, bombs, locks, and cars. Unusual combo in a scholar. He's also a great sky diver, he has a good pal with a plane, he's got a computer, he really doesn't like drug dealers—but for some reason he *does* like Messing. He's also fearless, and it seems that everybody he's come into contact with likes him."

"Except, of course, the people he's murdered."

"Yeah, except for them, but they don't count. I wouldn't like anybody they like."

"And his connection to law enforcement?" McKenna asked.

"Probable."

"An unusual man?"

"A remarkable man."

"Somebody who should be famous on this job, if he were a cop?"

"He's certainly someone I'd remember."

"Yet we have no idea who he is, do we?" McKenna asked.

"Brian, you've been around this job longer than me, been more places, and probably know more people than I do," Cisco countered. "Do you have any idea on who he is?"

"Not an inkling."

"And neither do I."

"I think maybe Chipmunk does," McKenna announced.

"He does?" Cisco asked, apparently astounded.

"Yeah."

Cisco thought that over for a moment. "I guess it's possible. He's been around longer than us, and he knows more people than both of us put together. Why don't you ask him what he thinks?"

"Because he wouldn't tell me. Not yet, anyway. Not until I'm ready to pull my hair out."

"Why not? You're one of his best pals, aren't you?"

"Yeah, but I think Justice is also a pal, someone he really likes, and you know Chip and his concept of loyalty."

"Yeah, when it comes to his pals, he's loyal to a fault. But consider this: Maybe Chip also likes Justice's act and thinks he's doing a pretty good job at it," Cisco suggested.

"Maybe."

"Good for him."

ELEVEN

Since Lela Cruz was reputed to be such a gracious hostess, Cisco thought it appropriate they set the mood by displaying their own social graces right at the outset of the interview, so he insisted on picking up a cake on the way to her house. In Cisco-fashion, he naturally chose Henry Pool's as the place to buy their cake. Pool was the very expensive baker to the rich and famous, so Cisco was sure Lela would recognize his name on the cake box and appreciate that she was indeed dealing with two classy guys.

McKenna hated driving, so as usual it was Cisco at the wheel for the trip. It was a short half-hour drive, and Cisco drove in silence for most of it. McKenna figured he was plotting his strategy for the interview, and he knew Cisco had his plan in place when he turned on the radio, tuned in a classical station, and began humming along to the music as he drove.

"Okay, what do we lead with?"

"First we ask her about the gun and the safe, and we let her lie to *our* faces," Cisco said. "Then we tell her we know Gaston kept the gun under his pillow, right next to where she slept, and that the combination for the safe is taped to the bottom of the tray in her jewelry box. That should get a reaction from her."

"We can't tell her that Walsh was snooping around her bedroom, so how do we explain how we know that?"

"We lie."

"You got a specific lie in mind?"

They both recognized that lying to witnesses and suspects was often a necessary part of police work, so
McKenna didn't expect Cisco to be insulted by his statement. Cisco wasn't. "I would tell her that the information
was contained in Justice's letter to Messing, sort of a P.S.
that won't be printed," Cisco said, apparently satisfied with
himself. "What's yours?"

"The same."

"Really?"

"Yeah, Cisco. Really. You think you're the only one who
could come up with a whopper like that?"

"I guess not, and I'm proud of you."

"Thank you, I think. The question is, will she buy it?"

"Properly presented, of course she will. Since I'm a better liar than you, and certainly more charming, you better
leave that part to me. Then I'll leave it to you to set the scene
so that she'll see it's in her best interest to stop with her lies
and tell us what we want to know."

"So, according to your plan, you *do* have something for
me to do?" McKenna asked.

"Yeah, something you should be good at with those Boy
Scout looks and that Boy Scout attitude of yours. A subtle,
reluctant threat coming from you won't be that offensive to
her. She'll think it over, and then we'll get her talking."

"That subtle threat being *money*?"

"That's it, the big one. Since Gaston trusted her enough to
give her the combination to his safe, he might also have
trusted her enough to tell her how and where he's hiding his
fortune. If so, she has to be worth billions. One of the richest
women in the country, but you'll explain to her that she has a
big problem brewing."

"Yeah, she sure does," McKenna said. "Gaston's money,
wherever it is and however it's been laundered, is still very
illicit and subject to attack. Once we get the goods on Gaston's operation and prove he's just the guy the Narcotics Division always thought he was, all that loot will be subject to
RICO forfeiture. So I tell her that, if she cooperates with us,

we'll try to make sure there's something left over for her after the feds raid the funds."

"Exactly what you tell her, and you have to sound convincing."

"We don't have the authority to offer her that kind of deal, so I'll be lying again."

"Of course you will. Can't let her know that if things work out right, she ends her days in poverty."

"That doesn't bother you?"

"Not much," Cisco said.

There was only one car parked in the wide Cruz driveway, a late-model black Mercedes, but Cisco still elected to park in the street. The lights were on downstairs in the house, but the upstairs floors were dark.

Cisco carried the cake. They were on the walkway, headed to the front door, when McKenna happened to notice the rear vanity license plate on the Mercedes. He stopped, grabbed Cisco's arm, and pointed to the car.

"Aarghh! That bitch ambushed us," Cisco said when he saw the lettering on the vanity plate, DONT WORRY. The car signaled the presence of Murray Plenheim, possibly the best, and certainly the slickest criminal defense attorney New York had to offer, who enjoyed a fine reputation in criminal circles. Those able to afford his stiff fees soon learned that they didn't have much to worry about if they were arrested, and it was one of them who had given him the nickname that stuck—Murray Don't Worry. He was recognized among successful criminals as the complete attorney.

McKenna and Cisco knew there were two reasons for Murray's success. First was his ability as a trial lawyer. Murray had developed and perfected a bag of tricks and legal maneuvers designed to delay proceedings, intimidate and discredit witnesses, malign cops, confuse juries, and ridicule prosecutors. Therefore, most experienced ADAs would rather quit and go into private practice before taking a risk on having their reputations ruined by facing him in open court.

That led to the second reason for Murray's success, the one that most concerned McKenna and Cisco. Since smart prosecutors feared Murray like the devil and would do almost anything rather than bring one of his clients to trial, Murray had become the acknowledged master of the deal in the criminal justice system, a consummate negotiator. Consequently, even if prosecutors were graced with a strong case against one of his clients, any barely reasonable plea bargain offered by Murray was usually found to be acceptable.

"Do you feel like negotiating with Murray?" McKenna asked.

"No. Don't even know if I feel up to negotiating with the Widow Cruz, at the moment. Pretty sharp lady," Cisco replied. "That whole bit about 'Come right over after I put the kids to bed' was just a ploy to give her time to set up this ambush."

"Maybe time to rethink your plan?" McKenna suggested.

"Good idea," Cisco replied. He then turned and headed back to the car, and McKenna followed.

It was a tough five-minute session, starting with the fact that their previous plan was no longer viable. Since Cisco's girlfriend, Agnes, was also Murray's wife's favorite niece and Murray's receptionist, the first idea to go was that Cisco would be exercising the slightest bit of charm on Lela Cruz. Murray doted on Agnes, so any such display would likely have a negative effect on both Cisco's personal and professional life.

The next idea to be discarded was that they could corner Lela on her lies to MacFarlane. Murray knew Messing, so if they tried that approach, Murray would naturally want to know the source of their information. McKenna and Cisco agreed that Messing might not hold up under questioning by Murray, so their "P.S. on Justice's letter to Messing" lie entailed too many risks.

To avoid letting Murray enjoy a chuckle, the third leg of their strategy was also out. Murray knew all the ins and outs on RICO proceedings, and he could find out with a simple phone call that any offer of special consideration they might present to Lela Cruz would be unauthorized and probably worthless.

"Too bad," Cisco said. "They were some pretty good lies we had cooked up."

"So what do we do now?" McKenna asked.

"We need some better lies."

"I wouldn't want to try it."

"So then we have no plan?"

"Nope. Looks like we're here just to drink her coffee and eat our cake."

"Maybe something will come to us when we get inside," Cisco said hopefully.

"Maybe."

Again carrying the cake, Cisco led the way to the front door and rang the bell. Lela answered, and McKenna's first thought was that her photo in the *Post* didn't do her proper justice. She was a tall woman, perhaps thirty years old, dressed in black slacks and a V-necked tan sweater with matching tan heels. Her long, dark blonde hair was pulled back into a simple ponytail, and the only makeup evident was lipstick in a subdued shade of red. She also wore a single strand of pearls around her neck and a polite smile on her face, but her eyes were puffy, leading McKenna to conclude she had been crying sometime in the past few hours, and maybe for the past few days.

"Detective McKenna, Detective Sanchez, so pleased to meet you," Lela said, offering her hand.

McKenna shook her hand without a word, but not Cisco. "Please accept our condolences on your loss," he said, and then he handed her the cake.

She accepted it, and then noticed the name on the box. "Henry Pool's? How very thoughtful of you," she commented, and for the first time ever McKenna saw Cisco beam like a schoolboy.

Then the smile left Lela's face, and McKenna thought she looked uncomfortable. "Before we go in, there's something I have to tell you. There's somebody else here, somebody you know."

"Yeah, we saw Murray's car—and yeah, we do know him," Cisco said.

"Does it bother you that he's here?"

"Not at all," McKenna said. "If you think you need a lawyer to talk to us, that's fine if it makes you more comfortable. Besides, it's always good to see our old pal Murray."

"He also speaks highly of the both of you. Says you're the two best detectives he knows and nice men as well."

McKenna didn't know how to handle that, but Cisco did. "I've never known Murray to be wrong."

Lela then turned abruptly, and they followed her to the parlor. It was a large, formal room, expensively furnished with two sofas facing each other on either side of an ornate coffee table. Hanging from the walls were large tapestries depicting pastoral mountain scenes of, McKenna guessed, Colombia. There were many potted tropical trees around the room, and the large, stuffed jaguar crouched on top of the fireplace mantel gave the impression they could be in a hacienda far from Queens.

Murray was there, seated on one of the sofas, sipping brandy from a snifter. Lying at his feet was a large black German shepherd who warily watched them enter but made no move to get up. Neither did Murray, but he did acknowledge their presence with a nod.

McKenna hadn't seen Murray in over a year, but he thought Murray hadn't changed much in the twenty years he had known him. His appearance and temperament still reminded McKenna of a stocky James Cagney. He was short, sharp, pugnacious, and he could, when in a friendly setting, be considered entertaining and gregarious. Murray's perfunctory greeting and his expensive pinstriped suit told McKenna that he didn't consider himself to be in a friendly setting at the moment. He was all business.

Lela placed their cake on the coffee table, and then McKenna and Cisco got their second jolt of the evening. Next to their cake box was another, much larger cake box, also from Henry Pool's. McKenna and Cisco both realized that before the game even began, Murray was already one up on them.

"Might I get you anything?" Lela asked. "Coffee or tea with your cake, or maybe something stronger?"

McKenna wanted to speak to Murray before making any attempt at interviewing Lela, so he was happy to send her on a mission. "Let's save the cake for later, but I'd love a cup of coffee," he said.

"And I'd like whatever Murray's having," Cisco said.

"Good choice, Cisco," Murray said, nodding approvingly. "Hennessy Reserve, top shelf."

"Please make yourselves at home," Lela said. "I shouldn't be long."

Cisco watched Lela leave, and McKenna watched Murray watching Cisco. Then Murray decided it was time to get to work. "She'll be gone for five minutes, at least. Why don't you do like she suggested and make yourselves at home?" Murray said, indicating the sofa opposite him.

McKenna and Cisco ignored the suggestion for the moment and remained standing. "At *least* five minutes? Your idea, Murray?" McKenna asked.

"Yeah, mine. I told her I'd like to establish some ground rules with my two old pals before you got to your business with her. She thought it might be a good idea."

"We weren't aware you were representing her," Cisco noted. "Mind telling us how that happened?"

"Did my presence here tonight surprise you?"

"Yeah, we were surprised," Cisco admitted.

"And thrown into a state of confusion?" Murray asked.

Cisco didn't want to answer that one. Instead, he looked to McKenna. "Yeah, Murray, we had to do some rethinking," McKenna admitted. "Happy?"

Murray savored a sip of his cognac before answering, then faced them with a smile. "Delighted."

"Now answer the question, please," McKenna insisted. "Just between us old pals, how'd it happen that you're here?"

"You're aware of that fishing expedition the Narcotics

Division pulled on her husband last year? Got search warrants on the flimsiest of pretexts to search his house and seize his business records?"

No use trying to defend that with Murray, McKenna thought. "We're aware of it."

"Well, at the time Mr. Cruz was represented by less-competent counsel. He didn't like the service he was getting, so he showed up in my office. I didn't know who he was at the time, but he knew who I was. He proposed a monthly retainer agreement I found satisfying."

"*Very* satisfying?" Cisco asked.

"Very. Matter of fact, since that was the only time I ever spoke to him, I'd say that retainer agreement was one for the books. Never had to do a thing for that very generous man."

"Until now," McKenna noted.

"To tell you the truth, services to Mr. Cruz's family weren't specifically covered in the retainer agreement. However, when I read about the murder and saw Mrs. Cruz's picture in the paper, it struck a chord with me. Then, when I heard you gentlemen were to be assigned to the case, I felt obligated to give her a call to offer my assistance."

So Cisco blabbed to Agnes why we were coming back from Florida. Then she happened to mention it to Uncle Murray, and now we're stuck with him, McKenna thought as he stared at Cisco.

Cisco had suddenly found something interesting on one of his fingernails, and he ignored McKenna's gaze as he gave whatever it was a close examination.

A bad turn of events, but understandable, McKenna decided, and he returned his attention to Murray. "So Gaston's death was initially very bad news for you, but you thought about your new circumstances until you found a silver lining?"

Murray managed to look offended as he returned McKenna's stare. "I realize I have a certain well-founded reputation, so it might surprise you to learn that I also have a conscience."

Murray Don't Worry with a conscience? That was a novel

idea for McKenna, and he tried to keep the disbelief off his face. He didn't succeed, so Murray felt the need to explain further. "Up to now, I've been paid well for doing nothing. Therefore, Mrs. Cruz will receive no bill for my services," he announced.

"So you've decided to make us miserable for free?" Cisco asked.

"Not exactly. I consider your misery to be ample payment for my services."

"Then you're paid," McKenna said. "Before we get to your ground rules, I'd be interested to hear why you think a witness needs a lawyer in this case."

"At first, I didn't know whether she did or not. After talking to her, I've decided that my presence will move things along."

"Move things along? Isn't that rather a new role for you, Murray?" McKenna asked.

"Yes, it is," Murray admitted. "Now for the ground rules, if you don't mind. We'll agree that knowledge of a crime does not in itself constitute a crime?"

"What crime are we talking about here?" Cisco asked.

"Any crime, but in this case, wholesale importation and distribution of narcotics." Murray paused for a moment to make sure he had McKenna and Cisco's total attention. He did. "We'll also agree that, for all practical purposes, lying to a local police officer is not a crime in the United States?"

"Are we talking specifically about lying to George Mac-Farlane?" McKenna asked.

"Not a crime?" Murray countered.

Possibly obstruction of justice, McKenna thought, but in Lela Cruz's case it was a stretch no DA would ever entertain. "No, not a crime, and maybe understandable at the time," he conceded. "After all, when she was talking to MacFarlane, her dead husband was a bloody mess in the next room. I'm sure she wasn't thinking straight, and maybe she told Mac-Farlane a few things she shouldn't have."

"Thank you, Brian. Very understanding of you. I was sure you'd have a few questions about some of the things she told

him that would strike an experienced investigator like yourself as patently false."

"Like the forty-four magnum, for instance, found outside
the house at the point where her husband was shot?"

"His gun, and she knew it. He slept with it under his pillow," Murray stated. "Anything else?"

"The safe."

"She knew about the safe."

"And the combination?"

"She has it."

Well, that was easy, McKenna thought. Maybe Murray
being here isn't such a bad thing after all.

"Does she know what was in the safe?"

"Not that night, but she assumes it was the usual. Money
and a few computer disks."

"How much money?"

"Probably lots, by our standards. She said he always had
at least a few hundred thousand in there."

"Does she know what was on the computer disks?"

"She can't say for sure, but she'll concede it had something to do with her husband's business."

"How about when she told MacFarlane her husband had
no enemies she knows of? Was that accurate?" McKenna
asked.

"She is aware of the nature of her husband's business,
and she assumes he must have enemies. However, she knows
of no specific enemy, and she has no idea who killed him—
or why," Murray said. "I hope that clears the air a bit."

"Somewhat, but tell me this: If you weren't here, would
she have cleared up the air on her own?"

"Eventually, but maybe with some embarrassment, so I
thought it would be better if I did it. I want this interview to
be entirely nonconfrontational."

"Why's that?" Cisco asked. "I thought you thrived on
confrontation."

"I usually do, but it would be counterproductive under the
circumstances we find ourselves in right now."

"What exactly are those circumstances?" McKenna asked.

"Have you two figured out yet how this killer is able to operate so successfully?"

"We're assuming he snatched someone high up in Gaston's operation and is squeezing him hard for information."

"And you intend to ask her if she has any idea who this person is?"

"Yes."

"Then those are the circumstances we find ourselves in."

"She knows who he snatched?"

"Yes. She'll tell you all about him herself, but I've advised her she should do so only under certain circumstances."

"What might those circumstances be?"

"That you both promise me you'll do everything within your power to rescue him as soon as possible."

"That's an easy promise to make," McKenna said. "Rescuing him is part of our job."

"I realize that, but there's a lot going on with your case, and as this thing goes on there might be much more you'll have to worry about. I want you to promise me that rescuing him will always be foremost in your mind."

"Why all the concern for this guy?" McKenna asked.

"Because he *is* part of my retainer agreement with Mr. Cruz, and I feel it only right that I do everything I can to keep him alive and in one piece."

"Might be too late for that," Cisco said.

"You don't think he's still alive?"

"That's not what I'm saying. Justice probably still has some use for him, so it's probable he's still alive. I just don't know if he's still in one piece."

"I see." Murray finished his drink, put the glass on the coffee table, and then focused on McKenna. "In any event, do I have your promise?"

"Yeah, you have our promise," McKenna said.

"Thank you, Brian," Murray said, and then he turned his gaze to Cisco. "How about you?"

"Yeah, Murray. You have my promise. I'll do everything possible to rescue this major drug-dealing client of yours before Justice damages him beyond repair."

"Thank you."

"Feel better?" Cisco asked.

"Yes, as a matter of fact I do. With those promises from you two in my pocket, I feel it's now more likely than not that I'll finally be meeting Jorge Rodriguez. Matter of fact, I'll probably be representing him in the problems I'm sure the feds and the Narcotics Division will have for him once he's free."

"Jorge Rodriguez? That's his name?" McKenna asked.

"Yes, but I'll let Mrs. Cruz tell you about him." Murray appeared content, and the time passed in silence until Lela returned carrying a tray loaded with a coffeepot, cups, plates, a silver tea service, Cisco's drink, and another one for Murray. As expected, she was the perfectly solicitous hostess as she served the coffee and drinks. She also prepared herself a coffee with cream and sugar, took a sip, and placed the cup on the coffee table. She then sat next to Murray on the sofa, folded her hands on her lap, and began.

"I guess Murray told you I wasn't entirely truthful with Detective MacFarlane. Stupid on my part, really, and I regretted each lie as soon as I told it."

"But you continued telling them," McKenna noted.

"Yes."

"Why?"

"Naïveté, I guess. For the children's sake, I was hoping Gaston's death would be treated as an ordinary murder, if there is such a thing. I didn't want his business dealings brought up in the newspapers, along with their reporters' descriptions of the type of man some people thought he was."

What kind of man does she think he was? McKenna wondered, but he knew the time wasn't yet right for that question. "I see," he said. "You figured that ordinary people who get murdered don't carry around forty-four–magnum revolvers and keep hundreds of thousands in cash in their safes, so when those questions came up, you tried leading our Detective MacFarlane down the wrong path."

"Yes, I tried," Lela said, and she lowered her eyes to stare at her hands. "Like I said, stupid, but it seemed to me he believed everything I told him, so I kept on lying."

"Your husband trusted you?"

"Completely. He loved me very much, and I'd never given him any reason not to trust me."

"What I mean is, did he trust you with details of his business?"

"He would tell me anything I wanted to know."

"So you're aware of at least some aspects of his business?"

"I knew he was involved with the cocaine trade, but never once did I ask him a single question about his business," Lela said, still staring at her hands. "And never once did he volunteer any particular information."

"How long have you known him?"

"My whole life. My parents and his had been best friends for more than fifty years. He's eleven years older than me, and he watched me grow up in Colombia—at least, I like to think he was watching."

"You loved him?"

"Since I was five, I think."

"Right until the day he died?"

Lela looked up from her hands and looked McKenna in the eyes. "My love for him never changed."

Because Gaston Cruz had the total, unquestioning love of a woman like this one, he was beginning to intrigue McKenna. But McKenna thought it time to get to the big question. "Murray's told you that we think the man who killed your husband has also kidnapped someone high up in your husband's organization?"

"Yes, he's told me."

"And that we think the killer is torturing this person to get information from him on your husband's business dealings, and also to get him to set up the meetings with the drug dealers he's killing and robbing?"

"He told me you two would reach that conclusion."

"And Murray's also told us you think you know who this man is, a guy named Jorge Rodriguez?"

"It's Jorge he has. I'm sure of it."

"What makes you so sure?"

"Jorge's my brother, and he would have been here for me after Gaston was killed. He wasn't, and I haven't been able to reach him."

Her brother? Justice is torturing her brother on a daily basis, and she knows it? This woman is operating under a lot of stress, McKenna thought, especially since she's seen first-hand the type of painful damage Justice does to people.

McKenna looked to Cisco for his reaction, and found that his partner and Murray were staring at each other. Cisco was frowning and appeared annoyed, but Murray was smiling smugly as he returned Cisco's stare.

What's the deal here? McKenna wondered, but then he got it. Cisco's thinking quicker than I am, but Murray, operating with some inside information, has been thinking quicker than both of us. The reason Lela was so happy to hear from me this afternoon is that she figures we're the best hope for freeing her brother. She was dying to tell us it was Jorge who Justice snatched. Enter Murray on the scene, and that simple piece of information is no longer good enough. Even though Lela would have told us about Jorge no matter what, Murray being Murray had to first extract promises from us that freeing him would be foremost in our minds, our primary concern.

Murray then nodded graciously to Cisco, and looked to McKenna with his eyebrows raised, waiting for a reaction. McKenna decided to ignore him and focus on the next question. "What was your brother's role in your husband's operation?"

"If I had to guess, I'd say second in command."

"You'd have to guess? You didn't discuss your husband's business with your brother, either?"

"The only discussion I had with him about it wasn't what

you'd really call a discussion. From time to time I'd just ask him to get out of it."

"His reaction?"

"He'd just laugh at me," Lela said sadly. "You have to understand that Gaston treated him well, and Jorge adored him since they were children. The truth of the matter is that Jorge liked working for Gaston, and he couldn't imagine any other life."

"Was Jorge in charge of the dirty work?" Cisco asked.

"I'd say no. Jorge's very smart and probably tough enough, but he's not a violent person. If he weren't working for Gaston, you'd probably call him a kind man."

"A kind, nonviolent drug dealer? He'd be the first one I know of," Cisco said, and he couldn't keep the sarcasm out of his voice.

"All the same, that's the way I think of him," Lela retorted.

This isn't going well, McKenna thought. Let's get back on track. "Your brother knew all the details on your security system here?"

"Of course he did," Lela said, and then a thought struck her. "What are you saying, that Jorge gave those details to the killer?"

"Had to be. The killer hit this place with inside knowledge on the alarm system, the dog, and he knew all about Carlos."

"He didn't get that information from Jorge," she stated with conviction. "Once he was kidnapped, Jorge would realize the kind of man he was dealing with, and no amount of torture would get him to reveal anything that might harm me or Gaston."

You have to be wrong, Lela. Your brother caved in under pain and pressure, McKenna thought, but he saw no reason to push that issue. "Okay, let's talk about things we're sure your brother told him. Jorge would know all the ins and outs of your husband's business?" he asked.

"I guess. My impression is that Gaston made all the major decisions, but Jorge ran both businesses on a day-to-day basis."

"Both businesses? You're talking about Exito Seguros?"

"Yes. He went to the office almost every day."

"Where does Jorge live?"

"Eight eighty-eight Park Avenue, Penthouse A."

"What day is it you think he was kidnapped?"

"He was here last Sunday afternoon for dinner, and Gaston was killed that night, so sometime before or shortly after the murder."

"When did you first try calling him?"

"He was the first one I called after I found Gaston dead. Called him even before I found Carlos."

"No answer?"

"No answer at home or on his cell phone. I left messages on his voice mail and with his service, but he never got back to me. I've been calling constantly, going frantic. On Monday I went to his apartment, not knowing what I'd find. He wasn't there, and the doormen hadn't seen him since Sunday."

"Sunday afternoon, or Sunday night?" McKenna asked.

"Sunday afternoon, presumably when he was on his way here."

"Does he have a car?"

"A red Volvo, new. I checked his garage and spoke with the people there, too. Last time they saw the car was when he checked it out Sunday afternoon."

So he was kidnapped after he left here on Sunday but before he got home. How would Justice pull that off? McKenna wondered, and quickly came up with an answer.

So did Cisco. "Bump and grab?" he asked McKenna.

"That's the way I'd do it, if I were him. He might've needed an accomplice, but we know he has at least one," McKenna said, and then he had another question for Lela. "Did Jorge have dinner here every Sunday?"

"Just about. How'd you know?"

"Justice had to have Jorge's routine down in order to snatch him. That means he had a loose surveillance on your brother for a while and knew he usually came here on Sundays. Perfect neighborhood for a small accident. Quiet, nobody on the streets. Justice bumps your brother's car, then pulls a gun and kidnaps him when Jorge gets out to exchange information."

Cisco added nothing to the explanation, but he had a few questions of his own. "You have the keys for Jorge's apartment?"

"Yes. I can give them to you, if you like."

"Later. Any signs of a struggle there?"

"No, everything was in order. Jorge is very neat."

"I guess he's not married?"

"No. Too busy."

"How about your folks?" McKenna asked. "Do they know he's missing?"

"Yes, I told them. They're as worried as I am."

"You never considered filing a missing persons report?"

"Considered it, and talked it over with my folks. They were all for it, at first, but then we gave it a lot of thought and decided against it. We were forced to come to the conclusion that Jorge was dead, killed by the same man who killed Gaston, so what good would it do to file a missing persons report?"

McKenna could see the logic of their decision, but only in light of their special circumstances. He would discuss those circumstances with Lela if he had to, but he was counting on Cisco to carry the ball instead. He waited, but not a sound came from his partner, so he discreetly nudged him with his elbow.

At last. "Did the fact that you wouldn't want the police snooping around Jorge's apartment and going through his things enter into your decision not to file that missing persons report?" Cisco asked.

"Yes, I'll admit it did."

"Because Jorge might've had evidence of a crime lying around somewhere, to wit, illegal importation and sale of narcotics?"

Murray decided it was time to be Murray. "I'll let your imaginations run with that one," he interjected. "What's important is that she's filing the missing persons report now, and she's filing it with you two."

"Thank you, Murray, but I'll answer the question," Lela said, surprising McKenna, Cisco, and certainly Murray. "We thought that would be a major problem for us, and to a certain extent it still is, but the most important thing for us is getting Jorge back alive. If and when that happens, Jorge might have to face the consequences of his actions—but at least he'll be alive."

"Sensible decision," McKenna said, then got on to a delicate matter that had to be addressed. "Did you remove anything from the apartment while you were there?"

"No, and I tried not to touch anything either."

"Is there a safe in the apartment?"

"In the master bedroom, behind the bookcase."

"Do you have the combination?"

"Wait a minute," Murray said, and turned to Lela, "and I really must insist on this. I represent your brother, and as far as I'm concerned, this is still a missing persons case when it comes to him. Based on what you've told them, they can get a warrant to search his apartment for anything that might help them locate him. That has nothing to do with whatever's in that safe. They might find something in there they could use to build a case against him."

That stopped Lela, and she appeared to be lost in thought.

"We'd be able to build a presumptive case against him, no matter what," Cisco said. "After all, Justice's information has to be coming from someone, and from the statements we've already received here tonight, we know who that someone is."

"Unsupported statements, speculative in nature," Murray said. "You don't have enough for a warrant to search that safe."

"How about the apartment? Will we need a warrant to search it?" McKenna asked.

"No. As long as Lela concurs, you have permission for a consensual search, and I'll go with you when you do it."

Then Lela came back to life. "What do you think you might find in that safe?" she asked.

"Records indicating who your brother's been dealing

with when he's helping to peddle your husband's product," McKenna said. "In order to free your brother, we have to capture Justice. If we have an idea who his next target might be, that could certainly be helpful."

"Tell her what else you might find in that safe, and please have the grace to be truthful," Murray said.

"Records of financial transactions."

"In other words, where Gaston has deposited his profits," Murray said.

"Yeah, the money-laundering records," Cisco replied.

"And what could you do with those records?"

"Us, personally, not our area of responsibility," McKenna said. "However, I'm sure Narcotics and the feds will be interested in them."

"And they'd use those records, if they exist, to seize the funds under the RICO statutes?"

"I imagine so."

"And that could conceivably be millions of dollars?"

"By our estimation, maybe billions," McKenna said.

That surprised Murray, and for a brief instant McKenna got a chance to see him at his very greediest. "Billions?" he asked.

"That's right, Murray," Cisco said. "Thousands of millions. We have information leading us to believe your client was a hellava drug dealer, had the East Coast market cornered for the past couple of years."

"But *billions*?" Murray said, still stunned by the prospect. "Now you can be sure I'll be with you when you enter that apartment, and you may certainly not touch that safe."

"Sorry, Murray," Lela said, and she patted his arm before addressing McKenna and Cisco. "It's the same combination as our safe. Right nine, left twenty, right thirty-seven. You have my permission to search it."

"You can't give that permission," Murray protested.

"I believe I can. Would you excuse me for a moment?"

"Do you know what you're doing?" Murray asked. "They'll take everything, and you'll be left with nothing."

"Not exactly," Lela said, then got up. "I'll be right back."

She left the room, leaving Murray in a state of consternation. "You know, giving billions to the feds goes against every fiber of my being," he commented.

"She wants her brother back, Murray, and she'll do anything that might help get him back," McKenna observed. "Besides, she's figured out that he's being tortured every day, and she sure wants that to stop."

"But billions?" Murray said. "Remarkable."

When Lela returned, she was carrying a small metal box. She took her seat again next to Murray and opened it. "I wasn't lying when I told you my husband didn't discuss his business affairs with me, but he did insist I know certain things in case something happened to him." She took out a document consisting of many pages, folded and tied with a ribbon, and she passed it to Murray.

Murray undid the bow, opened it, and began to read.

"What is it?" McKenna asked.

"A will," Murray replied, and he began thumbing through the pages.

"Yes, Gaston's will," Lela said. "Murray will find that Jorge's apartment is owned by Exito Seguros, a legitimate company totally owned by my husband, and willed entirely to me." She then reached into the box, rummaged through it, took out a document consisting of a single sheet of paper, and she gave that to Murray. "I think this will clear up my position," she said.

Murray took just a moment to read that document, and disgust registered on his face as he did.

"What is it, Murray?" McKenna asked.

"Basically, a signed and notarized consent form from Jorge Rodriguez authorizing Gaston Cruz or Lela Cruz to enter his apartment at any time and remove anything they like."

"Any more goodies of interest in that box?" Cisco asked.

"Two more. Maybe I shouldn't be showing this to you, but it'll eventually come out anyway, and I don't want Murray to think I'm a complete idiot," she said, then reached into the box and passed Murray two more bulky documents.

"Two life insurance policies on my husband's life for ten million each, listing my brother and myself as the beneficiaries," she said. "According to Gaston, they were purchased as part of his compensation package with Exito Seguros. He explained to me that all the funds in that company are legitimate, obtained from the sale of his lands in Colombia, and not subject to attack by the federal government."

"I think he explained correctly," Murray said. "Otherwise, the feds would have figured out a way to seize the company after they went through his business records."

"Ten million and the company?" McKenna said. "You should be able to manage, no matter what the feds do."

McKenna had meant it as a joke, but Lela didn't take it that way. "I think so. As you can see, Gaston insisted we live simply here so as not to attract attention to ourselves, and I never minded. I'm probably the only woman in the neighborhood without a maid."

Simply? McKenna asked himself, looking around the large, expensively furnished room. What would her version of extravagant be?

"It's still a lot of money you're giving up, and maybe you wouldn't have to," Murray said.

"I don't look at it that way," Lela retorted. "I'd like to lead a respectable life with my children from this point on, and I want nothing to do with that drug money."

"You mind if I ask a personal question?" Cisco asked.

"I don't know. Ask it first, and we'll see."

"Knowing the business Gaston was involved in and the things he did, you never questioned your love for him?"

"Not for an instant," she replied, and then lowered her eyes. "I guess Gaston was my character defect," she said, then stood up and looked from Cisco to McKenna to Murray. "I hope we're all still friends when this is over. Would you like me to serve the cake now?"

"Please do," McKenna said, and then a disturbing thought struck him: With Lela, fine, but friends with Murray?

TWELVE

Before McKenna, Cisco, and Murray left, Lela gave McKenna two photos of Jorge and the keys to his apartment. She also called the building's concierge, and authorized their admission to the apartment.

As it turned out, Murray's Park Avenue apartment was just two blocks from Jorge's, so McKenna and Cisco followed him home and waited while he parked his car in his building's garage. They then drove him to Jorge's building, and to their complete surprise, found a legal parking spot right outside.

After McKenna identified himself to the doorman, they were politely escorted to the private penthouse elevator, and the concierge activated it. When they left the elevator, Cisco stopped for a moment to admire the three small statues set on pedestals in the marbled hallway. "I'd say Jorge was doing pretty good for himself before he ran into Justice," was his comment. "Very nice."

"Pretty routine décor for Park Avenue penthouse lobbies," Murray said.

"I guess you live in one of the penthouses in your building?"

"Yeah, but my floor has just two apartments."

McKenna didn't want to hear any more, so he opened the door with the keys Lela had given him and stepped into a large central foyer with marble walls and a marble floor. To their left was a combination library and office, and Cisco immediately focused on the computer on the desk. "You might wanna call Lela," he said to Murray. "I wanna take the hard drive from that computer with us when we leave."

"Why should I waste her time and mine?" Murray replied. "She'll just say, 'Sure, Cisco, take it if you want.'"

In front of them was the living room, and to their right was the dining room and a hallway that led to the kitchen. Off the hallway was a bathroom. The apartment was a duplex, and a wide stairway led to the bedrooms upstairs. All the rooms were large, with fourteen-foot ceilings.

"Is yours a duplex, Murray?" Cisco had to ask.

"Yep."

"As nice as this?"

"I'd say so."

As they walked through the downstairs rooms, they saw absolutely no signs of a struggle. On the contrary, the apartment was spotless and orderly, with not so much as a doily out of place. They climbed the stairs to the second floor and found the bedrooms in the same condition. The bed in the master bedroom was neatly made; framed family photos including pictures of Jorge, Gaston, and Lela were arranged in a straight line on the dresser; there was no dust on the books in the seven-foot-high built-in bookcase; and even the towels in the master bath were perfectly aligned on the towel racks.

"Let's see if he's as neat as we think he is," Cisco said, and he opened the top drawer of the dresser to expose rows of neatly folded socks and handkerchiefs.

"Well, what do you think?" McKenna asked.

"Yeah, he is," Cisco said, closing the drawer. "Top drawer is where most of us keep our odds and ends, but Jorge doesn't even have a junk drawer."

Lela had told them about the electric switch hidden behind the headboard, and McKenna activated it. The bookcase slowly swung open on a hinge to reveal a two-foot-by-two-foot safe built into the wall behind. McKenna opened it and found that it contained six stacks of wrapped hundred-dollar bills. As he removed the stacks and passed them to Cisco, he noticed that most of the bills were used. Cisco made two trips to the bed with his arms loaded to dump the bundles of bills on it.

Underneath the stacks McKenna found what they had come for, three computer disks. He held them up for Cisco and Murray to see, then put them in his pocket.

"What do we do with the loot? Put it back?" Cisco asked.

"I guess. You got a count?"

"Pocket change in his business, two hundred sixty thousand even."

It had been a long day for Cisco and McKenna, and it wasn't over yet. Brunette was still waiting for McKenna in his office, and the interview with Lela and the search of Jorge's apartment still had to be documented in reports. At midnight they were headed downtown when McKenna's cell phone rang. "Sorry to say it didn't take us as long as I thought to trace that C-Four and those blasting caps," Dennis Hunt said. "That stuff has a history, and it rang all the bells when we entered the signature code in the computer. Part of a shipment to the Colombian army in ninety-three to—get this—be used by them to blow up drug labs they found. Apparently at least part of the shipment was waylaid, because the last time that stuff went off, it blew a drug runner's plane outta the sky over Guatemala. Unfortunately, the copilot was an undercover DEA agent."

"When did this happen?"

"Ancient history. Nineteen ninety-five."

"Where did that flight originate?"

"Panama."

"Was the bombing tied to Gaston Cruz in any way?"

"Don't know. We don't have the paperwork on the investigation, but it's still being carried as an open case."

"Is the agent's name listed?"

"Along with a brief bio. Consuela Andersen."

"A female agent?"

"Yeah, sounds like a real sad case. Twenty-nine years old, left a husband and two kids."

McKenna took out his notepad and pen. "Give me the DEA file number on the case."

After ending Hunt's call, McKenna next called Brunette. He gave him a brief synopsis of the day's events and ended the conversation with a few requests for files that Brunette could get much easier and faster than he could, especially at that hour. However, even for Brunette it would still take some time, so McKenna thought it best to waste some of their own time. He looked to Cisco and found him lost in thought as he drove. "You hungry?" McKenna asked.

"Cisco did Piggy with that wonderful cake he selected, but he is always a manly man. He could eat," Cisco replied without looking at McKenna.

What did I do to provoke this? McKenna wondered, but it took him only seconds to come up with the answer. He hadn't been including Cisco in his thought process—always a mistake—and he had just called Brunette with a number of requests without first filling Cisco in and asking his advice. More mistakes. "Market Diner?"

"A plebeian choice, as expected. Cisco has not eaten at the Market Diner since his father raised his allowance to a dollar, but it will do," Cisco said, and then he finally looked at McKenna. "As a fairly intelligent man, you will, of course, be seeking Cisco's guidance while we dine?"

"Of course."

"Fortunately for you, Cisco is a generous, forgiving man. He will therefore deign to enlighten his acolyte over a couple of greasy burgers."

Good God! How do I take this day after day? McKenna wondered for the umpteenth time, and he came up with the usual answer. Because. "Thank you, O Wise One."

"You're welcome."

Brunette was seated at his desk watching a videotape of the news conference on TV when McKenna entered. McKenna thought his friend looked even worse than he had that afternoon, with bags under his eyes and lines on his forehead he

had never noticed before. He was unshaven and dressed beyond casual, wearing jeans, a pajama top, and slippers. If he
felt as bad as he looked, he didn't show it; he had a smile and
a warm greeting for McKenna.

"You better get some sleep soon," McKenna advised.

"Tried lying down at ten, but I couldn't sleep," Brunette
replied, and clicked off the TV. "How's the cop theory
looking?"

"More likely than not, but still not certain. You get any of
those reports for me yet?"

"You're sure not winning me any popularity contests.
I've been annoying people here and waking up big shots in
Washington ever since you called, but nothing back yet.
However, I do have this for you," he said, then took a bulky
folder from his top desk drawer and put it on his desk.

"What is it?"

"Believe it or not, those are just summary reports on the
internal investigations in Narcotics, the Joint Drug Task
Force, and the DEA. Searched everywhere, looked hard at
everyone, found nothing substantive on any of the troops."

"That's it? All that paper to say nothing?"

"A few suspicions, a couple of minor points that don't
add up quite correctly, and a few personal problems uncovered that are really none of our business, but you get all that
in any comprehensive internal investigation. Whoever the
greedy turncoat is, he's smart, he's careful, and he's covered
his tracks well."

"And he's still above suspicion," McKenna added, then
leaned over Brunette's desk and tapped the folder. "But he's
in here somewhere, the richest cop or agent in the history of
this city."

"The richest ever? Are you sure about that?"

"Can't be certain, but I feel pretty strong about it."

"Why?"

"Because I have a good assessment on how much Gaston
was making, a good analysis of his business practices, and
an inside look at his personality from the person who knew
him best. Gaston was a generous guy, and he didn't mind

spending money to make money. Whoever it was Gaston bought, he paid him very well—and probably on a continuing basis."

"How well, do you think?"

"Say two or three million a month, and Gaston would've considered that a bargain for the constantly updated information that kept him safe and helped make him maybe the biggest drug dealer to ever operate in this country."

McKenna's analysis hit Brunette hard, and he slumped in his chair, thinking. "Two or three million a month could corrupt almost anyone, so all these reports might be worthless," he said after a few moments.

"Why does the amount make them worthless?"

"Because I have to now face the possibility Gaston bought someone I personally trust, one of the people who helped write these reports."

"A chief?"

"The worst possibility, but yes, it could be a chief."

"Well, whoever it is, I don't think we have too long to identify him and quickly bag him."

"Why? With Gaston dead, I'd think we'd have all the time we need," Brunette said, and then he got McKenna's meaning. "Justice knows who it is."

"Knows now, or soon will after Jorge suffers a bit more."

"Jorge was Gaston's paymaster?"

"Looks that way, and he had Gaston's complete confidence. He knows who it is, so it's just a matter of time before Messing gets another letter giving him the name and probably some proof. Think what that would do to this Job's reputation and prestige if we have to count on a murdering vigilante to uncover our dirty laundry for us."

Brunette laughed at the thought, but there was no mirth in it. "We really do know how to conjure up the worst-case scenario, don't we?" he asked. "What a recipe! First start off with a fabulously wealthy corrupt chief we can't catch, and let it simmer for a year or two. Next, add in that other guy we can't catch—you know, the murdering fun-filled vigilante cop who'll probably have a few fan clubs in place and cheering him on by tomorrow. Then, for the pièce de résistance, our vigilante-cop-we-can't-catch, he helps us out by sending a letter to Messing, telling the world just who our corrupt-chief-we-can't-catch really is. Absolutely wonderful, a recipe designed to have me cleaning out my desk and sent packing!"

Wow! This guy's in trouble, McKenna thought. What do I say to that? "It's bad, but you might be overreacting a bit. We *are* still in the game, you know."

"Yeah, but it's late in the game, we're down by a couple of goals, and we're still on defense deep in enemy territory. Is that overstating the case?"

Is it? McKenna wondered. No. "Pretty concise analogy, but there's still hope." He took Jorge's computer disks and hard drive from his pocket and put them on Brunette's desk.

"What's on them?" Brunette asked.

"Can't say for sure. I can get on-line and do basic stuff, but I'm no computer whiz."

"No problem. We've got computer whizzes aplenty in this building. What do you *think* is on them?"

"Gaston's books, his complete drug-dealing business records."

"Including the record of payments to the cop he bought?"

"If the amounts are large enough to be considered significant, I'd say so."

"Buddy, you're a ray of sunshine," Brunette said, and his mood visibly brightened. "While we're waiting for your reports to come in, why don't you tell me all about your day?"

McKenna did, spending half an hour talking. Brunette had only an occasional question, most of them centering on Gaston and the amount of money McKenna thought he had been making. McKenna had finished and was pouring himself a cup of coffee when Brunette's phone rang. A short conversation ensued, and McKenna could tell Brunette was talking to a chief.

"Unfortunately, you were right," Brunette announced after he hung up. "Somebody in Narcotics *did* do a report after the search warrant. Long and detailed, with photos.

Completely describes the house, the security system, Montoya's role, and even mentions the dog."

"That's not good news, you know. It's another indication that Justice is a cop."

"But it brings us closer to catching him. If he is a cop, he has to be a cop in a position to get his hands on that report. Narrows our search considerably, report was locked away in a file cabinet in the Narcotic Division's Intelligence Section."

"How many people had access to it?"

"Don't know, but I'll sure find out," Brunette replied. "My question for you is, What made you think such a report existed?"

"Lela, and common sense."

"Lela?"

"When she told me she was sure her brother hadn't given Justice the information he needed to circumvent their security system, neutralize Carlos, and kill her husband, I'd thought she was overestimating Jorge's courage under pressure. Where else could Justice have gotten that information? I asked myself. Only other place I could figure was from the Narcotics Division, and I wasn't sure about that."

"That's the common-sense part?"

"Sure. Narcotics was hot on Gaston. When they came up blank on that search warrant, they had to be hoping someone would be hitting that place again, maybe with a No Knock warrant at night. Maybe them, maybe another team, or maybe the feds. Common sense dictates they'd describe everything they saw there that another team would find nice to know the next time the place was hit."

"And you were right."

"Who found the report?" McKenna asked.

"O'Shaughnessy. He's bringing it over."

"Dog Dick's coming here?" McKenna moaned.

"Yeah, and please try to be nice to him. He did a good job, and chances are we're gonna have more need of him as this thing goes on," Brunette said, then stood up. "Can't have him seeing me like this. I'm gonna freshen up, shave, and get dressed."

"Put a rush on it, Ray. Him and I don't have much to talk about, and I don't think he cares much for my act."

"Why's that, do you think? Because sometimes you bend the rules to get the job done?"

"That, and the fact that you and I are pals."

"That's because he doesn't have any friends, and I'll tell you what I sometimes find myself thinking whenever I run into him. If he was a chief when I was a detective, he would have fired me for my version of police work."

"I dunno," McKenna said. "Things were different then."

"But he's always been the same." Brunette went to his bathroom and closed the door behind him.

McKenna made a fresh pot of coffee. He could hear the sound of Brunette's electric razor in the bathroom, and was pouring himself a cup when there was a knock at the door. "Come in," he yelled, and Chief Jeremiah O'Shaughnessy entered in full uniform. He nodded to McKenna, then looked around the room. "Where's the commissioner?" he asked.

"In the bathroom, but he should be out in a couple of minutes. Can I see the report while we're waiting?"

"I was instructed to bring it to the police commissioner," O'Shaughnessy said.

"Yeah, I know, but it's for me."

O'Shaughnessy appeared flustered, which delighted McKenna. "I'd rather wait and give it to him first," he said.

"Suit yourself. Coffee?"

"No, thank you." O'Shaughnessy then stood in front of Brunette's desk at the military position of attention, waiting.

O'Shaughnessy was the CO of the Internal Affairs Bureau. In his late fifties, tall, and in shape, with a full head of slicked-back gray hair that still had a touch of red at the edges, he cut an impressive figure with his erect, military bearing.

Appearances can be deceiving, McKenna thought every time he saw O'Shaughnessy. He had always considered O'Shaughnessy to be a procedural maniac totally lacking common sense. He was a stickler for the rules, even the silly or archaic rules sensible bosses ignored, and he enforced all rules with vigor and without mercy. He was, consequently, the most hated man in the department, but he didn't seem to mind. What he did mind was his nickname, Dog Dick, so naturally that was how every cop in the department referred to him.

Legend had it O'Shaughnessy had received the name years ago when he was a lieutenant with a full head of bright red hair working as a desk officer in a Harlem precinct. A prisoner had been brought before him, and O'Shaughnessy was booking him while simultaneously berating the arresting officer for some minor procedural infraction. It was then that the forever-beloved prisoner loudly noted to the delight of all the cops in the station house, "Lieutenant, you're as red on the head as the dick on a dog." That was it; among the cops O'Shaughnessy was Dog Dick forevermore.

McKenna was still at the coffeepot, finishing his first cup, when Brunette finally emerged from the bathroom. He looked like a new man, clean-shaven and in a fresh suit, but there was no disguising the bags under his eyes. McKenna thought he would be amused to see O'Shaughnessy still standing at attention in front of his desk, but apparently Brunette had become accustomed to such bizarre conduct from O'Shaughnessy. As he took his position behind his desk, O'Shaughnessy saluted and held the salute. "Chief O'Shaughnessy reporting to the police commissioner as ordered."

Brunette then astonished McKenna when he also assumed the position of attention and returned the salute. "Thank you, Chief," he said. "Now, please cut it out and sit down."

"Yes, sir." O'Shaughnessy dropped into one of the chairs in front of Brunette's desk, and McKenna noted that he even sat at attention.

"You got it?" Brunette asked.

"Yes, sir." O'Shaughnessy reached into his breast pocket, extracted an envelope, and placed it on Brunette's desk. Brunette then sat down and nodded to McKenna.

McKenna couldn't remember ever feeling better as he walked to the desk, picked up the envelope, opened it, and took out a copy of the search warrant, the three-page report, and the ten photos. O'Shaughnessy ignored him, staring at a spot on the wall over Brunette's head as McKenna read.

The report was well-written and detailed, McKenna concluded after he read it and examined the photos showing the inside and outside of the Cruz house. Everything Justice needed to know was in it.

McKenna replaced the report and the photos in the envelope and put it in his pocket. "Chief, does anyone know you removed the report?"

"No. There was one detective in the office when I got there, but I told him to get out. Then I searched the office and found it."

"Did it take you long?"

"About fifteen minutes. Pretty easy, really, it was in a file cabinet marked 'Executed Search Warrants.'"

"You did good, Jerry, but now I have another mission for you," Brunette said. "I want a discreet investigation done, and at the end of it I want the personnel folders of everyone on the team who executed the warrant, and anyone who would have access to that file cabinet. Can you do that?"

"How long do I have?"

"I know it's a tall order, but I need those folders on my desk by tomorrow night."

"What time tomorrow?"

"Say six."

"They'll be here."

That sure was a tall order, McKenna thought. How the hell is he gonna conduct an investigation like that without anybody finding out about it, and do it all in under fourteen hours?

Apparently, Brunette was wondering the same thing. "Mind telling me how you plan to proceed?" he asked.

O'Shaughnessy looked extremely uncomfortable at the question, and he looked back and forth from Brunette to McKenna. "I know you trust him, but I'd rather not say in the presence of Detective McKenna," he said at last.

"It's his case, and he's in charge of saving my bacon. Let's have the plan, Jerry."

"Commissioner, I feel obligated to advise you that divulging my plan on this matter in the presence of Detective McKenna would be an extreme violation of procedure."

"Jerry!"

"May I write it down and give it to you?"

"When?"

"Right now."

"If you insist." Brunette looked exasperated as he took a sheet of paper and a pen from his desk and passed them to O'Shaughnessy. O'Shaughnessy moved his chair so the back was to McKenna, and he began writing. It took him under a minute to write his plan. When he finished, he folded up the paper and passed it to Brunette.

Brunette unfolded the note, and he looked surprised as he read it. "Really?" he asked.

"Yes, sir," O'Shaughnessy replied.

"For how long?"

"Nine years."

Because of O'Shaughnessy's unusual conduct and the brevity of his plan, McKenna thought he knew how O'Shaughnessy intended to conduct his investigation. Brunette's questions told him he was right, but it still surprised him. O'Shaughnessy had a field associate planted somewhere in the Narcotics Division, a cop usually recruited in the police academy who throughout his or her career secretly reported to the Internal Affairs Bureau on the conduct of the cops with whom they worked. It was a program begun in the early seventies when corruption was rampant in the department, and it had produced many results. However, except for the occasional rumor of its continued existence, McKenna hadn't heard a concrete word about the program in years, and like most cops, he had assumed it had been discontinued.

"Good job, Jerry, and quite a piece of luck for us," Brunette said.

"Thank you, sir. Will that be all?"

"Yeah, that's it for now. See you tomorrow night."

"Yes, sir."

O'Shaughnessy stood up, again came to attention, and saluted. "Enough, already, Jerry," Brunette said, but he still returned the salute. O'Shaughnessy did an about-face and headed for the door, but Brunette stopped him before he reached it. "Jerry, make sure his folder is in with the others."

"Yes, sir."

"He's got a field associate in the Narcotics Division?" McKenna asked after the door closed behind O'Shaughnessy.

"Yeah, right in the Intelligence Section. Been reporting directly to O'Shaughnessy for nine years."

"Since he came on the job?"

"I imagine so."

"Did he write down the name?"

"No, but you'll be able to figure it out."

"Sure. Just look for the guy who made detective quick, then spends his career in sensitive jobs where cops have an opportunity to steal."

"When you find out who it is, let me know."

"You looked surprised to learn O'Shaughnessy had a field associate in Narcotics," McKenna noted.

"No, I knew we had them in there. What surprised me was we had one in the Intelligence Section. Don't imagine there's much opportunity for stealing drugs or cash there. If I was in IAB and running a field associate, I'd want him in the street, where the action and the opportunities are."

"I'm sure that's where he started out, but Narcotics is a tough, dangerous assignment at street level. Maybe he burned out and wanted a change."

"And the assignment to the Intelligence Section was his reward? Maybe," Brunette said, then tapped the internal-investigation folder. "How long is it gonna take you to go through this?"

"I'm not gonna be the one to do it. Cisco's been in Narcotics, and he's got a much more devious mind than I do. He volunteered for the mission, and I'm glad to let him have a go at it."

"Ferreting out a turncoat no one else could find is quite a mission."

"If anyone can do it, he can."

"What's he doing now?"

"Today's paperwork. He wants to have it all on Sheeran's desk when he comes in," McKenna said, and then a thought made him chuckle.

"What is it?" Brunette asked.

"I just thought it funny that it's possible there's three spies operating in the Narcotics Division—Gaston's, O'Shaughnessy's, and Justice's—and we have to uncover all of them to do this case right."

Cisco had finished the paperwork and was taking a snooze at his desk when McKenna entered the Major Case Squad office, but he woke up and was instantly alert when McKenna placed the internal-investigation folder on his desk. He picked it up and immediately began thumbing through the thick file. "Even for me, this is gonna take a while," he commented. "How'd it go with Ray?"

"Okay, but I gotta go back up. He still hasn't gotten in everything I need yet."

"Did you tell him how much we think Gaston's bought cop was making?"

"Yeah, I told him."

"I bet that set him on his ear."

"Certainly disturbed him. He thinks now it's possible the turncoat might even be a chief."

That thought caused Cisco to smile. "Me bag a chief? That'd be something, and I'd sure have some fun with it. I can hear myself saying, 'You have the right to remain silent, so shut up, Your Holiness, before you really piss Cisco off.' Or how's this? 'Oh, did Cisco put those cuffs on too tight, Exalted One? Damn! Of all days to forget my cuff key. Sorry, Chief.' Or how about . . ."

"How about this?" McKenna said, seeking to bring Cisco out of his fantasy. "I've given it a little more thought, and now I'm also inclined to think it's a chief, or at least somebody high up."

"Why's that?"

"Because whoever it is, he gave Gaston information on two of our informants, but he also gave up a DEA informant. Gave Gaston enough info to whack all three of them. If he's in our Narcotics or the Joint Drug Task Force, I figure he'd have to be pretty high up to have all the info on a federal informant."

"Hate to say it, but not necessarily. What do informants do?"

"Obviously, they provide information to whoever they're reporting to."

Cisco smiled and shook his head in a way that made McKenna feel like the kid who didn't know his colors in kindergarten. "Very good, Brian, but what else do they do?"

"Drugs?"

"Even better, Brian," Cisco said, nodding approvingly. "They do drugs. They're involved in buying or selling drugs, and most of them put bad things in their bodies on a regular basis. Now tell me, what happens to people like that, sooner or later?"

McKenna got Cisco's point, but he could see no way to avoid continuing the game. "They get arrested."

"Right. They get arrested, which is how most of them got to be informants in the first place. Now, what do you think happens when we lock up one of the feds' informants?"

"The DEA gets somebody to the station house right away, and the guy's released. Case closed, it never happened."

"Almost correct, but you know our job and the way we love to document everything. There's still one form filled out, a voided arrest form, and where do you think all those types of voided arrest forms are kept?"

"The Narcotics Division's Intelligence Section?"

"You're learning," Cisco said, then reached across his desk and patted McKenna's arm.

"Gotta go," McKenna said.

"Already? You just got here."

"Yeah, but you just gave me an idea that has to be checked out right now. What was the DEA guy's name?"

Cisco opened up the folder and quickly scanned through the first page of the first report, the overview of the investigation. "Reginald Crawford. You gonna check to see if he was the subject of a voided arrest?"

"No, I'm gonna tell Ray about it, and he's probably gonna have Dog Dick get the information for us."

"When will that happen?"

"Almost immediately."

Cisco liked that idea. "He's gonna wake up Dog Dick and have him come in?"

"Actually, he's already had him come in for another mission, but he's probably on his way home by now. Might even be there already, tucked snug into his crib," McKenna said, and even he had to smile at the thought.

"I love your life. Are you ready for some more good news?"

"I could use some."

"We were right in thinking Justice took Jorge in a bump and grab after he left Cruz's house Sunday night."

"How do you know?" McKenna asked.

"Because I called the One-Oh-Nine Precinct desk officer to find out if they recovered any stolen cars in the Cruz neighborhood that night, and they did. A ninety-eight Olds blocking the intersection on North Avenue, just two blocks from the Cruz house."

"Damage?"

"Slight front-end damage."

"Paint?"

Cisco smiled. "Red paint on the front bumper. Justice smacked Jorge's red Volvo, then jumped him. Left the Olds right there, and took Jorge away in the Volvo."

"Any witnesses?"

"None. Very quiet block, houses set back from the street, so we don't know if Justice was by himself when he did the deed."

"Where was the Olds stolen from?" McKenna asked.

"Railroad parking lot in Harriman. Owner got off the train Saturday night and discovered he was a pedestrian."

Harriman? About thirty miles north of the city line, McKenna thought. What would Justice be doing up there? "Where's the car now?"

"Still drivable, so it was returned to the owner."

"Probably a waste of time, but it has to be checked for prints," McKenna said. "I'll ask Sheeran to arrange it in the morning."

As frequently happens, when the police commissioner is working ungodly hours, so are many of the chiefs. The chief of detectives brought in the personnel folders of every black detective and supervisor who had served in the Bomb Squad in the last twenty years.

Five minutes after the chief of detectives left, the chief of the Scientific Research Division was in Brunette's office. Brunette gave him Jorge's computer disks and hard drive, and then the instructions: "We think there are financial records detailing many high-level drug transactions on those disks. I want all the records printed out and on my desk by six o'clock tonight."

"Six o'clock tonight? Could be easy, but it could also be a tough order, Commissioner," the chief protested. "My people have some experience with these computerized drug transaction records, and the dealers are sometimes very security conscious. They build in quite a few obstacles to prevent people like us from reading them."

"Obstacles? Such as?"

"The files might require a password to access them."

"Password? Circumvent it."

"And the records could also be in code."

"Code? Break it. Do whatever you have to do to get me those records by six."

Under the circumstances, there was only one answer the chief could possibly give: "Yes, sir."

Next into Brunette's office was the chief of personnel. At

Brunette's request, the FAA had sent him the complete list of all persons holding pilots' licenses in the United States. The chief had computer-matched the list to the department's personnel roster, resulting in another list of 232 cops.

"How many of them didn't notify the Personnel Bureau when they got their licenses?" McKenna asked the chief.

"Three, which I consider a high number," the chief reported. "First thing they usually do when they get the license is notify us, then apply for the Aviation Unit."

"Get me the personnel folders on those three," Brunette ordered. "How many are in Narcotics or the Bomb Squad?"

The chief had to consult his list and do a count. "None in the Bomb Squad, sixteen in Narcotics. Do you want their folders as well?"

"Please."

While the chief of personnel was completing his task, O'Shaughnessy returned from his second raid of the evening on the Intelligence Section office, and he had five voided arrest forms with him. Three documented Reginald Crawford's run-ins with the police, and the other two documented the voided arrests of the Narcotics Division informants killed by Gaston.

"This knucklehead got locked up three times for drugs?" Brunette asked, holding up Crawford's voided arrest forms.

"He's got a total of six arrests for sale or possession between ninety-one and ninety-eight, and the last one on his rap sheet was a heavy. A-One felony, so that's probably the one the feds used to turn him. After that, there's just the voided arrests," O'Shaughnessy said. "Two for sale, one for simple possession."

"I don't recall seeing any mention of those arrests in the internal-investigation report your people did," Brunette noted.

"Neither do I. Is it important?" O'Shaughnessy asked.

"Could be very important. It could be the main factor that exculpates the feds and puts us in the box, because it leads me to believe now that the turncoat is one of ours, not one of theirs. Matter of fact, we could've saved the feds a lot of headaches and wasted investigative time if one of your sleuths would've connected the dots and thought of looking for these voided arrest reports."

O'Shaughnessy was suddenly under the gun, and he knew it. "I agree, sir, and you can rest assured I'll address the problem. In my own defense, may I say that it's very hard to attract and keep good investigators in Internal Affairs."

"You may, and I know it is."

So did McKenna, and he was surprised to find himself feeling sorry for O'Shaughnessy. It was widely believed in the Detective Bureau that the cops who sought assignment as investigators in IAB were untalented folks who couldn't get the detective's shield any other way. Once there, they stayed there, and there were few shining lights among them.

But then O'Shaughnessy had something else to add that quickly evaporated any compassion McKenna was feeling for him. "Would you also keep in mind that they're just detectives, and certainly couldn't be expected to have the same degree of investigative insight as, say, the police commissioner."

"I didn't come up with the idea of looking for the voided arrest reports," Brunette said.

"Then who?" O'Shaughnessy asked, then turned to McKenna. "You?"

"No, Chief. Not me, either."

"Then who?"

"I'll give you a hint, Jerry," Brunette said. "Who's the most arrogant detective we have?"

"That's a tough one. We have so many arrogant detectives who think very highly of themselves."

"Last hint. He's probably the man you hate most in the department."

That did it, and he turned again to McKenna. "Your partner, of course. Detective Herman Sanchez. Thinks of himself as the world's greatest detective, and the only rules he thinks worth following are the ones he makes for himself."

Pretty good assessment, McKenna had to admit, and he was reminded once again of one of the reasons Cisco dis-

liked O'Shaughnessy more than he disliked most of the
other chiefs. Cisco's given name was actually Herman,
but he hated the name, and very few dared call him anything but Cisco. O'Shaughnessy, however, felt he was in a
position to call Cisco anything he liked, and he liked calling Cisco "Herman" at every conceivable opportunity.
With the exception of O'Shaughnessy, everyone who knew
Cisco expected that, sooner or later, Cisco would make
O'Shaughnessy suffer for his impertinence. The only questions were when would it happen and how bad would it be
for O'Shaughnessy?

By 3:45 A.M. McKenna and Brunette had gone through all
the personnel files and had found only one person that interested them, so they studied his again. Sergeant Craig North
of Brooklyn's 83rd Precinct Detective Squad had been
granted a single-engine pilot's license in 1997, and he hadn't
reported it to the Personnel Bureau. He was under no re-
quirement to do so, but what they found even more curious
was that North was black, and he had only been promoted to
sergeant the previous October. Before that, he had been a detective in the Manhattan South Narcotics District. That unit
was headquartered in the same building that housed the Narcotics Division Intelligence Section, 345 Hudson Street. Interesting coincidences? they wondered, but they knew North
couldn't possibly be Justice. He wasn't tall enough or heavy
enough: When North had entered the department his height
and weight were 5'7" and 145 pounds.
      At twenty-nine years of age and with just eight years on
the Job, both Brunette and McKenna initially thought he was
young to be a sergeant in the Detective Bureau, but then they
read his annual performance evaluations and decided he was
an asset to the Bureau. Over the years he had been consistently rated "Well Above Standards" by his supervisors, his
arrest activity and investigative skills were considered excellent, he spoke Spanish, in 1999 he had earned a B.A. in police science from John Jay College of Criminal Justice,

graduating with honors, and he had not taken a single sick day since joining the department. He had also been awarded the Medal for Valor, the department's second-highest honor, for his performance during a shoot-out with drug dealers in 1997. He lived in Bayside, Queens, and he was still single.

North was doing the job he was always meant to do, McKenna and Brunette decided, and that impression was reinforced when they studied the report on his background investigation performed when he had first applied to the department. It listed his father as a retired New York State Police captain.

"Do you remember giving him that medal?" McKenna asked when they had finally decided they knew everything important contained in the file.

"I'm ashamed to say I don't, and we only give out a handful of Medals for Valor a year," Brunette replied. "Too long ago, and I bet I've been to a hundred award ceremonies since then. Don't remember the man, and I don't remember the shoot-out that got him the medal."

"He sounds like a pretty impressive guy."

"Then let's talk to somebody who should know him," Brunette said, then called the chief of detectives' cell phone. That chief, at least, had finally made it home and was asleep in bed when Brunette called. No problem, of course; chiefs are always delighted when the police commissioner calls them at 4:00 A.M. with arcane personnel questions, which is one of the reasons they get to stay chiefs.

The chief knew North, and according to him, Craig North was an excellent man, a great detective supervisor who should go far in the department. According to the rules, a newly promoted sergeant must serve at least a year in a uniformed patrol command before being eligible for assignment to the Detective Bureau. Both Brunette and the chief knew that the rules were meant for the cops and detectives, but certainly not the chiefs, so the chief admitted that it was he himself who had put North in the 83rd Precinct Detective Squad after just two months of uniformed patrol duty.

"What kind of guy is he, personally?" Brunette asked. He got a short reply before he hung up.

"Nice guy?" McKenna asked.

"Says he wished a guy like North would marry one of his daughters."

That prompted McKenna to take a close look at North's ID photo. Not a bad-looking guy, he decided. Strong jaw, but he looks like he's always ready to smile.

By 4:30 McKenna was feeling tired, and he thought Brunette looked exhausted. Then Brunette got the call he expected from the director of the DEA, telling Brunette he had just sent him an e-mail with the complete file of the investigation on the murder of Consuela Andersen attached. Brunette was printing out the long file when his phone rang again. "Uh, oh. Batphone," he said when he saw which button on his phone was flashing. "Only people who have that number are you, the mayor, the cardinal, and my wife."

Brunette took a breath, and picked up the phone. It was the cardinal of the Archdiocese of New York, a very important man in New York politics. "Good morning, Your Eminence, always a pleasure to hear from you," McKenna heard Brunette say. "Not at all, I was up and working."

McKenna didn't imagine a call from the cardinal could have anything to do with his case, so he tried not to pay attention. Instead, he took the lengthy Andersen file to the copy machine in the small room off Brunette's office, and he made a copy of it. When he returned, Brunette had finished the call and was sitting at his desk, looking dejected. "Problem?" McKenna asked.

"A big one, for both of us," Brunette replied. "There's been a new development."

"Justice hit again?"

"In a manner of speaking. Do you know the pastor of St. Cecilia's?"

"Used to be Father Lima."

"Still is, but now it's Monsignor Lima. Know him?"

"Met him a few times years ago, when I was in the Two-Five Squad."

"What do you think of him?"

"Good man doing a great job with limited resources."

"What's the basis of that opinion?" Brunette asked.

"It's not just my opinion. Ask anybody in that neighborhood. St. Cecilia's is the heart and soul of Spanish Harlem, and the school is its main hope. One of the city's poorest neighborhoods, but more than half the kids who graduate from St. Cecilia's grammar school go on to graduate from college. Somehow, Monsignor Lima makes sure they have the basic tools to proceed and succeed."

"Then, fortunately for him, and probably unfortunately for us, his resources are no longer all that limited. Half an hour ago he got a call from Justice. Congratulated the monsignor on the fine work he was doing, and told him there was money for St. Cecilia's stacked in front of the poor box in the church. Told the monsignor to use it as he saw fit."

"Just wonderful. That's drug money, and it came from the dealers he murdered," McKenna said.

"That's what I figured."

"Was the church locked?"

"Since confessions last night, and it was locked again when the monsignor got to it."

"So Justice picked the lock," McKenna said. "How do we know about this so quick?"

"The monsignor called the cardinal first thing, and he felt I should know right away."

"How much money did he leave?"

"A lot. The monsignor hasn't counted it yet, but he said it looks like millions."

"Millions? Gotta be wrong," McKenna said. "Justice has made a lot of money from those drug dealers, but not millions."

"You'll be the first one to count it and tell me for sure. The cardinal told the monsignor to wait and see if we wanna dust the cash for prints first."

"Why do that? Waste of time, because I'll guarantee that Justice didn't leave a single print on that money. All we'd get are the prints of every junkie, crackhead, and drug dealer in

Spanish Harlem, and we probably already have all their prints," McKenna said, and then he had another thought. "Only the monsignor, the cardinal, and us know about the money at this point?"

"That's right. The cardinal is keeping it under wraps until he hears from me."

"Good," McKenna said, then checked his cell phone for a number.

"Who you calling at this hour?" Brunette asked.

"Messing."

"Messing? Why? I don't know if we want press on this before we know more and allow ourselves some time to try to put the proper spin on it."

"Ray, there is no proper spin for this. The guy I said in front of all the cameras was basically just a clever thief murdering drug dealers for his own purposes just made a liar outta me. He's doing the Robin Hood thing, so my only hope is that Messing can salvage some credibility for himself."

"How?"

"By stopping the presses. In the story he filed I got him to go with my version of Justice. You know, greedy, murdering vigilante acting solely on his own behalf. The early edition's already printed, but I'm hoping he still has time to change his slant for the later editions."

"And if there isn't time?"

"Then he looks as stupid as me, and that would make for an angry reporter with lots of influence and an inside track on Justice."

"That wouldn't be good."

"Very bad, I'd say. He'd be concentrating on all the questions we don't want asked at this point."

"Then we have to make amends, so let's try giving him some religion," Brunette suggested. "Invite him to the church for an exclusive, and tell him to bring a photographer if he wants."

"It'll piss off the other reporters, but Justice isn't writing to them," McKenna said. "To keep Messing really happy, he'd like a peek at our file on Gaston."

"Then keep him really happy."

That was easy, McKenna thought. "Last question, a touchy one, and Messing will sure want it answered. What happens to the money?"

"The money? Let's see. Robin Hood gives a poor, inner-city church a fortune to continue its good work, and then that uncaring, insensitive police department takes it away. How's that sound?"

"Bad."

"Aside from all our other problems, do we need the cardinal for an enemy?"

"Of course not. The monsignor keeps the loot."

THIRTEEN

Messing *would* be bringing a photographer, so McKenna decided a bit of a show was necessary for the *Post*'s late-edition front-page photo. He called the Crime Scene Unit, and they would be there to provide some hocus pocus for the camera.

Cisco parked the car in the 25th Precinct's parking lot, and they set out to walk the block and a half to the church. They lingered a few minutes at the corner of East 117th Street and Lexington Avenue to take in the St. Cecilia's complex from a distance of half a city block.

The church, the rectory, and the school playground were on one side of East 117th Street, and the school and convent were on the other. All the buildings were constructed of brick that had been painted red many times over the years, and McKenna guessed they had to be a hundred years old. He also thought it shouldn't take Monsignor Lima too long to come up with a few ideas on how to spend the money Justice had given his church. There were shingles missing from the roofs of both the church and the convent, the gutters were hanging from the side of the school, all the windows were old with panes framed in wood, and McKenna doubted if any of the buildings had been renovated in fifty years, if ever.

Then they saw the Crime Scene Unit van pull up, and first out was Joe Walsh. His presence at that hour meant he had been working since McKenna had seen him last, the afternoon before, so Walsh being there was a surprise for him.

But not for Cisco. "I knew it," he said. "Front-page photo in the *Post*, and Walsh figured a way to get his fat ass in it."

The rest of Walsh's team went to the rectory's front door, but not Walsh. He had seen McKenna and Cisco standing on the corner, and he stood waiting for them.

"He's got something for us," McKenna guessed.

"Sure he does. I can see his dopey I'm-so-great grin from here."

Then Messing and his photographer pulled in behind the Crime Scene Unit van, and Walsh apparently forgot all about McKenna and Cisco. Messing was driving, and Walsh was at his door and talking to him before he even got out of the car. That got McKenna and Cisco hurrying down the block, but not fast enough. Walsh had finished talking and Messing was out of his car and writing in his notepad by the time they arrived.

Messing finished writing, then reread his notes, and McKenna could see there was almost a full page. "Amazing amount of work you did, Joe," Messing commented as he put his notepad back in his pocket. "Glad you got some results outta it."

"What results?" McKenna asked Walsh, but it was Messing who answered. "The blood. Walsh found Justice's blood, type B negative. Did an amazing amount of work, might help narrow your search considerably if he's a cop."

He's right, McKenna thought. B negative has to be a rare type, and we must have all the cops' blood types on a computer file somewhere. "Joe, now why don't you tell *us* about all this work you did?" McKenna asked.

"I was just about to do that. Really wanted to tell you first," Walsh replied. "It's just that Phil had so many questions for me, and you know how good he is. I guess I just caved in under the pressure."

"Yeah, he's a monster. The work?"

"Did everything you wanted done. Last night I went upstate to Harriman and dusted the Olds Justice stole and left in Malba after he snatched Jorge. Worked hard, found lots of prints, but they all belonged to . . ."

"The owner or his family. No surprise there," McKenna said. "What else?"

"Dusted the Messing letters and the envelope. Only Phil's prints on the letter, but plenty on the envelope. Twelve, in fact, four of them Phil's. Went to the *Post* and took elimination prints in the mail room. Turns out that all but two of the remaining latents belonged to those guys."

"And those two? Some postal employee?"

"I'd say so, but that would take me much longer to check out. Might be a good deal of overtime involved."

"Forget it. If Justice didn't leave any prints on the letter, he didn't leave any on the envelope." Then McKenna noticed that the rest of Walsh's team had left the front door of the rectory and were headed toward the church, which told him that was where Monsignor Lima was. He didn't want to waste too much more time with Walsh. "How about the blood?"

"I'm getting to that," Walsh said. "I also dusted all the drug packages from Marginal Street. Found lots of prints there, too, but they all belong to . . ."

"Garcia or one of his henchmen," Cisco said impatiently. "Now get to the blood before I bury my fist in that fat gut of yours and grab your spine."

"Okay, the blood," Walsh said, unperturbed. "As we expected, Justice left no prints in or on the limo. That took me a while to ascertain for sure because I had to go all the way out to Oyster Bay Cove to take elimination prints from the ambassador . . ."

"Does that have anything to do with the blood?" Cisco asked in a way that made McKenna get ready to grab him.

"I found most of it in the right front door well of the limo," Walsh said at last.

"Most of it? Was there a lot?" McKenna asked.

"By my standards, quite a bit. Four drops."

"And the rest? Where was it?"

"A small smear on the point where he cut himself. Less than a drop on a small piece of sharp metal that sticks out from one of the clamps that secures the armor plating to the inside of the door. Justice probably didn't realize it at the time, but he cut himself on it when he was attaching his bomb to the armor plating. Small cut. He was wearing gloves, so it's probably on his arm. While he was working, four drops dripped from his arm into the door well."

"So he does make mistakes," McKenna said.

"They all do. Small mistakes they don't realize they made. They usually go unnoticed, unless some smart detective has the foresight to request my assistance. Then that minuscule mistake is uncovered, and the crime is ultimately solved."

Cisco didn't want to hear any more, and neither did McKenna. They turned and headed for the church. Walsh, Messing, and his photographer followed. As he entered the church, McKenna saw a photo flash reflect from inside, so he knew the rest of Walsh's team was already at work.

Or so he thought. Inside, he found that one of the detectives in Walsh's team was taking a picture of the other two posed and smiling on either side of the biggest pile of money McKenna had ever seen in his police career. The pile of wrapped bills formed a cross, with the top of the ten-foot-long cross pointing to the poor box. A quick glance told McKenna that quite a few of the wrapped packets of bills were hundreds, but he also saw many packets of fifties, twenties, and even a few packets of ten-dollar bills.

McKenna couldn't venture a guess on how much money was there, but it didn't make sense to him. Justice had robbed major drug dealers, and those people conduct most of their drug acquisitions by paying with packets of hundred-dollar bills. Besides, Justice had robbed only hundreds of thousands of dollars, but the pile looked like it contained more than that in cash. Much more. "What do you think?" he asked Cisco.

"Millions, for sure, and we got a problem."

"Millions? Where would he get millions?"

"Only one place."

Then it came to McKenna. "De Sales! He got De Sales's stash."

"Has to be, and he beat us out of a great photo opportunity. I was sorta counting on us setting the new seizure record, but he was quicker," Cisco said, but he was smiling when he said it.

What's so funny about that? McKenna wondered. "Doesn't it bother you that he's been outpacing us since we got to town, and he's been going at it longer than us?"

"Sure it does. What doesn't bother me is what he's doing with the money he's making while he's running circles around us," Cisco said, nodding toward the pile. "You gotta admit, this is pretty classy."

McKenna searched his mind for a rebuttal, but couldn't come up with one. It is pretty classy, he finally was forced to admit to himself, so what do I tell Cisco? "Doesn't this guy ever get tired?"

"Nah, not when he's having so much fun."

With McKenna, Cisco, and Messing counting while Monsignor Lima kept track of the process, it still took them another hour to arrive at the total figure. Justice had left St. Cecilia's three million dollars even.

"Now what?" the monsignor asked.

"Now you have to get this money to a bank, and then you have to figure out what to do with it," McKenna replied.

"That's it?" he asked, obviously delighted. "There aren't any technical procedures I have to go through first?"

"None," Cisco said. "Like Justice said, use it to continue your good work."

"And use it I will. The church roof, the school roof, and the rectory roof are all leaking, so we'll get them fixed straight away. We'll hire more teachers so we can reduce class size. Of course, we'll have to give our old teachers a raise. They're such good people, and I know they've been working for peanuts," Monsignor Lima said, and McKenna watched him go into a sort of trance as he continued. "We'll finally be able to get some modern computers for the kids to learn on. We have only four now, and they're so old and outdated. We'll get the sisters a new car, one that works all the time. We'll get all the classrooms painted before school starts. We'll lower the tuition, and we'll be able to provide so many more scholarships for those parents who can't afford to pay. We'll simply have to . . ."

"Monsignor, does it bother you that this is drug money you'll be spending to implement your admirable plans?" Messing asked, breaking the monsignor's gleeful mood and evoking a thoughtful frown from him.

But it was only a moment before the smile returned. "Not if I look at it right. This money left our community the wrong way to do bad things, and now it came back the right way to do good things."

"Hold on. I gotta write that down," Messing said, and he fumbled in his pocket for his pen.

It was then that McKenna's cell phone rang. "He hit again," Brunette said.

"How many dead?" McKenna asked.

"Dead? None. He hit us worse than that. He's giving away money again. Congregation Beth El this time, Lower East Side. Division Street between East Broadway and Rivington."

Division Street? That's Cisco's synagogue, McKenna thought. If he liked St. Cecilia's, he's gonna love this. "Was the synagogue locked?"

"Locked up tight. Justice picked one of the locks, and locked the building when he left."

"Did anybody see him?"

"The rabbi sure didn't. Justice woke him up with a phone call a couple of hours ago, told him there was a surprise in his synagogue he'd love. Just like he told the monsignor, he told him to use the money as he saw fit to continue his good work. The rabbi went down, and he had a fit. Stacks of money piled up in the foyer."

"A couple of hours ago? Justice must've went there right after he left here."

"Looks that way."

"Why the delay before we found out?"

"The rabbi doesn't have a cardinal, so he called the

precinct. The sergeant took one look at the loot and called the duty captain. Then the duty captain called the only chief who didn't know I was working tonight, so it took a while before I got the word."

I bet that chief knows *now* that Brunette's working, and I'm sure it was a bad piece of news for him, McKenna thought. "So the press already knows about it?"

"I imagine so. The job went out as a radio run, and good reporters always listen in. The press is gonna love it because Justice had some fun while he was there. He arranged the money into a Star of David."

We're really in trouble, McKenna thought.

Before leaving St. Cecilia's, McKenna called the desk officer at the 25th Precinct and requested that he assign two cops to guard the money. No problem, and since the church had an account with Chase, he next called Dave Fitzsimmons at home. Fitzsimmons was a retired captain who headed the security department for Chase's New York operations. It took McKenna only seconds to convince him that Chase, of course, would be delighted to send an armored truck to pick up that large cash deposit for the monsignor.

Once Cisco heard about Justice's visit to his synagogue, he was anxious to get there. Messing had the jump on the story at St. Cecilia's, but he was way behind his colleagues covering the story at Beth El. Consequently, he also wanted to get to the synagogue fast, so McKenna granted his request for a ride downtown. His photographer would pack up his gear and take Messing's car down at a more leisurely pace.

Aside from skydiving, Cisco was the kind of guy who engaged in other potentially life-threatening pastimes such as cliff climbing, hang gliding, and scuba diving. Whatever he did, McKenna knew Cisco always managed to emerge from his fun unscathed. So as he drove with lights and sirens down the East River Drive at a terrifying speed, McKenna had to constantly remind himself that stock-car racing was another of Cisco's pastimes. Still, he wanted Cisco's total attention on the road in front of them, and he hoped Messing would delay any questions he might have for him about the old synagogue and his connection to it.

McKenna glanced into the backseat in time to catch Messing tightening up his seat belt. Messing was pale and wide-eyed, so McKenna expected no questions from him for a while. He was wrong; Messing was a reporter first and foremost, and it wasn't long before he conquered his fear and the questions began. McKenna was happy they were just background questions that required little thinking on Cisco's part, so Cisco kept his eyes and mind on the road. The sun had come up, and the rush-hour traffic was just beginning.

As it turned out, Cisco knew just about everything there was to know about Congregation Beth El and its history, and it seemed to McKenna that Messing wrote down just about everything Cisco said.

The synagogue had been built in the 1890s by the city's first big wave of Jewish emigrants who fled to America to escape the pogroms raging at the time in Russia and Eastern Europe. There was nothing architecturally significant about the synagogue; it was a simple building built by poor people to serve their religious and social needs in their new and sometimes hostile country. Within a few years the tenements of the Lower East Side became the city's principal Jewish neighborhood, and the congregation's membership slowly increased. Some prospered and left the neighborhood, but the high birth rate kept the congregation large.

Then, in the late 1940s, came the second large wave of Jewish immigration, which consisted of the survivors of the Holocaust, displaced persons fleeing the devastation of Europe after World War II. Many were educated, well-to-do people, but all had lost everything to the Nazis. The population of the already crowded Lower East Side swelled, and the members of Congregation Beth El pitched in and did everything they could to help the new arrivals. Everyone got by for a few years, and then most prospered in the booming economy the United States enjoyed in the 1950s. Queens and the suburbs were developed, and the new houses set on tree-lined streets beckoned to the Jews of the Lower East Side.

By the 1960s the neighborhood had changed, and those who left were replaced by a new wave of immigrants from Puerto Rico. Most who stayed were the survivors of the concentration camps, people without families who were content to remain and live out their days among their friends from the Old Country. Congregation Beth El fell by default to them, and the congregation shrunk as, one by one, death claimed its members.

By 1995 there were only nine left, and they had a problem. Under Jewish law they needed a quorum of ten people to hold services, and that's when Cisco, a Cuban Jew, heard of their plight. He left his congregation and joined theirs. Since that time, he had attended the funerals of five of the old members, but he had managed by hook or crook to recruit replacements to keep the quorum going for the four remaining old-timers.

McKenna had always wondered why Cisco attended the old, decidedly unfashionable synagogue located at least a mile from his apartment, but he had never asked. Cisco's account, therefore, was all news to him, and it left him with a few perplexing questions.

Cisco knew McKenna and had noticed his pensive mood. "What's on your mind?" he asked.

McKenna would have preferred to wait until they left the East River Drive in order to discuss the matter at a slower speed, but that was no longer possible. "Why do you think Justice gave all that money to that synagogue?"

"What? You'd be happier if he gave it to another Catholic church?" Cisco replied defensively.

"That's not what I'm asking. I don't mind if he spreads it around, but why that particular synagogue?"

"Because he could see it needed help, and you'll agree when you see the building. Needs lots of work, makes St. Cecilia's look like Notre Dame."

"Does the synagogue have a school?"

"Not for the past thirty years. No kids."

"Does the congregation do anything special for the neighborhood?"

"Those old folks? Not much energy left, and I don't think they ever had much money to give. They help each other out as much as they can, though."

"How old is the youngest?"

"That'd be the rabbi. Someplace in his late seventies, early eighties."

"And what happens after the last one kicks off? Are you and your recruits going to keep the congregation going?"

"Before this, probably not. Sooner or later, that synagogue would've fallen down around our ears."

"But now?"

"Don't know," Cisco said, and McKenna could see that he hadn't given the matter any thought. "I guess it depends on how much Justice left, and how much is left over after we make the building habitable again."

"Suppose he left three million. How much would it take to fix the building?"

"To keep it plain and simple, no more than a couple of hundred thousand."

"So what do you do with the rest?"

"I dunno. I think it has to stay in the neighborhood, but there's no other synagogues close by. Maybe we'd wind up giving it to one of the churches."

"So that brings me back to my point," McKenna said. "Why'd he give to that particular synagogue? St. Cecilia's is kinda famous in Spanish Harlem, and anybody could see the church needed help. But even without Justice's gift, it's still a going concern that would've gone on serving the neighborhood for many more years. Not so your synagogue, and anybody who knows it would know that."

Cisco gave the matter some thought before answering. "Good point. I can't figure out why he did it."

"Me neither, but from what we know about him, he does everything for a reason that's well thought out."

Messing came up with a reason as Cisco slowed down and got off the East River Drive at the Houston Street exit.

"Maybe Justice knows somebody in the congregation, and he wants to make the old geezer and his pals happy for their last days."

A variation of that explanation had also crossed McKenna's mind, but it wasn't one he wanted to think about.

FOURTEEN

Since McKenna didn't want it to appear that Messing was getting preferential treatment, Cisco parked a block away from the synagogue to allow Messing to get there ahead of them. From their vantage point they saw the crowd of reporters hanging out in front of the synagogue part to let Messing climb the steps, only to be stopped at the door by a uniformed sergeant. He then rejoined his colleagues and was immediately the focus of their attention.

"You know what they're all waiting for?" Cisco asked.

"Yeah. They're planning a barbecue, and I'm the chicken they're gonna grill."

"Yeah, your 'Justice is just a murderous thief out only for himself' theory has been put to the torch, and they're gonna roast you good."

"I need an out, something to distract them and keep them off my back. Any ideas?"

"Titillate them. First tell them about St. Cecilia's."

Had to do that anyway, McKenna thought, but how does that help? If anything, telling them about that other three million Justice gave away makes me look even dopier. "And then? What do I add that will distract them?"

"That later today the great Detective McKenna and his even greater partner are gonna tell them where Justice got all his money from, and that we'll probably uncover another murder in the process."

"Another murder?"

"The murder of an innocent—sort of."

"Who?"

"De Sales had a live-in boyfriend, didn't he?"

He's right, McKenna thought. If Justice ransacked De Sales's house to get the loot, what happened to the boyfriend? Murdered, most likely, and still there. "Suppose Justice kept his loot stashed in his apartment? The boyfriend lives at the house, right?"

"Right. You have to hope he kept it at the house."

"And then suppose De Sales didn't keep his loot at his apartment or at his house. I'd look like a fool."

"A fool? That's putting it mildly."

I had to ask, didn't I? McKenna thought.

"Be a man and roll the dice, Sissypants," Cisco insisted.

"You sure this is the way to go?"

"Not certain, but any beating later is always better than a beating now."

"Okay, I'll go with it," McKenna said. He took out his phone, and dialed Chmil. "Where are you?" McKenna asked.

"Still at work."

That surprised McKenna. "Doing what?"

"Doing what you wanted me to do. Interviewing witnesses from the Classon Hotel, and running down the other three notches on Ramsey's rifle."

"Making any progress?"

"Got a married couple, but not married to each other, who saw him in the stairwell."

"Would they be able to recognize him if they saw him again?"

"They say they can. He's a bruiser, no neck. Scary-looking guy, but he gave them a smile and a 'Good evening' when he passed them."

"How old?"

"That's where they don't jibe. He says fortyish, she says maybe fifty-five, sixty."

"That's a big difference," McKenna noted. "Sketch?"

"Took them to the Artists Unit. Had a different artist for each witness. There's some differences in the sketches, but you can see it's the same guy."

So we're doing pretty good, McKenna thought. The age differences they give him are a problem, but not a big one. With the blood Walsh found and these two witnesses, once we get Justice ID'd, we have enough to collar him. "How about the three old notches on Ramsey's rifle?"

"Got them all accounted for, and I think he was a contract killer for drug dealers before he went to the slammer the last time. Always worked as a sniper. Matched the bullets to a killing in Coney Island, one in Yonkers, and another in Peekskill. All the victims had priors for sale of drugs. We're gonna be closing homicide cases all over the state."

"Great!" McKenna said. Yeah, just great, he thought. "Did you get the address of De Sales's Freeport place?"

"Piece of cake. Phone there is listed in his name. Both his places have fashionable addresses. His Brooklyn apartment is in a building off Grand Army Plaza, and his Freeport house is on the water off Atlantic Avenue."

"Where are De Sales's keys?"

"Property Room, Seven-Nine Precinct."

"You feel up to staying at it for a while longer?"

"As long as I get a nap someplace in the middle. I'm beat, been working since four yesterday afternoon."

"You'll get one, I promise, but first go get the keys. Get right out to Freeport and try the keys on the house."

"Why the rush?" Chmil asked.

"Turn on a radio and listen to the news. Justice has been giving away De Sales's millions. Gave to a church and a synagogue, so far, and I don't think he's done yet. If none of the keys fit the Freeport locks, we think De Sales's dead boyfriend might be rotting in the house."

"Killed by Justice?"

"Uh-huh."

"Makes sense. Is that what we're gonna use as the basis for a search warrant?"

"That, and Justice's letter to Messing. He's already proven himself a reliable informant, so it'll be easy for us to convince a judge that De Sales was an actively engaged major drug dealer. The warrant should also list drugs and proceeds from the sale of drugs as the items we're looking for."

"Sounds good. I'll be in touch."

McKenna next called Brunette to tell him his plan to deal with the press. "Great idea," Brunette said after he heard it. "While you're telling them why they're gonna love you tonight, please don't mention my name."

"You think it's that risky?" McKenna asked.

"You're in for a spanking this morning from them, but it won't be that bad. If you're right about the loot and the boyfriend, the next time you talk to them you'll look like Sherlock Holmes."

"And if I'm wrong?"

"They'll pound you into mush, of course," Brunette replied. "Did you get a chance to look at that plane-bombing file yet?"

"Not yet."

"How about Cisco? Did he look at the internal-investigation file yet?"

"He started it, but I'm sure he's not finished yet."

"Don't take this the wrong way. I know you guys have been busy, and you both must be beat by now," Brunette said. "I also appreciate that you're handling the press and keeping the pressure off me, but I can't hide forever. This case calls for a press conference by me soon, and it'll get national coverage. We're on the defensive, and I need some answers for the press that put us on offense."

McKenna understood Brunette's plight, and he didn't feel slighted by his friend's implied request to try harder. "We'll get to those files, Ray, and I hope we'll have those answers for you."

"What'd he say?" Cisco asked after McKenna ended the call.

"Keep up the good work."

There were many police cars parked outside the synagogue, and McKenna noticed a chief's unmarked car. He also noticed that the synagogue was in bad shape: The roof was sagging, a few of the upper windows were broken and covered with plastic sheeting, and the exterior of the grimy yellow brick building was in need of a sandblasting.

With Cisco smiling graciously at his side, on their way into the synagogue McKenna issued a series of "No comments" to all the reporters' shouted questions, but he did promise them he would have something to say once he was briefed on what was going on inside. The sergeant opened the door for them, and McKenna saw why the reporters were being kept outside. The money was right there, stacked on the floor to form a Star of David so large that they had to hug the walls of the foyer to get by it. Just as in the case of St. Cecilia's, a quick glance told McKenna that many of the packets of wrapped bills were hundreds and fifties, but there were many more wrapped packets of twenty- and ten-dollar bills. Four uniformed cops and another sergeant were at the interior doors leading to the foyer, guarding the loot.

Chief Rowe was once again the man in charge, and he was at the front of the synagogue talking to a frail-looking, elderly, bearded man whom McKenna assumed was the rabbi. As soon as the rabbi saw Cisco, he left the chief without a word and rushed forward to greet him with a hug. Cisco responded, hugging the rabbi while they patted each other's backs. "Cisco, so good to see you," the rabbi said. "Isn't it wonderful what that man did for us?"

"Let me go and I'll tell you," Cisco replied.

"You first."

Cisco released the rabbi, and then the rabbi released him. "Yes, it is wonderful," Cisco replied. "It's almost a shame that we have to find him, lock him up, and throw away the key."

"Will you be able to do that?"

"Of course."

"Well, when you do, please give him our heartfelt thanks for his generosity."

"I'll be sure to do that," Cisco said, and then introduced

McKenna to Rabbi Shlomo Green. "So good to finally meet you, Detective McKenna," the rabbi said. "I've heard so much about you."

"From Cisco?"

"Yes, he speaks very highly of you. Says you're turning out to be a fine detective."

"So nice of him to say so. I'm trying hard, and under his guidance, how could I go wrong?"

"You can't," the rabbi said. "I expect we'll be able to keep the money?"

"What did Chief Rowe tell you?"

"He said he thought it likely, but the final decision is yours. He said it's your case, and you're in charge."

"You can keep the money."

"God bless you, Detective McKenna."

"He always does."

McKenna then noticed that Rowe was waiting for him, so he left Cisco with the rabbi. "Seems you're working a lot of hours, Chief," McKenna noted.

"My choice, happens a couple of times a month," Rowe said. "Get assigned as the late-tour duty chief for the city, so I usually do a double."

So Rowe must be the chief who didn't notify Ray about this, McKenna thought. "How's it going, Chief?"

"Not so good. Who'd expect your pal to be in his office at five in the morning?"

"Don't sweat it; it'll pass. This case has him under a lot of pressure."

"It's already passed. He was a little harsh with me, but then he called an hour later to apologize. Pretty big of him, I think."

"I've found that, given enough time, he'll always do the right thing."

Walsh arrived with his team, and it took him only an hour as the cameras clicked to discover that Justice had entered the synagogue by picking a padlock securing a steel door that led to the basement.

With the help of four uniformed cops, it took McKenna
and Cisco another two hours of counting to find it was a repeat performance. As he had at St. Cecilia's, Justice had left
three million even for Congregation Beth El. The amount of
time it took them to count the money led McKenna to an unpleasant realization. Justice wasn't giving away the money
as a reaction to the nasty things McKenna had said about
him at the press conference; he was only one man, and he
wouldn't have had the time after the press conference to
count out the exactly three-million-dollar gifts for St. Cecilia's and Congregation Beth El, and then deliver them. No,
McKenna concluded, giving the money away was and always had been Justice's plan.

Messing had filed his St. Cecilia's story in time for it to
make the *Post*'s morning edition, and the paper was already
out, so that gift from Justice was no longer a secret for the
rest of the reporters gathered outside. They had all been
scooped—which always makes reporters angry—and
McKenna knew they had to suspect Messing had done it
with his connivance. It would be a painful press conference,
so McKenna hoped to make it as short as possible.

When he was ready to start, McKenna opened the synagogue's front door a crack and took a peek outside. There
were two dozen reporters out there, including three TV news
crews set to broadcast live. All were looking at him peeking
at them. McKenna closed the door and took three deep
breaths.

If McKenna had expected any sympathy from his partner,
Cisco's derisive smile told him he wasn't getting any. "Want
me to go out and check them for rotten tomatoes and anything else they can throw at you?"

"No thanks, but kind of you to offer," McKenna said.
Then he opened the door and stepped into the sunlight.
Cisco, of course, stayed inside. McKenna stood on the stairs,
and before a question could be asked, he began by stating he
had been wrong about Justice's motives. Justice was not
killing drug dealers for personal profit. He had given three
million to St. Cecilia's, another three million to Congrega-

tion Beth El, and McKenna told them he now thought that Justice had always intended to give away whatever money he stole from the drug dealers he killed. He ended his statement by telling them he expected Justice would give away even more, probably to other religious institutions.

"How much more?" was the first shouted question.

"I can't say for sure. Three million, six million, maybe even nine million," McKenna replied.

"That has to be more than he took from the drug dealers he killed in Brooklyn and Uptown, isn't it?" was the next shouted question.

"Much more."

"And much more than he could've taken when he killed Gaston Cruz?"

"Yes, he's already given away much more than he could have taken at the scenes of all the crimes we know about."

"So where's he getting it from?"

"That matter is under investigation."

The next question came from Messing. "Do you think you know where he's getting it from?"

"Yes."

"Are you going to tell us?"

"Not yet."

"When?"

"If I'm right, there will be another press conference tonight. I'll tell you at that time where he's been getting all this money from," McKenna said, and then he asked himself the big question: I'm already out on a limb and the branch is shaking, so should I climb way out? I look like a dope either way if this doesn't work out, he decided. "In addition, if I'm right, I expect to uncover evidence of another murder Justice has committed."

"Another drug dealer?" one of the TV reporters asked.

"No, an innocent."

"Totally innocent?"

"I expect it's someone who might've had knowledge of some aspects of the drug trade, but if so, he took no part in it."

"Then why did Justice kill him?"

"He killed this innocent to make it easier for him to get the money he's been giving away."

There were more shouted questions, most of them concerning the identity of this innocent, and McKenna decided to answer just one more.

"If he's not killing them for profit, what's his motive?" was shouted by a reporter from the *Daily News*.

"Revenge."

"Revenge for what?"

"When we figure it out, we'll be that much closer to catching him," McKenna replied.

It was then that Cisco finally emerged from the synagogue. "You did good, as good as could be expected," he whispered to McKenna. "Now it's time to cut bait and run."

McKenna agreed. Together, they walked down the steps and through the crowd of reporters, ignoring all the questions. They left the throng behind, and halfway expected to be followed as they headed for their car, but they weren't.

Messing knew where their car was parked, so he didn't have to follow them. McKenna hadn't seen him leave the front of the synagogue, but there he was, leaning against their car, waiting.

"Very good, Brian," Messing said. "You changed their whole focus from beating you up now to really pummeling you tonight."

"Yeah. Thanks, Phil. We're real geniuses," McKenna said. "Make sure you're there for the fun tonight."

"Tonight? I don't think I have to wait for my fun."

"Yes, you do. You see how mad they are at us already because we let you scoop them?"

"And they're gonna be even madder," Messing said cheerfully. "Who's this innocent, and where are we going?"

"Get off the car, Phil," Cisco said. "We're getting outta here."

"So we're not sharing anymore?"

"Sure we are," McKenna said. "You'll know what I'm gonna say before I say it tonight, but not much before."

"So that's the deal?"

"Yes."

"Too bad. Then I guess you'll know what Justice's letter to me says before it's printed in tomorrow's paper—but not much before."

Damn! I figured he already sent Messing another letter, but I forgot all about it, McKenna thought. "Where is this letter?"

"My editor tells me another one of those white envelopes with the computer-printed address is waiting for me on my desk."

Cisco unlocked the door Messing was leaning against. "Get in, Phil."

FIFTEEN

Although most of the reporters in town strongly suspected Messing had official help on his story, McKenna didn't think it necessary to confirm it with Messing's editor. Therefore, he sent Messing into the *Post*'s building for the letter while he and Cisco remained parked outside.

McKenna settled into his seat to take a catnap until Messing returned. Cisco woke him when Joe Walsh and his team pulled up behind them. Walsh got out of the van and walked to McKenna's window.

McKenna thought Walsh looked much worse than usual. He needed a shave, his pants and shirt were wrinkled and spotted with fingerprint powder, his jacket smelled of sweat, and his bloodshot eyes and the bags under them illustrated his fatigue. "How you guys holding up?" he asked.

"Tired, but still functioning," McKenna replied.

"You two look beat to shit, and I'm done for, too," Walsh said. "After I dust Messing's new letter and envelope, I'm going home and going to bed."

"For how long?"

"Until I wake up on my own."

"If you sleep long enough, chances are you'll miss some good photo opportunities."

"I don't care if they want me to pose for the cover of *Time*," Walsh said, and McKenna could see it hurt him to say it. "I'm going home, and staying a while."

· · ·

By the time Messing came out with the envelope, Walsh was back in his van and taking a nap with his head on the dashboard. Messing got in the backseat, dropped the envelope in McKenna's lap, and took off the pair of latex gloves McKenna had given him. He passed the gloves forward, and McKenna put them on.

The envelope was identical to the last one Justice had sent Messing, but it was the postmark that held McKenna's attention. It was stamped July 16, the day before he blew up Ramon Garcia and his crew in Spanish Harlem.

McKenna opened up the envelope and read the letter. As expected, the message for Messing was succinct, literate, and to the point:

> *Dear Mr. Messing:*
> *As you know by now, I intend to put Ramon Garcia out of business. This will necessarily involve killing him and an as yet undetermined number of his hirelings. Rest assured that, whatever the opposition, I will continue my work for some time. For your information, listed below in columns are the dates of transactions, the quantities and types of drugs obtained, and the prices paid by Garcia during his dealings with Gaston Cruz.*

As he had in his last letter to Messing, Justice had signed it in red ink.

McKenna saw at once that Garcia had been an even bigger dealer than De Sales, and the amounts of drugs he had purchased from Cruz were higher. In fourteen separate transactions, including Garcia's last fatal purchase, he had bought from Cruz 28 kilos of heroin and 168 kilos of cocaine for a total of $5,880,000.

Messing had been reading over McKenna's shoulder and was ready with a math test. "How much did De Sales pay Cruz for the stuff he bought?"

"Roughly four and a half million," McKenna replied.

"And we figured De Sales made what on that? Thirteen million in profit?"

"Give or take a million."

"And here we have Garcia buying even more from Cruz than De Sales did. Almost a million and a half dollars more."

"Don't ask the question, and I'll give you the answer," McKenna said.

"Okay, let's see how good you are."

Messing took out his pen and scribbled numbers on his hand while McKenna did the math on the cover of his notepad. Messing finished as McKenna was still working his way through the proportion formula he had learned in Catholic school long ago. Then Messing hummed and pointedly glanced at his watch whenever he caught McKenna looking. It took McKenna another two minutes to finish, and then he quickly rechecked his figures. "Garcia made about seventeen million dollars' profit for himself in the last fourteen months," he announced.

"Seventeen million? That sounds about right," Messing said, checking his hand.

"*About* right? What number did you come up with?"

"No number. Brian, for the past ten years I haven't been able to balance my checkbook even once."

McKenna, Cisco, and Messing were finishing breakfast in a diner near the *Post* building when Chmil called again. "How'd we make out?" McKenna asked, and he closed his eyes for the answer.

"Maybe great," Chmil replied. "None of the keys fit any of the doors, and the back door is unlocked."

McKenna opened his eyes, and said a small prayer of thanks. "Could you see inside?"

"Levolor blinds on all the downstairs windows, closed, but I could see inside the kitchen from the back-door window. Big kitchen, looks like nothing's outta place."

"What kind of house is it?"

"Nice neighborhood, but De Sales had himself the nicest place on the block. Big house, two stories, maybe twenty years old, but it looks like it's been totally renovated recently. Oversize lot on a canal, big cabin cruiser up on an electric davit, three-car garage."

"Any cars in the garage?"

"I'm way ahead of you. Vintage Land Rover, fully restored. I ran the plate, found it's registered to an Ismael Bopp at this address. Male, Asian, twenty-six years old."

"Any signs of life at the house?"

"The house has got central air, and the air conditioner on the side of the house is humming. Also, the lawn sprinkler system was watering the back lawn when I got here, but it's off now. Works on a timer, I think. Aside from that, nothing."

"Alarm system?"

"There's a sign on the front lawn from Sentry Alarms saying the house is protected, and I'd guess it is."

If I'm right, that should make no difference to us, McKenna thought. Either the alarm was off, or Justice bypassed it when he entered to take De Sales's loot and, incidentally, kill boyfriend Bopp. "Do you know where their courts are out there?"

"Sure. Mineola, maybe a half hour from here."

"Start heading there, and I'll call you back."

"When do I get my nap?" Chmil asked.

"Soon."

Next McKenna called Brunette. As it turned out, Brunette knew both the Nassau County District Attorney and the Nassau County police commissioner. He promised that when Chmil arrived at the Nassau County DA's office, he would be escorted through the cumbersome search-warrant process.

McKenna called Chmil back with the news. After he got the warrant, they would all meet in the parking lot of the Freeport Police Department's station house.

Neither McKenna nor Cisco knew exactly where the Freeport police station was located, but Messing did. He took his car, with McKenna and Cisco following. It was only a forty-five-minute trip, and McKenna planned to nap on the way, but then Cisco fell asleep at a traffic light before they even left Manhattan. McKenna woke him up with a forced cough, and spent the rest of the trip watching Cisco. When they arrived, Cisco parked in the lot behind the police station.

McKenna knew they both desperately needed a nap, but then Cisco surprised him when he took the internal-investigation folder from his briefcase and began studying it. Not to be outdone, McKenna began reading the DEA's file on the investigation of the plane bombing, but he found it difficult to concentrate. After two readings of the first five pages, the overview of the investigation, he knew that the DEA, in conjunction with the FAA and with some help from the Panamanian and the Guatemalan national police forces, had been able to draw no firm conclusions. The overview report, however, was rife with suspicions that placed the bombing at Gaston Cruz's door.

The report described Consuela Andersen as an accomplished pilot who was bilingual in Spanish and English. When she had four years' experience with the DEA, she went undercover in Panama, masquerading as Consuela Cook, a Belize national with an identity and documentation provided by the DEA. This documentation included a legitimate Belize pilot's license and driver's license in her Cook name, and her identity came with a history contrived in court records by the DEA. If anyone checked, Cook had a conviction in Florida for sale of cocaine. The records stated she was an illegal alien in the United States, and after serving five months of a six-month sentence in the Dade County Jail, she was released and deported back to Belize.

Three months after Consuela went undercover, the DEA was delighted when someone *did* check Cook's arrest record and her pilot's license. The investigation was done by a Miami-based PI after she had applied for a pilot's position with Aviones Turísticas y Cargas, a Panama-based air charter service suspected by the DEA of being a front for drug running into Mexico and the United States.

The report didn't go into many specifics of her employment with the air service, but it did note a few items McKenna found interesting. One was Andersen's awards: During her assignment she was cited once for bravery and once for extreme dedication to duty. The other was that her fatal flight was her third drug-running excursion as a copilot to remote, improvised airstrips in Sonora Province in Northern Mexico, and all were described as orientation flights for her. It had been anticipated by her superiors in the DEA that she would pilot solo her next trip to Sonora.

The DEA was able to monitor by radar most of Consuela's last flight. As happened on her previous two flights, they landed at a clandestine airstrip in El Salvador to refuel, and the FAA investigators speculated that was where the small bomb was attached to the tail section of the plane. It was found to be a timed device, and it exploded over the jungles of Guatemala half an hour after the plane took off again. The bodies of Consuela, the pilot, and most pieces of the plane were found, along with much of the cargo, estimated to be half a ton of cocaine. The FAA's investigation disclosed that the explosion had caused the tail section to separate from the main fuselage of the plane. Exploded C-4 residue was found and determined to be part of the shipment of explosives and blasting caps that had been sent to the Colombian Army.

Consuela's body was released to her family for burial, but since the DEA had another agent infiltrated into Aviones Turísticas y Cargas whose role would be jeopardized if it were known Consuela was an agent, the family agreed to a small, private burial without publicity. However, for a month there were no suspects in the bombing. The DEA and the El Salvadoran police conducted a raid on the airstrip where the refueling had taken place, and they found it deserted. Then a series of additional tragedies befell Aviones Turísticas y Cargas. While two of their planes were being unloaded in Sonora, the airstrip was attacked by a large group of heavily armed, masked gunmen. After one Aviones employee was killed in the ensuing firefight, the rest fled, and the gunmen burned the planes and the cargo before vanishing into the desert. The next day the Noriega government suspended the operating license of Aviones Turísticas y Cargas and grounded its planes. When the suspension was lifted two weeks later after a deal had been made with officials of the company, Gaston Cruz was the new government-approved man in charge of it.

That was when Cruz had first appeared on the DEA's screens, and it was speculated—but never proven—that he was behind the destructive campaign against Aviones Turísticas y Cargas that led to his installation.

Cruz began his tenure by immediately firing and replacing all employees of the company, including the remaining DEA agent. He next added new, bigger, and faster planes to the company's remaining fleet, and then he resumed operations, presumably under Noriega's protection.

The DEA was never again able to infiltrate the company, but they watched from a distance, and with mounting anger and frustration as Cruz apparently expanded and improved the company's legal operations as well as its illicit side. He ensured his employees' loyalty by paying them extremely well, and the DEA received reports that he had constructed many additional remote airstrips in El Salvador, Guatemala, and Mexico. His pilots were also better and more daring than the replaced pilots; they flew lower through the mountains to avoid and confuse radar detection as they headed north, and they rigged their cargo so that it could be unloaded in just minutes. The DEA was not even close to mounting a successful prosecution against Cruz by the time he left Panama and moved to New York.

So Jorge told Justice where Cruz stored his explosives, McKenna concluded. Probably the same place he stored his drugs, and maybe this DEA investigation needs another look.

McKenna didn't realize he had fallen asleep until Chmil woke him with a knock on his window. Cisco had also fallen asleep with his file on his lap, and he didn't wake up until McKenna rolled down the window.

Chmil looked beat and ready to fall asleep on his feet as he leaned against the top of the car. "How'd you make out?" McKenna asked.

Chmil held up the search warrant. "Easiest warrant I ever got. Had plenty of help, and I don't think it took half an hour, start to finish."

"Then let's get started." McKenna got out of the car and saw that Messing was asleep behind the wheel of his car, snoring with his mouth open. He and Chmil walked into the police station, showed the desk officer the search warrant, and told him they would be executing it immediately. The desk officer offered his department's assistance, and they tried politely declining, but they wound up with a uniformed two-man Freeport Police unit assigned to them. The desk officer contacted his unit by radio and told them to meet McKenna in the parking lot.

Cisco was napping again behind the wheel when McKenna and Chmil got back outside. Since Chmil didn't feel up to driving again, he decided he would ride with McKenna and Cisco, and they would drop him off at his car after executing the warrant. He climbed into the backseat and began his own nap.

Messing was also still asleep, and while waiting for the Freeport unit McKenna saw an opportunity. Messing would keep his jump on the story, but McKenna didn't want him around De Sales's house until he knew just what the story was. He wrote a note telling Messing he would call him after the police work was done, and left it on Messing's windshield.

SIXTEEN

Cisco parked in De Sales's driveway, and the Freeport cops pulled in next to them. The house was set up perfectly for Justice. The property was edged on the front and sides by a six-foot-high hemlock hedge that gave him the privacy to accomplish his mission with little fear of detection by De Sales's neighbors, and the canal in back ended at the house.

Chmil hadn't opened his eyes or even budged during the ride, and McKenna saw no reason to disrupt the nap he had promised him. He and Cisco left him sleeping in the backseat, and they decided to check the garage first. The Freeport cops waved, but made no move to get out of their car.

The garage side door was unlocked, and as Chmil had said, the old, completely restored Land Rover was there, occupying the first bay of the three-car garage. What Chmil hadn't mentioned occupied the rest of the garage. There was a pallet loaded with Sheetrock, another loaded with two-by-six wood beams, and a variety of tools, including a bench saw, an air compressor, and a pneumatic nail gun. On the far wall hung a large assortment of hand tools, neatly arranged on a Peg-Board. The tools all looked fairly new, but the sawdust on the bench saw indicated they had been used.

"This doesn't make sense," Cisco said. "A major drug dealer who's also a handyman?"

"There's enough lumber and Sheetrock here to finish the interiors of two good-size rooms," McKenna noted, "but the two-by-sixes don't make sense, either. You usually use two-by-fours to frame interior walls."

"You would, unless you wanted extra space in your walls."

Extra space for what? McKenna almost asked, but then he noticed he was getting that Cisco I-know-something-you-don't smile. That caused him to rethink his question, and then he came up with a plausible answer. "Yeah, extra space if you plan to hide millions in cash in your walls."

"I think we're heading into a very messy house. Let's go see how smart we are."

McKenna followed Cisco to the rear door. As Chmil had said, it was unlocked, but as soon as they entered they saw things in the kitchen he hadn't been able to see from outside. It was a large modern kitchen, with stainless steel and black marble as the main décor features, but there were round holes punched in the bottom of every exposed wall, and plaster dust covered the floor. There were many footprints in the dust, and Cisco put his foot next to one of them. The footprints were a little larger than Cisco's shoe. "What's your shoe size?" McKenna asked.

"Ten and a half."

"So he's what? Eleven, eleven and a half?"

"Yeah, but that tells us nothing. We already know he's big and strong," Cisco said, and then he pointed to the ceiling. "Ever see a residential home with a commercial sprinkler system installed?"

McKenna looked up and saw the four sprinkler heads protruding from the kitchen ceiling. "No, but it makes sense. If you buried millions in your walls, would you want to take a chance with fire?"

"No. So what does this room tell us?"

"The same thing it told Justice after he checked by knocking holes in the walls in here, probably with a hammer. De Sales was handy, but not handy enough to renovate a kitchen by himself. He hired a contractor to do it, so there was no money in the walls here."

"What do you wanna do first? See where it was, or find the body?"

"No rush, we'll come across Bopp in our travels. Let's go room by room till we find him."

Adjoining the kitchen through a swinging door was the dining room, and it was immediately apparent that De Sales had had lots of cash hidden in the walls of that large room before Justice got to it. Every wall had been pulled down to reveal the two-by-six studs De Sales had used to frame out the room, and chunks of Sheetrock and a layer of plaster dust covered the floor. Once again, the room was protected by sprinklers mounted in the ceiling, and there were many footprints outlined in the dust.

"Think you could hide a couple of million in those walls?" Cisco asked.

"We know he did."

They walked through the first floor of the house, finding the living room, the den, an office, and a bedroom in the same shape as the dining room. The walls of the downstairs bathroom, however, were intact, but Justice had checked them by punching a series of holes in them.

Upstairs, McKenna and Cisco found that Justice hadn't punched any holes in the hallway walls, and when they opened the first door they learned why. It was a bedroom, and the walls had been attacked from that side. All four had been pulled down by Justice, and the room was in the same partially demolished state as the rooms downstairs.

Cisco led the way to the next room. He opened the door, looked in, and then quickly closed it. "Brace yourself," he told McKenna. "I have some real bad news for you."

"What?"

"Good for him, bad for you. Bopp's in there, and he's alive."

"Damn!" McKenna was surprised to hear himself say. He pushed open the door, and there was Ismael Bopp, very uncomfortable but alive. He was wearing red silk pajamas and lying on his side on the floor next to the bed amid the pieces of shattered Sheetrock littering the room, his hands were secured somehow behind his back, and he was tightly wrapped in rope from his ankles to his elbows. There was a piece of duct tape across his mouth, but his eyes were wide open as he stared at McKenna with a mixture of hope and fear on his face. McKenna guessed he was either Indonesian or Filipino, and probably good-looking before his ordeal had begun, but McKenna thought *pretty* would be a more accurate word than *handsome*. Although he was covered in plaster dust, McKenna thought his long, straight black hair ordinarily had a lustrous shine, and he had the wiry build of an athlete.

"In his own way, De Sales wasn't doing bad for himself," Cisco commented.

McKenna took out his shield and held it up for Bopp to see. "We're the police, and we're here to help you."

The fear left Bopp's face, and he nodded his understanding.

McKenna looked up and saw that this bedroom was also protected by the sprinkler system. It was the master bedroom, and to his left he saw it had its own bathroom. He could see the punched holes in the bathroom walls, but they were otherwise intact. He then stood over Bopp, reached down, and pulled the tape from his mouth. Bopp immediately tried to say something, but his tongue was too swollen from thirst to speak.

"Don't worry," McKenna said. "We'll talk as soon as we get you untied and get you some water. But first, just try to answer one question for me. Are you Ismael Bopp?"

Bopp nodded. Cisco took out his Swiss Army knife and began cutting through the rope. Then he gave the knife to McKenna and went downstairs to get Bopp something to drink, leaving to McKenna the job of completing Bopp's release. Once he had all the rope cut and removed, he used the knife to cut the plastic strip securing Bopp's wrists behind his back. Bopp's hands were deep red, his fingers were swollen, and he still didn't move after McKenna had him completely free to do so.

Cisco returned with two cans of vanilla Slim-Fast. "We can kill two birds with one stone. It's cold and wet, and drinking this stuff might get him feeling better."

"I'm not sure it's the right thing to do in his condition, but we'll let him have it if he wants."

Cisco put the cans on the nightstand and brushed the pieces of shattered Sheetrock off the bed.

"I don't think he can move," McKenna said. "His circulation must be all screwed up."

"I already figured as much, so I talked to the Freeport cops and told them to get an ambulance here," Cisco said. "While we're waiting, let's see if we can walk him around a bit to get his legs going."

"That's worth a try."

Together, they lifted Bopp to his feet. At first, Bopp wasn't able to stand on his own, so McKenna and Cisco held him up by his elbows and guided him around the large, plaster-strewn bedroom until he was able to move his legs. Then they sat him on the bed and massaged his arms until he was able to move them as well.

"You wanna try drinking some Slim-Fast now?" McKenna asked, and Bopp enthusiastically nodded in reply. McKenna opened a can and put it in Bopp's hands, but he had to help him hold the can while he drank. When McKenna asked him if he wanted more, Bopp again nodded yes. He was regaining some strength, however, and was able to drink the second can on his own.

"Can you talk yet?" McKenna asked.

Bopp wet his lips with his tongue before he tried. "Yes, I can," he said softly, but his swollen tongue slurred his speech. "What day is it?"

"Friday," McKenna said.

"I thought so."

"How long have you been tied up?"

"I think it was early Wednesday morning. Two days. I'm still starving."

"I'm sure you are, but let's wait until we hear what a doctor has to say before you eat anything solid," McKenna suggested.

Bopp nodded.

"What happened in here?" Cisco asked, looking around the room.

"There was money in the walls, so much money," Bopp replied. "He took it all."

"You didn't know the walls were filled with money?"

"No. I was surprised, but he wasn't. He knew it was there."

"Do you know where the money came from?"

"It must be Ruben's. He's the one who did the house over, but I don't know where he could have gotten so much money."

"Do you know what Ruben does for a living?"

"He's some kind of a consultant. He gives rich people business advice, but I never imagined they paid him in cash."

"What do you do for a living?"

"I'm a graduate student."

"Where?"

"The School of Fashion and Design in the city."

"What are you studying?"

"Business administration, but as it applies to the fashion industry."

"Where are you from?"

"Manila, the Philippines."

"Are you going back?"

"I don't want to, but I have to go back when I finish school next year. I'm here on a student visa."

"When did Ruben do the renovations on the house?"

"This room he did last February after he sent me home during spring break."

"And the other rooms? Were you ever here while he was doing his renovations?"

"Never. Every time he sent me home, when I came back there were so many changes. It was always a surprise to me. I don't think he's that good with colors, but he certainly knows how to work with construction materials."

Bopp paused, and McKenna could see a question forming in his mind, one he didn't want to ask. McKenna didn't want him to ask it yet either, so he figured it was time to change the subject. "The man who did this to you and wrecked this place, could you recognize him if you saw him again?"

"Any place, any time."

"You saw his face?" McKenna asked.

"No. He was wearing a ski mask, but I'd still know him. He's black, very strong, and he has no neck. Just muscles."

"Was he wearing gloves?"

"Yes, rubber gloves. You know, the kind dentists wear."

"How did he get you tied up?"

"It was very early in the morning, and I got up to pee. When I came out of the bathroom, he was standing here with a gun in his hand. Biggest gun I've ever seen, and he had it pointed at my chest."

"A handgun?"

"Yes, but very complicated. It had something on the front, a silencer, I think, and some type of apparatus mounted on top."

"A laser sight?"

Bopp shrugged. "I wouldn't know."

"What happened next?"

"He told me to lie on the floor. I saw that he had already put all the rope on the bed, so I knew what he was going to do, and I was terrified. He must've seen that, because that's when he told me he wouldn't hurt me as long as I didn't resist. Oh, I forgot to mention. He has a very deep voice, but somehow he makes himself sound nice."

McKenna looked at Cisco in time to catch him smirking. He decided that this time he had the willpower to ignore Cisco, and returned his attention to Bopp. "Go on. What happened next?"

"Then he tied me up like you found me, so quick I couldn't believe it. Quick, like they tie up calves in the rodeo. It took you much longer to get me loose than it took him to tie me up."

"And then he left you on the floor?"

"No, he picked me up and put me on the bed. Picked me up so easy, like I weighed nothing."

"Did he say anything else to you?"

"Only when he was leaving."

"When was that?"

"Sometime Wednesday afternoon. Late afternoon, I think, because it got dark soon after."

"What did he say?"

"A few things. First he asked me if I required any medication on a daily basis, and I shook my head no."

"Damned nice of him to ask that, wouldn't you say?" Cisco asked.

McKenna didn't answer, but Bopp did. "I remember thinking at the time that, yes, that was a nice thing to ask me."

It was an answer McKenna didn't want to hear. "All right. What'd he tell you next?"

"That I'd probably be all right," Bopp replied, and then a look of embarrassment came over his face.

"You can tell us," McKenna said. "What else did he say to you?"

"That if the police were smart enough, they'd be here to get me by Friday at the latest. If not, he'd call them and tell them I was here."

"So it's Friday," Cisco said. "Friday the latest."

"Yes," Bopp replied, and he lowered his eyes.

"Meaning we're barely smart enough?"

"That's not what I said; it's what he said."

McKenna heard the siren of the approaching ambulance, but there were a few more questions he wanted to ask Bopp before he was treated by the ambulance crew. He nodded to Cisco, and Cisco knew what he meant. "Keep going. I'll take care of it," he said, and then left to delay the arrival of the ambulance crew. He closed the bedroom door behind him.

"Ismael, what did he do after he tied you up and put you on the bed?" McKenna asked.

"He ignored me. It was like I wasn't here. He tore this room up until he had it like you see it now."

"How long did that take him?"

"Not as long as you'd think. Like I said, he's very strong, and he works very fast. An hour, maybe. At first, I thought he was crazy when he hit the wall with the hammer. Then he pulled some of the wall down, and money fell out."

"Did you say anything to him?"

"I couldn't. He had that tape on my mouth."

"And then?"

"He just kept pulling the walls apart, and the money kept falling on the floor. He didn't touch it until he was done. Then he left and came back with big green trash bags. Put the money in, and threw the bags into the hallway."

"How many bags of money did he take out of this room?"

"He managed to fit it all in three bags, but he had to really squeeze it in."

"And then he left you?"

"Yes, but I knew he was still in the house. I could hear him tearing up the place for hours."

"And you didn't see him again until he left?"

"Not until he finally left the house, but I know he made lots of trips outside. I heard a door downstairs open and close many times right before he was getting ready to leave."

"And then? Did you hear his car when he left?"

"Not just then, and I don't think it was a car he had. The motor sounded deeper, like a truck's motor."

Makes sense, McKenna thought. He had too many bags of money to fit them all in a car. But he thought far enough ahead to bring a truck? "So do you have any idea what he was doing between the time he left the house and when you first heard the truck start?"

"He went into the garage, and he stayed there for about an hour."

"How would you know that?"

"I heard Ruben's air compressor go on in the garage. It's pretty loud, makes kind of a tinny sound, and the garage is right outside that window," Bopp said, nodding toward the window behind the bed. "I heard the compressor, but I couldn't imagine what he was doing with it."

"He was blowing the plaster dust off the money, taking

his time like he didn't have another care in the world," McKenna said.

"Really? He didn't appear to be a sloppy man, but he didn't strike me as the fastidious type."

"Maybe not by your standards, but he's fastidious enough by mine. And after the air compressor went off, you heard his truck?"

"Yes. I think he had it in the driveway."

"But you didn't hear it when he first pulled in?"

"No, it had to be while I was still sleeping. I'm a pretty sound sleeper."

"Can you think of anything else he did that might be important for us to know? Anything at all?"

McKenna could see that Bopp really was thinking, and it was a minute before he replied. "Something strange I forgot to mention, but I don't see how it could be important. Right before he left me the last time, he went through all the dresser drawers. Both Ruben's dresser and mine, and I couldn't imagine what he was looking for. After all, he already had all the money."

"Did Ruben keep any guns in the house?"

"I don't think so, and I never saw him with one."

Going through the dresser drawers? Not too strange, but what was he looking for? McKenna wondered. "When did you fall off the bed?"

"This morning, but I didn't fall. I rolled off on purpose, thought maybe I could somehow get the door open and get out of here. That's when I found out that I really couldn't move."

McKenna then saw the pensive look return to Bopp's face. "Okay, I'm done. Go ahead and ask, Ismael," he said. "I'll answer all the questions I can."

Bopp remained silent for a few moments, and McKenna knew he was carefully framing his words. "Is Ruben into something illegal?"

"Yes."

"Is it something to do with drugs?"

"Yes."

"Is he in trouble?"

"No."

"Is he all right?"

"No."

And there they were, at the question Bopp didn't want to ask—even though McKenna thought that by then Bopp already knew the answer. He watched as the young man quivered and his eyes filled with tears. "Is he dead?"

"Sorry, Ismael. Yes, he's dead, murdered by the same nice man who tied you up."

"I thought so," Bopp said softly. "Did he suffer?"

"Yes."

Bopp didn't say anything, and McKenna thought he was going to be all right. "Ruben! My Ruben!" Bopp suddenly wailed so loudly that he startled McKenna. Then he broke down, wailing uncontrollably while he beat his legs with his fists.

McKenna's heart went out to the picture of abject misery sitting on the bed in front of him. He got behind Bopp, patted his back, and tried every consoling phrase he knew. Bopp stopped pounding his legs, but he didn't stop crying, and he didn't stop shaking. Then McKenna got in front of him, bent over him, and held his hands. That stopped the shaking, but then Bopp surprised McKenna once again when he leaned forward and buried his face in McKenna's chest. McKenna let go of Bopp's hands and held him like a child. "I know it's tough, Ismael, and it's probably going to take a long time before it gets better."

That also seemed to work, and Bopp's wails quieted down to sobs. "He was so good to me, just so good to me," he said between his tears.

"I bet he was."

"Just so good."

"I know."

Then McKenna heard the sound of many footsteps coming up the stairs, followed by a knock at the door.

"Wait a minute," McKenna yelled.

"A minute? How much time you really need?" Cisco yelled through the door.

"Maybe a while," McKenna yelled back. "You got the ambulance crew with you?"

"Yeah, but they're real gentlemen. They won't mind waiting."

"Detective?" Bopp said softly.

"Yes."

"What's your name?"

"Brian."

"Brian, please don't let anybody see me like this. I feel so pathetic."

"I won't."

Bopp turned out to be quite good at recovery. It took a few more minutes, but he managed to bring his emotions under control. He was still shaky, but without any assistance from McKenna he got up, selected a clean pair of jeans and a T-shirt from his dresser, and then he turned to McKenna. "If you don't mind, I'd like to just rinse off. I won't be five minutes," he said.

"I don't mind. How about underwear?"

"Sometimes, but not today. Too restrictive, and I've been tied up long enough," Bopp replied, and McKenna thought he sounded serious when he said it. Bopp went to the bathroom and closed the door behind him. "Okay, I don't mind if you let them in now," he yelled through the door as the sound of the shower began.

Cisco opened the bedroom door and came in, followed by two male ambulance attendants. "He'll be out in five minutes," McKenna told them.

"What kind of guy is he?" one of the attendants asked.

"Soft and shattered, but not a bad guy," McKenna replied. He then motioned for Cisco to follow, and they left to finish their inspection of the house. There were three more upstairs bedrooms. One was in the same condition as the room in

which they had found Bopp, but the walls of the last two
they checked were unfinished and stripped to the beams. The
ceilings were finished, however, and the stripped rooms were
protected by the sprinkler system.

"Two-by-fours," McKenna said, eyeing the old, exposed
beams. "I guess De Sales intended to store future profits
here."

"Which I guess he planned to make soon, maybe from
the load of dope he thought he was getting from Cruz,"
Cisco added. "That's why he already had all the material he
needed stored in the garage."

"You're probably right," McKenna said, and then he noticed something on the floor of the stripped room. It was faint,
but he thought it might be a partial plaster dust footprint in the
middle of the room. He surprised Cisco when he lay down on
the hallway floor and inspected the floor of the room from that
perspective. From there he could make out the footprint, and
there were many more of them, barely visible. "Justice spent
some time in this room, walking all over," he told Cisco.

"Why would he do that? One look will tell him there's
nothing here."

McKenna stood up. "Let's see." He walked to a section of
framed-out timbers that had once been a closet, and looked
up. It was there, a small trapdoor that accessed the eaves of
the house. "I think he went up there," McKenna said.

"Then I guess we should, too," Cisco replied. "Wait
here." He left the room and returned a minute later carrying
two nightstands he had obtained from one of the demolished
bedrooms. He stacked them one on top of the other under
the trapdoor, and McKenna helped him to climb up and
stand on top of them. As he pushed the door up and slid it to
the side, four wrapped packets of cash fell from the opening.
Cisco caught one of them, McKenna caught another, and the
remaining two hit the ground. The bills were covered in
plaster dust, and all the packets consisted of hundred-dollar
bills.

"Why the hell did he leave those up there?" McKenna
asked.

"Because he's a nice guy, and he always tries to make amends," Cisco said. "Balanced the cash so it would fall out as soon as anyone moved the door."

"A gift for Bopp?"

"I doubt if he meant it for us," Cisco said. "Now let's do some thinking. How does Justice usually tell people he's giving them money?"

"With a note."

"But did Bopp mention anything about a note?"

"No, and I'm sure he would've if he knew about it."

"So he's got a note he doesn't know about?"

"Yep. Justice left it in a place where he thought Bopp—and only Bopp—would be likely to find it."

Cisco eyed McKenna closely. "Do you have any idea where that might be?"

"Your swami knows all."

"Where?"

"I'll show you after they take Bopp to the hospital."

"Why wait?"

"Because we have to talk some things over first."

"Is it possible we might be breaking some rules?"

"We might," McKenna said. "What do you think of Bopp?"

"Tough enough guy for a pansy."

"You like him?"

"He seems okay, in his own weird way. Let's go see how he's doing."

Bopp was again seated on the bed in the master bedroom, and he was putting on his shirt. The paramedics were packing up their gear. "How is he?" McKenna asked.

"Dehydrated, slight fever, but I think he should have no lasting ill effects," one of the paramedics said. "I advised him that he should come with us to get looked over good by a doctor, but he's not sure if he wants to go to the hospital."

"Ismael, you should go with them," McKenna said.

"Are you sure?" Bopp asked.

"Yes. Better safe than sorry."

"Then I'll go."

"Make sure you take keys with you. We'll probably be gone by the time you get back, and we'll lock the house when we leave."

"Thank you. I will."

"You realize that you're going to become something of a celebrity for a day or two and that there will be lots of reporters trying to talk to you?"

McKenna saw that was bad news for Bopp. "Do I have to talk to them?"

"No, but it will be hard to escape them. They're relentless, and they'll be camped out on your doorstep."

"I'm really a very private person, and I think I'll be subject to ridicule because of my relationship with Ruben. I don't want to talk to them."

"Then don't, but if you change your mind, I have a favor to ask. I have a friend who's a reporter, and I owe him a debt."

"Do you want me to talk to him?" Bopp asked.

"Only if you decide you can't stand the pressure anymore."

"What's his name?"

"Phil Messing. He works for the *Post*."

"Is he a nice man?"

"No, he's a reporter," McKenna said. "If he wasn't a reporter, maybe I'd call him a nice guy."

"Will he be fair with me?"

"Fairer than the rest."

"Then please tell your friend I'd be happy to talk to him, and only him."

"Thank you, Ismael. Good luck to you."

"And thank you, Brian. May I shake your hand?"

"Sure." McKenna offered his hand, and Bopp shook it briefly. Then he shocked Cisco. "May I shake yours as well?"

"Surely. It's Detective First Grade Cisco Sanchez you're meeting, and you might be interested to know you're about to shake the hand that shook the hand of Andy Warhol, Barbra Streisand, and the Dalai Lama," Cisco said as he offered his hand.

"Really? Then I'm especially honored to meet you," Bopp said, and he fervently shook Cisco's hand with reverence in his eyes.

"The Dalai Lama?" McKenna said sarcastically as soon as Bopp left with the paramedics.

"Yeah. He was in town one day, and he felt the urge to finally look me up. Dresses funny, but not a bad guy," Cisco replied offhandedly. "Now, where's this note?"

McKenna went to Bopp's dresser and tapped it. "In here, somewhere."

"Mind telling me why you think that?"

"Because one of the last things Justice did before leaving was to go through these drawers and the drawers in De Sales's dresser. For Bopp's benefit, he pretended he was looking for something."

"But what he was really doing was putting the note in there?"

"If I'm right, yes."

"And he knew that this dresser was Bopp's after he saw the contents?"

"Presumably."

"The note, please."

McKenna opened the top drawer and, as he expected, saw that Bopp was a neatnik. The drawer contained handkerchiefs and socks in all colors, folded and perfectly stacked. He rifled through the stacks. No note, so he closed the drawer and opened the next one. It was Bopp's underwear drawer, and it contained a perfectly folded assortment of underpants and undershirts in styles and colors McKenna couldn't begin to describe.

The note was there, in a plain white envelope, tucked between two silk undershirts. In contrast to Justice's other laser-printed notes, the lettering "Ismael" on the outside of the envelope was neatly handprinted in blue ink.

"Ah, his first lack of foresight. He didn't know he'd be leaving this note when he came here," Cisco said.

"Yeah, but everybody gets afterthoughts they act on. Besides, he didn't know the house before he came here, so he couldn't know where he'd hide any gifts he might leave," McKenna said. He briefly thought about putting on his latex gloves before opening the envelope, but he was so sure Justice had left no prints on the letter or envelope that he decided against it. He ripped open the envelope and took out the note. It was a long message, neatly handprinted on both sides of the sheet of plain white paper.

> *Ismael:*
>
> *It's possible you loved him, but Ruben De Sales was a malignant cancer that had to be excised from society and destroyed. However, I learned that he did have his good points. Even when he was under painful pressure from me, he would not reveal the location of his money unless I promised not to harm you. He told me you were unaware of his true nature and his business, and I believed him and gave my promise. After inspecting your house, I believe I would have found the money anyway, but you are still alive thanks to that promise, your lack of knowledge about the true De Sales, and his willingness to withstand considerable pain in order to save you.*
>
> *De Sales asked me to tell you that he loves you and that the house and his car are willed to you. That might repay any debt he owes you, but I realize that I have caused you pain and discomfort in order to advance my purposes. I have therefore attempted to make some restitution, and this attempt may succeed if the police are not astute enough to prevent it. I have left money for you in the eaves of this house near the access door in one of the barren rooms.*
>
> *Do as you like with the money, but I advise that you show this note to no one and that you do not tell the police about the money. If you fail to heed this advice, in all likelihood the police will confiscate the money as proceeds of*

criminal activity. I hope the following observa-
tion doesn't pain you too much, but I feel you
should know: Ruben De Sales died better than
he lived.

The note was signed "Justice" in the same blue ink.

After reading it twice, McKenna passed the note to Cisco. "Still quite the literate fellow, isn't he?" he asked as he was reading it.

"He knows how to get his point across in writing," McKenna said.

Cisco finished reading the note and gave it back to McKenna. "Now, what do we have to talk about?" he asked.

"We have in total four packets of one-hundred-dollar bills. Probably fifty bills in each packet, twenty thousand dollars total."

"Correct, and intended for our dopey and naive Mr. Bopp as some recompense for his pain and suffering."

"*Just* recompense?" McKenna asked.

"I think so."

"For the sake of argument, what will happen to that twenty thousand dollars when we turn it in?"

"*If* we turn it in, we would be starting a horrific and de-structive dispute between our job and the Freeport PD over which one gets the cash. On one hand, it comes as a result of a Nassau County search warrant. On the other hand, it was recovered by officers of the NYPD."

"How long do you think this dispute would drag on and fester?" McKenna asked.

"It'll take years before it's decided one way or the other. By then, it's probable that irreparable damage will have been done to the relationship between our department and theirs."

"So what do we do with the money?"

"Put it back in the rafters."

"And the note?" McKenna asked.

"After we wipe our prints off it, goes back in the drawer for Bopp to find."

"And what happens after we capture Justice? What do you think he'll have to say about the money?"

"We won't have to worry about that."

"Why not?"

"Because Justice will never be taken alive. If we get close enough to capturing him, he'll see to it that we have to kill him."

McKenna had already reached the same conclusion, though he hated to agree with Cisco. He took out his handkerchief and wiped down the note with it. He gave the envelope the same treatment before putting the note back in it. Then he opened the top drawer, and put the envelope under a stack of Bopp's socks.

"Why not put it back in the underwear drawer?" Cisco asked.

"Because it might take Bopp a very long time to find it there."

"He doesn't wear underwear?"

"Too restrictive."

"Ah," was all Cisco said.

SEVENTEEN

McKenna called Messing's cell phone, and it wasn't until the fifth ring that Messing answered. "Still sleeping?" McKenna asked.

"Yeah. What time is it?"

"Almost three. I expected to see you here sooner, and I left a note on your windshield."

"I see it," Messing said. "I guess I was beat. How'd you make out?"

"Found where De Sales had his money before Justice got it, but he didn't kill the boyfriend. Tied up, but he's fine now."

"Any chance of getting an interview with him?"

"If there is, it's only you he'll talk to."

"Love ya, Brian. I'll be there soon."

Since it was Chmil's warrant and since Chmil would be going back to the judge who signed it to describe what had been found, McKenna thought it was time to bring him back into the loop. He woke up Chmil and began briefing him on the search.

Cisco set out to ring doorbells and found a witness at the first house he tried, directly across the street from De Sales's house. She had noticed a Ryder rental truck parked in De Sales's driveway on Wednesday, and she thought it had been there for most of the day. She knew De Sales and Bopp by sight, but since she thought them to be "strange people who kept to themselves," she had never spoken to them. She knew, however, that De Sales frequently received deliveries of construction supplies, so she hadn't given the Ryder truck a second thought.

Cisco then told her that her neighbor was one of the major drug dealers murdered by Justice, and that news flashed around the neighborhood and set it abuzz. Soon there were no more doorbells to be rung; Cisco had set up shop on De Sales's front lawn, and he was busy taking statements from the line of neighbors who had also seen the Ryder truck parked in the driveway on Wednesday. Two of them had also noticed a well-built black man loading trash bags into the rear of the truck, and both stated they thought they could recognize him if they saw him again.

As Messing pulled up, Cisco was finishing with his last witness. Messing wanted to interview the neighbors, so Cisco left him and went back into the house. McKenna was in the master bedroom, walking Chmil through the crime. "It was a Ryder truck he used, probably stolen," Cisco told McKenna. "I'll make a few phone calls and let you know for sure in a couple of minutes."

By the time McKenna had Chmil fully briefed, Cisco did let him know. "A Ryder truck was stolen from their lot in Queens sometime Tuesday night," Cisco said. "Not an unusual event. What was unusual was that the truck was returned to the lot sometime Wednesday night, undamaged, clean, and with a full tank of gas."

"How many miles did he put on the truck?" McKenna asked.

"A lot. Two hundred thirty-six. Figure it's only about twenty-five miles from here to Manhattan, and what conclusion may we draw?"

"That Justice isn't keeping his cash anyplace close to the city."

"And I'll bet his cash, Jorge Rodriguez, and Jorge's red Volvo are all in the same place. Someplace secluded in the woods, probably upstate, far from the places we usually find our bad guys."

McKenna had figured it would happen eventually, but not quite so soon. Rarely a day passes without a demonstration

being held somewhere in the city to protest something, and
the city's press corps eagerly covers these events. Organized
by groups and committees that seem to form spontaneously,
the demonstrations are always news, and the press corps
never fails to publicize them, interview spokespersons, and
generate controversy over the demonstrators' grievances and
views, no matter how trivial the issue.

A group calling itself Mothers for Justice had already
formed to hold a demonstration at police headquarters, but
McKenna *was* surprised at the number of people demonstrating and at just how organized they were. Cisco parked at
a fire hydrant half a block from headquarters so he and
McKenna could take in the demonstration from a distance.

McKenna estimated there were three hundred people
demonstrating in an orderly fashion on the sidewalk next to
the headquarters' garage, most of them women with young
children in baby carriages or at their sides. Some carried
signs that read "We Need Justice," "Harlem Mothers for Justice," "Brooklyn Mothers for Justice," "Justice, Please Visit
the Bronx," or "Finally, Justice!" They also had a chant,
"Leave Him Alone," a message for the police, which they repeated over and over.

There were only twenty cops policing the demonstration,
but there wasn't much for them to do. The demonstrators
marched around in the space allotted for them inside a long
enclosure formed by wooden police barriers. The press covering the demonstration far outnumbered the police, and
McKenna could see television news crews from ABC, NBC,
CBS, CNN, and Fox.

The demonstration bothered McKenna, but what bothered him more were the two hundred people gathered across
the street from the demonstration, watching it. Many were
people who lived or worked in the area around police headquarters, and quite a few of them showed their support for
the demonstrators by applauding or shouting words of en-
couragement; in that crowd of supporters he counted nine
people he recognized, all detectives or civilian employees of
the department who worked at headquarters.

Cisco had also seen them. "We're in trouble," he said. "This has become a no-win situation."

"I know. We're in trouble if we don't get him, and we're in trouble if we do," McKenna replied. "Let's go."

Cisco pulled out, and they got caught by the red light at the corner. McKenna locked eyes with one of the demonstrators, a young, pretty black woman holding her son's shoulder with one hand and a loudspeaker with the other, and he felt she recognized him. She said something to the women marching closest to her, pointed in his direction, and then she raised the loudspeaker to her lips to inspire the demonstrators' new chant. It immediately caught on. "No Justice for McKenna!" was ringing in McKenna's ears when Cisco finally drove into the headquarters' garage.

The press conference at headquarters didn't go well. McKenna was able to tell the press where Justice had gotten the six million he had given away. Justice, however, had not left another body; Ismael Bopp was alive and well, and, the last McKenna heard, talking to Phil Messing.

McKenna tried to keep it short, and in answer to questions about the progress of the investigation, he said it was proceeding on course. The inference was that Justice was closer to being captured, and reporters made McKenna say just that, but he refused to tell them what made him believe it.

Then came a series of questions on the demonstration still going on outside, and McKenna felt pompous when he told them that the protesters were well-intentioned good people—but misguided.

The last question concerned Brunette. A reporter wanted to know when they would be hearing from him. Soon, McKenna had to say, and then added a few words he immediately regretted. He expected Brunette would have something positive to report, and that generated the question McKenna didn't answer: So we won't see the police commissioner again until you do something good?

• • •

McKenna was completely exhausted by the press conference. When he got to Brunette's office, he found him at his window, looking down at the demonstration fourteen floors below. Brunette also looked exhausted, but not as bad as he had at four that morning. "Looks like you got a nap someplace along the way," McKenna told him.

"And it looks like you really need one," Brunette replied. "Saw your press conference. Not bad."

"Is the next one yours?"

"Yeah, and it'll be a long one."

"You got good news?"

"I have plenty of news, spectacular stuff, but I don't know how good it is for us with Justice still running around. The worse we make Gaston look, the better Justice looks for whacking him."

"They were able to get Cruz's financial records off the disks?" McKenna asked.

"That they did, once I gave them a hint and some help. The records were written in a code they couldn't crack, but after I told them what some of the numbers were, they were able to come up with the key for the whole thing."

"You gave them the letters he wrote Messing?"

"That's all it took. Justice's figures were right on the money. Once they knew what a few coded lines in the records were, they were able to extrapolate and crack it."

"How much?"

"Gaston blew into town with just under a billion in seed money. Nine hundred forty million, most of it made with his air-freight operation. Since then, far as we can tell, he's made himself another four billion, three hundred forty million in pure, tax-free profit."

"Do we know where the money is?"

"Uh-huh. Laundered in many places offshore. We don't have the account numbers for the accounts it's stashed in, but we do know which banks he used. Way beyond our capabilities, so I gave it to the feds."

"They'll be able to identify the accounts and attach the money?"

"In time. There's people dancing around all over Washington right now, ready to kiss us."

"Do we know who he's been dealing with?" McKenna asked.

"Not precisely. In the records he used nicknames or names he gave his suppliers and his vendors, but the figures are all there. Dates, amounts, and what he paid for his drugs. Dates, amounts, and how much he sold the stuff for."

"So now we just have to attach names to the buyers and sellers?"

"And between us and the feds, we will. Most of them, anyway. What do you think he called De Sales in his records?"

"I couldn't begin to imagine."

"*Rey Maricón.*"

King Homosexual? Makes sense, McKenna thought. De Sales was gay, and he operated in Brooklyn. Kings County. "And Ramon Garcia. What name did he give him?"

"Simple one for us; used the name by which Garcia is known in Spanish Harlem: *El puro malo.* Pure bad."

Now for the big question, McKenna thought. "Did the cop he bought show up in his records?"

"He has a line in the first week of every month, and the amount never varies. Two million a month for the past twenty-two months."

"Forty-four million dollars? Can that be right?"

"All in cash."

"What name did he give him?"

"*Trompeta melodiosa.* The melodious trumpet, the one who gave Gaston enough information to make him one of the richest drug dealers in the world."

So how do we get this guy? And what does a person do with forty-four million in cash? McKenna asked himself. "Do you have the personnel folders?"

Brunette nodded toward his bathroom. "Don't want anyone seeing them, but there's three hundred forty of them. Everyone who might've had access to the Intelligence Section's files on a continuing basis, either officially or by sneaking into the office at night. That's everyone in the Intelligence Section and everyone in Manhattan South Narcotics."

Three hundred forty? How long is it gonna take Cisco and me to go through three hundred forty personnel files? "Too many. I'm gonna need some help."

"And you got it. Give Sheeran a list of everybody in the Major Case Squad you think is sharp when it comes to winding through a paper trail, and then we'll get them right to work on it."

"They're all sharp, but we can't start on it right away."

"Why not?"

"I have another job in mind for them for tonight."

"Doing what?"

"Maybe catching Justice dropping off some more cash."

"Where?"

"He's already given to the Christians and the Jews, so who's he missing?"

"The Muslims."

"He seems to be an ecumenical kind of guy, and he's got more cash to give. He already gave to a poor church and a poor synagogue, so I'd like every poor mosque in the city staked out tonight."

"Do you have any idea how many mosques that is?"

"No. Do you?"

"I know we had close to two hundred mosques the last time I checked, and I'm betting a good percentage of them could be considered poor."

"Too big a job," McKenna said. "We should be looking only at old, poor mosques in poor neighborhoods."

"That'll still be an enormous manpower commitment on short notice, and the whole thing will have to be kept secret."

"I know, but we only get one shot at this. It has to be done."

"And it will be. You got any more ideas?"

"A few. The type B blood?"

"Roughly ten percent of the population, and the files reflect that exactly. Three hundred forty personnel files, thirty-four of them for people with type B blood. They're in a separate box. What else?"

"A big map that accurately reflects mileage, with the Ryder lot in Queens right in the middle of it. Justice stole the truck from them right after he killed De Sales and Ramsey. We measured it on the way back, it's exactly twenty-two point two miles from De Sales's house to their lot, and he put two hundred thirty-six miles on that truck before he returned it. That leaves us with two hundred fourteen miles unaccounted for."

"I get it," Brunette said. "He went round-trip, so he dropped the cash at a spot that's close to a hundred and seven miles from the lot. We make a circle on that map . . ."

"A circle with a radius of a hundred seven miles, with the Ryder lot in the middle. The place where Justice brought the cash is sitting somewhere near the edge of that circle, and we're hoping for more."

"That it's the place where he lives?"

"And the place where he's holding Jorge Rodriguez."

"He might've put extra miles on that truck just to confuse us," Brunette said.

"He might've, if he had the time. But don't forget, he's been operating on a pretty tight, very busy schedule, and there has to be a lot of driving in the middle of it. Late Sunday afternoon he kidnaps Jorge, brings him to the hideout. He then has to get to wherever his pal keeps his plane and take a flight in time to drop in on Gaston early Monday morning. Gets the cash and the records, drives back to the hideout, and . . ."

"He tortures Jorge into translating the records, revealing where Gaston stores his drugs, and setting up the meeting with De Sales."

"Then he has to get the drugs, but he still finds the time to get to his computer and drop a letter to Messing that pretty much describes his plans for De Sales and Ramsey. That night he whacks them, and then he steals the truck."

"Then all day Wednesday he's doing heavy labor at De Sales's house," Brunette said.

"Followed by a lot of driving, but he still finds the time to drop another letter to Messing, this one with Ramon Garcia as the subject. Then, Wednesday night, he drives the truck back to the Ryder lot, and next he shows up at the ambassador's house in Glen Cove to steal his limo. He takes that back to the hideout to do his major, time-consuming modifications and have Jorge set up the meeting with Garcia. He blows up him and his crew, and then you'd think he'd give himself a break."

"But he doesn't," Brunette said. "Instead, he spent a lot of time last night dropping off his gifts. That's five days and nights straight with little or no sleep. How's he do it?"

"He's driven by hate, and hate can be like a drug."

"No drug's that strong. Don't forget, he's doing dangerous, physically demanding work, and it seems he's always sharp and thinking straight."

"So what conclusion can we draw?" McKenna asked.

"That his accomplice does more than just pilot his flights. He does most of the driving while Justice sleeps, he helps out in taking apart limos and building bombs, and he probably helps load and unload money."

"So this would be a guy who might be just about as good as Justice at all the things Justice does," McKenna said.

"Might be. Picks locks, makes bombs, and very good with cars."

"And he'd be a guy who's been going just as long and hard as Justice."

"With the same goals and the same level of commitment," Brunette added. "Meaning?"

"Meaning he's also driven by hate."

McKenna and Cisco had just finished their paperwork documenting their day at De Sales's house when Brunette called McKenna. "Just got some more bad news," he said.

"He hit again?" McKenna asked.

"No, but almost as bad. Mike Brennan just called to give me a heads-up on the column he's writing for tomorrow's paper. The piece will be titled 'Is Justice a Cop?' "

McKenna knew Brennan well, and both he and Brunette considered him a friend. The *Post* columnist was smart, intuitive, and well-informed—a dangerous combination for any official trying to hide something important in the city of New York.

Did Messing tip our hand to Brennan? McKenna wondered, but he quickly dismissed the notion. Messing was a reporter, but Brennan was a couple of steps up on the ladder, a columnist holding the position McKenna knew Messing aspired to hold for himself when he finally tired of haunting the police stations, bars, and back alleys of the city. No, he decided, Brennan looked at all angles and came up with the idea himself. "Did he want a comment from you on the piece?" McKenna asked.

"Sure he did."

"And what did you tell him?" McKenna asked, knowing that a simple 'No comment' was an almost impossible phrase to push past the influential columnist.

"I had to come clean. I had to tell him we've already considered the possibility that the man who's driving us crazy might be one of our own, and we're working on it."

"You didn't say *remote* possibility?"

"I try never to peddle remote possibilities when there's a good chance they're true. *Possibility*, plain and simple."

"Between his piece and Messing's exclusive interview with Bopp, the *Post* might set a record in copies sold tomorrow," McKenna noted.

"You're right, and I intend to get a copy right off the press and read it here—if this is still my office tomorrow morning."

"Have you heard from the mayor?"

"Every couple of hours."

"And?"

"He's been fairly supportive, but his calls are getting shorter, and I think I'd now describe his attitude as *brusque*."

"I guess it's you who'll be calling him now?"

"Next call, and I don't think it'll be a short one after I tell him about this. I'm already in trouble, and Brennan's piece might push me into the *expendable* category."

"But only if Brennan's column turns out to be true?"

"That would be the best possible slant. We now have a murderer who everybody's rooting for, the case has gone national, and it seems we're nowhere close to catching him. This is a political town, and heads roll in a time of crisis when it seems nothing good is happening to resolve it."

"Suppose we catch him soon?"

"If he's one of us, I'm probably out. If he hits again before we catch him, might be out. Best possible result—we catch him soon and he's not a cop—and there's still a chance I'll eventually be out."

"Small chance?"

"Small chance, unless something else screws up on me."

"Why any chance at all, if everything works out right?" McKenna asked.

"Because Justice, indirectly or not, has produced more big-time, effective results in one week than my entire Narcotics Division has in years. It's because of him we got those disks, and it's because of him we broke the code. The feds are gonna wind up confiscating billions, and once we attach real names to the monikers Gaston gave all those big-time drug dealers and wholesalers, it's just a matter of time before they're all in the soup."

He's right, McKenna thought, so what do I tell him that'll cheer him up?

Nothing came to mind.

EIGHTEEN

McKenna wanted to keep working but found he was too tired to read the files. It was time to go home to get a couple of hours' sleep before the stakeouts that night, and Cisco agreed.

McKenna was able to get only three hours' sleep, but when he returned to the office at midnight, showered, shaved, and wearing a fresh suit, he felt refreshed and eager to get to work.

Cisco was already at his desk, reading one of the personnel folders. He had also shaved and was wearing a fresh suit, and he looked better than he had when McKenna last saw him, but he still looked like he needed more sleep. "How long you been here?" he asked.

"Long enough to find the field associate," Cisco replied, and he passed the folder to McKenna. "John Fahey, nine years on the Job, and already he's a second-grader. Been in the Intelligence Section for three years. Started out with only two years on patrol in Midtown South before he was transferred to Manhattan South Narcotics. Spent four years there."

"Medals?"

"A few, but he's no hero. Two EPDs and one MPD."

"You're sure he's the field associate?"

"Think about it."

McKenna did, and found it unusual that with just two awards for Excellent Police Duty and one for Meritorious Police Duty, the lowest medals granted by the NYPD, and with only nine years on the Job, Fahey had managed to win promotion to detective second grade. Even more unusual was his transfer to Narcotics when he had just two years on the Job. "Arrest activity?"

"He knows how to get to Central Booking, but nothing special."

"Evaluations?"

"Plays well with others, but he never got a 'Well Above Standards' overall rating. The only thing his bosses thought he did great was paperwork. He's a whiz at reports," Cisco said. "Well?"

"More likely than not, it's him."

"Then let me show you why it's definitely him," Cisco said. "Go to his PA-One."

The PA-1 was the report on the background investigation performed on Fahey when he had applied to the department. It was at the back of the folder, and McKenna was reading it when Cisco gave him a hint. "Look at his mother."

McKenna turned the page and studied the information compiled on Fahey's family. Janet Fahey was married to John Fahey, and she had been forty-three years old at the time of the investigation. He went through the family history until he came to the item that stopped him: Before she married Fahey's father at age twenty, Janet Fahey had been Janet O'Shaughnessy. "Fahey is O'Shaughnessy's nephew?" he asked.

"Look at who recommended him for Narcotics."

McKenna turned back the pages until he found the endorsements on Fahey's application for the Narcotics Division, seven years before, and there it was: Inspector Jeremiah O'Shaughnessy had described Fahey in glowing terms and then approved the application. "Well, I'll be damned," McKenna said. "I didn't know O'Shaughnessy had a nephew on the Job."

"Nobody does, so look at it two ways," Cisco said. "If you managed to recruit a field associate, and he was reporting directly to you, would you tell anyone he was your nephew?"

"No, I guess not."

"Of course you wouldn't. Recruiting field associates has to be a hard job, so why would O'Shaughnessy make a hard job look easy? Now look at it from Fahey's point of view. If Dog Dick were your uncle, would you ever tell anyone?"

"Not even my wife."

"So there you have it."

"Very good. You found the field associate, but that's not the main mission. Are you any closer to finding out who Gaston bought?"

"Much closer."

That astounded McKenna. "You know who it is?"

"Not yet, but I will."

"How many folders have you gone through?"

"Ten, all people assigned to the Intelligence Section."

"And you think it's one of those ten?" McKenna asked.

"Can't say for sure. Nothing jumped out of those folders and grabbed me. It could just as easily be one of the Manhattan South Narcotics people, somebody who snuck into the Intelligence Section's office from time to time to get Gaston his information."

"That means we still have to go through another three hundred thirty folders."

"Cisco is bored with going through folders, so he has thought of a better way. A brilliant idea, really."

"Are you going to tell me about this brilliant idea?"

"In due course, but first you tell me a few things. Suppose you were getting two million a month from Gaston. In order to avoid suspicion, how would you live?"

"Frugally."

"Right, frugally. Even though you're sitting on a fortune, you're living like a church mouse. Would that drive you crazy?"

"I guess it might."

"Now add in that you're getting two million more each month, and we know now how much space that takes up. So much cash, and you're running out of places to put it. What do you do?"

McKenna got it. "You travel."

"A lot?"

"As much as you can."

"Where?"

"To places with loose banking laws. You leave the country with as much cash as you can hide in your luggage without raising suspicion, you live like a king overseas, and you open up bank accounts there to keep your basement clear of cash."

"So what do we do?"

"INS Passport Control," McKenna said. "We run the names on those folders and see who's been leaving the country a lot."

"Very good," Cisco said. "It heartens me to know that, with a little bit of prompting, you can be almost as brilliant as Cisco. Now, go up and see your pal, and get him working on our brilliant idea."

"Yes, sir."

In order to prevent the press, and then Justice, from learning that mosques would be staked out, absolute secrecy had to be maintained, and that directly affected the number of people available for the assignment on such short notice. The Major Case Squad, the Manhattan North Homicide Squad, and the Brooklyn Homicide Squad were assigned, but that provided only thirty-four detectives operating in seventeen teams to surveil the city's one hundred eighty-one mosques, and the mosques were spread throughout the city's black and Muslim neighborhoods.

Sheeran's instructions were brief and provided the detectives with quite a bit of discretion: Find a mosque that looks poor, find a good hiding spot for yourselves and your car, and stake it out. If Justice shows up, first call for backup, and then get him.

Rather than having his people try to stake out the mosques with detectives sitting in unmarked cars that still looked like police cars, Sheeran had been able to borrow from IAB's fleet. McKenna and Cisco were assigned a 1999

two-door Mitsubishi. They headed Uptown, and found a
mosque on West 126th Street in Harlem that looked promising. McKenna guessed the old building had once served as a
church; there was another building next to it that served as
the mosque's school and day-care center, and all the buildings were in need of repair. Between the school and the
mosque was an alley with a side door for the mosque.

Cisco parked half a block from the mosque. They
slouched down in their seats and began the long wait. After
three boring hours, both began doubting their chances for
success. "He's home sleeping, just like we should be," Cisco
said. Five minutes later, he said it again. Then McKenna got
a call from Brunette. "Just heard from the vicar at St. John
the Divine. He's been there."

St. John the Divine? So close, McKenna thought. Just a
mile from where we're sitting. "When?" McKenna asked.

"Justice called him half an hour ago," Brunette replied.
"Usual message: Told him to use it as he sees fit. Then the
vicar went to the church to check. The money's there, in
front of the altar, stacked like a cross."

"I'll get back to you, Ray. Got some thinking to do."
McKenna ended the call.

"Where?" Cisco asked.

"St. John the Divine."

"Protestant, isn't it?"

"Yeah, Episcopalian. Biggest church in the country, famous. There goes my poor little mosque theory."

"He's given to the Catholics, the Protestants, and the
Jews. If he has any loot left, the Muslims have to be next."

"Yeah, but we're at the wrong mosque."

"Why? When was he there?"

"More than a half hour ago."

"Then he should've been here by now. Where do you
want to go?"

"A big mosque."

"How about East Ninety-sixth and First? That's the
biggest mosque I know, and we can be there in five minutes."

"Get us there, please."

• • •

It was a large, new mosque built in the Islamic style and architecturally striking. It fronted on First Avenue, and because it was set back from the street in a wooded, parklike setting, it was the only structure on its side of the street between East 96th and East 97th Streets, occupying half the short block between First Avenue and the East River Drive.

Cisco drove around the block, looking for a suitable place to park, and he settled on a spot on East 96th Street, west of First Avenue, that gave them a good view of the building.

"I'm gonna go check the doors," McKenna said.

"Good idea," Cisco replied.

McKenna got out and was walking toward the mosque when Cisco pulled up and motioned for McKenna to get into the car. "He's here," Cisco said as McKenna got in.

McKenna searched the scene in front of him. "Where? I don't see him."

"You will. You can't see it from here, but he just left by the side door on Ninety-seventh Street."

McKenna understood. He had been able to see that door from their parking spot, but as he had walked toward the mosque, his view of the door had become blocked by the building.

Cisco drove to First Avenue, made a right, and pulled up slowly to the corner of East 97th Street. Then McKenna saw him, a muscular black man wearing a windbreaker, a black woolen cap, and latex gloves. He was standing halfway down the block, looking at them. East 97th Street was a one-way street that ran against them, but traffic was very light at that hour.

"What's he waiting for?" Cisco asked.

"His ride." McKenna took out his pistol. "You cut him off with the car. I'll get out behind him and make the grab," he said.

Cisco just nodded. It was their standard procedure.

Justice took off running toward the East River Drive as soon as Cisco turned the corner. As Cisco drove after Justice, McKenna opened his door, ready to jump out. When they were twenty feet behind Justice, Cisco slowed, and turned slightly toward the curb. Then they heard the sound of a car behind them, coming fast up the one-way street. Cisco checked the rearview mirror. "Stay in," he yelled, an instant before the car clipped the left rear of their car.

It was a spinout maneuver, and it worked perfectly. The old, green four-door Chevrolet kept going toward the East River Drive, but the force of the impact deployed the Mitsubishi's front and side air bags, and turned it completely around so that it was facing First Avenue.

The air bags were deflating, but Cisco still wasn't able to move. McKenna's door was still open, and he could get out, but he had dropped his pistol onto the street. "You all right?" he asked Cisco.

"Fine, I think."

McKenna got out and looked toward the East River Drive. The Chevrolet was stopped next to Justice, and he had the passenger door open but was still on the sidewalk, looking at McKenna and the Mitsubishi.

McKenna was too far away to make out the plate number, but he could see that the driver was also black. He spent a moment looking around for his gun, and then Justice surprised him. "McKenna! Are you all right?"

"Fine," McKenna yelled back.

"How about your partner?"

"He's okay, too."

"Glad to hear it. Sorry about your car," Justice yelled. Then he calmly got into the car, and the driver made a right turn onto the East River Drive service road.

Sorry? What kind of guy is this? McKenna wondered, and then he spotted his pistol on the ground behind the Mitsubishi. He picked it up and checked it. It looked fine, so he put it in his holster and got back into the car. The air bag had deflated enough to permit Cisco to move, and he was searching under his seat with his hand. "Can't find the radio," he said.

It took McKenna another minute, but he found it on the

floor behind his seat. By that time a civilian car had pulled up next to them, and the driver asked if they were all right. "Fine, thank you," McKenna said, and he waved the driver on.

"Oh, yeah, we're fine. Just dandy," Cisco said. "They made us look like a couple of boobs."

"True, and unfortunately we can't keep it a secret," McKenna said, and then he keyed the radio. "Team One to Major Case CO."

Sheeran answered at once. "Major Case CO. Go ahead, Team One."

"Subject is southbound on either the East River Drive or the service road as a passenger in the old green Chevy he had on West Hundred Twenty-sixth Street, vehicle driven by another male black. Car should be damaged on right front."

"Are you in pursuit?" Sheeran asked.

"Aaaagh," Cisco said, and it was the exact reply McKenna wished he could give Sheeran.

"Negative. The driver rammed our car before we could grab the subject."

"What's your location?"

"I wish we could tell him we were still in Florida," Cisco said.

Wouldn't that be wonderful? McKenna thought. "Our car's disabled, Inspector. We're on East Ninety-seventh between First and the Drive."

"Are you hurt?"

"Only our pride and our reputations," Cisco said. "Injured beyond repair."

"Negative, Inspector," McKenna transmitted. "We're fine."

"I'll transmit the description on the citywide band. I'm in Brooklyn, but I should be at your location in fifteen minutes."

"We'll be here," McKenna transmitted, and then he put the radio on the seat next to him.

"That was a pretty fancy move the driver pulled on us, wouldn't you say?" Cisco asked.

"The spinout? I'd say it was."

"Where do you think he learned it?"

"Our driver training course."

. . .

The mosque's side door was locked, and Justice had left it to McKenna to notify the mosque's imam about his visit and his gift. McKenna got his number from the IN CASE OF EMERGENCY sign on the mosque's side door, and the imam arrived ten minutes after Sheeran. The imam unlocked the door, and McKenna saw it had a push-bar mechanism, so Justice didn't have to take the time to pick the lock closed; when he left the mosque, the door locked behind him.

The money was in the center of the mosque, stacked in the shape of a crescent. As expected, it was the usual large load of cash.

"You know, I'm really beginning to hate counting money," Cisco said.

"Me, too, especially since we already know exactly how much is there," McKenna said.

McKenna did know, but it took another six hours of counting before he could announce to all the reporters gathered outside the 23rd Precinct that Justice had given three million each to the mosque and St. John the Divine. That was all he told the press. His answer to their other questions was that they should be addressed to the police commissioner during a press conference he would be holding at 6:00 P.M.

McKenna didn't envy Brunette that chore, and after taking time out from his paperwork to read the *Post*, he couldn't imagine how Brunette could handle it without getting mauled. While Brennan's column didn't take Brunette to task, his speculation that Justice was a cop was bound to raise many direct questions at the press conference, questions that couldn't yet be answered.

One thing was certain: The press conference would be well attended. Public interest in the case was at fever pitch, and articles related to Justice filled the first six pages of the *Post*. Four of the articles carried the Messing byline, and McKenna couldn't figure how he had found the time to write the pieces.

The feature article, naturally, was about the second letter Justice had sent him, and Messing savaged the drug trade in general and Ramon Garcia in particular. That didn't bother McKenna, but it disturbed him that Messing had managed to indirectly cast Justice in a positive light.

Justice also occupied top billing in the *Post*'s editorial pages and in the Letters to the Editor. The op-ed people just barely fulfilled their civic responsibility by softly condemning vigilante action and calling for Justice's arrest as soon as possible, but they also noted he was causing more damage to the drug trade in New York than the NYPD and the federal government combined.

As McKenna expected after reading the *Post*, the letters featured in the Letters to the Editor section were overwhelmingly in Justice's favor, seven to one. The lone dissenter complained about Justice's disregard for the rule of law, and he wrote that it was just a matter of time before an innocent was injured or killed in the crossfire.

McKenna closed the paper thinking that the editors and reporters at the *Post* had been overly favorable to Justice, but he was grateful they had also been fair with him. Since McKenna had given Messing the inside track, he didn't expect to receive the same generous treatment from the jealous reporters writing for the other newspapers, so he decided that the *Post* would be the only paper he would be reading that day.

McKenna and Cisco typed all their reports in the 23rd Precinct Detective Squad office, and it wasn't until noon that they finished the chore. By then, they were beat. They decided that, once again, it was time to get home for a nap, and Sheeran agreed. He offered to drop them both off. Cisco accepted, but McKenna declined the offer.

After Sheeran and Cisco left, McKenna took a taxi, but not home. Instead, he took it to The Wicked Wolf and looked in the window before he went in. The bar was crowded, and Chipmunk had another bartender working with him to help out, but the restaurant was only half full. Chipmunk didn't see him enter, so he went to a table where Chip would eventually see him, and sat down.

Chip was there a few minutes later. "Not going so good?"

"Going terrible. I'm desperate, and I'm ready to pull my hair out—the exact state of mind we talked about the last time I was here," McKenna said, and he saw by the look on Chip's face that it was bad news for him.

"I was hoping it wouldn't come to this," Chip said.

"It has. Sit down, please, and talk to me."

Chip did sit. He placed his hands on the table in front of him, but he didn't say a word.

"Do you know who Justice is?" McKenna asked.

"I'm pretty sure I do."

"Are you gonna tell me?"

"No."

"Why not?"

"Two reasons. One, because he's a friend, a great person who I know even longer than I know you. Much longer."

Much longer? How can that be? McKenna wondered. I know Chip for thirty years. "And the other reason?"

"The other reason is that I'm not the one you should be asking."

"Who should I be asking?"

"Your partner."

It was something McKenna had suspected, but Chip's assessment still caught him by surprise. "My partner? Cisco knows him?"

"He's Cisco's hero."

Cisco has a hero? was the first question that popped into McKenna's mind. "How do you know?"

"Because after they had some fun doing the hero stuff they do together, they stopped in to see me a few times. They've also gone on vacation together a few times to do the hero stuff they can't do here in the wintertime."

"What kind of hero stuff do they do together?"

"Skydiving, skin diving, stock-car racing."

"Is Justice a cop?"

"Used to be. One of the best, but he retired years ago."

Retired cop? Still bad, but not as bad as if he were still on the Job, McKenna thought. "Years ago? How old is he?"

"I dunno, exactly. Maybe five years older than me."

McKenna did the math, and the number shocked him. "Sixty-six, and he's still able to do all the things he's been doing to us?"

"He's in great shape, but not for too much longer."

"Why not?"

"Because he just found out he has a spot on his pancreas. Cancer."

"He told you that?"

"No, I haven't seen him in a couple of years. He doesn't live in town anymore."

"Has Cisco seen him?"

"I wouldn't know. It's been a long time since they were in here together."

"Then how do you know about the cancer?"

"We have the same doctor."

McKenna knew Chip's doctor. John Daley was also one of Chip's customers and doctor to many of the cops living in Manhattan. He was also a determined madman who held black belts in many of the martial arts. McKenna realized that if he couldn't crack Chip, he never stood a chance at cracking Daley, but he felt at least a try might be in order. "Is John another good pal of Justice's?"

"They're tight. Birds of a feather."

"And where's John been lately? Haven't see him around in a while."

"That's because he hasn't been here. Retired to Bermuda last April. Skin diving and fishing are all he's doing now."

"Are you still in touch with him?"

"We talk from time to time. Gave me the scoop on a new drug to treat my gout, and it works wonders for me."

So Daley's out, and it's probably just as well, McKenna thought. Next issue. "What makes you think that Justice is Cisco's hero?"

"Would you say Cisco likes to talk?"

"Yes."

"And what's his favorite subject?"

"Himself."

"Not when he's with his hero. Cisco listens to every word he says, laughs at all his jokes, and never lets him buy a drink."

"Do you know why he's killing the drug dealers?"

"Revenge."

"Revenge for what?"

"Ask your partner."

"You won't tell me?"

"Brian, I've already told you more than I ever wanted to. Everybody involved is a friend of mine, and there's loyalty issues in this for all of us. It's been driving me crazy."

"I'm sure it's also been driving Cisco crazy."

"Sure it has. He's a pain in the ass, but he's also a good man."

"Why do you think Cisco wanted us involved in this case?"

"I've given that a lot of thought, and I think it goes like this: Cisco figured that once his hero knew he was involved, he'd stop killing and just disappear."

"Because he wouldn't want to do anything that would hurt Cisco's reputation?"

"That's it. You might think of him as a killer who has to be caught, so you might not believe this . . ."

"Are you going to tell me he's really a nice guy?"

"Yes, and he really is."

"I believe you," McKenna said. "Last item. Now that he knows Cisco's involved, *will* he stop killing and try to disappear?"

"He'll stop killing, but I don't know if he'll disappear."

McKenna left The Wicked Wolf almost wishing he hadn't talked to Chipmunk. He had put his friend in a difficult spot, and what he had learned had put him in a tougher spot. What should he do about Cisco? He needed time to think, and he started walking down First Avenue.

McKenna knew Cisco as a moral man who would never do anything he considered wrong. The problem was that Cisco's concept of right and wrong differed at times from society's, but that never bothered Cisco. He always did what *he* thought was right, and then he let the chips fall where they may. Like Chipmunk, Cisco considered loyalty to be the most desirable trait a person could have, and he considered it a two-way street; he was unswervingly loyal to his friends, but he demanded total loyalty in return.

So why didn't Cisco tell me he knew Justice? was another question McKenna had to consider, but he reached a quick answer. Two reasons, and it had to do with split loyalty: He was Cisco's friend, but he was also Brunette's friend.

By the time McKenna reached East 57th Street, he decided that, no matter the personal cost, Cisco deserved his loyalty. He would keep it a close secret that he knew Cisco knew, and he wouldn't tell Brunette, even though Brunette also deserved his loyalty.

So what do I do about Ray? McKenna asked himself. This case is hurting him, and it may ruin him. Only one thing to do, he decided. Catch Justice, and do it quick.

McKenna headed west on East 57th Street, and he quickened his pace. He had to do something sneaky and underhanded, and that meant immediately enlisting the help of the most sneaky and underhanded man in town.

Bob Hurley was a retired detective with loose ethics who had found his perfect niche in life. After retiring, he became a PI, and he subsequently advanced himself in a business in which his loose ethics were consistently rewarded. The substance of the PI business is information, and Hurley could get information from every source imaginable—sometimes legally but usually not—and it was that ability that had made him the best and most successful PI in town. He had risen to become the president of the Holmes Detective Bureau, the company the rich and the famous visit when they just *have* to know something.

McKenna had known Hurley for twenty years, since the time when they were young detectives together. However, he had never worked with Hurley when he was on the Job, and, because of their contrasting ethics, he was grateful for that. Still, Hurley was a friend who could be counted on, and he had done many favors for McKenna.

McKenna walked past Hurley's office and decided that was not the place to discuss the matter he had in mind. Hurley employed many retired detectives, and in their eyes his request would not bear the light of day. He decided it was best to meet Hurley in his other office, the end stool of the back bar at Kennedy's. He called Hurley's office to arrange the meeting, and his secretary told him the boss was already there.

Kennedy's is a famous Irish pub on West 57th Street, a block west of Hurley's office. The long bar and restaurant in Kennedy's large front room was always crowded with tourists, businesspeople, and a sprinkling of neighborhood folks, but McKenna had never stopped there. His business was always in the back bar, the section of Kennedy's frequented by the same people who visited The Wicked Wolf. It was another one of the few police sanctuaries left in town, a place where detectives met to talk over their lives and brag about their cases with each other.

It was rare that McKenna didn't know everybody at the bar, and it wasn't one of those rare times. Hurley was there, holding court with his cronies at the end of the bar, but it took McKenna five minutes of handshaking and backslapping to make his way down to him.

McKenna caught Hurley's eyes, but didn't stop. Instead, he walked past the end of the bar and opened the door that led to Kennedy's third feature, a large private room with a service bar that was used exclusively for parties. He closed the door behind him and waited, but not for long. Hurley opened the door a few minutes later, carrying a fresh drink for himself and a bottle of O'Doul's for McKenna. He was casually dressed, but in an expensive manner that made him look the picture of success. "Secret stuff?" he asked McKenna.

"Very," McKenna replied.

"Profitable stuff?"

"You'll make a few bucks."

Hurley closed the door with his foot and handed the O'Doul's to McKenna. "Who's the client?"

"Me."

"No. I mean, who's paying?"

"Me."

Hurley appeared shocked at that. "Brian, you can't afford me."

"It's not that big a job for you, but it has to remain just between us. You have to do it yourself, and never whisper a word to anyone about it."

"I'm listening."

McKenna took a piece of paper from his pocket, and passed it to Hurley. "It's a phone number, a cell phone," he said. "I need to know every call made from that phone in the past week. Can you do that?"

"Expensive, but not exorbitant. Yeah, I can do it. Does this have anything to do with your case?"

"Indirectly."

"Whose phone is it?"

"Cisco's."

"Whoa!" Hurley said, and he tried giving the piece of paper back to McKenna. "I'm not up for the kind of beating he'd give me."

McKenna didn't take the paper. "He'll never know."

"What do you think he's doing, boffing Angelita while you're at work?"

"Worse."

"Worse than that?"

"Cisco has known Justice for years," McKenna said. "Matter of fact, Justice is his hero."

"Cisco has a hero?"

"Yes."

"And he didn't tell you?"

"No."

"Whoa!" Hurley repeated. "I'm not getting involved in this."

"Just listen," McKenna said. "This thing has put Cisco under tremendous internal pressure, and it has to be eating him up. I'm gonna use whatever you can give me to end it, without hurting him. You have to tell me who he's been calling."

"You think Cisco's been calling Justice?"

"Yes."

"And if he has, you're promising me he comes out of this without a scratch?"

"Some internal damage he's already suffering, but nothing that'll show on the outside."

Hurley finished most of his drink in small sips while he thought over McKenna's request. Then he reached his decision. "Wait here."

"How long will it take you?" McKenna asked.

"Depends. Who's his service provider?"

"Sprint."

"Half hour, tops. I'll see to it that you're not disturbed."

McKenna was sound asleep with his head on a table when Hurley returned and woke him up. He had the up-to-date monthly billing printout for the calls made from Cisco's phone, and McKenna could make sense out of most of it. In the past week there had been three calls to Agnes in Florida, and Hurley had listed Mike McCormick as the subscriber. There was also a call to Miami, and Cisco's father was listed as the subscriber.

What intrigued McKenna were the seventeen one-minute calls he had made to a number with an 804 area code that had no subscriber listed. The first one was made the previous Wednesday at 7:33 in the morning, and if he was right, that made sense to McKenna. Wednesday they were all in Florida together, and it was that morning Cisco had bought the New

York papers and learned that Justice had begun his murderous spree. The last call was made at 12:22 that afternoon, the time McKenna figured he was just getting to The Wicked Wolf for his chat with Chipmunk. "How come there's no subscriber listed for all these short calls?" he asked Hurley.

"Because even I can't find out who it is. No one can," Hurley said. "It's one of those prepaid cell phones, the kind all the drug dealers are using now. Go into a phone store, buy the phone, prepay the bill, and the phone works as long as the money lasts."

"What does the eight-oh-four area code cover?"

"Northern Florida."

"Let's see if I can find out who it is," McKenna said.

"Don't you know?"

"Yeah. Just making sure." McKenna took out his phone, and dialed the number. The response was immediate: "Leave me alone. I'm busy." The voice on the message was very deep.

Yeah, Justice, you sure have been busy, McKenna thought, and he ended the call. So Cisco's been going frantic trying to get in touch with Justice. Seventeen calls, all billed at one minute, so all he got was the same message I just got.

McKenna looked up to find Hurley watching him with undisguised interest. "Were you right?" he asked.

"Unfortunately, yes," McKenna replied. "Thanks, Bob. What do I owe you?"

"Just your eternal silence about this, and I consider that a bargain for me."

NINETEEN

Cisco always said that he would rather be an hour early for work than a minute late, so McKenna was waiting outside Cisco's apartment building at 4:30, an hour and a half before they were due in the office.

Cisco came out at 4:45, looking refreshed until he saw McKenna. He stopped in his tracks, then forced a smile as he approached his partner. "Looks like you didn't get any sleep."

"I slept, but not much," McKenna replied.

"You know?" Cisco asked, appearing unconcerned.

"Uh-huh."

"Chipmunk?"

"He just confirmed what I already suspected in the back of my mind."

"Suspected since Justice dropped off the loot at Congregation Beth El?"

"Yeah, since he dropped three million off at an obscure synagogue most people didn't know even existed. Your synagogue."

"So where do we go from here?" Cisco asked.

"First we have an enlightening chat, and then we go to the office."

"So I can either resign, get fired, or maybe even get arrested?" Cisco asked, smiling.

"Arrested for what?"

"Something to do with obstructing justice."

"You didn't obstruct justice. Matter of fact, you've been trying your best to catch Justice all along."

"You sure?"

"Certain. It was you who came up with the idea that he dropped onto the Cruz garage by parachute, it was you who suggested where De Sales was keeping his loot, and it was you who figured out the way Cruz's spy had been able to identify the three informants."

"All things you would have figured out yourself, sooner or later," Cisco countered, still smiling. "You're not me, but you're still no dummy."

McKenna wanted to keep the process on track, so he didn't reply to Cisco's taunt. "Not only am I certain you've been doing everything you can to wind up this investigation . . ."

"Everything but tell you who Justice is," Cisco countered.

"But you will?"

"Chipmunk didn't tell you?"

"No. He figures it's your place to tell me."

"He's right," Cisco stated.

McKenna waited for Cisco to tell him who Justice really was, but Cisco wasn't ready yet. "So I've been helpful in the beginning, but are you sure I'll be there for you at the end?"

"Certain. When push finally comes to shove, you'll be there, doing everything you can to help me put Justice in the box."

"What makes you so sure?"

"The mosque. If you weren't trying just as hard as I am to catch him, you wouldn't have told me when you saw him leave by the side door. If you didn't, we wouldn't have found out he'd been there until the imam opened up in the morning."

"So I'm still okay in your book?"

"A good partner operating under some tough rules I'm trying to understand."

"How about a good friend?" Cisco asked, and for the first time the smile left his face.

"That, too, and I know you're a man who values his friends," McKenna said.

"All of them?"

"You don't have many."

"I don't?" Cisco asked, appearing surprised at the statement.

"Of course not. There aren't many people who can put up with you."

"Royal pain in the ass?" Cisco asked, and the smile returned.

"Most of the time."

"But you can put up with me?"

"Most of the time," McKenna said. "Game's over, Cisco. Who is he?"

Cisco hesitated, and McKenna thought for a moment that he wasn't going to answer, but he finally did. "Donny North is my other good friend. He's a retired state police captain. Years ago he was the CO of their Violent Felony Apprehension Squad, spent quite a bit of time in town working with our cops."

"North? Then Craig North is his son?"

"Yeah, it was Craig who was driving the Chevy at the mosque last night."

"Good God! What a scandal we have shaping up here," McKenna said. "A retired state police captain committing murders all over town with the help of his son, an active NYPD detective sergeant?"

"I wish it wasn't so, but that's what we have."

"Motive?"

"Consuela Andersen, the DEA pilot. Donny's daughter and Craig's sister. She was quite a girl. When Cruz had the bomb put on her plane, he signed his own death warrant."

"You knew North was planning to kill him?"

"I didn't really know he was planning it, but I knew he wanted to kill him."

"When did you know it was North who did it?"

"When I read the headline, 'Murder in Malba.' Knew at that instant Donny had finally gotten to Cruz," Cisco said.

"How?"

"Something Donny said once, a couple of years ago. We

went on a skin-diving trip to Belize. One night on the beach we had a few too many, and Donny got real serious on me. Rare occurrence. Told me, 'You know, if I had my way, those murdering bloodsuckers wouldn't be safe in their mansions in Malba.'"

"You knew he was talking about Cruz?"

"Yeah, I knew. He doesn't have a mean bone in his body—except when it comes to Cruz and anyone else connected to the drug trade."

"And Craig? Right from the beginning, you knew he was in on it?"

"Strongly suspected but didn't know for sure. Only met the kid once, but I liked his style."

"What made you suspect?"

"I knew he was a pilot, and I knew he was a sergeant in the Eight-Three Squad, so I called there. They told me he's out sick right now."

"Did you know he's never been out sick before?"

"No."

"Do you have his home number?"

"No, and I didn't ask for it."

"Did you ever meet Consuela?"

"Just once, the same time I met Craig. Went to her wedding in St. Augustine."

"St. Augustine? Is that where Donny North is living now?"

"Yeah, he moved down there a couple of years ago to be close to his grandkids. Consuela's husband was from there, and that's where he settled with the kids after she was killed."

"What does the husband do?"

"Runs a martial arts school of some kind."

"Have you tried getting in touch with Donny?"

"I'm constantly trying his cell phone but no good. All I get is his smartass message for me: I'm busy; leave me alone."

"What would you have told him, if you could've gotten hold of him?"

"He knew I was going on vacation, and I think he waited for me to be gone before he started. I would've told him that I'm in the game now, so it's time to pack up and run."

"And if he did run?"

"Then he got away."

"You wouldn't have said a word about him?"

"Not a peep, but it's too late for that now."

Well, I'm glad that's on the table, McKenna thought. "Donny's going down?"

"Unless he leaves the country, yeah, he is."

"And Craig?"

"I hope not," Cisco said. "He's helping his father, but he hasn't killed anybody."

"Helping him plenty. Technically, he's an accessory to murder and just as guilty as his father."

"I don't care. He's still a good kid in my book."

McKenna decided to leave that subject alone for the moment. "Tell me about Donny."

"Simply put, he's the best at just about everything he does."

Coming from Cisco, that statement shocked McKenna. "I thought you were the best."

"At most things, only when Donny's not around. He's tough as nails . . ."

"Tougher than you?"

"He's got me by twenty years, but in his day, maybe. He's also a better sky diver and a better skin diver than I am, and we both know he's a better shot."

"How old is he?"

"I dunno. Early sixties, I guess."

"Does he golf?"

"Scratch golfer, beats me every time."

Beats Cisco at golf? That's certainly a redeeming quality, McKenna thought. "What are you better at?"

"Police work. He'd give me an argument on that, but he has to learn that I'm the best detective ever."

"Give me his history."

"U.S. citizen born in Panama, the Canal Zone. His father ran one of the tugs down there."

"Speaks Spanish?"

"Perfectly."

"When did he come to New York?"

"He did a stint in the army, joined in Panama, caught the end of the Korean War. Bronze star. Then he headed to New York and did odd jobs for a while."

"Odd jobs?"

"Very handy guy. Did construction, worked for an autobody shop, and then worked a while for a locksmith. Says he really liked that job."

"He's still liking it, and running us in circles while he's at it," McKenna noted. "When did he join the troopers?"

"Don't know, exactly. Must have been in the late fifties, because he was retired when I met him. Did twenty-five years with the troopers."

"And I guess he wound up in the Bomb Squad?"

"For a while, back in the sixties, but he spent most of his time in their Criminal Investigation Bureau as he worked his way up on the Job. Made captain, and was made CO of their Violent Felony Apprehension Squad. Worked all over the state, but his office was in the World Trade Center."

"Wife?"

"Died before I met him, when the kids were young. Breast cancer."

"How long have you known him?"

"Met him in eighty-nine during a skin-diving trip to Key West. Both from New York, both cops, and both fun-loving manly men, so we hit it right off."

"Did you know that Donny has a spot on his pancreas?" McKenna asked, and he saw that the news hit Cisco hard.

"Cancer?" he asked.

"Can't say for sure, but I assume so."

"How does Chipmunk know about this?"

"John Daley is still Donny's doctor."

Cisco also knew Daley and understood how Chipmunk had become so well informed. "Isn't pancreatic cancer the one that's always fatal? A painful, debilitating death?"

"Yeah, it is."

Cisco smiled and shook his head. "Then I guess that's not the death Donny has in mind for himself."

McKenna agreed, but he didn't want to comment on it. Instead, he thought it was time to ask the question that most needed answering. "You have any idea where he's hiding out?"

"Not a precise idea, but I'd bet someplace upstate. We know he put a lotta miles on that truck, and he used to live upstate."

"Where upstate?"

"He had a place in Orange County, near Middletown."

"And how far would that be from the Ryder lot?"

"Close enough, I think. Maybe eighty miles," Cisco said. "Upstate is where we should be looking for him."

McKenna knew the next problem would be a tough one that would stretch his friendship with Brunette to the limit. He wasn't sure how Brunette would react to the news that Cisco had known Justice's identity all along, but he strongly suspected that he would consider Cisco's role a dereliction of duty that couldn't be pardoned—and the timing couldn't be worse. In an hour Brunette would be holding a press conference in which most of the reporters would be holding his feet to the fire, and that wouldn't do. McKenna had to let Brunette know about Donny and Craig North, but he couldn't let him know the source of the information. Maybe someday he could, when they were all long retired, but not now. In the meantime, Brunette would have to be given a story. By the time Cisco and McKenna got to Police Headquarters, McKenna had come up with a plan.

McKenna squared his tie, knocked on the door, and entered Brunette's office. He had expected to find his friend worried and in a state of some consternation, but Brunette looked relaxed. "You get some sleep?" McKenna asked.

"More than you, I can see. You could use a complete makeover," Brunette replied. "Got any good news for me?"

"Maybe. You got any for me?"

"News, but I don't know how good it is for us. We got a detective in the Narcotics Intelligence Section who's been doing quite a bit of traveling over the past year. Been to the Caymans twice, the Bahamas four times, and Switzerland five."

"All countries noted for their secretive banking policies," McKenna noted. "Cash havens, with no questions asked."

"I imagine he's also been having some fun with his millions in other places. Took a two-week Asian tour with his family, and they spent another week in Mexico."

"So he's crooked, but at least he's a family man," McKenna said.

"His wife is in on it, too, helping him to hide the cash. She made nine trips to either Switzerland, the Caymans, or the Bahamas without him."

"What's his name?"

"Fahey. Detective Second Grade John Fahey."

McKenna laughed, and it caught Brunette by surprise. "Something funny about a bought cop who's gonna cost me and this department a lot of embarrassment?"

"It's only funny when you consider: Once a spy, always a spy."

"Meaning?"

"Fahey is also Dog Dick's spy, and spying for Cruz must have come natural to him after spying and reporting to Internal Affairs for nine years."

"You sure he's the field associate?"

"He's the one, and there's a bonus. He's also Dog Dick's nephew."

Even Brunette had to smile at that, but McKenna knew it was gallows humor. The fact that the crooked cop who had been spying for both IAB and Gaston Cruz was also the nephew of a trusted but universally despised chief was bound to come out. The cops would love the news, but McKenna could think of more than one reporter who would run with it and cause Brunette even more grief.

"You said you had some news?" Brunette asked.

"Might have some news," McKenna said, and then he settled into his story. "I think it's possible the guy who drove Justice's getaway car this morning was Craig North."

"Really? When did this come to you?"

"I only caught a glimpse of him when he smacked our car, and I didn't recognize him at the time. But after I got home, I couldn't get to sleep because I couldn't stop thinking, 'Where have I seen that guy before?' Then it came to me."

"His personnel folder?" Brunette asked.

"Yeah, his picture."

"How sure are you?"

"At first, not too sure. Then I called the Eight-Three Squad. Craig North, a guy who never went sick before, is now out sick."

"Out sick? If it's him, why didn't he just take off?" Brunette asked, and then he answered his own question. "New sergeant, no seniority, so it'd be almost impossible for him to get any time off in the summer."

McKenna had anticipated Brunette's next move, one that he, as a detective, didn't have the authority to request. Under the rules, a cop out sick had to remain in his residence, and compliance with that rule was sometimes checked with visits to the sick cop's home by a boss from the Health Services Division. Brunette took North's personnel folder from the pile of folders still stacked along his wall and got North's address from it. He next called the CO of the Health Services Division and instructed him to immediately send a sergeant to North's home for a routine residency check.

Brunette next did something else that McKenna didn't have the authority to do. He called the commandant of the state police in Albany and requested that retired Captain North's personnel folder be immediately faxed to him.

Then Brunette called Chmil and instructed him to bring his two witnesses from the Classon Hotel to the Major Case Squad's office.

Brunette's last call was to O'Shaughnessy, with a short, direct message that caused McKenna to smile: "I want you and your nephew in my office within an hour. I don't care

how you do it, but don't fail to get him here." He then hung
up without giving O'Shaughnessy a chance to respond, but
his next action gave McKenna a strong indication of where
Brunette was headed. He called his secretary in and told her
to make arrangements to have a lawyer from the detectives'
union and a tough, experienced ADA from the Manhattan
District Attorney's Narcotics Bureau standing by and waiting for his summons to police headquarters.

TWENTY

Because there was so much to be done, the press conference necessarily had to be postponed until eight o'clock. McKenna, of course, *knew* they were on the right track, but appearances had to be maintained with Brunette in order to save Cisco. He thought it best to let Brunette digest the information as it came in and then let him form his own conclusions.

Brunette began with a reexamination of Craig North's personnel folder, and the first thing he noticed was that, like Justice, Craig North had type B blood. Then he received the phone call from the CO of the Health Services Division. Craig North was not home.

When Donny North's personnel folder was faxed from Albany, Brunette attacked it with gusto. There was a facsimile of North's photo taken for the retired ID card he had been issued when he left the state police, and Brunette examined it for a moment. "Retired in eighty-five, so that's what he looked like then," he said as he passed it to McKenna.

North was smiling slightly as he stared at the camera, as if someone had just told him a good joke he had heard before. Except for the powerful, thick neck just visible at the bottom of the photo, McKenna would describe him as an average-looking fellow, with no particularly distinguishing characteristics visible on his face. North *did* look like a nice guy, and certainly not a bloodthirsty killer. "How old was he when this picture was taken?" he asked Brunette.

Brunette thumbed through the top pages until he found

something that made him smile. "Date of birth: July 19, 1934."

"So today's his birthday."

"That's right, buddy," Brunette said, and his smile broadened. "His seventieth birthday. He was fifty-one when that picture was taken."

"A seventy-year-old man is running us ragged?"

"Doesn't make us look too good, does it?"

"No, it doesn't," McKenna replied as he stared at the photo. "Fifty-one, and he doesn't look a day over forty."

"So what's he look like now?"

"Pretty good, we know, and not too much older. This picture is almost twenty years old, and one of Chmil's witnesses from the Classon Hotel thought he might've been fifty."

"And the other one?"

"Maybe sixty. Let's do something with this picture so we can use it in a photo array to show them. Might as well get him positively identified for the record."

"Good idea."

Brunette had the CO of the Photo Section standing tall in his office five minutes later. He wanted a photo taken from the facsimile, and then he wanted North's features in that photo altered to age North twenty years. The CO assured Brunette that it would be done, and done quickly.

Then Brunette returned to the folder. As he went through it, he noted that North's blood type was B, that he was from the Canal Zone and spoke Spanish, and that his occupations before joining the state police were auto-body mechanic and locksmith. North had graduated from the State Police Academy as number one in his class, and he had also earned the top prizes in the physical fitness and shooting categories.

Brunette found that North had always been highly evaluated by his superiors and found especially relevant the comments made on North's evaluations during his four years with the state police's Bomb Squad. His CO had twice stated on paper that "this investigator is the best bomb technician in the unit."

Then, near the end of the folder, Brunette found something that really piqued his interest. "What was that female DEA agent's name, the one whose plane Cruz had blown out of the sky?" he asked McKenna.

"Consuela Andersen. Why?"

"Because on November 21, 1966, Donald North's wife Jasmine gave birth to their second child at the Upstate Medical Center, a daughter they named Consuela." Brunette reached into his bottom desk drawer and took out the DEA case folder on the investigation into the death of Consuela Andersen. He thumbed through it until he found what he was looking for, then closed the folder and smiled.

"We got motive?" McKenna asked.

"Or an incredible coincidence. Another Consuela in this case, Consuela Andersen, was also born on November 21, 1966. I don't think I'd be going out on a limb if I said that we definitely do have motive. Next to greed, the most common motive when it comes to murder."

"Yeah, revenge," McKenna agreed. "When Cruz ordered Consuela's death, he didn't know that her father was a smart, tough, and very talented man with a long memory."

McKenna was making himself and Brunette another cup of coffee when O'Shaughnessy knocked and entered. He was alone, and once again he was in full uniform, but the summons to Brunette's office had affected his composure. O'Shaughnessy nodded to McKenna, and McKenna thought the chief looked worried—worried and confused.

"Where's your nephew?" Brunette barked before O'Shaughnessy even reached his desk.

"Outside, sir. I have him waiting outside," O'Shaughnessy said, and then he brought himself to attention in front of Brunette's desk and rendered his customary salute.

Brunette ignored the salute. "The time for military courtesies is over. Sit down, Jerry," he ordered, and O'Shaughnessy complied. He sat in the chair facing Brunette's desk, waiting for the bad news.

Brunette let O'Shaughnessy stew for a minute before hitting him with the first question. "You travel a lot, Jerry?"

McKenna could see at once that O'Shaughnessy didn't see the relevance of the question. "No, not much," the chief said, confused. "My wife's sister has a condo in Myrtle Beach, and we try to get down there every couple of years."

"What I mean is, do you travel much out of the country?"

"Not counting a couple of visits to Canada, I've been abroad twice."

"When and where?"

"Years ago the wife and I went on a package tour of the British Isles. That would be sometime in the eighties. Then, four years ago we spent a week together in Ireland. We were in Dublin for the millennium celebration."

"Is your passport still valid?"

"I think so," O'Shaughnessy replied, and McKenna could see that his confusion was mounting. "My wife takes care of those things, and she would've told me if it was set to expire."

"If I wanted to see your passport, would that present any problem for you?"

"None whatsoever. If you like, I'll call my wife, and you can send someone to my house to pick it up."

"That won't be necessary, Chief. I believe you. How about your nephew? Does he travel much?"

"He's away a lot, but I don't know if you'd call it traveling. Him and his wife have a cabin in the Poconos, and they get there whenever they can."

"When did he get this cabin?"

"January of last year."

"What makes you so sure of the time frame?"

"Because I loaned him part of the money for the down payment. Four thousand dollars, and he pays me back two hundred a month—always right on time," O'Shaughnessy said, and then he noted Brunette's smile. "He's very responsible, never a problem," O'Shaughnessy felt a need to add.

"So, to your knowledge, he doesn't travel much out of the country?"

"He took the wife and kids to someplace in Mexico last year. Cozumel, I think. Told me they had a vacation package there too good to resist."

"Does he get along with his wife?"

"Lovely couple, Beth and John were childhood sweethearts. They're still crazy about each other."

"So that's it, as far as travel is concerned? Just a bargain-priced family trip to Cozumel?" Brunette asked.

"That's it," O'Shaughnessy replied with certainty.

"No short trips every couple of weeks to Switzerland, the Cayman Islands, or the Bahamas?"

"Of course not. How could a detective afford that kind of lifestyle?" O'Shaughnessy quickly replied, and then McKenna watched his face as realization dawned on him. The chief lost his military bearing and slouched in his chair, and to McKenna, the stickler-for-the-rules commanding officer of the Internal Affairs Bureau suddenly seemed a pathetic and broken old man.

Brunette passed O'Shaughnessy the INS Passport Control report on John Fahey. O'Shaughnessy studied it intently for a few seconds, and disgust registered on his face. Then he gave up and placed the report face-down on Brunette's desk. He appeared to be at a loss for words, and he moved his tongue across his lips until he managed to form the question that had to be asked. "He's Gaston Cruz's spy?"

"And an accessory to murder," Brunette replied.

"The three informants?"

"Yeah, them. He sealed their fate when he sold their names to Cruz."

"How much did he get?"

"Two million a month for the past twenty-two months. Forty-four million, all in cash."

"Stashed overseas?"

"Most of it, but I'm sure he still has a few million hidden in either his house or his Poconos cabin."

"So he traded honor and trust for money," O'Shaughnessy said, more to himself than to Brunette, and the statement seemed to steel him. "His honor, and mine."

"Lots of money, but the concept's the same. The way I see it, he's a bought, dirty cop, a despicable character deserving no mercy, who was able to operate right under the nose of the CO of my Internal Affairs Bureau."

McKenna had expected Brunette's assessment to stun O'Shaughnessy, but it didn't. He squared his shoulders and stared directly into Brunette's eyes. "Yes, sir, you're right. It's a totally unacceptable situation," he said. "Where do you suggest we go from here?"

"We have two options. With option one, I will have a grand jury convened this afternoon, I will have the facts in this case presented to the jurors, and then, acting pursuant to the Mutual Legal Assistance Treaty, that grand jury will immediately issue subpoenas to banks in Switzerland, the Cayman Islands, and the Bahamas requesting information on all accounts under the control of John Fahey or his wife, Beth Fahey."

"Is Beth in on this, too?" O'Shaughnessy asked.

"In up to her eyeballs," Brunette said, and he passed O'Shaughnessy the INS Passport Control report on Beth Fahey's travels. "She made nine separate, short trips overseas on her own, presumably to deposit millions in cash."

"I see," O'Shaughnessy said. He accepted the report from Brunette, barely glanced at it, and placed it face-down on top on his nephew's report on the desk. "Go on, please."

"Once that grand jury is in possession of the appropriate records, your nephew and his wife will be indicted and subsequently arrested."

"He won't be arrested until then?"

"No, not with option one, unless your nephew or his wife tries to flee. Instead, I will suspend him from all duties, without pay, and I will have all his and his wife's activities closely monitored so that they will not have the opportunity to remove any cash from their house or their cabin."

"What would they be looking at, with option one?"

"As much time as the DA can get for them, and I assure you, there will be no plea bargaining. The charges will be very serious, and the media scrutiny will be intense. In the end, they will both be going away for a long, long time."

Brunette paused a moment to let it all sink in, but O'Shaughnessy's facial expression and demeanor didn't change as he took in Brunette's predictions. He remained attentive, and certainly interested, but silent, so McKenna could only imagine what was going through his mind.

"They have how many kids?" Brunette asked. "Two?"

"Yes, sir, two. Dan is seven, and Eddie is five."

"Then that's just another bad consequence of option one. With both their parents in jail for a long time, those kids will be farmed out to relatives, almost like orphans. They did nothing wrong, so that's regrettable. Matter of fact, there's a lot about option one that I'd find regrettable, so it's not the option I'd prefer," Brunette said. "You can imagine why, can't you?"

"Yes, sir, I can."

"Describe for me, please, the other regrettable consequences of option one."

"First of all, without any possibility of a plea bargain, this mess will go to trial, meaning it will remain in the public eye for a long time. The department will suffer tremendous embarrassment and an enormous loss of prestige. Naturally, as the person responsible for putting my nephew in a position where he could dishonor himself and the department, John and Beth wouldn't be the only two who would deserve to suffer, and everyone would expect that. I imagine that I would be treated harshly."

"Yes, you would," Brunette said. "Regrettably, with option one, you could no longer serve in your present position. You would leave this office tonight with the rank of captain, a demotion of five ranks, to take your new assignment in a place far out of the public's eye. I'm thinking that maybe you could serve as the executive officer of the Building Maintenance Section."

"Quite appropriate, sir, and I would certainly understand," O'Shaughnessy said, without emotion. "However, I am ready to listen to option two."

"With option two, you fall honorably on your sword. For the present, I can no longer afford to keep you as the commanding officer of the Internal Affairs Bureau, so you would leave this office with the rank of assistant chief—a demotion of one rank."

"I understand, sir, and quite generous of you," O'Shaughnessy said. "Might I ask what my new duties would entail?"

"At the present, I don't have an opening commensurate with an assistant chief's rank, so I'll assign you as the duty chief until something comes up."

"When would I assume my new duties?"

"Tomorrow night. Of course, if that doesn't suit you, you could retire without prejudice, and I'd understand."

"Is that what you'd prefer I do?"

"Not at all. You're probably the most hated man in the department, but every large organization needs a man like you. You've always worked hard on my behalf, you've always been loyal to me, and I want you to know that I appreciate it."

"Thank you, sir. Then I'll be staying as long as you want me. What are my responsibilities with option two?"

"After you leave this office, you explain his new facts of life to your nephew. You will tell him that I guarantee that he will do ten years max and that he'll be poor and jobless when he gets out. However, his wife will not be charged with any crime."

"And what does he have to do to get this deal?"

"After you give him his Miranda warnings, he makes a full confession to you and provides you with banks, account numbers, and amounts. He will then immediately and voluntarily be interviewed by an ADA in the presence of his union lawyer. While the videotape rolls, he will repeat all the information he gave you. Then he will be arrested by Detective Sanchez."

At the mention of Cisco's name, O'Shaughnessy lost his composure for the first time. The muscles in his neck tensed, and he halfway stood up, but then he thought better of it. He relaxed into the chair, passed his hand across his brow, and then once again brought himself to the seated position of attention. "Detective Sanchez? Does it have to be him?" he asked.

"Sorry, but yes, it must be him," Brunette said. "He's the one who put this all together, the one who came up with the idea that enabled us to discover your nephew's role in this sordid affair. The piper must be paid, and the devil must be given his due."

It took O'Shaughnessy a minute to digest the news, and then he appeared to resign himself to it. "I can see how, in light of these circumstances, Detective Sanchez would be the appropriate choice," he said evenly. "Are there any other indignities in store for me?"

"Yes. At my press conference today, it will be necessary that I explain it was your nephew who was Cruz's bought cop. That fact would come out sooner or later, so I feel it would be better to be up-front with the press."

"And my demotion and reassignment would also be mentioned?"

"Necessary from the public's viewpoint, but I will endeavor to present you in the best possible light. You know, 'The chief is a victim of an unfortunate circumstance some might understand. You can choose your friends, but you can't choose your family.' I'll also go out of my way to explain that you still have my confidence."

"Very kind of you, sir. Thank you, but I have a question. What happens if my nephew doesn't take the deal?"

"I can't imagine he'd be that stupid, but then he'd be free to leave. That would bring him and his wife back to option one."

"I'll see to it that he isn't that stupid. And after he's arrested?"

"Based upon his statements, a search warrant will be obtained for wherever it is he has his loose cash stashed."

"Might I say that it's a very nice offer you're making him, Commissioner? Certainly better than he deserves."

"I'm taking into account the amount of money it took to turn him."

"The price for his treachery? For an honest man, no price should be high enough. It's a better deal than I'd offer him."

"I might be able to throw in a little more," Brunette said. "Maybe a prison close to the city, so it'd be easier for family to visit him."

"Nice of you to offer, but that won't be necessary, sir. I won't be visiting him, and his wife is just as guilty as he is, so why don't we let the chips fall where they may?"

"Whatever you say, Chief. Let's get on with it."

O'Shaughnessy stood up, assumed the position of attention, and saluted. Brunette then also stood and returned the salute. O'Shaughnessy nodded to McKenna and left.

"Wow! There's a guy with some style under fire," McKenna said. "A real soldier."

"Surprised?" Brunette asked.

"Yeah, you?"

"A bit, but it's nice to know he can take as well as he can give. He earned some respect from me today."

"Can't believe I'm saying this about O'Shaughnessy, but he earned some respect from me, too."

"O'Shaughnessy? So he's no longer Dog Dick to you?" Brunette asked.

Can I go that far? McKenna wondered. "For now, at least, I'll think of him as Chief O'Shaughnessy."

"Would you make sure you give Cisco your new opinion on the chief?"

"I will, but I don't think it will make much difference to him. Cisco hates him, and the fact that O'Shaughnessy showed some style today won't change that."

TWENTY-ONE

Fahey took the deal, and he was confessing to the ADA on video in Brunette's conference room when Chmil arrived at the Major Case Squad office with his two witnesses, the illicit romancing couple from the Classon Hotel. By then, the retouched photo of Donald North had arrived from the Photo Section. McKenna placed the photo in a photo array folder, along with the photos of five other late-middle-aged black men, and gave it to Chmil.

Chmil separated his witnesses and showed each one the photo array. Both picked out North and identified him as the man they had seen carrying a duffel bag in the stairwell of the Classon Hotel. Both, however, stated he looked older in the picture than he did in the flesh.

It was just minutes before eight by the time McKenna got back up to Brunette's office. He found Brunette on the phone with someone who was a "Sir" to him, so McKenna knew that could only be the mayor. The door to the conference room was closed.

"Is your ass out of the fire?" McKenna asked as soon as Brunette hung up.

"He's happy about us finally getting Fahey, but he left me with the definite impression he expects a quick resolution to the Justice matter."

"How's it going in there?" McKenna asked, nodding toward the conference room.

"Better now. That ADA's smart, and he had the right questions, but he didn't have the right attitude for a slickster like Fahey. It was like pulling teeth getting the story from him. Just yes-and-no answers, volunteering nothing, so it would've taken all night. Then Cisco stopped the tape and read Fahey the riot act."

"And now Fahey's going into detail?"

"Since Cisco decided it was him who should be asking the questions. Complete story, and Fahey hardly stops to take a breath."

"How did Cruz know Fahey was the cop he should make the big offer to?"

"Fahey doesn't know for sure, but he figures it might be because his name was on the search warrant they did on Cruz's house."

"They left Cruz a copy?"

"Had to. Cruz knew the rules. But, according to Fahey, it made no difference which cop Cruz picked. For the amount of money Cruz was prepared to pay for the info he wanted, he's saying that anyone would've taken it."

"So he still thinks that, for the right price, murder and wholesale drug dealing can be condoned?"

"And actively aided. That's why he's going to jail."

"How did Cruz get in touch with him?"

"Cruz didn't involve himself in it, and Fahey didn't know the paymaster's name until Cisco showed him the picture Lela Cruz gave you guys."

"So Jorge Rodriguez handled the negotiations and payments," McKenna said. "Makes sense."

"It started when Fahey got into his car to go to work one morning, and he noticed two packages on his backseat. One million in cash in the packages, plus a note with a phone number. Note was short and to the point: If you want a million in cash every month, call the number. Fahey thought about it and made the call."

"When?"

"He must've done some soul-searching, but not much. Says he called the number about a week later. Jorge arranged a meeting with him at Sheep Meadow in Central Park. Told

Fahey what he wanted, and Fahey said he'd do it, but only after holding him up for another million a month."

"What did Jorge want? Everything?"

"For that price, of course. The complete Cruz file, the files on all the active investigations being done by the Narcotics Division, and anything else Fahey thought useful."

"How was payment and the exchange of information made?"

"Fahey gave Jorge a set of his car keys. He's the only house on his block way out in Suffolk County, Wading River Hollow. Jorge drove out there once a month, put the cash in his trunk, and took the files that Fahey had copied and put there."

"Which included the names of the informants?"

"That was one of the things Fahey tried dancing around with the ADA, but Cisco got it right out of him."

So, thanks to Fahey, our Narcotics Division became Cruz's investigating agency, McKenna thought. Two million a month to the right cop, and Cruz was able to scare away the competition, become the top dog, and ensure his own safety. "Did Fahey have any further personal contact with Jorge?"

"I imagine so, but I can't say for sure. I had to leave the session to get ready for this press conference."

"Is O'Shaughnessy still in there?"

"No. He can't stand the sight of Fahey, left right after you did," Brunette said. "Next issue. How much do you think I should tell them on what we know about Justice?"

"It would be nice if you could convey the impression that we're going pretty good without telling them we know who he is."

"You're afraid he'd run?"

"If he did, you wouldn't get the quick resolution the mayor wants," McKenna said. "Besides, I'm sure he loves his son as much as he loved his daughter, so he must have some contingency plan in mind to protect him if things get hot."

"He *has* shown us he's exceptionally good at making and

carrying out his plans," Brunette noted. "Give me a timetable. When do we tell them we know who Justice is?"

"If he hits again, of course. That'll give you something to keep the press at bay."

"And suppose he doesn't? How much time do we need to capture him?"

"I'd appreciate another couple of days."

The press conference was held in the auditorium of police headquarters, and McKenna took it in from the wings of the stage. It started fifteen minutes late and went long.

Brunette started by saying that an arrest had been made of a detective assigned to a sensitive position in the Narcotics Division, and evidence had been developed that he had been paid forty-four million in cash by Gaston Cruz.

The figure astounded the reporters, and Justice was forgotten for the moment—which was exactly what Brunette had hoped would happen. He was prepared to go on, but let the flurry of questions stop him. He answered each one patiently and fully. Yes, it was probable that most of the major investigations launched by the Narcotics Division over the past two years had been compromised by Detective Fahey, Brunette admitted, and he went on to explain how Gaston Cruz had utilized the information provided by Fahey to become the narcotics kingpin of the East Coast.

There had been questions on how Fahey finally had been identified and captured, and Brunette explained that Cisco, McKenna, and Chief O'Shaughnessy had been instrumental in uncovering his role. Then he dropped the bombshell: Fahey was O'Shaughnessy's nephew, but that hadn't deterred the chief from actively aiding the investigation that resulted in his arrest. He added that O'Shaughnessy was responsible for getting Fahey to reveal the locations of the money he had received, and Brunette then stated that he expected most of the forty-four million would be seized from the offshore banks where Fahey had deposited his payoffs.

Then came the question Brunette knew had to come: "As

the commanding officer of the Internal Affairs Bureau, shouldn't Chief O'Shaughnessy have uncovered his nephew's conduct before he had been able to cause so much damage to the Narcotics Division?" Brunette replied that while the matter was still under review, it was possible O'Shaughnessy should have been able to do just that. Therefore, Brunette announced, while he appreciated O'Shaughnessy's recent efforts, and had never doubted his honesty and dedication to duty, he had felt it necessary to demote and reassign the chief.

That caused a stir which intensified when Brunette told them that, in addition to the millions to be seized from Fahey's overseas accounts, he expected that the Narcotics Division, in conjunction with the federal government, would soon be seizing *billions* from Cruz's hidden overseas accounts.

"Did information from Justice's letters to Messing help you develop this information?" was the next question. "In an incidental way," Brunette replied. "Most of the information was independently developed by Detective McKenna and Detective Sanchez, using the full resources of the police department as they conducted their investigation into the murder of Gaston Cruz."

"Would the same results have been obtained if Justice hadn't killed Cruz?" another reporter shouted.

"Probably not," Brunette was forced to admit. "Last question."

"Are you any closer to identifying and arresting Justice?"

The ambiguous question was all McKenna could have hoped for, and he knew Brunette was stifling a smile as he answered. "We believe we are, and we will fully report on all further developments as they occur."

"Have you identified him?" was shouted by three reporters at once, but Brunette had already left the podium and was headed for the wings. McKenna followed him out the side door. They hadn't reached the elevators before McKenna's cell phone rang, and he knew who was calling.

"Well, *do* you have him identified?" Messing asked.

"I didn't see you at the conference," McKenna replied.

"I took it in on TV. Do you?"

"Off the record?"

"You're hurting me, Brian, but yeah. Off the record."

"We have him ID'd, but I can't talk now."

"Where do you want to meet?"

"It can't be around here, and it can't be right away," McKenna said. "I'll be hiding from all your pals for the rest of the night, and I'll be busy here for a while."

"Sotto Cinque at eleven?" Messing suggested.

"I'll try to be there. If I can't make it, I'll give you a call."

"Messing?" Brunette asked when McKenna ended the call.

"Yeah, Messing."

"A deal's a deal," Brunette stated, and McKenna knew he would be meeting Messing on time. The elevator doors opened, but then McKenna's phone rang again. Brunette held the doors, and waited while McKenna answered it. "What now, Phil?"

But it wasn't Messing. "Just thought you'd like to know. Your partner gave me a call a couple of hours ago. Asked me to get him a Craig North's cell phone number," Hurley said.

"And did you?" McKenna asked him.

"Just did."

Brunette was watching him, and if he knew McKenna was talking to Hurley, he would naturally want to know what Hurley had to say. Under the circumstances, that wouldn't do, so McKenna decided a small subterfuge was called for. "Okay, Phil, you win. Eleven-thirty at the latest," McKenna said. He ended the call and joined Brunette on the elevator.

The Fahey session was over by the time McKenna and Brunette got back to Brunette's office, and the conference room was empty. That meant Cisco was at Central Booking with Fahey.

The first thing Brunette did was call Sheeran to his office. "What'd you think of the press conference?"

"Good just about throughout, but a little confusing at the

end," Sheeran replied. "We don't want them to know we have Justice identified?"

"Not just yet, but in the meantime I want a full-blown stakeout at his son's house."

"Already got that going," Sheeran said.

"What are their orders?" Brunette asked.

"Arrest him if he shows up, but put nothing over the air. He's to be brought directly to the Major Case Squad office without the press being made aware we have him."

Sheeran's statement told McKenna two things. One was that Cisco had brought the boss up to speed on recent developments in the case. The other was something McKenna expected, that Sheeran had been sharp enough to anticipate Brunette's order, right down to realizing that Brunette wanted no publicity in the event Craig North was arrested.

Brunette gave Sheeran a nod of approval and dismissed him. Then he produced the large map he had ordered. As he had directed, the Ryder rental lot in Queens was at the center, and a circle had been drawn around it to indicate the area falling within the one-hundred-seven–mile radius. "Let's go over this," Brunette suggested. "Why do we think he's upstate?"

"First of all, the car he used to kidnap Jorge was stolen from a parking lot upstate," McKenna said. "Then we have to take into account the fact that he's lived there, knows the area."

"Any ideas on where upstate?"

"None."

While Brunette made a fresh pot of coffee, McKenna stared at the map, but he couldn't concentrate on Justice. Cisco was foremost on his mind, and he wondered why his partner had obtained Craig North's cell phone number from Hurley without first consulting him. Was Cisco planning to tip off Donny and Craig if we got close to them? If so, that would be a violation of trust and a dereliction of duty that couldn't be tolerated.

The prospect bothered McKenna, but what bothered him more was that he was lying to one friend to protect the other.

He sympathized with the situation Cisco found himself in, but he wasn't sure if Brunette would. He realized that Brunette placed a high value on friendship, but McKenna was certain of one thing: Brunette would neither condone nor tolerate Cisco tipping off either of the Norths.

Then McKenna's phone rang again, and he answered it. "You going out of your mind?" Cisco asked.

"Yeah, thanks to you, I am," McKenna replied.

"Then why don't you give yourself some relief? You have my permission to tell your pal about me and Donny. Would that make things better for you and that pesky conscience of yours?"

"Sure would, but I don't know if it's a good idea."

"If it has to be done, the timing's perfect," Cisco countered. "I'm the one who got Fahey, Ray knows it, and he just about made a hero of me with the press. He won't kill me over this."

"You sure?"

"Reasonably. By the way, I got Craig's cell phone number from Hurley. Figured it might come in handy for us later, in case we decide to do the right thing."

McKenna was relieved that Cisco parted with that piece of information, but what did he mean by "the right thing"? Then he noticed that Brunette was leaning against a file cabinet, staring at him with a cup of coffee in each hand. "What's on your mind, Brian?"

McKenna ended the call and put the phone in his pocket. "Getting this guy, and wrapping up this case."

"There's nothing bothering you?"

Sharp, McKenna thought, but the question threw him into a state of indecision. He wanted to learn a thing or two about Brunette's thinking on the case before deciding whether or not Cisco was right. "When we get Donny North, suppose his son gets away. How would that affect you?"

Brunette gave McKenna his cup of coffee, then eyed him shrewdly while he took a sip of his own. "Not the optimum result, as far as the Job is concerned. Cop gone real bad is one way of looking at him," he said. "However, I wouldn't cry too much about it if he *did* get away."

McKenna put his cup on Brunette's desk. "You don't think he's a real bad guy?"

"We're just supposing here, right?"

"That's all we're doing."

"He's been a perfect soldier before this started. Smart, educated, hardworking, and dedicated, just the kind of guy we want, so I'm going to put myself in his shoes for a moment. I'm a great cop, and my sister, another great cop, has been murdered in the line of duty. We know who did it, but nothing bad is happening to the guy. Matter of fact, he's happy and prospering almost beyond belief, and I know he's corrupted somebody in the department to do it. You think that would be driving me out of my mind?"

"If you're any kind of guy, it would."

"Then you add in the fact that my father, another great cop who raised me and my sister by himself after my mother died—and did a good job at it—is a very sharp guy who's also going out of his mind over this, but he's prepared to do something about it, and accomplish quite a bit of good while he's at it."

"You'll admit that Justice's act hasn't been such a bad thing for this city?" McKenna asked.

"Not outside this room, I wouldn't. But just between us, he's the best thing to come along in ages. Made us look like real idiots at first, but if we get him soon, that's not too important. What is important is that, thanks to him, we're going to seize billions in drug assets, we're going to lock up many high-level drug dealers, and he got Cisco involved in this case, so now we got Fahey," Brunette said. "Giving those millions to the church, the mosque, and the synagogue wasn't such a bad thing, either—but these are all things we can't say."

"They'll be said anyway," McKenna predicted. "Despite our posturing, the press is making a hero out of him, and our citizens out there overwhelmingly agree with the points the press is making."

"So what's your point?"

"Just trying to think ahead a bit. If we manage to take him

alive, his trial will be a bigger media circus than O.J.'s. We have a great case against him, and everyone knows he's guilty of whatever we charge him with, but he's got massive public support—meaning, no matter what, we're going to come out of it looking like the bad guys."

"True, but you don't think that's something we'll have to worry about, do you?"

"No. I don't think he'll allow himself to be taken alive. But that still leaves us with Craig, and once we give out his story . . ."

"We still have a problem," Brunette said, and he took another sip of coffee while he thought out the scenario. "Suppose, just for the moment, Craig did get away. He'd still be one of the most wanted men in the world, face plastered on every front page. Where would he go, and what would he do?"

"Like we have to keep telling ourselves, his father's never without a plan. Before he started, I think he took into account the possibility that he was going down himself, but I'm sure he doesn't intend that fate for his son, and I'm just as sure he still has a few loose millions lying around. With enough money, anyone can disappear."

"If we screw up, and he somehow gets the opportunity," Brunette said. Then he smiled and shook his head. "Good for him, and maybe not too bad for us, but let's stop all this supposing."

McKenna made his decision. "I think he will get the opportunity."

"How?"

"Cisco."

"Cisco?"

"Donny North is his good friend. He knew right from the start that Donny is Justice."

"Whaaat?"

"That's right, and he put himself in the position of trying to catch his good friend."

"When did he tell you this?"

"He didn't. I had to figure it out for myself."

"Does he know you know?"

"Yeah, we had a chat."

"Does he know you're telling me?"

"He's the one who suggested I do."

Brunette finished his cup of coffee in one swallow, then picked up McKenna's. He took another long sip and sat behind his desk. "Give me this from the beginning."

McKenna told the story, and Brunette didn't have a single question until the end. "So you think Cisco might plan on tipping off Craig if we get close to him?"

"I think he may," McKenna replied.

"Do you approve?"

"Like you said, it wouldn't break my heart. But no, I don't approve."

"And neither do I. However, we both know Cisco always manages to get done whatever he intends to do—and he somehow manages to emerge unscathed," Brunette said, and then he stared hard at McKenna. "Therefore, if he does make that call someplace along the line, I, for one, don't want to know about it."

So Cisco has his tacit license to operate, McKenna thought. "Neither do I."

TWENTY-TWO

Cisco arrived back at the office just as McKenna was leaving for his meeting with Messing. Cisco was hungry, and he liked the food at Sotto Cinque, so he decided he wanted to tag along, especially since Messing would be picking up the tab.

Sotto Cinque was located at Third Avenue and East 29th Street, and Cisco had just found a parking spot around the corner from the restaurant when his phone rang. He answered it, smiled to McKenna, and said, "Good to hear from you, Donny. Nice of you to finally remember your old pal, the one you're running ragged while you're having your fun. Nice job you're doing."

Cisco had McKenna's total interest as he listened to North. "Yeah, my partner has you and your kid identified. I didn't tell him it was you, he figured it out on his own. I'd like to tell you more, but you know the rules," Cisco told North. "Why don't we get together for a drink, and have a couple of laughs before I introduce you to your millions of adoring fans?"

Cisco listened to North's short response and then said, "Have it your way, Donny, but I'm not sure that's the way to go. Probably very messy, and there's a big downside to your plan. We both know you have a story to tell, and your public's dying to hear it—and they're all prepared to believe whatever you have to say."

As Cisco listened to North's reply, McKenna was gesturing that he wanted to talk to North. Cisco waved him off. "Just tell me this one thing, and I'll try to find a way to pay you back," Cisco said to North. "Are you gonna be dealing with any more drug lords in the near future, or will I finally be able to get a good night's sleep tonight?"

North's reply was short. "Thanks for the heads-up, Donny. I appreciate it," Cisco said. "Hold on, will ya? My partner's becoming a real fan of yours, and he's dying to talk to you." He then passed the phone to McKenna.

"Donny? It's Brian McKenna," McKenna said.

"I know who you are, Brian, and I'd like to congratulate you on the job you're doing. First rate," North said, and McKenna was impressed by how deep his voice was. "If Cisco didn't blab, and I figured he wouldn't, I thought it would have taken a while longer to get me ID'd."

"Pretty first-rate job you're doing yourself," McKenna replied. "Very impressive, but I don't want a messy ending. I know about that spot on your pancreas, and I know what you're thinking."

"Who told you about the spot?"

"Chipmunk. He got it from John Daley."

"Is Chip the one who ID'd me for you?"

"No, and Lord knows I tried. He knew it was you, and he gave me some bits and pieces but not a name. You've got some good pals, tried and true."

"Yeah, Chip's good. Mind telling me how you put it together?"

"Got a glimpse of your son when he rammed us. Turns out I was studying his personnel folder just hours before. Didn't recognize him at first, but it finally came to me," McKenna explained. "How's he holding up?"

"He's strong, he's dedicated, and he's tireless. Good man, and I'm proud of him."

"You know you're putting him in the box, don't you?"

"I know, and he knows, but he wouldn't have it any other way."

"How are you holding up?"

"I've had better days, and I could sure use a good night's sleep, but I'm probably not going to get it. We're in endgame."

"More fun tonight?"

"If everything works out for me."

"Will you listen to a deal?"

"Brian, I know what you're going to say, and it won't make much difference to me, but I'm listening."

"If you and your son come in, you'll have to fend for yourself. But I promise you won't be put in the general population once you're in, and I'll make sure you get the best medical care available."

"Nice offer, and thanks. You realize that pancreatic cancer is incurable, don't you?"

"Yeah, I saw the Jimmy Carter pieces on TV. But think about being famous during your sunshine years, and I promise to get you as much access to the press as possible."

"You mean as much access as you can get me, don't you?"

"I've got some weight, and you'll be heard."

"Get to the part about my son," North said. "What's your offer on him?"

"He's gonna wind up being just about as popular as you are, and he also has a story to tell. The police commissioner is as sympathetic as he can be under the circumstances, and he has even more weight than me. Much more, and if I present the deal to him, he'll go for it. Have him come in, and I promise we'll both be speaking good and speaking often to the press about your son way before sentencing time, and that has to have an effect on the judge and the DA. They're all politicians, so that's sure to have an effect."

"Nice offer, Brian, and thanks, but I don't think he'll go for it. See ya."

"So you're both gonna go out in a blaze of glory?" McKenna asked, but North had ended the call. McKenna couldn't let Cisco know he had North's cell phone number, so he passed the phone to Cisco. "Call him back, please."

Cisco dialed the number and waited, but North didn't answer.

"Damn!" McKenna said. "I'm beat, and it looks like he has a big night in store for us."

"I'd say so," Cisco replied. "We might as well endure it on a full stomach."

Messing was already there, enjoying a martini at a table in the rear of the restaurant. He appeared to be in a good mood, and McKenna knew it was going to get better. Messing's take on them, however, was somewhat different. "You guys look like shit," he observed. "Eat hearty, then go home and get a day and a night of sleep."

"Like to, Phil, but we're gonna be going through the night and probably most of tomorrow—and you'll probably be just as busy as us," McKenna predicted as they took their seats. "Justice is gonna hit again tonight."

"How do you know?"

"Because he told us."

"You talked to him?"

"Just now. He gave Cisco a call, and then he talked to me for a while."

"Called you on your cell phone?" Messing asked Cisco.

"Yeah, he called my cell phone," Cisco said, and McKenna knew what was coming next. "How'd he get your number?"

"We're way, way off the record on this, now and forever. Right, Phil?" Cisco asked.

"Yeah, we're off," Messing said, but it appeared he didn't like the idea.

"He always had my cell phone number. We've been good pals for years."

"Years?"

"About fifteen."

"And when did you first know it was your pal who was doing the killing?"

"As soon as I read the first headline down in Florida."

"And did you know he knew?" Messing asked McKenna.

"Not until today."

"And your feelings about your partner withholding that tidbit from you, if you don't mind?"

"Complicated situation for Cisco, and I understand it. There are no hard feelings."

"Aaghh, you guys are really hurting me," Messing moaned. "If I could only run with this story, I could top any Dear Abby column. Could out-rate Oprah, too, if I could get you guys to act out a bit."

"Well, you can't, so Abby and Oprah are safe," Cisco said.

"You gonna tell me about this pal of yours?"

"It's not news if you can't print it," Cisco countered.

"Not even the background you'll give me on Justice?"

"Only if you can find a way to attribute it to another source, and then only when we give you the word that you can go public with his identity."

"Which will be when?"

Cisco looked to McKenna for the answer. "If he acts up tonight, you can run with his identity tomorrow."

"In time for tomorrow's edition?"

"Maybe," Cisco said. "If so, you can also run with his son's identity—as long as you can put the proper slant on him."

"His son? Is that his accomplice?" Messing asked.

"That's him. A highly decorated, well-respected, and very well-liked NYPD detective sergeant."

"Oh, boy! What a story—as long as I'm the firstest with the mostest," Messing said, and then a thought hit him. "Well-liked by who?" he asked Cisco. "You?"

McKenna answered, "By both of us, and keep that in mind."

"Foremost in my mind. Who are they?"

"Donald and Craig North," McKenna said. "Donny was a captain with . . ."

"The state police," Messing said, cutting in with a smile. "Haven't heard his name in years. Guess I lost track of him."

"You know him?" McKenna asked.

"Met him a few times when I was starting out in this business."

"Here?"

"No, I was still making my bones. Cub reporter with the *Albany Times Union* back in the early seventies, and he was doing some newsworthy things up there. I did a piece on a push-in robbery crew he locked up."

"Did you know he'd been in their bomb squad in the sixties?"

"I don't recall that I did," Messing said. "Maybe another reason he didn't ring any bells with me is that he wasn't a bruiser back then. In shape, but a skinny guy. Marathon runner."

"Did you like him?" Cisco asked Messing, but he was smiling at McKenna when he did.

"Everybody did. Real nice guy," Messing said with a smirk for McKenna. "I hope you two fine gentlemen are very, very hungry, because by tomorrow my editor won't be able to whimper about any outlandish bill I might give him."

Cisco and McKenna explained the developments in the case throughout their hearty dinners, and espressos had been ordered when Messing decided to call his editor to suggest he save the front page for his story. The editor, however, was the one with the news; Justice had just sent the *Post* a fax addressed to Messing. After getting Sotto Cinque's fax number from the waitress, Messing asked his editor to send the fax to him there. It arrived a few minutes later, and the waitress delivered it to him. He began reading, and seconds later he was smiling.

"What's so funny?" Cisco had to ask.

"Looks like I don't have to wait for your approval before identifying Justice for my readers," Messing replied as he continued reading. "Donny tells me who he is and why he's doing it. The way I see it, that places his story in the public domain."

"Anything in there you don't already know?" McKenna asked.

"Not so far," Messing said. "You guys have been real

straight with me, but forget that nonsense about me trying to make him look like a bad guy."

"You will mention that, for whatever reasons he has, he's made himself into a mass murderer?" McKenna asked.

"You wanna keep yourselves as the good guys?"

"That'd be nice."

"It would, but forget it. I'm sure my editor read this before he sent it to me, and he'd never go for it."

"Why not? Doesn't the *Post* still have a sense of civic responsibility?"

"They have a sense of circulation, and I predict we're not gonna piss off our readers and side with the police on this one. Not with his story," Messing said, waving the fax.

"Is it that good?" Cisco asked.

"How's this? He asks that he be buried next to his daughter in St. Augustine. That'll jerk some tears outta my readers, and it sounds like you *are* gonna be busy tonight," Messing said. "This letter reads like the script from *Death Wish*. You see any of those movies?"

McKenna didn't answer, but Cisco did. "All of them. The first one was great, and even the sequels weren't real bad flicks."

"So here's a question for you two, and answer me honestly. When Charles Bronson was doing his thing, who were you rooting for? The cops, or him?"

"Charles Bronson, of course," Cisco said at once. "An aggrieved manly man doing manly things in a manly way."

Messing nodded, but he still wasn't satisfied. "Brian? Tell me the truth. Who were you rooting for?"

McKenna couldn't bring himself to tell the truth on that one, so he opted for a lesser lie. "Never saw the movies."

"Yeah, sure," was Messing's reaction. Then he studiously ignored McKenna as he resumed reading his fax.

On the drive back to One Police Plaza McKenna and Cisco decided they would get some sleep at their desks while waiting for Donny's next move. Cisco was stopped at a light when McKenna's phone rang. "Where are you?" Brunette asked.

"On the way back. Be there in five minutes," McKenna said, bracing himself. "What's he done now?"

"Nothing yet, but I just heard from MacFarlane. He's got a possible landing strip."

"Where?"

"Upstate, just outside Monticello."

"That's within range. How'd he get it?"

"The local cops up there. They've been asking around, and they finally found an old codger who works in an all-night gas station. He heard a plane take off on Monday morning in the wee hours. Says it came back and landed a couple of hours later."

"And the cops there know of a private airstrip near that gas station?"

"Yeah, but they didn't think to check on it because they all know the guy who owns it and they know he hasn't been around for a while."

McKenna was getting a queasy feeling in his stomach, but he tried ignoring it. "Has he got a house up there near his airstrip?"

"With a barn, and a hangar for his plane. According to the cops, it's a single engine, kinda small."

"And the owner?"

"Respectable guy, very popular with them. Doctor from the city who only comes up every once in a while."

That queasy feeling intensified, and McKenna stifled a burp. How did Chip describe Donny's good doctor pal? Birds of a feather? McKenna thought. I didn't ask him anything about a plane, but was he dropping me a hint I didn't catch? Possible, he conceded, but then decided the best course of action was to recover and keep charging forward. "Are you ready for your swami to once again mystify you when he gives you this doctor's name?"

"I'm ready," Brunette said, "but I won't be mystified this time."

"Dr. John Daley."

"Yeah. How'd you know?"

"Sorry. No peeking up the magician's sleeve allowed, but John fits right into this case. You know him?"

"No, but don't tell me. Another nice guy?"

"Unfortunately, yeah. In a case loaded with them we have yet another nice guy who places a high value on friendship."

TWENTY-THREE

While Cisco gassed up the car, McKenna reported to Brunette and told him about his conversation with North and his meeting with Messing. Brunette was unhappy about North's fax to Messing and the amount of sympathy and understanding it would generate for the Norths soon after the *Post* hit the stands in the morning. That couldn't be helped, Brunette reasoned, but that was only the first problem he would be facing that evening.

Although it was the Monticello police who had reported the airstrip to MacFarlane, Daley's place was located outside town—and outside their jurisdiction—so further investigation there would have to be carried out under the auspices of the state police. That turned into another problem soon after Brunette got in touch with their superintendent at his home in Albany. To save time, Brunette wanted him to have one of his investigators obtain a search warrant for the Daley house, garage, hangar, airplane, and grounds from an Orange County magistrate. Evidentiary items listed on the warrant as subject to seizure were to be Jorge Rodriguez's red Volvo, cash, weapons, explosives, the computers and ink-jet printer Justice had used to write his notes and letters, the clothing witnesses described as having been worn by Justice during his murders, and his green Chevy. If Jorge Rodriguez was there and still alive, he would also be seized, along with Justice and his son.

"Fine, will do," the superintendent said. "Any idea yet on who this Justice character is?"

It was a question Brunette wanted to avoid, but he couldn't. "Unfortunately, he's one of yours. A retired state police captain," he replied. "Donald North."

Brunette was treated to a moment of stunned silence before the superintendent found his tongue. "Wait a minute! You mean Captain Nice?" he asked. "You want us to help you get Captain Nice?"

"If that's what you guys call Donny North, then yeah, I want you to help us get him—and help me save my bacon while you're at it. You know him?"

"Know him? He's a god to most of us old-timers. I actually had the privilege of working for him when I was a young sergeant. Taught me most of what I know."

"He's been teaching us a bit, too," Brunette admitted. "Have you seen him lately?"

"No, not in a long time. He just dropped out of sight, so I figured he went wherever old heroes go."

"When did he drop outta sight? After his daughter was killed?"

"His daughter was killed? When and how?"

Brunette didn't feel like chatting with the superintendent, so he described as briefly as he could the circumstances surrounding Consuela's murder. He then found that, apparently, the superintendent didn't feel much like chatting with him either, because his next request was one that usually prompted cops to answer in dull monotones: "Please spell out the probable cause you're proposing as the basis for this search warrant, Commissioner, and try to be specific."

Brunette had his probable cause, but he became increasingly irritated as the superintendent attempted to pick apart each point he made. Brunette prevailed, but it took some time. McKenna would have his search warrant, and the state police SWAT team would be meeting him in the rear of a diner five miles outside Monticello. Chosen by the superintendent to obtain the warrant was Sergeant Jay Schneider of his Criminal Investigations Bureau. He characterized Schneider as one of his best investigators and a man with influence in state police circles.

. . .

It would be a state police operation, but Brunette didn't entirely trust the superintendent's attitude—and maybe even his commitment—when it came to arresting Donny North. He therefore assigned two Emergency Service trucks to follow McKenna and Cisco upstate. He also ordered an NYPD helicopter to Stewart Field, about thirty miles from Monticello. He saw no reason to offend the superintendent without just reason, however, so the helicopter was to stay on the ground at Stewart Field, and the Emergency Service crews were to station themselves someplace dark and quiet ten miles outside Monticello. They would all be at McKenna's beck and call by radio, but only if he really needed them.

There was little traffic at that hour, so Cisco figured it should take them no more than an hour and a half to reach Monticello. With Cisco driving, McKenna figured that meant an hour and some minutes, but then Cisco surprised him. He showed some consideration for the drivers of the Emergency Service trucks behind them and drove at the speed limit.

McKenna napped in the car, and Cisco didn't have much to say until they left the Thruway and headed west on Route 17. Then he nudged McKenna awake, and he had his phone in his hand. "Just thought I'd let you know, I'm making a call," he said.

The statement threw McKenna into a state of panic. Why you doing this to me, Cisco? he wondered. If you're gonna call Craig, then just do it and keep it to yourself. "Who you calling at this hour?"

"Murray."

The mention of Murray Don't Worry's name had never been good news to McKenna before, but it was this time, and McKenna let out a little sigh of relief. "Go ahead, but why call Murray now? Jorge?"

"Yeah. I just wanna wake him up to let him know we're getting his client for him and Lela, and keeping our promises. Then, if Jorge's still alive, we'll do our duty."

"And do you know what Murray's gonna tell you?"

"Sure. 'Under no circumstances are you to question my client in my absence,' which is fine with me. We already got the goods on Jorge, so I can't think of a single question I'd like to ask him."

Cisco was right, McKenna knew, and the thought of waking up Murray with an annoying 2:00 A.M. phone call did have its appeal.

To McKenna's surprise, Cisco wasn't annoying. He handled the call to Murray in a perfunctory fashion, leading McKenna to conclude that he had something else on his mind. Cisco received the instructions from Murray they had expected. He also wanted to be called again if Jorge were found alive. If not, Murray asked Cisco to let him sleep, and he would read about Jorge in the morning papers.

Then they received a radio message from the pilot of the helicopter. He reported that he was on the ground at Stewart Field, waiting for further instructions from McKenna. That message was followed by another from the Emergency Service sergeant in one of the trucks behind them. He knew the area, and told them they would be pulling off on a dirt road five miles ahead to await McKenna's call.

Because Cisco sometimes took off on his skydiving ventures from a private airport in Ellenville, a town close to Monticello, he also knew the area and knew the meeting place. He pulled into the front of the parking lot outside the well-lighted diner. Parked in the rear of the lot was the state police SWAT team, next to an unmarked car they assumed belonged to Sergeant Schneider. Six black-clad troopers and their sergeant were standing outside their truck, casually talking among themselves over coffee. The SWAT sergeant acknowledged McKenna and Cisco with a nod, but their arrival seemed to provoke no more than passing interest from the rest of his team.

McKenna thought it was a good location to plan what was to come that evening. Only four other cars were in the parking lot, and visible inside the diner were just a few patrons.

"You deal with these guys," Cisco said. "I'm gonna go in, pee, and get a cup of coffee. You want anything?"

Just go in and make your call to Craig if you're going to, McKenna thought. "Thanks, Cisco," he said. "I'm beat, and a container of coffee would be great."

Cisco got out of the car, walked past the bank of pay phones outside the diner, went in, and McKenna was able to see him head straight for the rest rooms. Then McKenna noticed that Cisco's cell phone was still on the front seat, and he couldn't decide if that made him feel good or bad. He got out of the car and approached the troopers.

Once again, the sergeant was the only one to pay any attention to him. He appeared to be another old-timer, and McKenna sized him up as a no-nonsense tough guy. "Sergeant Schneider just got the warrant," he said without a hint of cordiality. "He'll be the reporting officer and the custodian of anything we seize. Until we have the house secured, I'm in charge."

The brief greeting reinforced McKenna's impression of the sergeant, and he mentally prepared himself for trouble. "That's fine by us," he said, and since it saved paperwork for him, the arrangement delighted him. "Where is Sergeant Schneider?"

"Doing one of the things he does best," he replied, nodding toward the diner.

"Eating?"

"Yeah, although I'm sure a place like this doesn't measure up to his standards. A real bon vivant. Best restaurants, best clothes, and so on," the sergeant said, and then he pointedly looked McKenna up and down. "You must know the type," he added.

Sure do, but what the hell's Schneider doing with the state police? He should be on our job with all the other bon vivants, McKenna thought, but didn't say. "Have you seen the place yet?"

"Passed by the house. It's set back from the road a bit, but we could make out a light on downstairs. Barn door's closed, and the airstrip is in the back behind the trees. Couldn't see it from the road, but we know it's there. Had one of the Monticello guys draw us a sketch of the grounds."

"Have you come up with a plan?" McKenna asked.

"You think the son's likely to shoot it out with us, if push came to shove?" the sergeant asked.

"No, I'm certain he wouldn't."

"Then we don't need much of a plan, because Captain Nice would never shoot a trooper. Surround the house, knock on the door, and ask him if he'd mind if we come in for a drink or two before you cart him away."

"You think it'll be that simple?"

"Should be, unless he really doesn't want to go with you. In that case, he might smack you and a couple of these young guys around if he's in a real hurry to get out. They're tough enough, but they're not in his league."

"But you'll get him?"

"If he's in there, we'll get him, but I'll tell you one thing, and you better take the time to listen to me: Barring something unimaginable and ungodly, nobody's shooting him or his son while I'm here."

"Then let's put this to rest," McKenna said. "Neither I nor my partner has any intention of shooting Donny North or Craig North."

"Then this'll be an unpleasant chore tonight, but we can get along," the sergeant said, and he offered McKenna his hand. "I'm Eddie Voehl."

"Pleased to meet you," McKenna said as he shook Voehl's hand. "I guess you know Donny?"

"Met him two or three times, and it was always my privilege."

"Then here's something I'd like you to keep in mind, Sarge," McKenna said. "I never met the man, but I've talked to him, and I've seen what he does to people he doesn't like. There's nothing nice about it—very cruel, very messy. He's been through a lot, he's tired and in pain, he's under a lot of pressure, and he might not be thinking straight."

"What's your point? That you think we have something to worry about here?"

"What I'm saying is that he might not be the same man you knew, and he's as much as told me he's not gonna be taken alive. I also don't think he'll permit you to prance in there and take his son to jail," McKenna said. "Put that all together, and a cavalier attitude might be the wrong approach when dealing with him."

It was apparent to McKenna that his assessment didn't sit well with Voehl. The crusty old sergeant stared hard at him for a moment and then walked past him to the middle of the parking lot for a few moments of quiet thinking.

McKenna kept his eyes on the pay phones outside the diner while he waited for Voehl's decision. Cisco came out carrying two containers of coffee, and he was accompanied by a large, rotund, middle-aged man wearing a suit that had to be as good as Cisco's and maybe better.

Cisco didn't even glance at the pay phones as they passed. He gave McKenna his container of coffee and introduced him to Schneider. "Pleased to meet you, Detective McKenna. Heard a lot about you, and it's a pleasure to work with you," Schneider said as he shook McKenna's hand, and then he noticed Voehl standing alone. "What's on his mind?" he asked McKenna.

Before McKenna could answer, Voehl made his decision and walked toward his men. "You win," he said softly to McKenna as he passed. When he reached his troopers, he had their full attention, and his message wasn't softly given. "Suit up. Full protective gear, full weapons load," he ordered. "It's possible the situation's not what I thought it was."

Voehl's command provoked an immediate flurry of activity as his men hastened to comply.

"Is that the result you were looking for?" Cisco asked McKenna.

The question irritated McKenna. "Don't give me a hard time on this, Cisco," he said brusquely. "Better safe than sorry."

"Never said it wasn't," Cisco said evenly. "Are we gonna sit back and enjoy the show, or are we gonna be in it?"

"I'd say you're gonna be out of it," Schneider offered. "Sergeant Voehl runs his own operations, and he doesn't like strangers hanging around while he's at it."

"How about you? You gonna be out of it?" Cisco asked.

"He doesn't much care for my act, so I expect I'll be sitting on the sidelines with you gentlemen," Schneider said.

"And if you object?"

"Wouldn't think of it."

"Why not?"

"Because I like my clothes, I like my face, and Voehl would ruin both while he's kicking my ass."

The sketch made by the Monticello cop was a good one, with approximate yardages indicated. Daley's place was an old farm he had converted over the years to his tastes. The barn and the two-story house were described as pleasant and well kept, but old and unpretentious. The house was set back fifty yards from the road, and the barn was next to it. A dirt road ran two hundred yards from the rear of the house and through the woods to the runway and hangar. The quarter-mile-long runway was also packed dirt, equipped with landing lights, with the hangar on its eastern end.

McKenna thought Voehl's new plan was sensible and well thought out, and it took into account Donny North's new state of mind and recent actions. Believing that North would not be taken alive and considering that North probably placed negative value on the hostage he might be holding, to save Jorge Rodriguez's life Voehl decided on surprise and quick action. The house would be assaulted and the occupants quickly subdued, hopefully denying Donny North an opportunity to kill Jorge Rodriguez.

Route 17 curved a few hundred yards from the Daley place, so Voehl decided to park the SWAT truck there, where it wouldn't be visible from the house. Schneider parked behind the truck, and Cisco pulled in behind him. Then he and McKenna got out.

McKenna noticed that Cisco again had left his cell phone on the front seat, so he knew they were headed into action as they followed Schneider, Voehl, and the troopers down the dark road toward the house. There was no moon, and the going was difficult for McKenna and Cisco, but easy for the troopers as they all wore night-vision goggles. The one extra set of goggles on the truck had gone to Schneider.

The SWAT team was equipped for action, armed with grenade launchers, tear gas and stun grenades, Ruger MP-9 submachine guns, and pistols. They wore flak vests, Kevlar helmets that had radio headsets and microphones mounted in them, and each trooper was equipped with a gas mask. In addition, two of the troopers carried a ladder, the other four carried two battering rams between them, and Voehl had a bullhorn.

Then McKenna saw the dim lights of the Daley house in the distance. It appeared that only one light was on downstairs; the rest of the grounds were in darkness.

"Don't you think it's time you got our people ready, just in case?" Cisco whispered to McKenna.

"Was just about to do that," McKenna said. They stopped, and he took out his radio. "Don't want our new pals to know what we're up to, so you'd better stay with them," McKenna suggested. "I'll catch up."

Cisco shrugged, then continued down the dark road.

McKenna first contacted the pilot and told him to get airborne. He described the location of the house just east of Monticello on Route 17, and asked the pilot if he could hover three miles from Monticello. "No problem. Will do," the pilot said.

McKenna had noticed a sign that read MONTICELLO 3 MILES on the way to the diner, so he next radioed the Emergency Service sergeant and asked him to bring the trucks to a point near that location, get them out of sight, but be prepared to either set up a roadblock on Route 17 or deploy at the Daley house on his command.

"Any landmarks near the house?" the sergeant asked.

"You'll see the state police SWAT truck and a couple of unmarked cars parked along the side of the road," McKenna replied. "The house is the next one past them, about two hundred yards up on the left."

"You got it. We'll be ready and awaiting further instructions."

McKenna turned off the radio, put it in his pocket, and hurried down the road to catch Cisco and the troopers. He found Cisco by bumping into him on Route 17, just before Daley's driveway. Schneider was standing next to him, watching something to the left of the house through his night-vision goggles.

"What's going on?" McKenna asked Cisco.

"The good news is that we're in the right place. Voehl was nice enough to run back and tell us Jorge's red Volvo is in the garage. Bad news is that he was pretty curt when he told us to wait here."

"No other cars?" McKenna asked.

"Nope. My guess is that Donny is in the city now, having his fun and getting ready to cause us another major problem. Might even have Craig with him, in which case they're gonna be hurting Jorge's ears and shaking him good just for the fun of it."

"What are they doing now?" McKenna asked, tapping Schneider on the arm. "Getting into position?"

"Yeah, should have the house surrounded in another minute," Schneider said. "Soon as they cut the power, the noise begins."

That was the plan, McKenna knew, and its pace was quickened when a dog inside the house began barking loudly. The power line was connected to the house at a point above the window in the room where the light was on, and McKenna was able to see two troopers place their ladder against the house. It took just seconds for one of them to climb to the power line and cut it, plunging the house into total darkness. Then they heard from Voehl. "Captain North! This is Sergeant Eddie Voehl of the state police," he said into his bullhorn, and it came over loud and clear. "Sorry, but we're firing stun grenades into the house, and then we're coming in. Please do not resist."

Instantly following was the sound of windows breaking, and then the muffled explosions of the stun grenades the troopers had fired through the windows. Seconds later, McKenna heard the sounds of the front and back doors of the Daley house being shattered off their hinges by the battering rams and then braced himself as he listened intently for the sounds of gunfire that would signify a violent end to the mission.

No gunfire, just the sound of the dog inside whining, but then McKenna heard something else, faint and far behind the house: the sound of an airplane engine. Somehow, minutes before the assault, Cisco had managed to tip off Craig North.

He took out his penlight, pointed it in Cisco's direction, and turned it on in time to catch him smiling. He took out his radio, and as he ran down the driveway by the faint light offered by his penlight, he keyed it. "McKenna to Aviation One," he transmitted.

"Aviation One, standing by," the pilot replied.

"There's a plane getting set to take off from that airstrip. Do whatever you can to prevent that."

"We'll try, McKenna, but it's gonna take us some minutes to get there."

"I'll do whatever I can to slow him down," McKenna transmitted. It took him a minute at the rear of the house to find the dirt road that led to the runway, and he saw no sign of the troopers. They were all in the house, and he thought he was on his own. Then he heard running footsteps behind him, and shone his light on Cisco approaching him.

"I'm with you," Cisco shouted. "Get going."

The sound of the plane's engine was much louder, and McKenna knew he didn't have much time. Craig North was revving up for takeoff.

With Cisco behind him, McKenna took off running down the dirt road through the woods, but the penlight didn't offer enough illumination to let him proceed at full speed. Then he almost stumbled on a rock wall that had been built across the road to prevent even a four-wheel-drive vehicle from proceeding to the runway. "Careful," he yelled as he cleared the wall and continued, but the warning was too late. A second later he heard Cisco stumble and fall.

McKenna continued on and saw a clearing ahead. Then the airplane with its headlights on briefly crossed his narrow field of vision. Craig was taking off, but a new engine sound gave him some small hope as he kept running. It was the helicopter, and it was getting closer fast. McKenna broke out of the woods just in time to see the airplane take flight near the end of the runway. To his right, flying in low, he could see the lights of Aviation One.

Then Craig North shut off his headlights, and there were no other lights showing on the airplane. McKenna could no longer see the plane, and the sound of its engine was growing faint. But he could see the helicopter turn, and it appeared to him it was in pursuit. He keyed his radio. "Aviation One, can you see him?"

"Just barely. He's headed north at about one thousand feet, flat out, but he'll have to get some altitude soon to clear the Catskills. Some of those mountains are over three thousand feet."

The helicopter was also headed north at low altitude, but its lights were fading from McKenna's view. "Aviation One, will you be able to keep up with him?"

"Looks like that's a negative, McKenna. Too fast," was the reply McKenna didn't want to hear. "He's gaining space on us, but we'll be able to keep him on radar for a while."

"Will you be able to get in touch with other radar stations to help you track him?"

"I'll have our base contact Air Defense Command and all the airports up here. Don't know their capabilities, but if they can keep him on radar, somebody can grab him when he lands wherever."

"Do what you can, and please keep me informed."

"Will do."

Then McKenna heard Cisco approaching, and he shined his light down the road. Cisco was limping and rubbing his elbow. "Are you okay, Cisco?"

"I'll live, but this sure isn't my lucky day," Cisco replied.

"Not *your* lucky day? How so?"

"Bought this four-hundred-dollar suit with two pairs of pants, and I just tore a hole in the jacket. Who'd have thought of building that wall across the road?"

By his tone, McKenna could tell that Cisco was genuinely steamed, and it gave him a perverse pleasure. "That good pal of yours, the one who plans for everything," McKenna replied.

"Well, that's one I owe him, but I gotta respect his foresight."

They stood in silence for a while, and then McKenna knew how Cisco had done it. Cisco would never want that phone call to Craig traced back to him, McKenna reasoned, so he had taken a page out of Donny North's book and bought another cell phone, the type that works on a prepaid phone card. Paid cash for the phone and the card, no questions asked. After he knew Voehl's plan of attack, he called Craig at the first opportunity, while I was on the radio with our Emergency Service Unit and Aviation One, but before he joined Schneider in front of the house and before the troopers were in position. Craig bolted right away, and Cisco has me here to testify that he didn't have his phone with him.

Just for fun, McKenna felt like asking Cisco to borrow his phone, but he quickly discarded that impulse because he really didn't want any concrete proof that would incriminate his partner.

"I betcha I know what you're thinking," Cisco said out of the blue.

Do I want to play this game? McKenna asked himself, but he couldn't resist. "Give it a try."

"You don't think I still have it, do you?"

The question caught McKenna by complete surprise and increased his respect for his partner. No, of course you don't, he thought. That was a one-call phone, and you either

threw it far into the woods or buried it under a rock somewhere along the way.

McKenna didn't answer, but that wasn't good enough for
Cisco. "Well, do I win?" he asked.

"Yeah, Cisco. Except for your suit, you're the winner all
around tonight, and I'm the loser."

"Don't take it so hard, Brian," Cisco said, and he punched
McKenna lightly on the arm. "You're pretty good, but nobody wins them all.".

"Not even you?"

"Hard as it might be for you to believe, no, not even me.
Cisco predicts he will wind up as one of the big losers by the
time this affair is over."

McKenna wanted to be annoyed at Cisco but found he
couldn't. He's right, McKenna thought. He's placed himself
in a no-win situation with implications that will affect him
for the rest of his life, no matter how it works out.

"Look at it this way," Cisco added. "If he's still alive, no
telling what would have happened to Jorge during that assault if Donny was there. We put his safety above getting
Donny, so we kept our promise to Murray and Lela."

"That's one way of looking at it," McKenna said, and he
resolved to keep it at that.

TWENTY-FOUR

During the walk back to the house, McKenna radioed the Emergency Service units and instructed them to return to the city, averting a possible diplomatic incident. Many of the lights were on in the house, so McKenna knew Voehl's men had restored the power. But Voehl was waiting for them at the rear of the house, so there was still a problem. He had heard the helicopter, and he had questions that required answers.

"Your operation, and our commissioner didn't feel it was his place to tell your superintendent how to run it. However, he's a careful man, and he took precautions," was McKenna's answer, and he expected Voehl to be offended.

Voehl wasn't. "Good thinking. Apparently we should have thought of it ourselves," he replied, showing McKenna that he valued practicality and insight over diplomacy.

"So there's no hard feelings between us?" McKenna asked.

"Can't vouch for what our superintendent will think about your commissioner, and I imagine he might have something to say to him. But between us, no, there's no hard feelings," Voehl said. "C'mon inside, and I'll show you what we got."

Jorge Rodriguez was alive, but it took him a while to recover from the disorientation suffered from the effects of the stun grenade fired through the window into the basement room that had served as his cell. He was found in bed, with one

wrist handcuffed to the bed rail, and he was further re-
strained by leg shackles, but also in his room were a TV and
VCR with a remote control and a bookcase loaded with
Spanish-language videotapes and books, mostly classics. It
appeared to McKenna that Jorge was none the worse for
wear.

Schneider had an ambulance dispatched to the house, and
Rodriguez was examined by a paramedic. According to him,
there was no visible evidence that Rodriguez had been tortured, and Jorge had no complaints of pain or injury to offer.
McKenna found him to be polite, especially after Jorge went
out of his way to thank each of the troopers for freeing him.

Owing to Murray's instructions, Jorge could not be questioned in his absence because any statements made by him
on what had caused him to give information to North, and
what type of information he had given, would necessarily be
self-incriminating because it would indicate knowledge of
Cruz's illicit affairs. No matter, the computer disks they had
seized from his apartment gave them enough on Jorge, so
Cisco placed him under arrest, handcuffed him, and read
him his rights.

Jorge didn't seem the least bit surprised, and he appeared
to be resigned to whatever fate was in store for him.
McKenna could see that Jorge, still polite, rose in Cisco's estimation when he recognized Cisco's damaged suit as a
Pierre Cardin and complimented him on his taste in clothes.

Voehl and his men had already searched the house for
booby traps, and they had found none. Voehl then decided to
check the barn with his men, and he returned minutes later.
"That's where he kept his explosives and tools," he reported
to Schneider. "Nothing's set to go off, but I called the Bomb
Squad to inventory it and cart the stuff away."

Schneider took the report in stride. "When will they get
here?"

"They say an hour, more or less. You wanna take a look at
it now?"

"Naw, it can wait. We'll search the house first."

Voehl shrugged. "Suit yourself. We're packing up and getting out of here."

Five minutes later, Voehl was gone with his men, and neither McKenna nor Schneider were sorry to see them go.

Cisco had again called Murray, and Murray was on his way to meet them at the state police's Harriman barracks, so McKenna expected to have a conversation there with Jorge that would be less cultured but much more informative.

The Norths' large German shepherd had also been disoriented for a while, but it proved to be no problem once it recovered under Cisco's care. The two of them quickly formed a bond, so while McKenna and Schneider searched the house, Cisco sat in the living room, stroking the dog's ears while he discussed ballet and opera with his congenial prisoner.

There was nothing on the main floor that McKenna or Schneider considered interesting, and they were on their way upstairs when McKenna heard from Aviation One. They hadn't been able to keep up with the airplane, but they had managed to keep it on radar until it reached the Adirondack Mountains, forty miles north of Albany. Then Craig North had demonstrated some flying skill when he dropped to one thousand feet, zigzagged between the mountains, and disappeared from their screen. Aviation One was returning to Stewart Field to refuel before heading back to base.

Schneider took a seat on the steps while McKenna called Brunette to report. Brunette had just one question after McKenna told the story. "You think Donny North was aboard that plane?"

"Couldn't see into the cockpit, but I don't think so," McKenna replied. "The only car in the barn is Jorge's Volvo, so I'd say Donny's closer to you than he is to us."

"If he is, he's not in his green Chevy. Got a report an hour ago that it was found in the Bronx. They took the plates off and parked it on the sidewalk alongside a junkyard fence.

Old car, damage to the front end, and the place is closed for the weekend, so it didn't arouse much interest."

"So they stole another car shortly after they rammed us," McKenna surmised. "Then they dropped off the Chevy, and headed home."

"I guess. How are you feeling?"

"Tired, and a little down."

"Down about what? Craig getting away?"

"We were pretty close to wrapping up a neat package here, but now we don't look quite that good."

"Get over it, buddy," Brunette said. "You can't win them all."

That advice was becoming familiar to McKenna, and it told him that Brunette didn't consider Craig's escape to be such a bad thing, especially when he considered that Brunette hadn't asked how Craig had known enough to be sitting in his plane when his house was hit.

The search of the first upstairs bedroom disclosed little in the way of evidence, but enough to connect Donny North to the house. The bedroom was his, because framed on the dresser was a photo of a much younger Donny with his arm around a good-looking young woman whom McKenna assumed was his long-dead wife. Also represented in pictures were Craig and Consuela; three showed them as children playing together in a park, one was a photo of Craig in his sergeant's uniform, and another showed a grown-up Consuela standing next to a twin-engine plane.

The Consuela photo held special interest for Schneider. He picked it up and stared at it for a moment, then held it in front of McKenna's face. "Tough job you got," he said. "Are you getting the picture here?"

"I already got the picture. You're preaching to the choir," McKenna was surprised to hear himself say. "I guess you knew Donny North?"

"Just by reputation. I was just a rookie when he got out,

but I'll tell you one thing: You and your partner are the first cops I've known who ever thought bad about him."

"He's doing bad things," McKenna offered.

"I guess, but what would you think if this picture found its way to some understanding reporter who's writing about Donny's exploits and misdeeds?"

McKenna was certain Schneider had just such an upstate reporter in mind. "Your search warrant, so you're in charge here," he replied, "and it wouldn't bother me if the right reporter got a hold of that picture."

Schneider smiled, stacked all the photos, and then it was on to the closet. Found hanging neatly among the clothes there was a tan checked sports jacket, and McKenna assumed it was the jacket Donny North was wearing when he had dealt with the crew on Marginal Street. At McKenna's request, Schneider took the jacket and the photos with him when they left the room.

As expected, Craig's bedroom demonstrated that he was another neat person. The bed was made, which led McKenna to believe Craig had been guarding Jorge and awaiting a report from his father when Cisco called with his warning. The quantity of clothes hanging in his closet and neatly folded in his dresser drawers indicated that Craig had known he was leaving his old life for good when he had joined his father on his mission, and that same Consuela picture on his dresser, this one larger and framed in black, told McKenna that it hadn't taken much for Donny to convince his son to join him.

As Voehl had reported, it was the search of the barn that yielded the bonanza. The red Volvo was there, and McKenna noted the dent in the rear quarter-panel caused when North had kidnapped Jorge with the bump-and-grab ploy. On the far wall there was a long workbench with many tools hanging on pegs over it. On the bench was a box that was marked "C-4," and Schneider went right to it. McKenna found an item Voehl hadn't mentioned, the computer and ink-jet printer sitting on the bench.

The computer had rebooted itself after the power was restored, and the desktop screen was displayed. The only folder on the screen was PROJECT LETTERS, and McKenna clicked on it. North's titles for the nine letters he had written came up.

McKenna had already seen seven of those letters and notes, so he focused on the titles of the last two: LETTER TO MESSING 7-20-03 and NOTE FOR POLICE 7-20-03. Since July 20 was today's date, McKenna knew that in the letter for Messing—a letter he figured had already been sent—were North's reasons behind the carnage he planned for the day. He opened the file, read the letter, then read it again. Next he opened the NOTE FOR POLICE, and he read that one. He then printed them both out and called Brunette while Schneider came over and read the paper version of the letter.

Brunette didn't answer until the sixth ring. "Sleeping?" McKenna asked.

"No. I'm on the other line with the superintendent. He tells me he has a report of a light plane crashing into a mountain in the Northern Adirondacks near the town of Elizabethtown. Set the woods on fire."

"Damn! I guess that's the end of Craig," McKenna said, and the thought saddened him. "Was he on anybody's radar when he crashed?"

"Aviation had it set up so that he would've been when he got out of the Adirondacks, but he didn't make it. Zigzagging through those mountains at night has to be a tough maneuver."

"Too tough for him, I guess. Have the troopers been able to get to the plane yet?"

"Not until the fire's brought under control."

"Well, tell the superintendent you have more important things to discuss with me and that you'll get back to him if you can find the time."

"He already doesn't like me much, and he sure won't like that. We got a big problem brewing?"

"Major. I'm into Donny's computer, and the note he plans to leave for us today reads: 'Sorry for the mess, but all the king's horses and all the king's men couldn't put these dirt-bags back together again.'"

"You find any bomb-making stuff?"

McKenna looked into the box of C-4, then looked down the bench. "I'm looking at it now. Timers, fuses, wires, pipes, electronic gizmos, and four packets of C-Four. That's what's left, but I'm sure Donny has all he needs with him right now."

"Hold on," Brunette said. It took him a minute to get rid of the superintendent before he came back on the line. "Tell me about it."

"He's going after a drug dealer named Antoine Clay. Name ring a bell for you?" McKenna asked.

"Sure does. Major player, always wears a Panama hat, reputedly controls most of the street-level heroin and cocaine operation in Harlem and further uptown, and maybe even the Bronx."

"Definitely the Bronx, according to Donny. Also mentions that he tried to get him by setting him up with a major sale, but since he went into action the big players have all gotten extremely suspicious and very health conscious. He knows Clay has to be just about out of product, but he wouldn't go for the sale meeting with Donny."

"So what does Clay plan to do, go out of business?"

"Donny doesn't say, but I think Clay plans to wait until we get Donny before he resumes operations."

"Maybe, but think about this," Brunette said. "Cruz supplied all the major operations in this town. If Clay's running out of product, the rest of them who are left must be in the same shape."

"Tickles you, doesn't it?"

"I'll admit it does. Does he detail how much Clay bought from Cruz?"

"Sure does, and he's the biggest fish Donny's dealt with yet. Thirteen separate transactions, bought forty keys of heroin and two hundred ten keys of coke. The total he paid Cruz was five million eight hundred thousand, so you can just imagine how much Clay made off all that stuff."

"A very rich man, if he survives. So how does Donny plan to take out Clay, and I guess whoever Clay has around him?"

"He doesn't say, but he must know where Clay's holed up. I'd guess he plans to go in blasting, cause maximum damage, and then blow the place when he leaves."

"And he gives no indication where that place is?"

"None."

"Then we'll have to ask someone else," Brunette said.

"Jorge?"

"Donny wouldn't have known where Clay's well-defended hideout is, so Jorge must've told him."

"That information's not gonna come cheap," McKenna said. "Murray's on his way up here right now to safeguard his client's rights."

"Damn! I hate that man. Do what you can with him, but don't give away the store."

"What will I be authorized to offer in exchange for the information?"

"Don't know yet. I gotta wake up the DA and lay it out for him."

"You might mention to him that time is of the essence and that we could be dealing with a Justice whose priorities have changed for the worse, as far as we're concerned. Much worse. No telling how he's thinking now and what he'll do if he's cornered."

"Craig?"

"Yeah, Craig. There's no way to keep our operation up here secret, and that crash will have to be on the news—if it isn't already. His second kid killed in another plane crash, the only kid he had left. Cruz was behind the first one, and you saw how he dealt with him."

"And we're behind this one?"

"That might be how he looks at it. If so, he won't be friendly old Captain Nice when he vents on us."

When they got back in the house, McKenna faced a chore he had been dreading. Cisco was still in the living room with

Jorge and North's dog when he and Schneider entered, and
he appeared to be in a good mood. That changed when
McKenna told him about the plane crash.

Cisco took the news on Craig very hard. He sat with a
blank look on his face for a few minutes, looking at no one
and saying nothing. Schneider watched Cisco, perplexed,
and McKenna understood. Schneider couldn't possibly
know the deep anguish the news was causing Cisco. "Too
bad about the kid. I feel bad, too. If he was still here when
the SWAT team hit the house, he'd be in trouble, but still
alive," Schneider remarked.

McKenna thought that unwitting remark was the exact
wrong thing to say, but it seemed to bring Cisco back to life.
"And what do you think he'd be facing? Accomplice to
many murders, maybe twenty years?"

"Technically," Schneider said.

"Then I think it's better this way. Any son of Donny
North's would rather go down fighting than get put in with
the real bad guys."

"Maybe you're right, but what makes you say that?"
Schneider asked. "Do you know Donny North?"

McKenna thought Cisco was about to spill the beans, but
he didn't. "No, but he strikes me as a solid guy who looks at
things the same way I do."

Schneider would be staying at the Daley place until the
Bomb Squad completed their inventory, but McKenna was
anxious to begin interrogating Jorge. That had to happen at
the Harriman Barracks, with Murray present and assenting
to whatever deal was reached. So McKenna went for the car
and encountered an immediate problem. Someone had noticed the SWAT truck and the two unmarked cars parked
alongside the road, and word had gotten to the press. There
were two reporters at the driveway entrance, and McKenna
was recognized. He declined comment and hurried down the
road, but by the time he got back with the car, two more reporters had arrived.

It was left to Schneider to handle the press and give them a statement, and he accepted the job. Just before dawn McKenna and Cisco loaded Jorge into the car for the half-hour drive to the Harriman Barracks.

Murray was sleeping in his car outside the Harriman barracks when McKenna and Cisco got there with Jorge. They let him sleep for the moment, and took Jorge inside to get the paperwork done before dealing with Murray. Since Schneider had called ahead on their behalf, no explanations were necessary for the desk sergeant. He handed Cisco the packet of arrest forms, and told him that Jorge's lawyer, a rather imperious and demanding character, had already been in asking for them. Cisco thanked the sergeant and got directions to the booking room.

Half an hour later, with the paperwork done and Jorge fingerprinted, Cisco went out to wake up Murray. He was back minutes later, and Cisco introduced Murray to his client. Murray then instructed Jorge to sit down and to say nothing without first saying it to him in private. Jorge just nodded his understanding and sat down. "Charges?" Murray then asked Cisco, getting right down to business.

"We tried to keep it simple, for the moment," Cisco said. "Just one count of Conspiracy to Sell a Controlled Substance, and lots of it. Class A-1 felony, and we got him good with the computer disks. Even with you in the picture, he could be looking at twenty-five to life."

"Could be?" Murray asked.

"Yeah, Murray, *could* be, and with all the publicity already surrounding this case, public interest will be high. If the DA succumbs to it, your client has a real problem."

"Let me get this straight," Murray said, smiling. "Are we already in negotiations?"

"Yeah, we are."

"Who authorized these negotiations?"

Cisco looked to McKenna to answer. "The PC, and he has the DA halfway onboard," McKenna said. "Still twisting his arm, and you know Ray. Ever know him to lose a serious match of wills?"

Murray ignored that question and replied with one of his own. "Negotiations at this stage of the proceedings are highly unusual, wouldn't you say?"

"It's rare, but it happens."

"Yes it does, but only when the police have a real problem—and that's always good for a client of mine," Murray said, obviously enjoying himself. "I take it he has information that you desperately need to know?"

"If we had it, we'd be in a position to save some lives," McKenna said.

"But this information, if he gave it to you, would tend to further incriminate him?"

"Not if we reach a deal."

Murray paused to think before responding. "What do you need to know?"

"Where Justice is right now."

"And he knows that?"

"Justice is planning on whacking another big player and his crew, and we're assuming your client told him where this player might be holed up."

"And Justice might be set to act as we sit here talking about it?"

"Yes."

"That puts my client and I in a position of some strength, wouldn't you say?" Murray asked.

"You're not all that strong, Murray," Cisco said, cutting in. "When Brian says we need that information to save lives, keep in mind that it's bad lives we're talking about. All of them are people the world would be better off without."

"Oh, I get it. Thank you, Cisco," Murray replied. "After Justice slaughters this major drug dealer and all his cronies—and generates a lot more positive publicity for himself while he's at it—are we pretending there'll be no political ramifications that will adversely affect Brunette and the mayor? Ramifications that would also, incidentally, further erode the public's already declining confidence in the whole criminal justice system? Is that the game we're playing here? If so, count me in. I like it."

Murray's got us good, McKenna realized, and so did Cisco. Neither answered.

Murray looked from one to the other, smiling broadly. Then he got serious. "So we're not pretending anymore? Just as well, if time is important," he said. "What's your offer?"

"If he truthfully tells everything he knows and testifies against all the dealers implicated by his disks, then it's five years max and a ten-million-dollar fine," McKenna said. "That's all the DA will give."

"He'll do better, but he just doesn't know it yet," Murray predicted. "He'll agree to two years in a minimum-security prison, followed by three years in the Witness Protection Program if Jorge's still testifying for the state, and a one-million-dollar fine."

"Ray might be able to talk him down on the jail time, and the Witness Protection Program doesn't sound like that bad an idea if he's still testifying."

"And the fine?"

"The DA won't budge on that. If he did, he'd be committing political suicide."

"How so? A million's not chump change, you know."

"Because in a case generating as much publicity as this one is, good reporters will be doing a lot of digging. It's bound to come out that Gaston Cruz had your client named as the beneficiary of a ten-million-dollar life insurance policy. The DA can't permit him to do a laughable sentence and then walk away a very wealthy man."

"Good point, so forget wealthy. How about he walks away as just a reasonably well-off guy who'd be able to keep up with his expenses?"

"Expenses like that Park Avenue apartment of his?"

"He will be unemployed, and he'll need a suitable place to live while he searches for a new job. Why be spiteful and force him to change residence at such a tough time in his life?"

"A number?" McKenna asked.

"Get me everything else, and I'll settle for an eight-million-dollar fine. That's my final offer, so you'd better get on the horn to your pal," Murray said, and then he headed for the door. "Now tell me, where's the bathroom in this place?"

TWENTY-FIVE

For the past couple of hours, Donny North had become increasingly amazed at the number of white people now living in Harlem, and these weren't the white hippies, white junkies, or the white avant-garde artists who had been sprinkled throughout the area in the seventies and eighties. As far as he could tell, most of the whites he had seen on the street below walking their dogs, taking their children to church or Sunday school, or going to the store for the Sunday papers were yuppies, and lining the curbs were their BMWs, Audis, and Volvos.

Although the neighborhood was still predominately black, North thought this small section of Harlem had been transformed into a decidedly upper-middle-class enclave, and he could see why people of all shades found it a desirable place to live. The streets were tree-lined, the brownstone private homes and co-op apartment buildings appeared to be well-maintained and solid, and the views were great. From his position on the roof of the small, private elementary school he could easily see the Hudson River, Grant's tomb on the near bank of the river and the Palisades on the other, the George Washington Bridge on his right, Central Park on his left, and Morningside Park behind him.

More important, North also had a perfect view of the front door and front windows of Antoine Clay's brownstone on the other side of Convent Avenue, but he hadn't seen the drug kingpin. There was, however, one small indication he might be inside: There was a security camera above the front door of the brownstone that was focused on the stoop, but that didn't provide enough security for a man like Clay. There was always a man watching the street from the second-floor front left window, and North had seen the guard change there three times that night.

That small sign was not enough to propel North into action, so it had been a long, hard, frustrating night—a night filled with doubt, apprehension, and some pain. He had a transistor radio tuned to 1010 WINS, the local all-news radio station, and he had been following McKenna and Cisco's activities since the raid on Daley's house had been announced. He had wondered how Craig had managed to get to the plane in time to get away, and then he had heard about the Adirondack plane crash.

The next few hours had been filled with anguish, apprehension, and self-recrimination. He regretted ever having allowed Craig to participate in the crusade, even though he knew that Craig was a big factor in the success they had enjoyed up till now. The kid had been persuasive, strong, and determined, and his arguments couldn't be denied. He had convinced North that, without his active participation, there would have been little chance of making a dent in the drug trade and avenging Consuela's death in a way that would eternalize the sacrifice she had made.

And Craig had been right, North realized. Craig had copied Cruz's file in the Narcotics Division Intelligence Section, thereby gaining the plans to his house; Craig had been the pilot that night; Craig had saved him at the mosque; and if Craig hadn't helped him with the driving, he wouldn't have had the strength to carry out each phase of the operation on schedule.

And then, just after dawn, Craig had called from Elizabethtown, bringing North's anguish, doubts, and self-recrimination to an immediate end. After Cisco had tipped him off to the impending raid, Craig had escaped in the plane with the duffel bag full of all the cash they had left. The police helicopter had been a surprise for him, but he had been able to outrun it. However, he had figured he was still on their radar, and suspected he would be on many radars when he got out of the Adirondacks. He had figured he would be arrested when he landed, so he had decided not to land.

Craig's skill and actions following that decision made North proud. In a valley near the northern edge of the Adirondacks, Craig had located Route 9 below him by the headlights of the few cars traveling the secondary road through the mountains. He rose to three thousand feet, put the plane on automatic pilot, and parachuted with the duffel bag strapped to his leg. Even from that low altitude, he had been good enough—or lucky enough—to have been able to guide himself to a meadow next to the road. He had immediately tried calling North, but found that his cell phone didn't work in the mountains. He had walked north for two hours on Route 9, hiding whenever he saw the lights of an approaching car or fire engine, until he had cleared the mountains at a point just outside Elizabethtown. Then he had made the call, the only bright spot in North's otherwise miserable night.

North longed to see his son again, hold him, and personally congratulate him, but both were strong men who knew and accepted the personal consequences of the course they had chosen. Their good-byes had already been said and wouldn't be repeated. "Get going, son, and run as far as you can" were North's final words to Craig.

North knew he had many other things to worry about, especially with men like Cisco and McKenna dogging his trail. First was the computer he had left, and he had chided himself countless times that night for not deleting the letters and messages he had left on the hard drive. He couldn't imagine how they had known about Daley's place, but he realized he had seriously underestimated his adversaries.

But what could they learn from his last message to Messing? he asked himself. That he was planning another mission as part of his crusade? They already knew that, so all they got from the letter was the name of his target, but not the location where the attack would occur. Unless the Narcotics Division's intelligence on Clay had dramatically improved since Craig had left the unit, they couldn't possibly know about his brownstone hideout.

Unless . . . And that brought North to his second mistake—Jorge. He couldn't bring himself to kill Cruz's paymaster after he had pumped him for all the information he needed to deal with Cruz's customers. A mistake, he knew, but not one he regretted, whatever the consequences. Contrary to all his expectations, he had liked Jorge and enjoyed his company. After a while, it had begun to amaze him that a man like Jorge would involve himself in such a nefarious business.

But Jorge alive left North with the big question to consider: Would Jorge give Cisco and McKenna the location of Clay's brownstone hideout? After pondering the question for hours, North could not come up with an answer.

At ten o'clock North decided that the pedestrian and vehicular traffic on the street below made continuing the surveillance of the brownstone too risky. Besides, he was exhausted, and the gnawing pain in his side was beginning to affect his thought processes. So North decided that a reprieve was in order and that he would award himself another day on earth that he hadn't originally planned or relished. He would sleep through most of it and end his days and his crusade at least reasonably well rested.

He took quick stock of his weapons and equipment, prepared to lug it all down four flights of stairs. Then he gave himself another reprieve. Since he considered it likely the small school was closed for the summer, he would hide his stuff someplace in the building before leaving.

There was a breeze coming off the Hudson, and the skies were clear. The day would be hot, he figured, but nowhere near as hot as the night he had planned for Antoine Clay and crew. The thought made him smile, and he left the roof whistling "O Solo Mio," one of his and Cisco's favorite tunes. On the stairwell down, he decided to call his friend to give him the good news that would set his mind at ease.

TWENTY-SIX

Of course, Murray's final offer wasn't his last word. He was the master of the deal, and the negotiations had continued for hours more. So far, despite all the cajoling Brunette could muster, Murray's terms were too stiff for the DA to accept. No deal, and the DA had his own line of rationale for refusing. Since Donny North hadn't struck that night, he reasoned that the assault on Daley's place and the subsequent death of his son had caused North to delay his plans, or maybe even to cancel them.

Brunette had presented that rationale to Cisco for his opinion. "No way. He's delayed for whatever reasons, but he's not stopped. Maybe he'll get some sleep and do some more thinking, but he'll be back charging hard," was Cisco's assessment.

In desperation, Brunette ordered half the Narcotics Division in on overtime. He would have the detectives locate and interview all their informants in an effort to learn Antoine Clay's location.

Murray and Jorge had been in the booking room's cell for the past hour while Murray fully debriefed his client. To give them privacy, McKenna and Cisco had taken chairs into the hallway. Cisco was asleep and snoring in his, leaving McKenna awake to await Murray's next offer.

Cisco's phone began ringing, but Cisco remained sound asleep. McKenna nudged him, and Cisco looked like he didn't know where he was for a moment, but then he took his phone from his pocket and answered the call. "Hello, Donny. Been hoping to hear from you," he said into the phone after a moment. "Can't tell you how sorry we are about the way things turned out."

Cisco then listened to North without saying a word for what seemed an eternity to McKenna. Cisco seemed passive while he listened, but McKenna knew his partner, and he suspected there was a smile tweaking at the corner of his lips. "Thanks for the heads-up," Cisco said at last. "You're a pal, and maybe we'll be running into each other tonight. In the meantime, get some sleep yourself." He then ended the call and put the phone back in his pocket.

"Well?" McKenna said.

"Called to say we should get as much sleep as we can to-day. Delay of plans, nothing doing until tonight. I'm gonna take his advice." Cisco leaned back in his chair and again closed his eyes.

That wasn't good enough for McKenna. "Seems it took him a long time to say only that."

"Yeah, he was exceptionally wordy this morning since he's of the opinion this might've been the last chat we'll ever be having," Cisco said, without opening his eyes.

"What about his son? What'd he have to say about Craig?"

"He said he accepts our apologies," Cisco replied, his eyes still closed.

"Elaborate, please."

Cisco finally opened his eyes and stared at McKenna. "We'll talk about this another time, Brian. For now, do me a big favor and please put it out of your mind."

"A big favor?"

"A very big favor," Cisco said. Then he settled into his chair again and closed his eyes. He was asleep in minutes, and McKenna kept his eyes on him. He expected more snoring, but not this time. The smile Cisco had struggled to hide came out as he slept.

McKenna walked down the hall to the men's room and

called Brunette. "How are the negotiations with the DA going?" he asked when Brunette answered.

"Still talking to him, but mostly going nowhere," Brunette replied.

"Too bad, but keep trying. Cisco just got another call from Donny. Tonight's the night, and Donny suggests we get plenty of sleep."

"Then you should listen to him, and I sure will. When you getting here?"

"Murray's debriefing Jorge now. Then we'll get Jorge arraigned at a court someplace up here, and after that we'll be bringing him back to town."

"You got any time frame for me?"

"Can't say. Don't know how long these things take up here," McKenna said, and then he got to the real reason for his call. "Anything new on the plane?"

"Troopers still haven't been able to get to it, and it's no longer their primary concern. It's been dry, and the wind's kicking up in the mountains. Fire's still going strong, and it was threatening some homes, but they now think that they have it contained. Route Nine's been closed though, so there are lots of troopers busy on traffic control duty."

"Tough situation," McKenna said, and then he decided it was best to change the subject. "You read the morning papers yet?"

"Just browsed through them enough to know that Messing's pulled out the stops and made Donny and Craig into heroes with a very understandable cause. You read about it yet?"

"Not yet."

"Then you're one of the few. Every cop I've seen around here today has his or her face buried in the paper, and they seem to be very interested in Messing's slant on Donny and Craig's antics."

McKenna thought back to the attitude of the cops on the sidelines at the last Justice demonstration outside headquarters. "You mean they're very *sympathetic*, right?"

"More than that. Everyone puts a straight face on when

they see me, but it's my strong impression that every cop in this building is rooting for them."

"I've been getting that attitude all along. We're the bad guys, even to our own people."

"For the time being, and we got the demonstrators outside again this morning. More than last time, and they're marching around with big posters with my picture on them," Brunette said, sounding despondent. "Care to guess the new name they have for me, printed in big letters right under my mug?"

"Don't even want to try."

"Pontius Pilate. How's that? To the hundreds of people marching around right under my window—and most of them look like real solid citizens—I'm their new Pontius Pilate."

Whoa! That's a tough one, McKenna said to himself. "Heavy's the head that wears the crown."

"Thanks, buddy. I gotta go wash my hands again. Call me when you're on your way back."

McKenna felt sorry for Brunette, but as he left the bathroom, Cisco was on his mind. McKenna thought he knew what North had really told Cisco, and why Cisco hadn't relayed that information to him. Craig North was alive, McKenna was sure, and at his father's request, Cisco was withholding that information until Craig had some time to put more distance between himself and the Adirondack Mountains.

So what do I do with this very strong suspicion? McKenna asked himself as he stared down at Cisco still smiling in his sleep.

Nothing, that's what I'll do, he decided. Keep it to myself and let the kid get as far away as he can.

The demonstration outside police headquarters was still going strong when McKenna and Cisco arrived from Harriman with Jorge, and McKenna saw at once why Brunette was feeling the heat. Brunette had said there were hundreds of demonstrators, but McKenna estimated there were a thousand of them filling the sidewalks outside the building. The demonstrators were orderly, again mostly women with young children, and the event was well covered by the press. McKenna saw news vans there from all the local TV channels, and the crew from a national news channel, Fox News, was filming while a Fox News reporter interviewed two of the protesters.

Cisco managed to get them into the headquarters garage without being noticed by the demonstrators, and they lodged Jorge in the old central booking facility in the building's basement. McKenna and Cisco then went to the Major Case Squad office and received instructions from Sheeran. Cisco was to sign out, go home, get some sleep, and report back to work at six that night; McKenna would also be going home, but after seeing Brunette.

McKenna found Brunette looking even more tired and run-down than he had been the night before. He had big bags under his red eyes, his shoulders were stooped, he was unshaven, and his shirt and pants were rumpled. McKenna decided not to comment on his friend's appearance. Instead, he asked about progress being made with the Narcotics Division's informants.

"Ran down a few leads and rumors, but got nothing concrete," Brunette replied. "Seems nobody at street level knows where Clay's holed up."

"Any progress with the DA?" McKenna asked.

"None. He's sticking to his last offer. Three years and the ten-million-dollar fine."

"Any plan on what to do tonight if we can't find Clay and the DA doesn't budge?"

"Yeah, I have an idea, but it would be a bitter pill for me to swallow. I could go on radio and TV with a message for Clay: Donny North knows where you are, and he plans to kill you tonight. If you want to live, call nine-one-one. We'll come and get you."

That *would* be a bitter pill to swallow, McKenna thought. Ray would basically be acknowledging to the press that we're powerless to find North or prevent his plans, and no

police commissioner could survive unscathed the assaults by
the press sure to come after a message like that goes out over
the airwaves. "Tough decision," McKenna offered.

"Yeah, one I'm hoping I don't have to make."

TWENTY-SEVEN

After having coffee with Cisco in the Major Case Squad office, McKenna was back in Brunette's office at 6:00. He was feeling much better after six solid hours of dreamless sleep at home, and he thought Brunette looked better, too. "I guess you got some sleep," McKenna noted.

"Had to, before I had the videotape shot," Brunette replied. "Couldn't very well be on TV looking like a beat man, could I?"

"You're not having a press conference to make your pitch to Clay?"

"No. There would be too many embarrassing questions I don't want to answer right now."

"Has this videotape been delivered yet?"

"No. I figured I'd wait until you have a final chat with Murray. Tell him that the DA's last offer was his final offer. Take it or leave it, and he wants an answer tonight."

"You haven't gotten the DA to budge?"

"Tried everything I could with him, but he won't give up any more. Says it would be political suicide for him to leave Jorge with two million, and he won't accept the idea of Murray beating him."

"Any luck with the informants?"

"Still running down rumors, but nothing yet."

McKenna called Murray's cell phone number, and Murray answered at once. "Where you been, Brian? It's been a long day, and I want to get home," Murray said.

"Been sleeping. I got a message for you from the DA.

Last offer was his final offer. Take it or leave it, and he wants an answer tonight."

Murray chuckled. "His final offer, you say?"

"And the commissioner believes him, so here's something for you to consider. If North gets a chance to kill Clay and his crew tonight—and we have every reason to believe he's gonna try to do just that—then the value of Jorge's information declines dramatically."

"For you and Brunette in your present situation it declines, but *dramatically*? I think not. There's billions to be seized, and many drug lords to be prosecuted. You have Jorge's computer disks, true, but that's the only evidence you'd have to present."

"It's good information, and I'm sure the DA can run with it and win," McKenna countered.

"Only if he's running unopposed. A lawyer like myself could get a jury, and maybe even a judge, to question the veracity of the information on those disks, and maybe even the authenticity of the disks themselves. To wrap it all up into a nice, tight package, what you need is Jorge himself—the man on the inside who made the disks. You see my point?"

McKenna did. Jorge could testify on the authenticity of the disks and the accuracy on the information on them. Better yet, testifying from personal experience and observations, he could tie all the other drug lords into Cruz's operation. "Yeah, Murray, I see your point."

"But the DA doesn't yet, so he's still not thinking correctly. All he'd have to do to assure that he'd be able to seize those billions and get those drug lords good is agree to let Jorge keep a couple of measly million of his own money."

And sooner or later, the DA would have to do just that. Murray's got us, McKenna thought. So where do I go from here? "Could you do me one favor, Murray?"

"Depends on what it is."

"Could you present the DA's offer to Jorge, and tell them he'd be saving lives if he accepts it now?"

"I don't think he's overly concerned about the lives of Antoine Clay and his associates."

"But maybe he has a little concern for Donny North's life. Tonight will be his last mission, and everything indicates he intends to go out in a blaze of glory. If Jorge tells us where Clay's holed up, I promise we'll do everything possible to save North's life."

"You think that would do it for Jorge? Exchange his two million for the life of the man who kidnapped him and murdered his brother-in-law?" Murray asked.

"It might. Despite everything that's happened, he likes Donny. And despite Jorge's occupation, he strikes me as a man with a conscience."

Murray paused before answering. "Okay, I'll do you that favor. I'll go see Jorge now, I'll give him the DA's latest offer, and I'll tell him about your promise. I will, however, advise him against taking the deal."

"But if he decides to take it anyway, you'll get right back to me with Clay's location?"

"You'll be hearing from me, one way or the other."

"Thanks, Murray. I'll make sure that you're expected at Central Booking."

At 7:30 McKenna was still in Brunette's office when Murray called back. "Jorge needs an hour or two to think about it, so I have a suggestion," Murray said. "He's hungry, and he's not overjoyed about the bologna and salami sandwiches they're serving here. I believe he'll be more inclined to think if he was enjoying a good meal while he's at it."

"And you'll go out and bring him back such a meal?" McKenna asked.

"It wouldn't bother me."

"Thank you, Murray. We'll arrange it."

Brunette called the desk sergeant at Central Booking and told him that Jorge would be eating in some style and comfort there tonight. Then he felt he could no longer procrastinate over the painful decision he had been dreading. "Can't take a chance on waiting another couple of hours," he told

McKenna. "I'm gonna have copies of my videotape delivered to every TV and radio station in town."

"Might be the right decision, but then again, it might not," McKenna said. "If Jorge gives it up in the next couple of hours, we get Donny, Clay gets saved, and . . ."

"And I don't have to make myself into a bigger target for the press," Brunette said. "It would be nice, but I can't afford to take the chance. If Donny hits while I'm waiting and hoping for that chance to save myself some embarrassment, what kind of a guy would I be?"

"Not that bad a guy," McKenna replied. "Remember, these are the lives of dirtbags we're talking about."

"So far, that's all he's been killing, dirtbags. But maybe he's been lucky. Suppose an innocent gets caught in the crossfire in the next couple of hours while we're sitting here dithering over a decision that should've been made already? That would be an innocent death I could've prevented. You think I could live with that on my conscience?"

"Many could, but no, you couldn't."

"Where do you think Clay's holed up?" Brunette asked. "Uptown somewhere?"

"Very likely. That's his backyard, the area he controls."

"Then get your partner and get up there, and I'll have some extra Emergency Service trucks, the Bomb Squad, and all the detectives I can muster assigned to Harlem for the night. When you hear from Murray, let me know."

"And in the meantime? Your video goes out?"

"Unfortunately, yeah. Keep your car radio tuned to a news station, and let me know what you think of it."

North was on the school roof again, well-rested, ready, and waiting. He still had received no positive sign that Clay was in the brownstone across the street, and he was running out of patience. The gnawing pain in his side had intensified, but he tried to ignore it as he checked his weapons for the third time that night. His old military scope-mounted Remington Model 70 sniper rifle was loaded with a magazine of twenty rounds, and he had another twenty-round magazine lying on the roof next to it. He cleaned the scope lens again and again checked the rifle action.

He next turned his attention to his 40-millimeter grenade launcher and assured himself that it was in good working order. Since he had reduced the explosive charge in each of his sixteen grenades in order to avoid damaging the brownstone to the extent that it would collapse and thereby endanger the lives of the occupants of the buildings on either side of it, those grenades received another minute inspection. He was satisfied that the charge remaining in each would accomplish his purpose but that the resulting shrapnel would not have sufficient force behind it to completely penetrate the brick double walls separating the brownstone from its neighbors.

Last to receive North's inspection were his two laser-sighted Beretta Model 92F 9-millimeter pistols. The laser sights were operating perfectly, and he ensured that each pistol's magazine was fully loaded with fourteen rounds. Since he was planning a noisy evening for Clay, to increase the pistols' accuracy he had unscrewed the silencers from each. He replaced the pistols in his shoulder holsters and continued his surveillance of the brownstone while he listened to 1010 WINS through the earpiece of his transistor radio.

At 8:30 North received a pleasant surprise when the 1010 WINS newscaster announced the police commissioner's message for Antoine Clay. North recognized it as an act of political courage by Brunette, but North also figured it should soon produce a side effect that would advance the fate of Antoine Clay and his henchmen. If Clay was inside, and if he had received the message—and North had every reason to believe he had since he could see the reflected lights of at least two TVs through the brownstone's second- and third-floor windows—then Clay would be responding in his own way. Since North was sure there were many incriminating items in his brownstone that Clay could not possibly explain away to the police, he wouldn't be following Brunette's advice to the letter. No, Clay wouldn't be calling

911 to invite the police to his brownstone to protect him and
his illegally well-armed crew, but what would he do?

If Clay believed Brunette's message and if he was inside,
North reasoned that the well-protected drug lord would soon
be leaving the brownstone for another location. When he did,
North would be ready, and there would be no missing this
target. Jorge had described Clay as a man who, in contrast to
most well-heeled drug kingpins, dressed in a fastidious and
conservative style. Clay favored expensive pin-striped suits,
tasteful power ties, and wing-tipped shoes. His only conces-
sion to uptown vanity was the white Panama hat he wore always, his trademark in the areas of the city he dominated.
North figured that hat and its contents would soon be in his
sights.

McKenna and Cisco were parked at the corner of West 135th
Street and Adam Clayton Powell Boulevard in Harlem.
There were many signs that the neighborhood was the subject of a sizable increase in police presence. Many Emergency Service trucks and unmarked cars had passed them as
well as many marked radio cars reassigned for the night
from Lower Manhattan and Bronx precincts. In addition,
earlier in the evening Cisco had driven to the 32nd Precinct
station house to check out two radios tuned to the frequency
used by the local precincts, and they saw parked outside two
more Emergency Service trucks, two Bomb Squad vans, the
Bomb Squad's bomb-disposal truck, and the large mobile
command-center truck.

At 8:45 Murray called McKenna, and his initial message
was brief: "Brownstone, one-thirty Convent Avenue. Good
luck, and you owe me for this," Murray said, and he ended
the call.

McKenna repeated the message to Cisco. "That's in the
Three-Oh Precinct, maybe ten blocks from here," Cisco
said. He pulled from the curb and began heading west on
West 135th Street, toward the Hudson River.

McKenna called Murray back.

"That's all I'm telling you," Murray said when he answered.

"Murray, please, I need a little more—and it's just between us," McKenna said.

"Totally off the record?"

"And never to be mentioned again by me to anyone."

"I'll trust you," Murray said. "Shoot."

"How does Jorge know this is the place where Clay's holed up?"

"Doesn't know for sure, but strongly suspects. On Cruz's first deal with Clay, it was Jorge who delivered the product. Clay's a naturally suspicious guy, so his men kidnapped Jorge from the deal site instead of giving him the cash. Brought him to the brownstone, and Clay had the product tested there. When it turned out to be superior stuff, Clay was delighted. He apologized to Jorge, gave him the cash, and showed him around the place. Very classy, and Clay even called it his 'secret hideaway.'"

"Thanks, Murray. I think we can proceed with some confidence," McKenna said. He ended the call as Cisco parked at a fire hydrant on Convent Hill Road, one block from Convent Avenue. McKenna was dialing Brunette's number when Brunette called him. "Got some news, buddy," Brunette said.

"Good or bad?"

"Can't decide just yet; it has both good and bad aspects. The state police finally got to Craig's plane, and he wasn't in it. The automatic pilot's still engaged, so he must've set it and bailed out before the crash."

McKenna could see why Craig alive was a problem for Brunette. It made Craig a fugitive to be captured in order to tie up the case. If and when that happened, it kept the whole Justice affair in the public eye, and the Craig case would draw public sympathy while it detracted from the NYPD's and Brunette's images. "What's the good aspect about this, as far as you're concerned?" McKenna asked.

"Two things: First of all, I think I like the kid, so I'm glad he's still alive. The other is that it'll make Donny North easier to deal with for us, once we get close to him."

McKenna thought it was time to play dumb. "Because you think he knows his son's still alive?"

"I'm sure the first thing the kid did when he hit the ground was call his father."

"And now Donny has no reason to be mad at us?"

"You can get Cisco's opinion, but I don't think Donny will be shooting at any cops if we can manage to corner him."

"Then I have some good news for you," McKenna said. "I just got a call from Murray, and he gave me the location. I think we're pretty close to Donny right now."

"Where are you?"

"Convent Hill Road, parked off the corner of Convent Avenue."

"And where's Clay's hideout?"

Before McKenna could answer, the sound of a gunshot reverberated through the air. The source of the sound was around the corner on Convent Avenue, and the first gunshot was quickly followed by another three, and then a steady crescendo of gunfire. There was an intense firefight taking place around the corner.

Cisco was already out of the car and running toward the corner, gun in hand, when McKenna finally answered Brunette. "One-thirty Convent Avenue, and get the cavalry here. There's a battle going on out here."

"I can hear it, buddy. Be careful."

Cisco was crouched behind a parked car on the corner by the time McKenna got to him. The steady sound of gunfire continued unabated, but McKenna could also hear the sounds of many sirens in the distance and getting closer.

McKenna took cover next to Cisco, and he peered over the top of the car to take in the scene on Convent Avenue. Visible in front of the brownstone across the street was a parked black limo with its right front and right rear passenger doors open. The engine was running, but McKenna could see no sign of the driver. What he could easily see was the source of the gunfire, and all of it was coming from the brownstone. From four separate open windows on the first and second floors were men firing pistols toward the roof of a building across the street. Then McKenna heard a popping sound echo down from the roof of a building on their side of the street, and it was instantly followed by an explosion on the first floor of the brownstone that blew one of the gunmen out the window to the small, gated front courtyard below. His bloody torso was peppered with shrapnel, and he wasn't moving.

McKenna had recognized that popping sound and knew what it meant. He had last heard it when he was a Marine Corps machine gunner serving in Vietnam in the late sixties, and it meant that Donny North had just taken out some of his opposition with his "bloop gun," a 40-millimeter grenade launcher, by firing grenades through the open brownstone windows.

The gunmen remaining at the windows continued firing toward the roof of the building across the street, but then North diminished their enthusiasm considerably. There was another pop, followed by another explosion, this time on the second floor of the brownstone. The gunman who had been firing from the left window was also blown out, and he fell headfirst to the courtyard, landing on top of the first victim. The man on top was a bloody mess, in even worse shape than his partner under him.

There was one gunman remaining on the first floor, and another on the second, but their return fire became sporadic, and they were no longer showing themselves. Instead, they crouched under the windowsills, and every few seconds they raised their guns to fire one or two unaimed shots in the general direction of the roof across the street.

It seemed to McKenna that a long time had passed since he and Cisco had arrived on Convent Avenue, but he knew they had been there for less than thirty seconds. The sirens were getting very close, and then McKenna saw the first unit arrive behind them on Convent Hill Road, outside the line of fire. It was an Emergency Service team, and they quickly got out of their truck, opened a side-panel door, and armed themselves with automatic weapons. They then headed for

McKenna and Cisco, but McKenna stopped them by raising his hand. He took the precinct radio from his pocket, turned it on, and keyed it. "Major Case Squad to Central. Emergency Message," he transmitted.

"Go ahead, Major Case Squad," the dispatcher replied.

"Shots being fired at One-thirty Convent Avenue in a big way. Responding units are not to drive onto Convent Avenue. Request they be assigned to block off Convent Avenue at Convent Hill Road and West One-two-nine Street."

"Understood, Major Case Squad," the dispatcher replied, and McKenna heard her directing the many responding units. North, however, didn't give him much time to listen to the radio. Another pop, followed by another explosion inside the first floor of the brownstone, and North whittled down his opposition by one more. That gunman wasn't ejected through the window by the force of the explosion, and McKenna couldn't see him, but he could hear him screaming in pain. Another pop, another explosion on the first floor, and those screams were silenced.

McKenna didn't know if the lone remaining gunman was still at his post at the second-floor window, but he had stopped firing. Down the street, McKenna saw the roof lights of two uniformed units blocking off the intersection of Convent Avenue and West 129th Street. Many more units were arriving behind them on Convent Hill Road, and McKenna had a thought. He keyed his radio again. "Major Case Squad to Central."

"Go ahead, Major Case Squad," the dispatcher replied.

"The subject is on the roof of a building across the street from One-thirty Convent Avenue, looks like it might be a school of some kind. Request you direct some responding uniformed units to cover the backyard entrance of that building, but they should use extreme caution."

"Understood, Major Case Squad. How about the backyard entrance to One-thirty Convent?"

"Probably unnecessary, Central," McKenna transmitted. "The subject has already neutralized most of the opposition inside, and I don't think he intends to let any of them live."

McKenna scanned the school roof but saw no sign of North. Then North proved him right and showed him he was still there. He fired another grenade into the second-floor window of the brownstone, then for good measure, another two through the closed third-floor windows. The building was shaken by the force of the explosions, and a section of the roof collapsed into the third floor. Silence followed, and McKenna figured there could be no one left alive inside.

It was then that McKenna and Cisco found that the limo wasn't unoccupied. The chauffeur had been hiding under the dashboard; and he decided to take advantage of the lull in the action. He peeked over the dash, put the car in "Drive," and the limo slowly left the curb. As it passed the Audi that had been in front of it, the limo's two open doors were slammed closed when they hit the Audi's rear bumper. As the limo proceeded slowly down Convent Avenue toward the two police cars blocking the intersection, McKenna and Cisco were able to see that North had been very busy before they arrived on the scene. The three bodies on the sidewalk, and the two pistols lying next to them, had all been hidden from their view by the parked limo. All three were well-dressed, all had been killed by shots to the head, and by the bloody Panama hat he was still wearing, McKenna knew who one of them was.

So did Cisco. "Great job, mission accomplished" was his take on the scene. "Got them when they were trying to bug out in the limo."

Then a voice sounded over McKenna's radio. "Duty Chief to Central."

"Go ahead, Duty Chief," the dispatcher replied.

"I'll be arriving on Convent Avenue in three minutes to take command. Have the Major Case Squad unit there transmit a status report."

McKenna knew who the duty chief was, and Cisco recognized the voice. "Christ! Dog Dick's coming here to fuck up this beautiful scene?" he muttered. "What a case of unbelievably bad fuckin' luck!"

Cisco didn't ordinarily use profanity, and McKenna knew

he considered it a form of speech used by lesser beings as they struggled to express themselves. His expletives told McKenna just how much Cisco dreaded O'Shaughnessy's impending arrival.

McKenna raised the radio to give O'Shaughnessy the status report, but Cisco took it from him. "Major Case Squad to Duty Chief. Everything's just peachy keen here," Cisco transmitted. "We got a drug lord and most of his henchmen lying around dead and bloody, and our prime subject is probably still on the scene, looking to take out any chief who comes into range."

"Is that you, Herman?" O'Shaughnessy asked, and McKenna could swear he felt the heat of Cisco's blood boiling.

Cisco, however, wasn't about to let O'Shaughnessy get the better of him. "Yes, Chief, it's me. Detective First Grade Cisco Sanchez, the famous investigator who has arrested many infamous criminals and a related rat or two," he transmitted in a calm, even voice.

O'Shaughnessy's next message told McKenna that the chief had evidently decided to ignore Cisco and his veiled reference to his nephew. "Duty Chief to Central. Have all units at the scene report in with their specific locations."

While keeping an eye on the front door of the school, McKenna kept a mental tally as the units reported in by radio. He learned he had plenty of help positioned at or near Convent Avenue. The back door of the school was being covered by five uniformed precinct units, there was a total of eight Emergency Service teams along with many detective units cordoning off each end of the block, and even the rear door of 130 Convent Avenue was being covered by three uniformed precinct units. The Bomb Squad was also there, awaiting orders at West 129th Street and Convent Avenue.

Since North had successfully transformed the scene from a battleground between himself and Clay's forces into a basic siege, with himself as the object, McKenna knew O'Shaughnessy would follow the rules for such a situation. He was right. "Duty Chief to Central. Direct all

non-uniformed units to leave the scene," was O'Shaughnessy's next transmission.

"That means us," McKenna told Cisco, but he knew his
partner would be unwilling to permit himself to be excluded
by O'Shaughnessy. Right again. "C'mon, Sissypants," Cisco
said. He left McKenna, bobbed and weaved his way across
the street, and continued in a crouch toward Clay's brownstone, shielded from the school by the cars parked at the
curb.

How many more rules and direct orders are we going to
violate today? McKenna wondered, but he followed Cisco.
Seconds later he was next to him, crouched behind a parked
BMW. On the sidewalk a few yards from them were the bodies of Clay and his two henchmen, and in the front courtyard
behind them were the bodies of the other two. "So what
now?" McKenna asked Cisco.

Cisco took a look around before answering with a smile.
"We enjoy the stark beauty of our surroundings while we
wait for Dog Dick to get the Emergency Service guys
arranged in some kind of tactical formation around the
school."

"And then?"

"That's up to Donny."

Events proceeded as Cisco had predicted. McKenna saw
O'Shaughnessy arrive at Convent Hill Road and Convent
Avenue, and he heard him on the radio directing the Emergency Service cops into position. A minute later, McKenna
and Cisco found themselves at the center of the line of sixteen heavily armed Emergency Service cops who had taken
cover behind parked cars across the street from the school.
O'Shaughnessy was slowly making his way toward them,
crouching behind parked cars as he moved down the block,
with a loudspeaker in his hand.

Then Donny North made his move. He opened the front
door of the school, removed his two laser-sighted pistols
from his shoulder holsters, and stood calmly waiting on the
landing just above the steps, arms at his sides with guns in
hand. He had been wounded at some point during his ex-

change of gunfire with Clay's men, and blood covered the right side of his shirt.

The Emergency Service cops on the line immediately reacted. Partially maintaining their positions of cover behind the parked cars, they sighted their MP-5 submachine guns on Donny North.

O'Shaughnessy had also seen North, and he stopped in place, three cars from McKenna and Cisco. He felt some kind of statement was in order, so he peered over the top of the parked car and brought the bullhorn to his lips. "Captain North! This is Chief Jeremiah O'Shaughnessy of the New York City Police Department. Drop your weapons and place your hands on your head."

"Chief Jeremiah O'Shaughnessy? Aren't you better known as Dog Dick?" North shouted back, bringing a smile to the lips of every cop there.

"You told him about O'Shaughnessy?" McKenna whispered to Cisco.

"His name might've come up once or twice," Cisco admitted.

"Captain North! You have ten seconds to drop your guns and place your hands on your head. If you don't comply, I will order my men to fire," O'Shaughnessy shouted into his loudspeaker, and his voice filled the street.

"Fuck you, Dog Dick," North shouted back, and then he raised his pistols and sighted on O'Shaughnessy. A small red dot appeared on O'Shaughnessy's exposed right shoulder, and another appeared on his bullhorn.

O'Shaughnessy should have dropped behind the car, but he didn't. Instead, he held his ground and yelled his command to the Emergency Service cops. "Fire!"

Nobody did.

O'Shaughnessy appeared confused, but he still held his ground and repeated his command. "Fire!"

Again, nobody did.

O'Shaughnessy finally came to his senses and dropped behind his parked car but an instant too late. North fired one shot, and the bullet caught O'Shaughnessy in the top of his right shoulder on his way down. O'Shaughnessy dropped the bullhorn and writhed in pain on the sidewalk, holding his wound. Still, none of the Emergency Service cops fired at North, even though he had shifted his aim to seriously threaten two of them. One red dot was centered on the Kevlar helmet of an Emergency Service cop on Cisco and McKenna's left, and the other red dot was centered on the helmet of an Emergency Service sergeant on their right.

"This is getting a little out of hand, wouldn't you say?" McKenna asked Cisco.

"A little, but relax. He won't shoot any of these cops, and they apparently know it," Cisco replied.

"How can you be so sure after he just shot the chief?"

"Dog Dick? Don't expect any tears from me on that one," Cisco said. "Donny just winged him, and did us all a favor, including Dog Dick himself. He'll be getting out on three-quarters. Hundred grand plus a year pension for him, tax free."

He's right, McKenna thought. Donny just gave Dog Dick a winning ticket in the civil service lottery, and he'll be smiling in some comfort while he recovers from his wound. Still, something has to be done here. "Why don't you just get up, walk across the street, and take his guns?" he asked Cisco. "He'd never shoot you."

"Sorry, Brian, that's not in his script," Cisco replied. "Why don't you?"

"Would he shoot me?"

"Wing you, maybe, if you didn't do your duty first. Might hurt a bit, but you'd live."

"Do my duty? You mean, you want me to shoot him?" McKenna asked.

"Not what *I* want; it's what *he* wants," Cisco said. He looked up and down the line of cops behind the parked cars, then focused on McKenna. "Looks like none of these sentimental bozos are gonna do their duty, either," he said, and McKenna saw the pain in his eyes.

"So?"

"So, as usual, the hard part falls to Cisco," Cisco said. He shook his head, stood up, and aimed his pistol at North's chest. North smiled, and responded by switching his aim to Cisco's chest. Two red dots showed there, both centered on Cisco's heart. The impasse continued for a few moments. Then North nodded, and Cisco fired two quick shots. Both hit North in the right side of his chest. He dropped his guns, clutched his chest with both hands, and slumped slowly to the landing.

Cisco was bending over North in an instant, and he was quickly joined by McKenna. North was on his back with his eyes open, still alive, but his breathing was labored. He moved his mouth, struggling to speak, and McKenna heard the sounds of many hurried footsteps. He turned to face the Emergency Service cops rushing toward them. "Stay back!" he yelled, and all of them complied, stopping in their tracks. Then two advanced slowly, weapons held at the ready and aimed at North until the Emergency Service sergeant took charge. "You heard the man. It's all over here," he shouted. "Get back across the street and clear your weapons."

All the cops complied, and McKenna watched them for a moment as they shuffled across the street behind the sergeant. Then he returned his attention to North and Cisco. North was staring up at Cisco, still struggling to speak, and then he finally managed it. "Are we alone?" he asked, his voice rasping with the pain showing through.

"Yeah, Donny, we're alone," Cisco replied softly. "Speak your piece."

"You never were much of a shot," North said softly, and he managed to smile through the pain.

"Never as good as you, amigo, but good enough. You're checking out—lung shot—and you don't have much time."

"You sure?"

"Yeah, Donny, I'm sure."

"Good." North continued smiling as he stared up at Cisco, and McKenna watched his eyes lose their focus as his breathing became even more labored. Then Donny North closed his eyes, his breathing stopped, and he died quietly with the smile still on his face.

McKenna figured they had been on Convent Avenue for under ten minutes, but Cisco wasn't prepared to waste any more time there. He turned and began walking quickly back up Convent Avenue toward their car. McKenna ran after him and slowed down when they were walking abreast. "Leave me alone, Brian," Cisco said. "You'll have plenty to do here, and I need some time by myself."

McKenna saw that Cisco's eyes were filling with tears. "You gonna be a baby?" he asked, still keeping pace with Cisco.

"Maybe, but not a word about this to anyone."

"Never." McKenna left Cisco and headed for the spot across the street where he had last seen O'Shaughnessy.

EPILOGUE

Since sightings of Craig North in countries ranging from Canada to Argentina were being reported every couple of days in the press, Brunette couldn't keep the case out of the headlines, and the demand by reporters for interviews with McKenna and Cisco remained high. They refused all requests, and then Brunette came up with a remedy for that situation. It had never happened before in the NYPD, but McKenna and Cisco didn't *go* back on vacation, they were *sent* back. "Get lost, and don't come back till I call for you," were his parting words to them, and they complied, rejoining their loved ones in Fort Myers Beach.

For the first week McKenna was able to thoroughly enjoy his time with Angelita and the kids, mainly because Cisco kept himself out of sight—presumably entertaining Agnes—but he wasn't out of McKenna's thoughts. It appeared to most other members of the Major Case Squad that Cisco had managed to deal with killing Donny North, but McKenna knew better, and he had noticed changes in his partner. McKenna hadn't heard him brag about anything since Convent Avenue; he was polite and reserved in his dealings with everyone, and he had little to say to anyone that wasn't directly job related.

That changed at 7:00 A.M. on their second Tuesday in Fort Myers Beach. McKenna and Mike McCormick were set to tee off on the third hole when Cisco unexpectedly showed up with his clubs. "Been watching you guys from my window, and it occurred to me you both could benefit from Cisco's expertise," he announced.

McCormick didn't appear to be happy at the prospect, but McKenna was. "You're back?" he asked.

"Yeah, couldn't stand myself any longer. I'm done moping around," Cisco said. "During your free lesson, Cisco will beat you both on every hole."

And he did.

The Craig North sightings continued in the press, generating enough public interest to compel Brunette to send teams of happy detectives on overtime from the Major Case Squad to countries all over the hemisphere to investigate and dispel each one. Most of the sightings were quickly determined to be "unsubstantiated," but, trying as hard as they could, the detectives couldn't manage to attach that wonderful label to every case. A few witnesses interviewed in Panama proved to be especially persistent and annoying, and once, quite by unlucky accident, one detective team thought they might actually be close to locating Craig. Brunette quickly recalled them to New York, and he reassigned them to duties in the Lost Property Section that didn't require quite so much misplaced competence.

It was then that the DA decided that a legal technicality had to be addressed. If Craig North were located anywhere outside the United States, he couldn't be legally arrested, and a request for his extradition couldn't be presented to the local government. What would be needed first was an arrest warrant naming Craig North, and that warrant could be obtained only after he was indicted by a grand jury.

The DA saw no choice but to convene a grand jury to hear Craig North's case, and McKenna was subpoenaed to New York to testify.

"What we have here is a runaway grand jury," the ADA told McKenna before he debriefed him. "The problem is, this grand jury is running in reverse."

"You don't think they'll indict Craig?" McKenna asked.

"They reluctantly might, if we can present an airtight case against him, but it's my strong suspicion that they'd much rather indict me."

"What makes you think that?"

"I got the feeling after I presented my only other two witnesses in this case, Jorge Rodriguez and Dr. John Daley," the ADA replied, and McKenna saw that he was reliving a bad experience. "Rodriguez testified that he never saw Craig North. When I tried to pin him down with a few more questions, the grand jury foreman stood up and accused me of badgering the witness. That's never happened to me before, and I had to back off."

"And Dr. Daley?"

"Worse. He testified that he had rented his house and loaned his plane to his good pal, Donny North. Fine, but it quickly went bad when he told the jury he had never seen Craig North in his life."

"You think he was lying?"

"Me and everyone in that room knew he was lying, but I was the only one who cared. I tried to pin him down with questions like 'Why would you loan your plane to Donny North, a man without a pilot's license?' The jury didn't like that line of questioning, and then the foreman stood up and ordered me outta the room."

"And?"

"The rest of the jurors clapped, and I left."

"The foreman can do that?"

"I had to check to be sure, but yeah, he can. Trouble for me is that, until now, it's never been done before to an ADA in this state. Kinda dubious distinction I have."

"So that leaves just me," McKenna said.

"Just you," the ADA agreed. "You're the only witness I have left who can physically connect Craig North to his father's crime spree, so tell me about your experience outside the mosque. At the time, how sure were you that the driver was Craig North?"

This poor guy's in trouble, and it's going to get worse for him, McKenna thought. "At the time?"

"Yeah, at the time. How sure were you?"

"Kinda thought it was him, but later I figured out it had to be him."

"*Later* won't count with this grand jury," the ADA said. "What counts is what you thought outside the mosque, and you're telling me you 'kinda thought' the driver might've been Craig?"

"Yeah, kinda thought."

"How about you were *pretty sure* at the time that it could be him?"

"No, I just kinda thought."

"Maybe you were *reasonably sure*?" the ADA suggested.

"No, not at the time."

The ADA didn't have another question for McKenna. He just cradled his head in his arms on his desk, and McKenna thought he might've been shaking a little.

Grand jury votes are conducted in secret, and after a vote is taken, a buzzer is sounded by the foreman to notify the ADA that a decision had been reached.

After McKenna's testimony, the buzzer sounded less than a minute after he and the ADA had left the grand jury room. The ADA went back in to get the results, and he emerged moments later to give McKenna the news. "Refused to indict, voted 'No True Bill.'"

McKenna tried to suppress his smile, and feared he might have failed. He felt the need to say something to distract the ADA. "No True Bill? What does that mean?"

"It means this case will probably never be presented to any grand jury ever again," the ADA replied, and he was staring at his shoes. "It also means that Craig North, wherever he might be, is a free man, and not wanted for any crime in the State of New York."

"Even though everyone knows he's guilty?" McKenna asked. The ADA continued staring at his shoes for a few moments more before replying, leading McKenna to fear he might have played it up too much.

He had. The ADA looked up, stared at McKenna, and obviously found something in his face he didn't like. "Yeah, free now and forevermore, even though everyone knows he's guilty," he said sardonically. "Now, Detective McKenna, would you kindly do me one last favor?"

"Sure."

"Please go away."

"Okay."